Making Faces

by

Amy Harmon

A quotation attributed to Edward Everett Hale (April 3, 1822 – June 10, 1909) appears in this work.

Excerpts from a variety of William Shakespeare's plays, sonnets, and poems appear in this work including: "Sonnet 116," "Hamlet," "Measure for Measure," and "Othello."

Excerpt from *King James Bible* "The Suffering Servant" Isaiah 53:2.

Please visit www.authoramyharmon.com

First Edition: October 2013
Amy Harmon

Making Faces: a novel / by Amy Harmon—1st ed.
ISBN: 978-1-63392-095-8
Library of Congress Cataloging-in-Publication Data available upon request

Summary: Ambrose Young was beautiful. The kind of beautiful that graced the covers of romance novels, and Fern Taylor would know. She'd been reading them since she was thirteen. But maybe because he was so beautiful he was never someone Fern thought she could have . . . until he wasn't beautiful anymore.

The Spencer Hill Press version of this book contains Bonus Content interviews not previously available.

Published in the United States by Spencer Hill Press.
For more information on our titles visit www.spencerhillpress.com

Distributed by Midpoint Trade Books
www.midpointtrade.com

Cover design by: Murphy Rae, for more information please visit www.murphyrae.net
Interior layout by: Scribe Inc.

Printed in the United States of America

For the Roos Family

David, Angie, Aaron, Garrett, and Cameron

I am only one,
But still I am one.
I cannot do everything,
But still I can do something;
And because I cannot do everything,
I will not refuse to do the something
that I can do.

—EDWARD EVERETT HALE

Contents

Prologue

"The ancient Greeks believed that after death, all souls, whether good or bad, would descend to the underworld, the kingdom of Hades, deep in the earth, and dwell there for eternity," Bailey read aloud, his eyes flying across the page.

"The underworld was guarded from the living world by Cerberus, an enormous, vicious, three-headed dog with a dragon for a tail and snake heads lining his back." Bailey shivered at the image that popped into his mind, imagining how Hercules would feel when he saw the beast for the first time, knowing he had to subdue the animal with nothing but his bare hands.

"It was Hercules's final task, his final labor to perform, and it would be the most difficult quest of all. Hercules knew that once he descended into the underworld, facing monsters and ghosts, wrestling demons and mythical creatures of every kind along his way, he might never be able to return to the land of the living.

"But death did not frighten him. Hercules had faced death many times, and longed for the day when he too would be delivered from his endless servitude. So Hercules went, secretly hoping to see in the kingdom of Hades, the souls of loved ones he had lost and now paid penance for."

1

Superstar or a Superhero

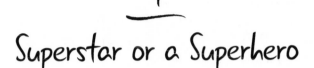

First Day of School—September 2001

The school gymnasium was so loud that Fern had to lean down next to Bailey's ear and shout to be heard. Bailey was more than capable of maneuvering his wheelchair through the teeming student body, but Fern pushed him so they could more easily stay together.

"Do you see Rita?" she yelled, eyes roving. Rita knew they had to sit on the bottom bleacher in order for Bailey to sit near them. Bailey pointed, and Fern followed his finger to where Rita was waving frantically, making her breasts bounce and her fluffy blonde hair swing wildly around her shoulders. They made their way to her, and Fern let Bailey take over control of his chair as she scrambled up to the second row, sitting just behind Rita so Bailey could position his chair at the end of the bench.

Fern hated pep rallies. She was small and tended to get bumped and squished no matter where she sat, and she had little interest in cheering and stomping her feet. She sighed, settling in for the half hour of screaming, loud music, and football players working themselves up into a frenzy.

"Please rise for the National Anthem," a voice boomed, and the mic shrieked in protest, causing people to wince and cover their ears, but effectively quieting the gymnasium.

"We have a special treat today, girls and boys." Connor O'Toole, also known as Beans, was holding the mic with a wicked grin on his face. Beans was always up to something, and he instantly had everyone's attention. He was part Irish, part Hispanic, and his upturned nose, sparkling hazel eyes, and devilish grin were at odds with his smoky coloring. And he was a talker; it was obvious that he relished his time at the microphone.

"Your friend and mine, Ambrose Young, has lost a bet. He said if we won our first game, he would sing the National Anthem at this pep assembly." Gasps were heard, and the volume in the bleachers rose immediately.

"But we didn't just win our first game, we won our second game too!" The audience roared and stomped their feet. "So, being a man of his word, here is Ambrose Young, singing the National Anthem," Beans said and waved the mic toward his friend.

Beans was small. Though he was a senior, he was one of the smaller players on the team and was more suited to wrestling than football. Ambrose was also a senior. But he wasn't small. He towered above Beans—one of his biceps was almost as big around as Beans's head—and he looked like one of those guys on the cover of a romance novel. Even his name sounded like a character from a steamy read. And Fern would know. She'd read thousands of them. Alpha males, tight abs, smoldering looks, happily-ever-afters. But no one had ever really compared to Ambrose Young. Not in fiction or in real life.

To Fern, Ambrose Young was absolutely beautiful, a Greek god among mortals, the stuff of fairy tales and movie screens. Unlike the other boys, he wore his dark hair in waves that brushed his shoulders, occasionally sweeping it back so it wouldn't fall into his heavily-lashed brown eyes. The squared-off edge of his sculpted jaw kept him from being too pretty, that and the fact he was six foot three in his socks, weighed a strapping 215 pounds by the age of eighteen, and had a body corded with muscle from his shoulders to his well-shaped calves.

Rumor was that Ambrose's mother, Lily Grafton, had tangled with an Italian underwear model in New York City during her quest to find fame. She became quickly untangled when he discovered she was carrying his child. Jilted and pregnant, she limped home and was swept up in the comforting arms of her old friend, Elliott Young, who gladly married her and welcomed her baby boy six months later. The town paid special attention to the handsome baby boy as he grew, especially when diminutive, blond Elliott Young ended up having a brawny son with dark hair and eyes and a build worthy of, well, an underwear model. Fourteen years later, when Lily left Elliott Young and moved to New York, no one was surprised that Lily was going back to find Ambrose's real father. The surprise came when fourteen-year-old Ambrose remained in Hannah Lake with Elliott.

By that time, Ambrose was already a fixture in the small town, and people speculated that was the reason he stayed. He could throw a javelin like a mythical warrior and barrel through opponents on the football field like they were made of paper. He pitched his little league team to a district championship and could slam-dunk a basketball by the time he was fifteen. All of these things were notable, but in Hannah Lake, Pennsylvania, where the town closed their businesses for local duels and followed the state rankings like winning lottery numbers, where wrestling was an obsession that rivaled football in Texas, it was Ambrose Young's ability on the mat that made him a celebrity.

The crowd went instantly quiet as Ambrose took the microphone, waiting for what was sure to be a highly entertaining massacre of the anthem. Ambrose was known for his strength, his good looks, and his athletic prowess, but nobody had ever heard him sing. The silence was saturated with giddy expectation. Ambrose pushed his hair back and then shoved his hand in his pocket as if he was uncomfortable. Then he fixed his eyes on the flag and began to sing.

"Oh, say can you see by the dawn's early light . . ." Again, there was an audible gasp from the audience. Not because it was bad, but because it was wonderful. Ambrose Young had a voice fitting of the package it was encased in. It was smooth and deep and impossibly rich. If dark chocolate could sing, it would sound like Ambrose Young. Fern shivered as his voice wrapped around her like an anchor, lodging deep in her belly, pulling her under. She found her eyes closing behind her thick glasses, and she let the sound wash over her. It was incredible.

"O'er the land of the free . . ." Ambrose's voice reached the summit, and Fern felt like she had climbed Everest, breathless and ebullient and triumphant. "And the home of the brave!" The crowd roared around her, but Fern was still hanging on that final note.

"Fern!" Rita's voice rang out. She shoved at Fern's leg. Fern ignored her. Fern was having a moment. A moment with, in her opinion, the most beautiful voice on the planet.

"Fern's having her first orgasm." One of Rita's girlfriends snickered. Fern's eyes shot open to see Rita, Bailey, and Cindy Miller looking at her with big grins on their faces. Fortunately, the applause and the cheers prevented the people around them from hearing Cindy's humiliating assessment.

Small and pale, with bright-red hair and forgettable features, Fern knew she was the kind of girl who was easily overlooked, easily ignored, and never dreamed about. She had floated through childhood without drama and with little fanfare, grounded in a perfect awareness of her own mediocrity.

Like Zacharias and Elizabeth, parents of the biblical John the Baptist, Fern's parents were far beyond their childbearing years when they suddenly found themselves in a family way.

Fifty-year-old Joshua Taylor, popular pastor in the small town of Hannah Lake, was struck dumb when his wife of fifteen years tearfully told him she was going to have a baby. His jaw hit the floor, his hands shook, and if it hadn't been for the serene joy stamped on his forty-five-year-old wife, Rachel's face, he might have thought she was pulling a prank for the first time in her life. Fern was born seven months later, an unexpected miracle, and the whole town celebrated with the well-loved couple. Fern found it ironic that she was once considered a miracle, since her life had been anything but miraculous.

Fern pulled off her glasses and began shining them on the hem of her T-shirt, effectively blinding herself to the amused faces around her. Let them laugh. Because the truth of the matter was, she felt euphoric and dizzy all at once, the way she sometimes felt after a particularly satisfying love scene in a favorite novel. Fern Taylor loved Ambrose Young, had loved him since she was ten years old and had heard his young voice lifted in a very different kind of song, but in that moment he reached a whole new level of beauty, and Fern was left reeling and dazed that one boy could be gifted with so much.

• • •

August 1994

Fern walked over to Bailey's house, bored, having finished every single book she'd checked out from the library the week before. She found Bailey sitting like a statue on the cement steps that led to his front door, eyes trained on something on the sidewalk in front of him. He was pulled from his reverie only when Fern's foot narrowly missed the object of his fascination. He yelped and Fern squealed when she saw the enormous brown spider just inches from her feet.

The spider continued on its way, slowly traversing the long stretch of concrete. Bailey said he had been tracking it for half an hour, never getting too close, because after all, it was a spider, and it was gross. It was the biggest spider Fern had ever seen. Its body was the size of a nickel, but with its gangly legs it was easily as big as a fifty-cent piece, and Bailey seemed awestruck by it. After all, he was a boy, and it was gross.

Fern sat beside him, watching the spider take his time crossing Bailey's front walk. The spider meandered like an old man on a stroll, unhurried, unafraid, with no apparent goal in mind, a seasoned citizen with long, spindly limbs, carefully unfolding each leg every time he took a step. They watched him, entranced by his terrifying beauty. The thought took Fern by surprise. He was beautiful even though he frightened her.

"He's cool," *she marveled.*

"Duh! He's awesome," *Bailey said, his eyes never wavering.* "I wish I had eight legs. I wonder why Spider-Man didn't get eight legs when he got bit by that radioactive spider. It gave him great eyesight and strength and the ability to make webs. Why not extra legs? Hey! Maybe spider venom heals muscular dystrophy, and if I let that guy bite me, I'll get big and strong," *Bailey wondered, scratching his chin like he was actually considering it.*

"Hmm. I wouldn't risk it." *Fern shuddered. They became entranced once more, and neither of them noticed the boy riding down the sidewalk on his bike.*

The boy saw Bailey and Fern sitting so still, so silent, and his interest was immediately piqued. He stepped off his bike and laid it on the grass, following their gazes to where a huge brown spider crept along the walkway in front of the house. The boy's mother was petrified of spiders. She always made him kill them immediately. He'd killed so many he wasn't even afraid of them anymore. Maybe Bailey and Fern were afraid. Maybe they were scared to death, so scared they couldn't even move. He could help them. He ran up the sidewalk and smashed the spider beneath his big white sneaker. There.

Two pairs of horrified eyes shot to his.

"Ambrose!" *Bailey shouted, horrified.*

"You killed him!" Fern whispered, shocked.

"You killed him!" Bailey roared, pushing up to his feet and stumbling down the sidewalk. He looked at the brown mess that had occupied the last hour of his life.

"I needed his venom!" Bailey was still caught up in his own imaginings of spider cures and superheroes. Then Bailey surprised them all by bursting into tears.

Ambrose gaped at Bailey, and then watched as Bailey walked on unsteady legs up the steps and into his house, slamming the door behind him. Ambrose closed his mouth and shoved his hands into the pockets of his shorts.

"I'm sorry," he said to Fern. "I thought . . . I thought you were scared. You were both just sitting there staring at it. I'm not scared of spiders. I was just trying to help."

"Should we bury him?" Fern asked, her eyes mournful behind her big glasses.

"Bury him?" Ambrose asked, stunned. "Was he a pet?"

"No. We just met," Fern said seriously. "But maybe it will make Bailey feel better."

"Why is he so sad?"

"Because the spider is dead."

"So?" Ambrose wasn't trying to be a jerk. He just didn't understand. And the little redhead with the crazy, curly hair was kind of freaking him out. He'd seen her before at school and knew her name. But he didn't know her. He wondered if she was special. His dad said he had to be nice to kids who were special, because they couldn't help the way they were.

"Bailey has a disease. It makes his muscles weak. It might kill him. He doesn't like it when things die. It's hard for him," Fern said simply, honestly. She actually sounded kinda smart. Suddenly, the events at the wrestling camp earlier that summer made sense to Ambrose. Bailey wasn't supposed to wrestle because he had a disease. Ambrose felt bad all over again.

Ambrose sat down beside Fern. "I'll help you bury him."

Fern was up and running across the grass to her own house before the words had left his mouth. "I have a perfect little box! See if you can scrape him off the sidewalk," she shouted over her shoulder.

Ambrose used a piece of bark from the Sheens' flowerbed to scoop up the spider's remains. Fern was back in thirty seconds. She held the white ring box open as Ambrose deposited the spider guts onto the pristine cotton. Fern put the lid on and gestured to him solemnly. He followed her to her backyard and together they scooped out handfuls of dirt from a corner of the garden.

"That should be big enough," Ambrose said, taking the box out of Fern's hand and placing it in the hole. They stared at the white box.

"Should we sing?" Fern asked.

"I only know one spider song."

"Itsy Bitsy?"

"Yeah."

"I know that one, too." Together Fern and Ambrose sang the song about the spider getting washed down the waterspout and getting a second chance to climb when the sun came out again.

When the song was over, Fern put her hand in Ambrose's. "We should say a little prayer. My dad is a pastor. I know how, so I'll say it."

Ambrose felt strange holding Fern's hand. It was moist and dirty from digging the grave and it was very small. But before he could protest, she was speaking, her eyes scrunched closed, her face screwed up in concentration.

"Father in Heaven, we're grateful for everything you have created. We loved watching this spider. He was cool and made us happy for a minute before Ambrose squished him. Thank you for making even ugly things beautiful. Amen."

Ambrose hadn't closed his eyes. He was staring at Fern. She opened her eyes and smiled at him sweetly, dropping his hand. She began pushing the dirt over the white box, covering it completely and tamping it down. Ambrose found some rocks and arranged them in an S *shape for spider. Fern added some rocks in the shape of a B in front of Ambrose's S.*

"What's the B for?" Ambrose wondered out loud. He thought maybe the spider had a name he didn't know about.

"Beautiful Spider," she said simply. "That's how I'm going to remember him."

2

Have Courage

September 2001

Fern loved summertime, the lazy days and the long hours with Bailey and her books, but fall in Pennsylvania was absolutely breathtaking. It was still early in the season, not quite mid-September, but the leaves had already started to change, and Hannah Lake was awash in splashes of color mixed in with the deep green of the fading summer. School was back in session. They were seniors now, the top of the heap, one year left before real life began.

But for Bailey, real life was now, this instant, because every day was a downhill slide. He didn't get stronger, he got weaker, he didn't get closer to adulthood, he got closer to the end, so he didn't look at life the way everyone else did. He had become very good at living in the moment, not looking too far ahead at what might come.

Bailey's disease had taken away his ability to raise his arms even to chest level, which made it impossible to do all the little things people did every day without thinking twice. His mom had worried about him staying in school. Most kids with Duchenne muscular dystrophy don't make it past twenty-one, and Bailey's days were numbered.

Being exposed to illness on a daily basis was a concern, but Bailey's inability to touch his face actually protected him from germs that the rest of the kids managed to wipe all over themselves, and he rarely missed a day of school. If he held a clipboard in his lap he could manage, but holding the clipboard was awkward and if it slipped and fell he couldn't lean down to retrieve it. It was a lot easier for him to work at a computer or slide his wheelchair in close to a table and rest his hands on the top. Hannah Lake High School was small and not very well-funded, but with a little help and some adjustments to the normal routine, Bailey would finish high school, and he would probably finish at the top of his class.

Second-hour precalculus was filled with seniors. Bailey and Fern sat in the back at a table high enough for Bailey to utilize, and Fern was his assigned aid, though he helped her more in the class than she helped him. Ambrose Young and Grant Nielson sat in the back of the room as well, and Fern was tickled to be so close to Ambrose, even though he didn't know she existed, three feet away from where he sat wedged in a desk that was too small for someone his size.

Mr. Hildy was late for class. He was habitually late to his second-hour class, and nobody minded really. He didn't have a class first hour and you could usually find him in the mornings with a cup of coffee in front of the TV in the teacher's lounge. But that Tuesday he came into class and flipped on the TV that hung in the corner of his classroom, just to the left of the chalkboard. The TVs were new, the chalkboards old, the teacher ancient, so nobody paid him much attention as he stood staring up at the screen, watching a newscaster talk about a plane crash. It was 9:00 a.m.

"Quiet, please!" Mr. Hildy barked, and the room reluctantly obeyed. The shot on the screen was trained on two tall buildings. One had black smoke and fire billowing out of the side.

"Is that New York, Mr. Hildy?" someone asked from the front row.

"Hey, isn't Knudsen in New York City?"

"That's the World Trade Center," Mr. Hildy said. "That wasn't a commuter plane, I don't care what they are saying."

"Look! There's another one!"

"Another plane?"

There was a collective gasp.

"Holy sh—!" Bailey's voice trailed off and Fern clamped a hand over her mouth as they all watched another plane burrow into the side of the other tower, the tower that wasn't already on fire.

The newscasters were reacting much like the students in the class—shocked, confused, scrambling for something intelligent to say as they stared with dawning horror at what was clearly not an accident.

There was no calculus assignment that day. Instead, Mr. Hildy's math class watched history unfold. Maybe Mr. Hildy considered the seniors old enough to see the images that played out in front of them, to hear the speculation.

Mr. Hildy was an old Vietnam vet, he didn't mince words, and he couldn't tolerate politics. He watched with his students as America was attacked and he didn't bat an eye. But he quaked inside. He knew, maybe better than anyone, what the cost would be. It would be young lives. War was coming. No way it couldn't after something like this. No way it couldn't.

"Wasn't Knudsen in New York?" someone asked. "He said his family was going to see the Statue of Liberty and a bunch of other stuff." Landon Knudsen was the student body vice-president, a member of the football team, and someone who was well-liked and well-known throughout the school.

"Brosey, doesn't your mom live in New York?" Grant asked suddenly, his eyes wide with the sudden realization.

Ambrose's eyes were fixed on the TV, his face tight. He nodded once. His stomach was hot with dread. His mom not only lived in New York City, but she worked as a secretary in an ad agency that was located in the North Tower of the World Trade Center. He kept telling himself she was fine; her office was on a lower floor.

"Maybe you should call her." Grant looked worried.

"I've been trying." Ambrose held up his cell phone, the one he wasn't supposed to have in class, but Mr. Hildy didn't protest. They all watched as Ambrose tried again.

"Busy. Everybody is probably trying to call." He snapped the phone closed. Nobody spoke. The bell rang, but everyone stayed in their seats. A few kids trickled in for their third-hour class, but word was spreading throughout the school and the regular schedule was no match for the unfolding drama. The incoming students sat atop desks and stood against the walls and watched the screen along with everyone else.

And then the South Tower collapsed. It was there and then it wasn't. It dissolved into a massive cloud that swept down and out, dirty white, thick and fat, bristling with debris, dense with devastation. Someone screamed and everyone was talking and pointing. Fern reached over and took Bailey's hand. A couple of girls started to cry.

Mr. Hildy's face was as chalky as the board he made his living writing on. He looked out over his students crammed into his classroom and wished he'd never turned on the TV. They didn't need to see this. Young, untried, innocent. His mouth opened to reassure them, but his intolerance for bullshit robbed him of speech. There was nothing he could say that wouldn't be a bald-faced lie or that wouldn't frighten them more. It wasn't real. It couldn't be. It was an illusion, a magic trick, just smoke and mirrors. But the tower was gone. The second tower to be hit, the first to go down. It took only fifty-six minutes from impact to collapse.

Fern clung to Bailey's hand. The billowing cloud of smoke and dust looked like the batting from Fern's old stuffed bear. It was a carnival prize, filled with cheap, fuzzy, synthetic cotton. She'd conked

Bailey in the head with it and the right arm had torn free, spewing fuzzy white fluff in all directions. But this wasn't a carnival. It was a spook alley, complete with maze-like city streets filled with people covered in ash. Like zombies. But these zombies wept and called out for help.

When they heard the news that a plane had gone down outside Shanksville—only sixty-five miles from Hannah Lake—students began leaving the classroom, unable to bear more. They ran out of the school in droves, needing reassurance that the world hadn't ended in Hannah Lake, needing their families. Ambrose Young stayed in Mr. Hildy's room and saw the North Tower go down an hour after the South Tower collapsed. His mother still wasn't answering. How could she when he couldn't get anything but an odd buzzing in his ear whenever he tried to call? He went to the wrestling room. There in the corner, in the place where he felt safest, sitting on the loosely rolled mat, he offered an awkward prayer. He was uncomfortable with asking God for anything when He so obviously had His hands full. With a choked "amen" he tried to reach his mother once more.

● ● ●

July 1994

High up in the rickety brown bleachers, Fern and Bailey sat slurping the purple Popsicles they'd pilfered from the freezer in the teacher's lounge, looking down at the bodies writhing and grappling on the mat with the fascination of the excluded. Bailey's dad, the high school wrestling coach, was holding his annual youth wrestling camp, and neither of them were participating; girls weren't encouraged to wrestle, and Bailey's disease had started to weaken his limbs significantly.

Basically, Bailey was born with all the muscle he was ever going to have, so his parents had to carefully consider how much activity he should participate in. Too much, and his muscles would tear down. In a normal person, muscles that are torn down repair themselves and rebuild stronger than before, which is what creates bigger muscles. Bailey's muscles couldn't rebuild. But if he didn't get enough activity, the muscle he did have would weaken more quickly. Since the age of four, when he was diagnosed with Duchenne muscular dystrophy, Bailey's mother had monitored Bailey's activity like a drill sergeant, making him swim with a life jacket even though Bailey could navigate the water like a fish, mandating nap time, quiet time, and sedate walks in her busy little boy's life so he maintained his ability to avoid a wheelchair for as long as possible. And they were beating the odds so far. At ten years old, most kids with Duchenne MD were already wheelchair-bound, but Bailey was still walking.

"I may not be as strong as Ambrose, but I still think I could beat him," Bailey said, his eyes narrowed on the match below them. Ambrose Young stood out like a sore thumb. He was in the same class as Bailey and Fern, but he was already eleven, old for his grade, and he stood several inches taller than all the other kids his age. He was tussling with some of the boys from the high school wrestling team who were assisting with the camp, and he was holding his own. Coach Sheen was watching him from the sidelines, shouting out instructions and stopping the action every so often to demonstrate a hold or a move.

Fern snorted and licked her purple Popsicle, wishing she had a book to read. If not for the Popsicle, she would have left a long time ago. Sweaty boys did not interest her very much.

"You couldn't beat Ambrose, Bailey. But don't feel bad. I couldn't beat him either."

Bailey looked at Fern in outrage, spinning so fast that his dripping Popsicle slid from his hand and bounced off his skinny knee. "I may not have big muscles, but I'm super smart and I know all the techniques. My dad has shown me all the moves, and he says I have a great wrestling mind!" Bailey parroted, his mouth turned down in an angry frown, his Popsicle forgotten.

Fern patted his knee and kept licking. "Your dad says that 'cause he loves you. Just like my mom tells me I'm pretty 'cause she loves me. I'm not pretty . . . and you can't beat Ambrose, buddy."

Bailey stood up suddenly and he wobbled a little, making Fern's stomach flop in fear as she imagined him falling from the bleachers.

"You aren't pretty!" Bailey shouted, making Fern instantly seethe. "But my dad would never lie to me like your mom does. You just wait! When I'm a grown-up, I will be the strongest, best wrestler in the universe!"

"My mom says you are going to die before you are a grown-up!" Fern shouted back, repeating the words she had heard her parents say when they didn't think she was listening.

Bailey's face crumpled, and he began to climb down the bleachers, hanging onto the railing as he teetered and tottered to the bottom. Fern felt the tears rise up in her eyes and her face crumple just as Bailey's had. She followed after him even though he refused to look at her again. They both cried all the way home, Bailey pedaling his bike as fast as he could, never looking over at Fern, never acknowledging her presence. Fern rode alongside him and kept wiping her nose with her sticky hands.

Her face was a mess with snot and purple Popsicle when she brokenly confessed to her mother what she had said. Fern's mother silently took her by the hand and they walked next door to Bailey's house.

Fern's aunt Angie, Bailey's mom, was holding Bailey on her lap and talking quietly to him on the front porch as Fern and her mother climbed the stairs. Rachel Taylor slid into the adjacent rocker and pulled Fern onto her lap as well. Angie looked at Fern and smiled a little, seeing the tear-stained cheeks streaked with purple. Bailey's face was hidden in her shoulder. Fern and Bailey were both a little too old to sit in their mothers' laps, but the occasion seemed to demand it.

"Fern," Aunt Angie said softly. "I was just telling Bailey that it's true. He is going to die."

Fern immediately started to cry again, and her mother pulled her against her chest. Fern could feel her mother's heart pounding beneath her cheek, but her aunt's face stayed serene, and she didn't cry. She seemed to have arrived at a conclusion that would take Fern years to accept. Bailey wrapped his arms around his mother and wailed.

Aunt Angie rubbed her son's back and kissed his head. "Bailey? Will you listen to me for a minute, son?"

Bailey was still crying as he lifted his face and looked at his mother and then looked at Fern, glowering like she had caused all of this to happen.

"You are going to die, and I am going to die, and Fern is going to die. Did you know that, Bailey? Aunt Rachel is going to die, too." Angie looked at Fern's mother and smiled apologetically, including her in the gloomy prediction.

Bailey and Fern looked at each other in horror, suddenly shocked beyond tears.

"Every living thing dies, Bailey. Some people live longer than others. We know that your illness will probably make your life shorter than some. But none of us ever know how long our lives are going to be."

Bailey looked up at her, some of the horror and despair relaxing from his expression. "Like Grandpa Sheen?"

Angie nodded, laying a kiss on his forehead. "Yes. Grandpa didn't have muscular dystrophy. But he got in a car accident, didn't he? He left us sooner than we wanted him to, but that's how life is. We don't get to choose when we go or how we go. None of us do." Angie looked her son squarely in the eyes and repeated herself firmly. "Do you hear me, Bailey? None of us do."

"So Fern might die before me?" Bailey asked hopefully.

Fern felt a rumble of laughter in her mom's chest and looked up at her in amazement. Rachel Taylor was smiling and biting her lip. Fern suddenly understood what Aunt Angie was doing.

"Yes!" Fern jumped in, nodding, her springy curls bouncing enthusiastically. "I might drown in the tub when I take my bath tonight. Or maybe I will fall down the stairs and break my neck, Bailey. I might even *get smashed by a car when I'm riding my bike tomorrow. See? You don't have to be sad. We're all going to croak sooner or later!"*

Angie and Rachel were giggling, and Bailey had a huge grin spreading across his face as he immediately joined in. "Or maybe you will fall out of the tree in your backyard, Fern. Or maybe you will read so many books that your head will explode!"

Angie wrapped her arms tightly around her son and chuckled. "I think that's enough, Bailey. We don't want Fern's head to explode, do we?"

Bailey looked at Fern, and everyone could see that he was considering this seriously. "No. I guess not. But I still hope she croaks before me." Then he challenged Fern to a wrestling match on his front lawn where he soundly pinned her in about five seconds. Who knew? Maybe he really could have whupped Ambrose Young.

● ● ●

2001

In the days and weeks following the attacks on 9/11, life returned to normal, but it felt wrong, like a favorite shirt worn inside out—still your shirt, still recognizable, but rubbing in all the wrong places, the seams revealed, the tags hanging out, the colors dulled, the words backward. But unlike the shirt, the sense of wrong couldn't be righted. It was permanent, the new normal.

Bailey watched the news with equal parts fascination and horror, tapping away at his computer, filling pages with his observations, recording the history, documenting the footage and the endless tragedies in his own words. Where Fern had always lost herself in romance, Bailey lost himself in history. Even as a child he would dive into stories of the past and wrap himself in the comfort of their timelessness, of their longevity. To read about King Arthur, who lived and died more than a thousand years before, was its own immortality, and for a boy who felt the sands of time slipping by in an endless countdown, immortality was an intoxicating concept.

Bailey had religiously kept a journal for as long as he could write. His journals filled a shelf in his bedroom bookcase, standing among the stories of other men, lining the wall with the highlights of a young life, the thoughts and dreams of an active mind. But in spite of his obsession with capturing history, Bailey was the only one who seemed to take it all in stride. He wasn't any more fearful or any more emotional than he ever was. He continued to enjoy the things he had always enjoyed, to tease Fern the way he always had, and when Fern could take no more of the history unfolding on the television screen, he was the one to talk her down from the emotional cliff everyone seemed to be teetering on.

It was Fern who found herself closer to tears, more fearful, more affectionate, and she wasn't the only one. A pervading sense of outrage and sorrow intruded on daily life. Death became very real, and in the senior class at Hannah Lake High School there was resentment mixed with the fear. It was senior year! It was supposed to be the best time of their lives. They didn't want to be afraid.

"I just wish life was more like my books," Fern complained, trying to hoist both her and Bailey's backpacks on her narrow shoulders as they left school for the day. "Main characters never die in books. If they did, the story would be ruined, or over."

"Everybody is a main character to someone," Bailey theorized, winding his way through the busy hall and out the nearest exit into the November afternoon. "There are no minor characters. Think how Ambrose must have felt watching the news in Mr. Hildy's class, knowing his mom worked in one of those towers. He's sitting there, watching it all on TV, probably wondering if he's watching his mother's death. She might be a minor character to us, but to him she's a leading lady."

Fern brooded, shaking her head at the memory. None of them had known until later how close up and personal 9/11 was for Ambrose Young. He'd been so composed, so quiet, sitting in math class, repeatedly dialing a number that had never been answered. None of them even suspected. Coach Sheen found him in the wrestling room more than five hours after the towers collapsed, after everyone else had long since gone home.

"I can't reach her, Coach." Ambrose whispered, as if the effort it took to increase his volume would crack his control. "I don't know what to do. She worked in the North Tower. It's gone now. What if she's gone?"

"Your dad is probably wondering where you are. Have you talked to him?"

"No. He's got to be going crazy too. He pretends like he doesn't love her anymore. But I know he does. I don't want to talk to him until there's good news."

Coach Sheen sat beside the boy who dwarfed him and put his arm around his shoulders. If Ambrose wasn't ready to go home, he would wait with him. He talked about random things—about the upcoming season, about the guys in Ambrose's weight, about the strengths of the teams in their district. He strategized with Ambrose about his teammates, distracting him with inconsequential things while the minutes ticked by. And Ambrose kept his emotions in check until his phone peeled out in shrill alarm, making them both jump and reach for their pockets.

"Son?" Elliott's voice was loud enough for Mike Sheen to hear it through the phone, and his heart seized, afraid of the words that hadn't been spoken. "She's okay, Brosey. She's okay. She's coming here."

Ambrose tried to speak, to thank his dad for the welcome news, but was unable to reply. Rising to his feet, he handed his phone to his coach. Then, overcome, he walked several steps and sat down once more. Mike Sheen told Elliot they were on their way to the house, snapped the phone shut, and put his arm around the shaking shoulders of his star wrestler.

There were no tears, but Ambrose shook like he was overcome with fever, like he'd been stricken with palsy, and Mike Sheen worried for a second that the emotion and stress of the day had made him genuinely sick. After a time, the manic shivering eased, and together they left the room, flipping off the lights behind them and closing the door on an agonizing afternoon, grateful that on a day of unprecedented tragedy, they had been granted a reprieve.

"My dad's worried about Ambrose," Bailey said. "He says he seems different, and he's distracted. I've noticed that even though he works as hard as he always has in practice, something's off."

"Wrestling season only started two weeks ago." Fern defended Ambrose even though she didn't need to. Ambrose had no bigger fan than Bailey Sheen.

"But September 11th was two months ago, Fern. And he's still not over it."

Fern looked up at the gray-streaked sky hanging heavily above their heads, tumultuous with the predicted storm. The clouds were churning, and the winds had just started to kick up. It was coming.

"None of us are, Bailey. And I don't think we ever will be."

3

Create a Disguise

Dear Ambrose,
  You are freakin' hot, and you're an amazing wrestler.
  I am soooo into you.
  I was wondering if maybe you want to hang out sometime?

xx Rita

Fern wrinkled her nose at the childish missive and looked at Rita's hopeful face. Fern was not the only one who had noticed Ambrose. Maybe because he was so involved with wrestling, constantly traveling and practicing with very little downtime, he hadn't had many girlfriends. His unavailability made him an even hotter commodity, and Rita had decided she was going after him. She showed Fern the note she had written for him, complete with pink paper, hearts, and lots of perfume.

"Um, this is fine, Rita. But don't you want to be original?"

Rita shrugged and looked confused. "I just want him to like me."

"But you wrote him a note because you want to get his attention, right?"

Rita nodded emphatically. Fern looked at Rita's angelic face, the way her long blonde hair swung around slim shoulders and perfect breasts, and felt a pang of despair. She was pretty sure Rita already had Ambrose's attention.

"She's such a beautiful child."

Fern heard her mother speaking from the kitchen, talking to Aunt Angie, who sat by the screen door watching Bailey and Rita sitting in the swings in Fern's backyard. Fern needed to use the bathroom, but had come in through the garage instead of the screen door so she could check on the turtle she and Bailey had captured by the creek that morning. He was in a box filled with leaves and everything else a turtle could ever want. He hadn't moved and Fern wondered if maybe they had made a mistake by taking him from his home.

"She almost doesn't look real." Fern's mother shook her head, pulling Fern's attention from the turtle. "Those bright-blue eyes and those perfect doll features."

"And that hair! It's white from root to tip. I don't think I've ever seen anything like it," Angie said. "And yet she's brown as can be. She's got that rare combination of white hair and golden skin."

Fern stood awkwardly in the hallway, listening to the two women talk about Rita, knowing that her mother and aunt thought she was still in the backyard. Rita had moved to Hannah Lake that summer with her mother, and Rachel Taylor, a pastor's wife to her core, was the first to welcome the young mother and her ten-year-old daughter. Before long, she was arranging lunch dates and inviting Rita to come play with Fern. Fern liked Rita. She was sweet and happy and willing to do whatever Fern was doing. She didn't have a very good imagination, but Fern had enough for both of them.

"I think Bailey's smitten." Angie laughed. "He hasn't blinked since he laid eyes on her. It's funny how kids are drawn to beauty just like the rest of us. Before you know it, he's going to start demonstrating his wrestling

skills and I'm going to have to find a way to distract him, bless his heart. He begged Mike to let him participate in the wrestling camp again. Every year it's the same thing. He begs, he cries, and we have to try to explain why he can't."

There was silence in the kitchen as Angie seemed lost in her thoughts and Rachel prepared sandwiches for the kids, unable to protect Angie from the realities of Bailey's disease.

"Fern seems to like Rita, doesn't she?" Angie changed the subject with a sigh but her eyes stayed fixed on her son swinging back and forth, talking nonstop to the lovely little blonde beside him. "It's good for her to have a girlfriend. She spends all her time with Bailey, but she's going to need a girlfriend as she gets older."

It was Rachel's turn to sigh. "Poor Fernie."

Fern had turned to walk back down the hall toward the restroom but stopped abruptly. Poor Fernie? She wondered with a jolt if she had some disease, a disease like Bailey's that her mother hadn't told her about. "Poor Fernie" sounded serious. She listened intently.

"She's not pretty the way that Rita is. Her teeth are going to need some major work, but she's still so small and she hasn't lost most of her baby teeth. Maybe when all her permanent teeth grow in it won't be as bad. At the rate she's growing, she's going to be in braces when she's twenty-five." Fern's mother laughed. "I wondered if she would be jealous of Rita. But so far, she seems unaware of their physical differences."

"Our little, funny Fernie," Angie said, a smile in her voice. "You can't find a better kid than Fern. I am thankful every day for her. She is such a blessing to Bailey. God knew what he was doing when he made them family, Rachel. He gave them each other. Such a tender mercy."

But Fern was rooted to the spot. She didn't hear the word blessing. She didn't stop to ponder what it meant to be one of God's tender mercies. She's not pretty. The words clanged around in her head like pots and pans being jostled and banged. She's not pretty. Little, funny Fernie. She's not pretty. Poor Fernie.

"Fern!" Rita shouted her name and waved her hand in front of Fern's face. "Hello? Where did you go? What should I say?"

Fern shook off the old memory. Funny how some things stuck with you.

"What if you say something like, 'Even when you're not around, you're all I see. You're all I think about. I wonder, is your heart as beautiful as your face? Is your mind as fascinating as the play of muscle beneath your skin? Is it possible that you might think about me too?'" Fern paused and looked at Rita.

Rita's eyes were very round. "Oh, that's good. Did you write that in one of your romance novels?" Rita was one of the only people who knew Fern wrote love stories and dreamed of having them published.

"I don't know. Probably." Fern smiled sheepishly.

"Here! Write it down," Rita squealed, pulling out a paper and a pencil and shoving them into Fern's hands.

Fern tried to remember what she had said. It came out even better the second time. Rita giggled and danced up and down as Fern finished the love note with a flourish. She signed Rita's name dramatically. Then she handed the note to Rita, who pulled some perfume from her backpack, gave the paper a spritz, folded it up, and addressed it to Ambrose.

Ambrose didn't respond immediately. In fact, it took him a few days. But on day four, there was an envelope in Rita's locker. She opened it with shaking hands. She read silently, her brow furrowed, and she clutched Fern's arm as if she was reading a winning lottery ticket.

"Fern! Listen!" she breathed.

"She walks in beauty, like the night
Of cloudless climes and starry skies;
And all that's best of dark and bright
Meet in her aspect and her eyes;"

Fern's eyebrows shot up and disappeared beneath her too-long bangs.

"He's almost as good a writer as you are, Fern!"

"He's better," Fern said dryly, blowing a stray curl out of her eyes. "The guy who wrote that is better anyway."

"He just signed it with an A," Rita whispered. "He wrote me a poem! I can't believe it!"

"Uh, Rita? That's by Lord Byron. It's very famous."

Rita's face fell, and Fern rushed to console her.

"But it's awesome that Ambrose would quote . . . Lord Byron . . . in a letter . . . to you, I mean," she reassured haltingly. Actually, it *was* pretty awesome. Fern didn't think many eighteen-year-old guys regularly quoted famous poetry to beautiful girls. She was suddenly very impressed. Rita was too.

"We have to write him back! Should we write a famous poem, too?"

"Maybe." Fern pondered, her head tilted to the side.

"I could make up my own poem." Rita looked doubtful for several seconds. Then her face lit up and she opened her mouth to speak.

"Don't start with roses are red, violets are blue!" Fern warned, knowing intuitively what was coming.

"Darn," Rita pouted, closing her mouth again. "I wasn't going to say violets are blue! I was going to say, 'Roses are red and sometimes pink. I'd really like to kiss you, I think.'"

Fern giggled and swatted her friend. "You can't say that after he's just sent you 'She Walks in Beauty.'"

"The bell is going to ring." Rita slammed her locker shut. "Will you please write something for me, Fern? Pleeeeeaase? You know I'm not going to be able to come up with anything good!" Rita saw Fern's hesitation and begged sweetly until Fern caved. And that's how Fern Taylor started writing love notes to Ambrose Young.

1994

"Whatcha doin'?" Fern asked, plopping down on Bailey's bed and look-ing around his room. It had been a while since she'd been in there. They usually played outside or in the family room. His room had wrestling paraphernalia, primarily from Penn State, all over his walls. Interspersed with the blue and white were pictures of his favorite athletes, shots of his family doing this and that, and piles of kids' books about everything from history to sports to Greek and Roman mythology.

"I'm making a list," Bailey said briefly, not lifting his eyes from his task.

"What kind of a list?"

"A list of all the things I want to do."

"What do you have so far?"

"I'm not telling."

"Why?"

"'Cause some of it's private," Bailey said, without rancor.

"Fine. Maybe I'll make a list too, and I won't tell you what's on it either."

"Go ahead." Bailey laughed. "But I can probably guess everything you're gonna write."

Fern snatched a piece of paper from Bailey's desk and found a Penn State pen in a jar of change, rocks, and randomness that sat on his night-stand. She wrote LIST at the top and stared at it.

"You won't just tell me one thing on your list?" she asked meekly after staring at the paper for several minutes without coming up with anything exciting.

Bailey sighed, a huge gust that sounded more like a perturbed par-ent than a ten-year-old boy. "Fine. But some of the things on my list I probably won't do right away. They might be things I do when I'm older . . . but I still want to do them. I'm going to do them!" he said emphatically.

"Okay. Just tell me one," Fern pleaded. *For being a girl with such a good imagination, she really couldn't think of anything she wanted to do, maybe because she went on new adventures every day in the books she read and lived through the characters in the stories she wrote.*

"I want to be a hero." Bailey looked at Fern gravely, as if he was disclosing highly classified information. *"I don't know what kind yet. Maybe like Hercules or Bruce Baumgartner."*

Fern knew who Hercules was and she knew who Bruce Baumgartner was too, simply because he was one of Bailey's favorite wrestlers and, according to Bailey, one of the best heavyweights of all time. She looked at her cousin doubtfully, but didn't voice her opinion. Hercules wasn't real and Bailey would never be as big and strong as Bruce Baumgartner.

"And if I can't be a hero like that, then maybe I could just save someone," Bailey continued, unaware of Fern's lack of faith. *"Then I could get my picture in the paper and everyone would know who I am."*

"I wouldn't want everyone to know who I am," Fern said after some thought. *"I want to be a famous writer, but I think I will use a pen name. A pen name is a name you use when you don't want everyone to know who you really are,"* she supplied, just in case Bailey wasn't aware.

"So you can keep your identity a secret, like Superman," he whispered, as if Fern's storytelling had just reached a whole new level of cool.

"And no one will ever know that it's me," Fern said softly.

• • •

They weren't typical love notes. They were love notes because Fern poured her heart and soul into them, and Ambrose seemed to do the same, answering with an honesty and a vulnerability she hadn't anticipated. Fern didn't innumerate all the things she/Rita loved about him, didn't rave on and on about his looks, his hair, his strength, his talent. She could have, but she was more interested in all the things she didn't know. So she carefully chose her words and crafted questions that would allow her access to his innermost thoughts. She knew it was a charade. But she couldn't help herself.

It started with simple questions. Easy things like sour or sweet, winter or fall, pizza or tacos. But then they veered into the deep, the personal, the revealing. Back and forth they went, asking and answering, and it felt a little like undressing—removing the unimportant things first, the jacket, the earrings, the baseball cap. Before long, buttons were undone, zippers were sliding down, and clothes were falling to the floor. Fern's heart would flutter and her breaths grew short with every barrier crossed, every piece of metaphorical clothing discarded.

Lost or Alone? Ambrose said alone, and Fern responded, "I would much rather be lost with you than alone without you, so I choose lost with a caveat." Ambrose responded, "No caveats," to which Fern replied, "Then lost, because alone feels permanent, and lost can be found."

Streetlights or Stoplights? Fern: Streetlights made me feel safe. Ambrose: Stoplights make me restless.

Nobody or Nowhere? Fern: I'd rather be nobody at home than somebody somewhere else. Ambrose: I'd rather be nowhere. Being nobody when you're expected to be somebody gets old. Fern: How would you know? Have you ever been nobody? Ambrose: Everybody who is somebody becomes nobody the moment they fail.

Smart or Beautiful? Ambrose claimed smart, but then proceeded to tell her how beautiful she (Rita) was. Fern claimed beautiful and went on to tell Ambrose how clever he was.

Before or After? Fern: Before, anticipation is usually better than the real thing. Ambrose: After. The real thing, when done right, is always better than a daydream. Fern wouldn't know, would she? She let that one slide.

Love songs or Poetry? Ambrose: Love songs—you get the best of both, poetry set to music. And you can't dance to poetry. He then made a list of his favorite ballads. It was an impressive list, and Fern spent one evening making a mix CD of all of them. Fern said poetry and sent him back some of the poems she'd written. It was risky, foolish, and she was completely naked by this point in the game, yet she played on.

Stickers or Crayons? Candles or Light bulbs? Church or School? Bells or Whistles? Old or New? The questions continued, the answers flew, and Fern would read each letter very slowly, perched on the toilet in the girl's restroom, and then spend the rest of the school day crafting a response.

She commanded Rita to read each missive, and with each note, Rita got more and more confused, both by the things Ambrose was saying and the answers Fern was giving. More than once she protested: "I don't know what you two are talking about! Can't you just talk about his abs? He's got amazing abs, Fern." Before long, Rita was handing over the notes to Fern with a shrug and delivering them back to Ambrose with complete disinterest.

Fern tried not to think about Ambrose's abs or the fact that Rita was intimately acquainted with them. About three weeks after the very first love note, she walked around the corner between classes, needing to retrieve an assignment from her locker only to see Rita pushed up against said locker, her arms wrapped around Ambrose. He was kissing her like they had just discovered they had lips . . . and tongues. Fern had gasped and turned immediately, retreating in the direction she had come. For a moment she thought she would be sick, and she swallowed the nausea rising in her throat. But it wasn't an upset stomach that made her ill, it was an upset heart. And she really had only herself to blame. She wondered if her letters simply made Ambrose love Rita more, making a mockery out of everything she revealed about herself.

4
Meet Hercules

It only took a little more than a month before the ruse was uncovered. Rita was acting funny. She wouldn't meet Fern's gaze when Fern handed her the love note for Ambrose that she had thoroughly enjoyed composing. Rita's eyes shot to Fern's outstretched hand, eyeballing the carefully folded paper like it was something to fear. She made no move to take it from Fern's hand.

"Um. I actually don't need it, Fern. We broke up. We're done."

"You broke up?" Fern asked, aghast. "What happened? Are you . . . okay?"

"Yeah. No big deal. I mean, really. He was getting weird."

"Weird? How?" Fern suddenly felt like she was going to cry, like she'd been dumped as well, and she worked at making her voice steady. Rita must have heard something though, because her eyebrows shot up beneath her swoopy bangs.

"It's really okay, Fern. He was kind of boring. Hot, but boring."

"Boring or weird? Usually weird isn't boring, Rita." Fern was thoroughly confused and growing a little angry that Rita had let Ambrose get away from them.

Rita sighed and shrugged, but this time she met Fern's eyes, apology in her gaze. "He figured out I wasn't writing the notes, Fern. The notes really didn't sound like me." It was Rita's turn to look accusing. "I'm not as smart as you are, Fern."

"Did you tell him it was me?" Fern squeaked, alarmed.

"Well . . ." Rita hedged, looking away again.

"Oh, my gosh! You did." Fern thought she was going to pass out right there in the crowded hallway. She pressed her forehead into the cool metal of her locker and willed herself to be calm.

"He wouldn't let it go, Fern. He was so pissed! He was kind of scary."

"You have to tell me everything. What did his face look like when you told him it was me?" Fern felt the bile rise.

"He looked a little . . . surprised." Rita bit her lip and played with the ring on her finger uncomfortably. Fern guessed "surprised" was an understatement. "I'm sorry, Fern. He wanted me to give him all the notes that he wrote you—um, me—whatever. But I don't have them, Fern. I gave them to you."

"Did you tell him that too?" Fern wailed, her hands hovering around her mouth in horror.

"Uh, yeah." Rita was shaking now, her misery evident on her pretty face. The altercation with Ambrose must have upset her more than she was willing to admit. "I didn't know what else to do."

Fern turned and ran straight for the girl's room, closing herself in a bathroom stall, her backpack in her lap, her head on her backpack. She squeezed her eyes closed, willing the tears away, chastising herself for getting into this situation. She was eighteen years old! Too old to hide in a bathroom stall. But she couldn't face precalculus right now. Ambrose would be there, and she didn't think she would be quite as invisible anymore.

The worst part was that every word had been real. Every word had been the truth. But she'd written the letters as if she had a face like Rita's and a body like hers too, like she was a woman who could woo a man with her figure and her smile and back it up with a brain to match. And that part was a lie. She was small and homely. Ugly.

Ambrose would feel like a fool for the words he'd given her. His words had been words for a beautiful girl. Not Fern.

● ● ●

Fern waited outside the wrestling room. She had placed the notes Ambrose had written Rita in a big, Manila envelope. Bailey had offered to return all the notes at practice. Bailey knew all along about the game Fern and Rita had played. He said he would be discreet and just give them to Ambrose after practice was over. Bailey was an honorary member of the team, the statistician, and the coach's sidekick, and he attended wrestling practice every day. But Bailey had a hard time with discreet, and Fern didn't want to make matters worse and embarrass Ambrose in front of his teammates. So she waited, cowering in a nearby hallway, watching the wrestling room door, waiting for practice to dismiss.

One by one, the boys trickled out in different states of dress or undress, wrestling shoes slung over their shoulders, shirts off even though it was ten below outside. They didn't really notice Fern. And for once she was glad to suffer from invisibility. Then Ambrose walked out, obviously freshly showered because his long hair was wet, though he'd combed it back from his face. Thankfully, he walked alongside Paul Kimball and Grant Nielson. Paulie was sweet and had always been nice to Fern, and Grant was in several of her classes and was a little nerdier than his friends. He wouldn't make a big deal about her wanting to talk to Ambrose.

Ambrose froze when he saw her standing there, and the smile that had been playing around his lips dissolved into a stiff line. His friends halted when he did, looking around in confusion, obviously not believing, even for a second, that it was Fern he had stopped for.

"Ambrose? Can I talk to you for a minute?" Fern asked, her voice faint, even to her own ears. She hoped she wouldn't have to repeat herself.

All it took was a brief jut of his chin and Ambrose's friends got the message, walking on without him, eyeing Fern curiously.

"I'll get a ride with Grant then, Brosey," Paulie called. "See you tomorrow."

Ambrose waved his friends off, but his eyes skimmed just above Fern's head as if he was eager to be away from her. Fern found herself wishing this confrontation had come even a week later. She was getting her braces off on Monday. She'd worn them for three long years. If she'd known this was going to happen, she might have tried to tame her hair. And she would have put her contacts in. As it was, she stood with her curly hair springing out in every direction, her glasses perched on her nose, wearing a sweater she'd worn for years, not because it was flattering but because it was cozy. It was thick wool in a pale shade of blue that did nothing for Fern's complexion or her slight frame. All this flashed through her mind as she took a deep breath and held the big envelope out in front of her.

"Here. All the notes you sent Rita. Here they are."

Ambrose reached out and took them, anger flashing across his face. And his eyes found hers then, pinning her back against the wall.

"So you had a good laugh, huh?"

"No." Fern winced at the childlike sound of her voice. It matched her childish figure and her bowed head.

"Why did you do it?"

"I made a suggestion. That was all. I thought I was helping Rita. She liked you. Then it got out of hand, I guess. I'm . . . sorry." And she was. Desperately sorry. Sorry that it was over. Sorry that she would never see his handwriting on paper again, read his thoughts, know him better with each line.

"Yeah. Whatever," he said. She and Rita had hurt and embarrassed him. And Fern's heart ached. She hadn't meant to hurt him. She hadn't meant to embarrass him. Ambrose walked toward the exit without another word.

"Did you like them?" she blurted.

Ambrose turned back, his face incredulous.

"I mean, until you found out I wrote them. Did you like them? The notes?" He despised her already. She might as well go for broke. And she needed to know.

Ambrose shook his head, dumbfounded, as if he couldn't believe she had the gall to ask. He ran one hand through his wet hair and shifted his weight in discomfort.

"I loved your notes," Fern rushed on, the words tumbling out like a dam had burst. "I know they weren't meant for me. But I loved them. You're funny. And smart. And you made me laugh. You even made me cry once. I wish they had been for me. So I was just wondering if you liked the things I wrote."

There was a softening around his eyes, the tight, embarrassed look he'd worn since he'd seen her standing in the hallway easing slightly.

"Why does it matter?" he asked softly.

Fern struggled to find the words. It did matter. Whether or not he knew it was her, if he liked her letters it meant he liked her. On some level. Didn't it?

"Because . . . I wrote them. And I meant them." And there it was. Her words filled the empty hallway, bouncing off the empty lockers and linoleum floors like a hundred bouncy balls, impossible to ignore or avoid. Fern felt naked and faint, completely exposed in front of the boy she had fallen in love with.

His expression was as stunned as her own must have been.

"Ambrose! Brosey! Man, you still here?" Beans sidled around the corner as if he'd just happened upon them. But Fern knew instantly that he'd heard every word. She could see it in his smirk. He must think he was saving his friend from being assaulted, or worse, asked to a girl's choice dance by an ugly girl.

"Hey, Fern." Beans acted surprised to see her there. She was surprised he knew her name. "I need a jump, Brose. My truck won't start."

"Yeah. Sure." Ambrose nodded, and Beans grasped him by his sleeve ushering him out the door. Fern's face flamed in embarrassment. She might be homely. But she wasn't stupid.

Ambrose let himself be pulled away, but then paused. Suddenly, he walked back to her and handed her the envelope that she'd given him only minutes before. Beans waited, curiosity flitting across his face.

"Here. They're yours. Just . . . don't share them. Okay?" Ambrose smiled briefly, just a sheepish twist of his well-formed lips. And then he turned and pushed out of the building, Beans on his heels. And Fern held the envelope close and wondered what it all meant.

● ● ●

"Get a net over that hair, son," Elliott Young reminded patiently as Ambrose dropped his gear by the back door of the bakery and headed to the sink to wash up.

Ambrose pulled his hair back with two hands and wrapped an elastic band around it so that it was out of his face and less likely to fall into a vat of cake batter or cookie dough. His hair was still damp from his shower after practice. He pulled a net over the dark ponytail and pulled on an apron, wrapping it around his torso the way Elliott had taught him long ago.

"Where do you want me, Dad?"

"Get started on the rolls. The dough is ready to go. I've got to finish decorating this cake. I told Daphne Nielson I'd have it ready at six-thirty, and it's six now."

"Grant said something about cake at practice. He said he thought he was close enough to weight that he would be able to steal a slice."

The cake was for Grant's little brother, Charlie, a birthday cake with characters from the animated *Hercules* on the top of three chocolate layers. It was cute and fanciful, with just enough color and chaos to appeal to a six-year-old boy. Elliott Young was good with details. His cakes always looked better than the pictures people could look at in the big cake book positioned in front of the bakery on a pedestal. Even the kids liked to peruse the laminated pages, pointing at the cake they wanted for their next big day.

Ambrose had tried his hand at decorating a few times, but his hands were big and the tools were small, and though Elliott was a patient teacher, Ambrose just didn't have the touch. He could do very basic decorating, but he was much better at baking, his strength and size more suited to labor than finesse.

He attacked the rising dough with competence, kneading and rolling and tucking each mound into a perfect roll without thought and with considerable speed. In the bigger bakeries there were machines that did what he was doing, but he didn't mind the rhythm of the operation, filling the huge sheets with handmade rolls. The smell of the first batch of rolls in the oven was killing him though. Working in the bakery during wrestling season sucked.

"Done." Elliott stepped back from the cake and checked the clock.

"Looks good," Ambrose said, his eyes on the bulging muscles of the mythical hero standing atop the cake with his arms raised. "The real Hercules wore a lion skin, though."

"Oh, yeah?" Elliott laughed. "How'd you know that?"

Ambrose shrugged. "Bailey Sheen told me once. He used to have a thing for Hercules."

Bailey had a book propped on his lap. When Ambrose peered over his shoulder to see what it was, he saw various pictures of a naked warrior fighting what looked to be mythical monsters. A few of those pictures could have been framed and put in the wrestling room. The warrior looked like he was wrestling a lion in one and a boar in another. That was probably why Sheen was reading it; Ambrose didn't know anyone who knew more about wrestling than Bailey Sheen.

Ambrose sat down on the mats beside Bailey's chair and started lacing up his wrestling shoes.

"Whatcha reading, Sheen?"

Bailey looked up, startled. He was so absorbed in his book that he hadn't even noticed Ambrose. He stared at Ambrose for a minute, his eyes lingering on his long hair and the T-shirt that was inside out. Fourteen-year-old boys were notorious for not caring about clothes and hair, but Bailey's mom wouldn't have let him leave the house like that. Then Bailey remembered that Lily Young didn't live with Ambrose anymore, and Bailey realized it was the first time he'd seen Ambrose all summer. But Ambrose had still shown up for Coach Sheen's wrestling camp, just like he did every summer.

"I'm reading a book about Hercules," Bailey said belatedly.

"I've heard of him." Ambrose finished tying his shoes and stood as Bailey turned the page.

"Hercules was the son of the Greek god Zeus," Bailey said. "But his mother was a human. He was known for his incredible strength. He was sent on a bunch of quests to kill all these different monsters. He defeated the bull of Crete. He killed a golden lion whose fur was impervious to mortal weapons. He slayed a nine-headed hydra, captured flesh-eating horses, and destroyed man-eating birds with bronze beaks, metallic feathers, and toxic poop." Ambrose chortled and Bailey beamed.

"That's what the story says! Hercules was awesome, man! Half god, half mortal, all hero. His favorite weapon was a club, and he always wore the skin from the lion, the golden lion that he killed on his very first quest." Bailey narrowed his eyes, studying Ambrose. "You kinda look like him, now that your hair is growing out. You should keep it like that, grow it even longer. Maybe it will make you even stronger, like Hercules. Plus, it makes you look meaner. The guys you wrestle will pee their pants when they see you coming."

Ambrose tugged on the hair that he'd neglected since last spring. With his mom gone now and two bachelors in the house, he had gone without *a lot of things he used to take for granted. His hair was the least of his concerns.*

"You know a lot, don't you, Sheen?"

"Yeah. I do. When you can't do much but read and study, you learn a few things, and I like reading about guys who knew a thing or two about wrestling. See this one?" Bailey pointed at the page. "Hercules on his first quest. Looks like he's working his tilt on that lion, doesn't it?"

Ambrose nodded, but his eyes were drawn to another image. It was a picture of another statue, but this one showed just the face and chest of the hero. Hercules looked serious, sad even, and his hand touched his heart, almost as if it hurt him.

"What's that picture about?"

Bailey screwed up his face and contemplated the image as if he wasn't sure.

"It's called Face of a Hero," *Bailey read the caption. He looked up at Ambrose. "Guess it wasn't all fun and games being a champion."*

Ambrose read aloud over Bailey's shoulder. "Hercules was the most famous of all the ancient heroes, and the most beloved, but many forget that his twelve labors were performed as penance. The goddess Hera caused him to lose his mind, and in his crazed state, he killed his wife and children. Grief-stricken and filled with guilt, Hercules sought out ways to balance the scales and ease his tormented soul."

Bailey groaned, "That's stupid. If I made a sculpture called Face of a Hero *I wouldn't make him sad. I'd give him a face like this." Bailey bared his teeth and gave Ambrose the crazy eye. With his tufty, light-brown curls, blue eyes, and ruddy cheeks, Bailey didn't pull off the mean face very well. Ambrose snorted and, with a quick wave to Bailey, hurried to join the other wrestlers already stretching out on the mats. But he couldn't get the bronzed face of the mourning Hercules out of his head.*

"Well, It's too late to make a lion skin out of fondant, but I think it'll pass muster." Elliott smiled. "I've got another cake to finish, and then we'll head out. You need to get home. Don't want you getting burned out."

"You're the one who has to come back tonight," Ambrose said amiably. Elliott Young staggered his hours so he could be at home in the evenings, which meant he was back at the bakery at around two in the morning. He would leave at seven when Mrs. Luebke came on shift and be back again around three in the afternoon when her shift ended, working until seven or eight again in the evening. Most days, Ambrose would join him after practice, making the work go a little quicker.

"Yeah. But I'm not trying to keep my grades up and going to wrestling practice before and after school. You don't even have any time for that pretty girlfriend."

"Pretty girlfriend is gone," Ambrose muttered.

"Oh yeah?" Elliott Young searched his son's face for signs of distress and found none. "What happened?"

Ambrose shrugged. "Let's just say she wasn't the girl I thought I knew."

"Ahh," Elliot sighed. "Sorry, Brosey."

"Beautiful or smart?" Ambrose asked his father after a long pause, never breaking his rhythm with the rolls.

"Smart," Elliott answered immediately.

"Yeah, right. That's why you chose mom, huh? 'Cause she was so ugly."

Elliott Young looked stricken for a heartbeat and Ambrose immediately apologized. "Sorry, Dad. I didn't mean it like that."

Elliott nodded and tried to smile, but Ambrose could tell he was hurt. Ambrose was really on a roll today. First Fern Taylor, now his dad. Maybe he would have to start doing penance like Hercules. Thoughts of the mournful champion rose up in his mind. He hadn't thought about him in years, yet Bailey's words rang in his mind like it had happened yesterday.

I guess being the champion isn't all fun and games, huh?

"Dad?"

"Yeah, Brosey?"

"Are you gonna be okay when I'm gone?"

"You mean to school? Sure, sure. Mrs. Luebke will help me, and Paul Kimball's mom, Jamie, came in today and filled out an application for part-time work. I think I'll hire her. Money's always an issue, but with a wrestling scholarship and with a little tightening up here and there, I think it's doable."

Ambrose didn't say anything. He didn't know if "gone" meant school. It just meant gone.

5

Tame a Lion

The marquee in front of the city offices, right on the corner of Main and Center, said *Going for Four! Take State, Ambrose!* It didn't say *Go Wrestlers!* or *Let's Go Lakers!* Just *Take State, Ambrose!* Jesse Jordan immediately took issue with the sign, but the other boys on the bus didn't seem to mind. Ambrose was one of them. He was their team captain. They all thought he would lead them to another state championship, and that was all that mattered to them.

But Ambrose was as bothered by the sign as Jesse was. He tried to shrug it off, the way he always did. They were on their way to Hershey, Pennsylvania, for the state tournament, and Ambrose couldn't wait until it was over. Then maybe he could breathe for a while, think for a while, have a little peace, just for a while.

If wrestling was just about what happened on the mat and in the wrestling room he would love the sport. He *did* love the sport. He loved the technique, the history, the sense of being in control of the outcome, the way it felt to execute the perfect takedown. He loved the simplicity of the sport. He loved the battle. He just didn't like the screaming fans or the accolades or the fact that people were always talking about Ambrose Young as if he were some kind of machine.

Elliott Young had taken Ambrose all over the country to wrestle. Since Ambrose was about eight years old, Elliott had invested every last cent into making his son into a champion, not because Elliott needed him to be, but because talent like Ambrose's deserved that kind of fostering. And Ambrose had loved that part too—being with his dad, being just one of a thousand great wrestlers on any given weekend, vying for the top spot on the medals podium. But in the last few years, as Ambrose garnered national attention and Hannah Lake Township realized they had a star on their hands, it had stopped being fun. He'd fallen out of love.

His mind tiptoed back to the army recruiter who had come into the school last month. He hadn't been able to get the visit out of his mind. Like the whole country, he wanted someone to pay for the deaths of three thousand people on 9/11. He wanted justice for the kids who lost their moms or dads. He remembered the feeling of not knowing if his own mom was all right. Flight 93 had gone down not so far away, just a little over an hour's drive from Hannah Lake, bringing the reality of the attack very close to home.

The United States was in Afghanistan, but some people thought Iraq was next. Someone had to go. Someone had to fight. If not him, then who? What if nobody went? Would it happen again? He didn't let himself think about it most of the time. But now he was anxious and jittery, his stomach empty and his mind full.

He would eat after weigh-ins. He had a hard time making 197 pounds and had to cut weight to get there. His natural, off-season weight was closer to 215. But wrestling down gave him an advantage. At 197 he was 215 pounds of power stripped down to pure, lean muscle and not much else. His height was uncommon in the wrestling world. His wingspan and the length of his torso and legs created leverage where his opponents had to rely on strength. But he had that too—in spades. And he'd been unstoppable for four seasons.

His mother had wanted him to be a football player because he was so big for his age. But football became second fiddle the first time he watched the Olympics. It was August 1992, Ambrose was nine years old, and John Smith won his second gold medal in Barcelona, beating a wrestler from Iran in the finals. Elliott Young had danced around the living room, a small man who had found his own solace on the mat. It was a sport that welcomed the big and small alike, and though he wasn't ever a serious contender, Elliott Young loved the sport and shared that love with his son. That night, they wrestled around on the family room rug, Elliott showing Ambrose the basics and promising him they would get him signed up for Coach Sheen's wrestling camp the following week.

The bus shuddered and jerked, hitting a pothole before it lumbered up onto the freeway, leaving Hannah Lake behind. When he came back home it would be done, over. But then the craziness would truly start and he would be expected to make a decision about which college to wrestle for and what to study and whether or not he could stand the pressure indefinitely. Right now he just felt tired. He thought about losing. If he lost, would it all just go away?

He shook his head adamantly and Beans caught the movement and wrinkled his brow in confusion, thinking Ambrose was trying to tell him something. Ambrose looked out the window, dismissing him. He wouldn't lose. That wasn't going to happen. He wouldn't let it.

Whenever Ambrose was tempted to just phone it in, the whistle would blow and he would start to wrestle, and the competitor in him wouldn't—couldn't—go down without leaving it all on the mat. The sport deserved that much. His dad, his coach, his team, the town. They deserved it, too. He just wished there was a way to leave it all behind . . . just for a while.

● ● ●

"Welcome to Hershey, Pennsylvania, the sweetest place on Earth, and welcome to the Giants Center where we are looking live at day one of the 2002 high school wrestling championships," the announcer's voice boomed out in the enormous arena that was packed with parents and wrestlers, friends and fans, all dressed in their school's colors, signs held high, hopes held higher. Bailey and Fern were positioned in prime seating, right on the arena floor with the mats that were spread from one end to the other.

According to Bailey, sometimes being in a wheelchair had its advantages. Plus, being a coach's kid and the top stat keeper gave him a job to do, and Bailey was all about doing it. Fern's job was to assist Bailey with stat-keeping—as well as making sure he had food and a set of legs and hands—and to let Coach Sheen know when Bailey needed a bathroom break or something she couldn't provide. They had it down to a science.

They would plan breaks between rounds, mapping out each day before it started. Sometimes it was Angie who played assistant, sometimes one of Bailey's older sisters, but most of the time it was Fern at Bailey's side. On bathroom breaks, Bailey filled his dad in on the team standings, the point spreads, the individual races, as his dad helped him do the things he couldn't do for himself.

Between all of them, with Coach Sheen doing the heavy lifting when it was needed, Bailey hadn't ever missed a tournament. Coach Sheen had gained a little notoriety and more than a little respect throughout the wrestling community as he'd juggled the responsibilities to his team with the needs of his son. Coach Sheen always claimed he got the better end of the deal—Bailey had an amazing mind for facts and figures and had made himself indispensable.

Bailey had witnessed every one of Ambrose Young's matches at every one of his state tournaments. Bailey loved to watch Ambrose wrestle more than anyone else on the team, and he hollered as Ambrose took the mat for his first match of the tournament. According to Bailey, it shouldn't be a contest. Ambrose was far superior in every way, but those first matches were always some of the scariest, and everyone was eager to get them out of the way.

In his first round, Ambrose was matched up with a kid from Altoona that was far better than his record. He'd clinched the third spot in his district, making it to state by the skin of his teeth in an overtime match. He was a senior, he was hungry, and everyone wants to knock the champion from the pedestal. To make things worse, Ambrose wasn't himself. He seemed tired, distracted, even unwell.

When the match started, more than half of the eyes in the arena were riveted on the action in the far left corner, even though there were almost a dozen other matches going on at the same time. Ambrose was his normal, offensive self, shooting first, moving more, constantly making contact, but he was off his game. He started his shots from too far back and then didn't finish them when he might have scored. The big kid from Altoona gained confidence as the first two minutes came to an end and the score was tied at zero. Two minutes with Ambrose Young with it all tied up was something to take pride in. Ambrose should be putting the hurt on him, but he wasn't, and everyone watching knew it.

The whistle started the second round and it was more of the same, except maybe worse. Ambrose kept trying to stir something up, but his attempts were halfhearted, and when his opponent chose down and was able to get an escape, it was Ambrose 0, the Altoona Lion 1. Bailey roared and moaned from the sidelines, and at the end of the second period with the score still 0–1, Bailey started to make efforts to get Ambrose's attention.

He started chanting, "Hercules! Hercules! Hercules!"

"Help me, Fern!" he urged. Fern wasn't much of a chanter or a yeller, but she was starting to feel sick, like something was way off with Ambrose. She didn't want him to lose this way. So she joined Bailey in the chant. A few of the fans were sitting close to the corner and without much urging, they chimed in too.

"Hercules, Hercules, Hercules," they roared, understanding that the demigod of Hannah Lake was about to be dethroned. Ambrose Young was losing.

With twenty seconds left in the match, the referee stopped the match for the second time because the 197-pound lion from Altoona needed to adjust the tape on his fingers. Because it was the second time the action had been stopped, Ambrose would be able to choose his position—up, down, or neutral—to end the match.

Bailey had maneuvered himself to the edge of the mat next to the two chairs designated for the Hannah Lake coaches. No one challenged him. Perks of being in a wheelchair. You got away with a lot more than you otherwise would.

"Hercules!" he shouted at Ambrose, and Ambrose shook his head in disbelief. He was listening to his coaches, but not listening. When Bailey interrupted, the frenzied instructions ceased and three sets of frustrated eyes turned on him.

"What are you yelling about, Sheen?" Ambrose was numb. In twenty seconds his shot at a four-peat would go up in smoke. And he couldn't seem to shake off the lethargy, the sense that none of this was real.

"Remember Hercules?" Bailey demanded. It really wasn't a question, the way he shoved the statement at Ambrose.

Ambrose looked incredulous and more than a little confused.

"Remember the story about the lion?" Bailey insisted impatiently.

"No . . ." Ambrose adjusted his headgear and looked over at his opponent who was still getting his fingers wrapped while his coaches threw instructions at him and tried not to look euphoric over the turn of events.

"This guy's a lion too. An Altoona Mountain Lion, right? Hercules's arrows weren't working on the lion. Your shots aren't working either."

"Thanks, man," Ambrose muttered dryly, and turned to walk back to the center of the mat.

"You know how Hercules beat the lion?" Bailey raised his voice to be heard.

"No, I don't," Ambrose said over his shoulder.

"He was stronger than the lion. He got on the lion's back, and he squeezed the shit out of him!" Bailey yelled after him.

Ambrose looked back at Bailey and something flickered across his face. When the referee asked Ambrose what position he would take, he chose top. His fans gasped, the entire township of Hannah Lake gasped, Elliott Young cursed, and Ambrose Young's coaches' mouths dropped along with their stomachs and their hopes for another team title. It was as if Ambrose wanted to lose. You didn't choose top when you were down by one with twenty seconds left in the match. All Altoona had to do was not get turned—or even worse, escape and get another point—and he would win the match.

When the whistle blew, it was as if someone hit slow motion. Even Ambrose's movements seemed slow and precise. His opponent scrambled, trying to push up and out, but instead found himself in a vise so tight he forgot for a moment about the twenty seconds on the clock, about the match that was his to win, and about the glory that would come with it. He sucked in a breath as he was shoved face first into the mat and his left arm was yanked out from under him. The vise grew even tighter and he thought about slapping the mat with his right hand, the way the UFC guys did when they were tapping out. His legs shot out, splaying for leverage as his left arm was threaded past his right armpit. He knew what was happening. And there wasn't a damn thing he could do about it.

Slowly, precisely, Ambrose wrapped himself around his opponent, tying up his legs as he tipped the lion onto his back, never releasing the pressure. In fact, Ambrose's arms trembled with the amount of power he was exerting. And then the count began, one, two, three, four, five. Three back points. Ambrose thought about Hercules and the lion with the golden fleece and stretched and tipped the lion from Altoona just a little more. With two seconds left on the clock, the referee slapped the mat.

Pinned.

The spectators went wild, and the whole town of Hannah Lake claimed they had believed in him all along. Coach Sheen looked at his son and grinned, Elliott Young fought back tears, Fern discovered her nails were shredded, and Ambrose helped his opponent stand. He didn't roar or leap into his coach's arms, but when he looked at Bailey, there was relief in his face, and a small smile played around his lips.

The tale of his first match spread like wildfire, and the chant of Hercules accompanied Ambrose in ever increasing volume from one match to the next, providing fodder for his longtime fans and flaming a whole new following. Ambrose didn't falter for the rest of the tournament. It was as if he'd flirted with the edge and decided it wasn't for him. By the time he took the mat in the finals, his last match in his unprecedented high school wrestling career, the whole arena roared the name Hercules.

But after he dominated his last match and the referee raised his right arm in victory, after the announcers went wild with speculation as to what came next for the incredible Ambrose Young, the four-time state champion found a quiet corner and without fanfare, slid his singlet around his waist, pulled on his royal blue Hannah Lake Wrestling T-shirt, and covered his head with his towel. His friends found him there when it was all over and the medals were being awarded.

6

See the World

It was in the middle of nowhere, just a big crater in the ground. But the wreckage had all been cleared away. People said charred paper, debris, bits of clothing and luggage, frames of some of the seats, and twisted metal had been scattered and spread around the crash in an eight-mile radius and into the wooded area south of the crater. Some people said there were pieces of wreckage in the treetops and in the bottom of a nearby lake. A farmer even found a piece of the fuselage in his field.

But there was no debris there now. It had all been cleared away. The cameras, the forensic teams, the yellow tape, all gone. The five boys thought they might have trouble getting close, but nobody was there to stop them from taking Grant's old car off the road and winding it down to where they knew they'd find the place Flight 93 had collided with the Pennsylvania earth.

There was a fence surrounding the area—a forty-foot chain-link fence that had withered flowers stuck through the links and signs and stuffed animals wedged here and there. It had been seven months since 9/11, and most of the signs and the candles, the gifts and the notes had been cleared away by volunteers, but there was something about the place that was so somber as to make even five eighteen-year-old boys sober up and listen to the wind that whispered through nearby trees.

It was April, and though the sun had peeked out briefly earlier in the day, spring hadn't found southern Pennsylvania, and the brittle fingers of winter found their way through their clothing to the young skin already prickling with the memory of death that hung in the air.

They stood next to the fence, linking their fingers through the holes and peering through the chinks to see if they could make out the crater in the earth, marking the resting place of forty people none of them had ever met. But they knew some of their names, some of their stories, and they were awed and silent, each one wrapped in his own thoughts.

"I can't see a damn thing," Jesse finally admitted after a long silence. He'd had plans with his girlfriend, Marley, and though he was always game for a night with the boys, he was suddenly wishing he'd stayed home this time. He was cold and making out was a whole hell of a lot more fun than staring out into a dark field where a bunch of people had died.

"Shhh!" Grant hissed, nervous about the prospect of capture and interrogation. He'd been certain driving down to Shanksville on a whim was a stupid idea. So he'd lectured and warned but had come along anyway, just like he always did.

"You might not be able to see anything . . . but . . . do you feel that?" Paulie had his eyes closed, his face lifted to the air, as if he was truly hearing something the rest of them couldn't. Paulie was the dreamer, the sensitive one, but nobody argued with him this time. There was something there, something almost sacred shimmered in the quiet—but it wasn't frightening. It was strangely peaceful, even in the cold darkness.

"Anyone need a drink? I need a drink," Beans whispered after another long stretch of silence. He fished in his jacket and pulled out a flask, jubilantly raising it in memorial. "Don't mind if I do."

"I thought you weren't drinking anymore!" Grant frowned.

"Season's over, man, and I am officially drinking again," Beans declared cheerfully, taking a long pull and wiping his grin with the back of his hand. He offered it to Jesse, and Jesse gladly took a swig, shuddering as the fiery liquid burned a path to his stomach.

The only one who didn't seem to have anything to say was Ambrose. But that wasn't abnormal. Ambrose spoke up rarely, and when he did, most people listened. In fact, he was the reason they were there, in the middle of nowhere on a Saturday night. Since the army recruiter had come to the school, Ambrose hadn't been able to think of anything else. The five of them had sat on the back row of the auditorium, snickering, making jokes about boot camp being a walk in the park compared to Coach Sheen's wrestling practices. Except Ambrose. He hadn't snickered or made jokes. He had listened quietly, his dark eyes fixed on the recruiter, his posture tense, his hands clasped in his lap.

They were all seniors, and they would all be graduating in a couple of months. Wrestling season had ended two weeks ago, and they were already restless—maybe more than they had ever been— because there would be no more seasons, nothing to train for, no more matches to dream about, no victories to enjoy. They were done. Done . . . except Ambrose, who had been highly recruited by several schools and who had the academics and the athletic record to go to Penn State on a full ride. He was the only one who had a way out.

They stood on the precipice of enormous change, and none of them, not even Ambrose—especially not Ambrose—were excited about the prospect. But whether or not they chose to take a step into the unknown, the unknown would still come, the yawning precipice would still swallow them whole, and life as they knew it would be over. And they had all become highly aware of the end.

"What are we doing here, Brosey?" Jesse finally said what they'd all been thinking. As a result, four pairs of eyes narrowed in on

Ambrose's face. It was a strong face, a face more prone to introspection than jest. It was a face the girls were drawn to and the guys secretly coveted. Ambrose Young was a guy's guy, though, and his friends had always felt safest in his presence, as if just by being near him, some of his luster would rub off on them. And it wasn't just his size or good looks or the Samson-like hair that he wore to his shoulders in defiance of the style or the fact that it bothered Coach Sheen. It was the fact that life had fallen into place for Ambrose Young, right from the start, and watching him, you believed it always would. There was something comforting in that.

"I signed up," Ambrose said, his words clipped and final.

"For what? School? Yeah. We know, Brosey. Don't rub it in." Grant laughed, but the sound was pained. There had been no scholarships for Grant Nielson, though he'd finished in the top of his class. Grant was a good wrestler, not a great wrestler, and Pennsylvania was known for their wrestlers. You had to be a great wrestler to get a scholarship. And there was no money in some savings account for college. Grant would get there, but he would have to work his way through . . . slowly.

"Nah. Not for school." Ambrose sighed, and Grant's face twisted in confusion.

"Ho-ly shit." Beans drew the words out on a long whisper. He may have been on his way to being drunk, but the kid wasn't slow. "That recruiter! I saw you talking to him. You wanna be a soldier?"

There was a shocked intake of breath as Ambrose Young met the stunned gazes of his four best friends. "I haven't even told Elliott. But I'm going. I'm just wondering if any of you want to come with me."

"So, what? You brought us out here to soften us up? Make us feel all patriotic or somethin'?" Jesse said. "'Cause that ain't enough, Brosey. Hell, what are you thinkin', man? You could get a leg blown off or something. Then how you gonna wrestle? Then it's over! You got it made! You got Penn freakin' State. What? You want the Hawkeyes?

They'd take you, ya know. A big guy that moves like a little guy—a 197-pounder that shoots like he's still 152? What you bench pressin' now, Brose? There isn't anyone who can hang with you, man! You gotta go to school!"

Jesse didn't stop talking as they left the makeshift memorial and pulled back out onto the highway heading for home. Jesse had been a state champ too, just like Ambrose. But Ambrose hadn't just done it once. Four-time state champ, undefeated the last three years, the first Pennsylvania wrestler to win a state championship as a freshman in the upper weights. He'd been 160 pounds as a freshman. His only loss had come early in the year at the hands of the reigning state champ, who was a senior. Ambrose pinned him at state. That win had put him in the record books.

Jesse threw his hands up and swore, letting loose a string of obscenities that made even Beans, Mr. Foul Mouth himself, feel a little uncomfortable. Jesse would kill to be in Ambrose's position.

"You got it made, man!" he said again, shaking his head. Beans handed Jesse the flask and patted his back, trying to soothe his incredulous friend.

They rode in silence once more. Grant was at the wheel out of habit. He never drank and had designated himself the driver and caretaker ever since they all started driving, even though Paulie and Ambrose hadn't partaken in the comfort that Beans had to offer that night.

"I'm in," Grant said quietly.

"What?" Jesse screeched, spilling what was left in the flask down the front of his shirt.

"I'm in," Grant repeated. "They'll help me pay for school, right? That's what the recruiter said. I gotta do something. I sure as hell don't want to farm for the rest of my life. At the rate I'm saving money, I'll finish college when I'm forty-five."

"You just swore, Grant," Paulie whispered. He'd never heard Grant swear. Ever. None of them had.

"It's about damn time," Beans howled, laughing. "Next we just gotta get him laid! He can't go to war without knowing the pleasure of a woman's body." Beans said this in his best Don Juan, Latin lover voice. Grant just sighed and shook his head.

"What about you, Beans?" Ambrose asked with a smirk.

"Me? Oh, I know all about the pleasure of a woman's body," Beans continued on in accented English, his eyebrows waggling.

"The army, Beans. The army. What about it?"

"Sure. Hell, yeah. Whatever." Beans acquiesced with a shrug. "I got nothin' better to do."

Jesse groaned loudly and put his head in his hands.

"Paulie?" Ambrose asked, ignoring Jesse's distress. "You in?"

Paulie looked a little stricken, his loyalty to his friends warring with his self-preservation. "Brose . . . I'm a lover. Not a fighter," he said seriously. "The only reason I wrestled was to be with you guys, and you know how much I hated it. I can't imagine combat."

"Paulie?" Beans interjected.

"Yeah, Beans?"

"You may not be a fighter, but you aren't a lover either. You need to get laid, too. Guys in uniform get laid. A lot."

"So do rock stars, and I am a lot better with a guitar than I am with a gun," Paulie countered. "Plus, you know my mom would never let me." Paul's dad had been killed in a mining accident when he was nine years old and his younger sister was a baby. His mom had moved back home to Hannah Lake with her two little kids to be closer to her parents and ended up staying.

"You may have hated wrestling, Paulie. But you were good at it. You'll be a good soldier, too."

Paulie chewed his lip but didn't answer and the car fell silent, each boy lost in his own thoughts.

"Marley wants to get married," Jesse said after a long lull. "I love her, but . . . everything is moving so damn fast. I just want to wrestle.

Surely some school out West wants a black kid that likes white people, right?"

"She wants to get married?" Beans was stunned. "We're only eighteen! You better come with us, Jess. You gotta grow up some before you let Marley put a collar on you. Plus, you know the saying. Brose Before Hos," he quipped, playing on Ambrose's name.

Jesse sighed in surrender. "Ah, hell. America needs me. How can I say no?"

Groans and laughter ensued. Jesse had always had a pretty inflated ego.

"Hey, doesn't the army have a wrestling team?" Jesse sounded almost cheerful at the thought.

"Paulie?" Ambrose asked again. Paulie was the lone holdout, and out of everyone, Paulie would be the hardest for him to leave behind. He hoped he wouldn't have to.

"I don't know, man. I guess I gotta grow up sometime. I bet my dad would be proud of me if I did. My great-grandpa served in World War II. I just don't know." He sighed. "Joining the army seems like a good way to get myself killed."

7

Dance with a Girl

There wasn't a fancy hotel or a posh location anywhere near Hannah Lake to have the prom, so Hannah Lake High School made do decorating their gymnasium with hundreds of balloons, twinkle lights, hay bales, fake trees, gazebos, or whatever the prom theme dictated.

This year's theme was "I Hope You Dance," an inspirational song that offered no inspiration with regard to decorating ideas. So the twinkle lights and balloons and gazebos made yet another appearance at yet another Hannah Lake High School prom, and as Fern sat next to Bailey, staring out onto the gymnasium floor filled with swirling couples, she wondered if the only thing that had changed in fifty years was the style of the dresses.

Fern fiddled with the neckline of her own dress, smoothing her hand over the creamy folds, swishing her legs back and forth, watching the way the skirt draped to the floor, thrilling at the hint of gold sparkle when the fabric caught the light. She and her mother had found the dress on a clearance rack at a Dillards in Pittsburgh. It had been marked down over and over again, most likely because it was a dress made for a tiny girl in a color that was not fashionable among tiny girls. But taupe looked good on red heads, and the dress looked wonderful on Fern.

She had posed for pictures with Bailey in the Taylors' living room with the bodice pulled up around her chin the way her mother liked it, but two seconds after she left the house she pushed the ruffled neckline off her shoulders and felt almost pretty for the first time in her life.

Fern hadn't been asked to the big dance. Bailey hadn't asked anyone either. He had joked that he didn't want to make any girl dread going to her prom. He'd said it with a smile, but there was a flash of something mournful in his face. Self-pity wasn't Bailey's style, and his comment surprised Fern. So she asked Bailey if he would go with her. It was prom, and they could sit home and sulk that they didn't have dates or they could go together. They were cousins, and it was completely lame, but being uncool was better than missing out. And it wasn't like going to prom together would cause any image problems. They were both the epitome of lame—literally in Bailey's case, figuratively in Fern's. It wouldn't be a night for romance, but Fern had a dress for her prom and a date too, even if it wasn't a conventional one.

Bailey was outfitted in a black tux with a pleated white shirt and a black bow tie. His curls were moussed and artfully placed, making him look a little like Justin from N'Sync . . . at least that's what Fern thought. Couples rocked back and forth, their feet barely moving, arms locked around each other.

Fern tried not to imagine how it would feel to be pressed up against someone special, dancing at her prom. She wished briefly that she was there with someone who could hold her. Fern felt a flash of remorse and looked at Bailey guiltily, but his eyes were locked on a girl in hot-pink sparkles with cascading blonde hair. Rita.

Becker Garth held her tightly and nuzzled her neck, whispering to her as they moved, his dark hair a striking contrast to her pale tresses. Becker, who had more confidence than he deserved and a swagger that some smaller men develop out of a need to make themselves seem bigger, was twenty-one and too old for a high school prom. But Rita was in the early stages of infatuation, and the dreamy look on her face as she gazed at him made her more beautiful still.

"Rita looks so pretty." Fern smiled, happy for their friend.

"Rita always looks pretty," Bailey said, his eyes still held captive. Something in his tone made Fern's heart constrict. Maybe it was the fact that she, Fern, never felt pretty. Maybe it was the fact that Bailey had noticed and was captured by something Fern thought he was immune to, something she thought he put little value in. Now here he was, her cousin, her best friend, her partner in crime, lured in like all the rest. And if Bailey Sheen fell for the pretty face, there was no hope for Fern. Ambrose Young would surely never look at one so plain.

It always came back to Ambrose.

He was there, surrounded by his friends. Ambrose, Grant, and Paulie seemed to have come without dates, much to the despair of the senior class girls who sat home, uninvited to their senior prom. Resplendent in black tuxes, young and handsome, slicked up and clean-shaven, they celebrated with everyone and no one in particular.

"I'm going to ask Rita to dance," Bailey said suddenly, his wheelchair lurching out onto the floor as if he had just stumbled on the decision and he was going for it before he lost his nerve.

"Wh-what?" Fern stuttered. She sincerely hoped Becker Garth wouldn't be a jerk. She watched in equal parts fascination and fear as Bailey motored up alongside Rita as she and Becker looped hands to walk off the floor.

Rita smiled at Bailey and laughed at something he said. Leave it to Bailey; he was definitely not short on charm. Becker scowled and walked right past Bailey, as if he wasn't worth stopping, but Rita dropped his hand and, without waiting for Becker's permission, sat gingerly on Bailey's lap and looped her arms around his shoulders. A new song pulsed from the speakers, Missy Elliott demanding to "Get Ur Freak On," and Bailey made his wheelchair spin in circles, round and round, until Rita was laughing and clinging to him, her hair a blonde wave across his thin chest.

Fern bobbed her head with the music, wiggling in place, laughing at her audacious friend. Bailey was fearless. Especially considering Becker Garth still stood on the dance floor, his arms crossed unhappily, waiting for the song to be over. If Fern were a beautiful girl, she might dare go up and try to distract him, maybe ask him to dance so that Bailey could have his moment without Becker chaperoning. But she wasn't. So she gnawed at her fingernail and hoped for the best.

"Hey, Fern."

"Uh . . . hi Grant." Fern straightened, hiding her jagged nails in her lap. Grant Nielson had his hands shoved into his pockets as if he were as comfortable in a tux as he was in blue jeans. He smiled at her and tossed his head toward the dance floor.

"Wanna dance? Bailey won't mind, right? Since he's dancing with Rita?"

"Sure! Okay!" Fern stood up a little too fast and wobbled in the heels that gave her three inches and made her a staggering five foot five. Grant grinned again, and his hand shot out to steady her.

"You look pretty, Fern." Grant sounded surprised. His eyes roved over her and settled on her face, his eyes narrowed as if he was trying to figure out what was different.

The song changed about twenty seconds after they started dancing, and Fern thought that was all she was going to get, but Grant looped his arms around her waist when a ballad began and seemed happy to partner up for another song. Fern swiveled her head around to see if Bailey had relinquished Rita, only to discover he hadn't. He was making lazy figure eights around the other dancers, Rita's head against his shoulder as they mimicked slow dancing as best they could. Becker was standing by the punch bowl, his mouth twisted and his face red.

"Sheen's gonna get pounded if he isn't careful." Grant laughed, following Fern's gaze.

"I'm more worried about Rita," Fern said, realizing suddenly that she was. Becker made her nervous.

"Yeah. Maybe you're right. You'd have to be pretty messed up to hit a kid in a wheelchair. Plus, if Garth touches him, all heck would break loose. No wrestler in here would allow it."

"Because of Coach Sheen?"

"Yeah. And because of Bailey. He's one of us."

Fern beamed, glad to know the feeling was mutual. Bailey loved every member of the wrestling team and considered himself the team's assistant coach, mascot, personal trainer, head statistician, and all-around wrestling guru.

Next, Paulie asked Fern to dance. He was his sweet, distracted self, and Fern enjoyed dancing with him, but when Beans sidled up and invited her onto the dance floor, Fern started wondering if maybe she wasn't the butt of a private joke, or worse, a bet. Maybe Ambrose would be next, and then they would all ask her to pose with them in a picture, laughing uproariously at their sham of a prom. Like she was a circus sideshow.

But Ambrose never asked her to dance. He never asked anyone. He stood head and shoulders above most of the crowd, his hair pulled back tightly in a sleek tail at his nape, accentuating the plains and valleys of his handsome face, the wide set of his dark eyes, the straight brows and the strong jaw. The one time he caught Fern looking at him he frowned and looked away and Fern wondered what she'd done.

On the way home, Bailey was unusually quiet. He claimed fatigue, but Fern knew better.

"You okay, B?"

Bailey sighed and Fern met his gaze in the rearview mirror. Bailey would never be able to drive, and he never sat in the front seat. Whenever he and Fern cruised around town, Fern would borrow the Sheens' van because it was rigged for wheelchair use. The middle seat of the van was pulled out so Bailey could drive his wheelchair up a ramp and into the body of the vehicle. Then his wheels were locked and he was strapped in with belts that were anchored to the floor so he wouldn't tip over in his chair. Dragging Main Street wasn't much fun with Bailey in the backseat, but Fern and Bailey were used to it, and sometimes Rita would come along so that Fern didn't feel like a chauffeur.

"Nah. Tonight's one of those nights, Fernie."

"Too much reality?"

"Way too much reality."

"Me too," Fern said softly, and felt her throat close against the emotion that rose in her chest. Sometimes life seemed particularly unfair, unduly harsh, and beyond bearing.

"You looked like you were having a good time. Bunch of the guys asked you to dance, right?"

"Did you ask them to dance with me, Bailey?" The realization slammed into her.

"Yeah . . . I did. Is that okay?" Bailey looked stricken and Fern sighed and forgave him instantly.

"Sure. It was fun."

"Ambrose didn't ask though, did he?"

"Nope."

"I'm sorry, Fern." Bailey was well-aware of Fern's feelings for Ambrose Young and her despair after the debacle with the love letters.

"Do you think there's any way someone like Ambrose could fall in love with someone like me?" Fern caught Bailey's gaze in the mirror again, knowing he would understand.

"Only if he's lucky."

"Oh, Bailey." Fern shook her head, but loved him for saying it . . . and even more for meaning it. She and Bailey had agreed they weren't ready to go home, so they cruised up and down the dark Main Street, the darkened windows of the businesses reflecting the bright head-lights of the old blue van and the dim prospects of the lonely pair inside. After a while, Fern turned off the main drag and headed for home, suddenly tired and ready for the uncomplicated comfort of her own bed.

"It's hard to come to terms with sometimes," Bailey said abruptly.

Fern waited for him to continue.

"It's hard to come to terms with the fact that you aren't ever going to be loved the way you want to be loved."

For a moment, Fern thought he was talking about her and Ambrose. But then she realized he wasn't talking about unrequited love . . . not really. He was talking about his illness. He was talking about Rita. He was talking about the things he could never give her and the things she would never want from him. Because he was sick. And he wouldn't be getting better.

"There are times when I think I just can't take it anymore." Bailey's voice cracked, and he stopped talking as suddenly as he had begun.

Fern's eyes filled with sympathetic tears, and she wiped at them as she pulled the van into the Sheens' dark garage, the automatic light flickering on in sleepy welcome overhead. She slid the car into park, unlatched her seat belt, and turned in her seat, looking at her cousin. Bailey's face looked haggard in the shadows, and Fern felt a flash of fear, reminded that he wouldn't be beside her forever—he wouldn't even be beside her for long. She reached out and grabbed his hand.

"There are times like that, Bailey. Times you don't think you can take it anymore. But then you discover that you can. You always do. You're tough. You'll take a deep breath, swallow just a little bit more, endure just a little longer, and eventually you'll get your second wind," Fern said, her smile wobbly and her teary eyes contradicting her encouraging words.

Bailey nodded, agreeing with her, but there were tears in his eyes too. "But there are times when you just need to acknowledge the shit, Fern, you know?"

Fern nodded, squeezing his hand a little tighter. "Yep. And that's okay, too."

"You just need to acknowledge it. Face the shit." Bailey's voice grew stronger, strident even. "Accept the truth in it. Own it, wallow in it, become one with the shit." Bailey sighed, the heavy mood lifting with his insistence on profanity. Swearing could be very therapeutic.

Fern smiled wanly. "Become one with the shit?"

"Yes! If that's what it takes."

"I've got Rocky Road ice cream. It looks a little like poop. Can we become one with the Rocky Road instead?"

"It does look a little like shit. Nuts and everything. Count me in."

"Sick, Bailey!"

Bailey cackled as Fern climbed in the back, unhooked the belts that secured his chair and shoved the sliding door open.

"Bailey?"

"Yeah?"

"I love you."

"I love you too, Fern."

• • •

That night, after her shimmery dress was put away, her curls unpinned from the complicated twist, and her face scrubbed free of makeup, Fern stood naked in front of her mirror and looked at herself in frank appraisal. She'd grown up some, hadn't she? She was almost five foot two. Not that small. She was still on the scrawny side, but at least she didn't look twelve anymore.

She smiled at herself, admiring the straight white teeth she'd suffered so long for. Her hair was recovering from last summer's hair disaster. Convinced shorter hair would be more manageable, she'd directed Connie at Hair She Blows to cut it short like a boy. Maybe it wasn't short enough, because it had sprung out from her head like a seventies fro, and she'd spent most of her senior year looking like Annie from the Broadway play, further accentuating her little girl persona. Now, it almost touched her shoulders, and she could force it into a ponytail. She promised herself she wouldn't cut it again. She would let it grow until it reached her waist, hoping the weight of longer hair would relax the curl. Think Nicole Kidman in *Days of Thunder*. Nicole Kidman was a beautiful redhead. But she was also tall. Fern sighed and pulled her pajamas on. Elmo stared back at her from the front of her top.

"Elmo loves you!" she said to herself in her best squeaky imitation of the puppet's voice. Maybe it was time to get some new clothes, maybe a new style. Maybe she would look older if she didn't wear Elmo pajamas. She should buy some jeans that fit and some T-shirts that actually revealed that she wasn't flat-chested . . . not anymore.

But was she still ugly? Or had she just been ugly for so long that everyone had already made up their minds? Everyone, meaning the guys she went to school with. Everyone, meaning Ambrose.

She sat at her little desk and turned on her computer. She was working on a new novel. A new novel with the same story line. In all her stories, either the prince fell in love with a commoner, the rock star lost his heart to a fan, the president was smitten by the lowly school teacher, or the billionaire became besotted with the sales clerk. There was a theme there, a pattern that Fern didn't want to examine too closely. And usually, Fern could easily imagine herself in the role of the female love interest. She always wrote in the first person and gave herself long limbs, flowing locks, big breasts, and blue eyes. But tonight her eyes kept straying to her mirror, to her own pale face with a smattering of freckles.

For a long time she sat, staring at the computer screen. She thought of the prom, the way Ambrose ignored her. She thought of the conversation afterward and Bailey's surrender to the "shit," even if it was only temporary surrender. She thought about the things she didn't understand and the way she felt about herself. And then she began to type, to rhyme, to pour her heart out on the page.

If God makes all our faces, did he laugh when he made me?
Does he make the legs that cannot walk and eyes that cannot see?
Does he curl the hair upon my head 'til it rebels in wild defiance?
Does he close the ears of the deaf man to make him more reliant?

Is the way I look coincidence or just a twist of fate?
If he made me this way, is it okay to blame him for the things I
        hate?
For the flaws that seem to worsen every time I see a mirror,
For the ugliness I see in me, for the loathing and the fear?

Does he sculpt us for his pleasure, for a reason I can't see?
If God makes all our faces, did he laugh when he made me?

Fern sighed and hit print. When her cheap printer spit out the poem, Fern stuck it to her wall, shoving a thumbtack through the plain white page. Then she crawled into bed and tried to turn off the words that kept repeating in her head. *If God makes all our faces, if God makes all our faces, if God makes all our faces . . .*

8
Party Hard

Ambrose didn't like alcohol. He didn't like the fuzziness in his head or the fear that he would do something monumentally stupid and embarrass himself, his dad, or his town. Coach Sheen didn't allow any alcohol during the season. No excuses. You got caught drinking and you were off the team, period. None of them would risk wrestling for a drink.

For Ambrose, wrestling was a year-round thing. He was always training, always competing. He wrestled during football and track, even though he was on the high school team for both sports. And because he was always training, he never drank.

But he wasn't training anymore, because he wasn't wrestling. He was done. And the town was in a quiet panic. Five of their boys, off to war. The news had spread like wildfire and though people professed pride and had clapped the boys on their backs, telling them they appreciated their sacrifice and their service, the underlying current was one of horror. Elliott had bowed his head as Ambrose had broken the news to him.

"Is this what you really want to do, son?" he asked quietly. When Ambrose said it was, Elliott patted him on the cheeks and said, "I love you, Brosey. And I will support you in whatever you do." But Ambrose had caught him on his knees several times, tearfully praying. He had a feeling his father was making all kinds of deals with God.

Coach Sanders at Penn State had said he respected Ambrose's choice. "God, country, family, wrestling," he'd said to Ambrose. He said if Ambrose felt the call to serve his country, that's what he should do.

After graduation, Mr. Hildy, his math teacher had pulled him aside and asked for a word. Mr. Hildy was a Vietnam vet. Ambrose had always respected him, always admired the way he conducted himself and ran his classes.

"I hear you signed up for the guard. You know you'll get called up, don't you? You'll be shipped out faster than you can say Saddam Hussein. Do you realize that?" Mr. Hildy asked, his arms folded, his bushy gray brows lifted in question.

"I know."

"Why you goin'?"

"Why did you go?"

"I was drafted," Mr. Hildy said bluntly.

"So you wouldn't have gone if you had a choice?"

"No. But I wouldn't change it either. The things I fought for, I'd fight for again. I'd fight for my family, my freedom to say whatever the hell I want, and for the guys I fought beside. That, most of all. You fight for the guys you serve with. In the middle of a firefight, that's all you think about."

Ambrose nodded as if he understood.

"But I'm just telling you right now. The lucky ones are the ones who don't come back. You hear me?"

Ambrose nodded again, shocked. Without another word, Mr. Hildy walked away, but he left doubt behind, and Ambrose experienced his first qualms. Maybe he was making a huge mistake. The doubt made him angry and restless. He was committed. And he wasn't turning back.

The United States and her allies were in Afghanistan. Iraq was next. Everyone knew it. Ambrose and his friends would enter basic training in September. Ambrose wished it was tomorrow. But that was what they'd all agreed to.

That summer was hell. Beans seemed intent on drinking himself to death, and Jesse might as well be married for as much time as he spent with his friends. Grant was farming, Paulie, writing endless songs about leaving home, working himself up into a blubbering mess. Ambrose spent all his time at the bakery or lifting weights. And summer dragged by.

Now, here they were, Saturday night, two days before they left for Fort Sill in Oklahoma, and they were all at the lake celebrating with every kid in the county. There was soda and beer, balloons, trucks with tailgates lowered, and food at every turn. Some kids swam, some kids danced at the water's edge, but the majority just talked and laughed and sat around the bonfire, reminiscing and trying to pack in one last summer memory to see them through the years ahead.

Bailey Sheen was there. Ambrose had helped Jesse hoist his chair and carry him down to the lake where he could mix and mingle. Fern was with him, as usual. She wasn't wearing her glasses and her curly hair was tamed into a braid with a few tendrils curling around her face. She didn't hold a candle to Rita, but she was cute, Ambrose had to admit that much. She had on a flowery sundress and flip flops, and try as he might, he found himself looking at her throughout the evening. He didn't know what it was about her. He could have started something with any number of girls he called friends who might like to send him off with a little something special. But sloppy coupling had never been his thing, and he didn't want to start now. And he kept looking at Fern.

He ended up drinking more beer than he should have, getting pulled into the lake by a bunch of guys from the wrestling team, and missing the moment when Fern left. He saw the Sheens' old blue van pull away, crunching across the gravel, and he felt a twist of regret slice through him.

He was wet and mad and a little drunk—and not enjoying himself at all. He stood next to the fire trying to squeeze the water from his clothes, and he wondered if the regret he felt over Fern was just his way of digging in his heels at the last moment, grabbing for something to hold onto as his old life slipped away and the future dawned, scary and new.

He let the fire dry the worst of the wet from his jeans and T-shirt and let the conversation flow around him. The flames looked like Fern's hair. He cursed aloud, causing Beans to pause in the middle of introducing a new game. He stood up abruptly, knocking the flimsy lawn chair over, and walked away from the fire, knowing he should just leave, knowing he wasn't himself. He was such an idiot. He'd twiddled his thumbs all summer long with not a damn thing to do. Now here he was, the night before his last day in town, and he was just discovering that he might like a girl who had all but thrown herself at him more than six months before.

He was parked at the top of the hill, and the cars that were nestled close to his were empty. Good. He could just sneak away. He was miserable, his crotch was wet, his shirt was stiff, and he was all partied out. He headed up the hill only to stop in his tracks. Fern was picking her way down the path to the lake. She was back. She smiled as she approached him and fingered a strand of her hair that had come loose and was curling against her neck.

"Bailey left his ball cap, and I offered to come back for it after I dropped him off. And I wanted to say good-bye. I got to talk to Paulie and Grant, but I didn't get to talk to you. I hope it's okay if I write you sometimes. I would want people to write me . . . if I were leaving . . . which I probably never will, but you know," she was growing more nervous as she spoke, and Ambrose realized he hadn't said a word. He'd just stared at her.

"Yeah. Yeah, I'd like that," he rushed to put her at ease. He ran his fingers through his long damp hair. Tomorrow the hair would go. His dad said he'd shave it off for him. No use waiting until Monday. He hadn't had short hair since Bailey Sheen told him he looked like Hercules.

"You're all wet." She smiled. "You should probably go back by the fire."

"You wanna stick around, maybe talk for a minute?" Ambrose asked. He smiled like it was no big deal, but his heart pounded like she was the first girl he had ever talked to. He wished suddenly that he'd had a few more beers to take the edge off.

"Are you drunk?" Fern narrowed her eyes at him, reading his thoughts. It made Ambrose sad that she thought he wouldn't want her around unless he was smashed.

"Hey Ambrose! Fern! Come 'ere! We're starting a new game. We need a couple more players," Beans called out from where he crouched by the fire.

Fern walked forward, excited that she was being included. Beans hadn't been exactly nice to Fern through the years. He usually ignored girls he didn't think were good-looking. Ambrose followed a little more slowly. He didn't want to play stupid games, and if Beans was running the show, it was sure to be mean or stupid.

It turned out the new game wasn't new at all. It was the same old version of spin the bottle they'd been playing since they were thirteen and needed an excuse to kiss the girl sitting next to them. But Fern seemed intent on the whole thing, her brown eyes wide and her hands clenched in her lap. Ambrose realized she probably hadn't ever played spin the bottle. It wasn't like she came to any of their parties. She hadn't been invited. Plus, she was the pastor's daughter. She probably hadn't ever done half the things everyone else sitting around the fire had done, multiple times. Ambrose laid his head in his hands, hoping Beans wasn't going to do something that would embarrass Fern or make it necessary to beat the shit out of him. He really didn't want that strain on their relationship heading into boot camp.

When the bottle landed on Fern, Ambrose held his breath. Beans whispered to the girl beside him, the girl who had spun the bottle. Ambrose glowered at Beans and waited for the axe to fall.

"Truth or dare, Fern?" Beans taunted. Fern seemed petrified of either one. As she should be. She bit her lip as twelve pairs of eyes watched her grapple with the choice.

"Truth!" she blurted out. Ambrose relaxed. Truth was easier. Plus, you could always lie.

Beans whispered again, and the girl giggled.

"Did you, or did you not, write love letters to Ambrose last year and pretend they were from Rita?"

Ambrose felt sick. Fern gasped beside him, and her eyes shot to his, the darkness and the dancing flames making them look black in her pale face.

"Time to go home, Fern." Ambrose stood and pulled Fern up beside him. "We're out. See you losers in six months. Don't miss me too much." Ambrose turned, clasping Fern's hand in his, pulling her along behind him. Without turning his head, he raised his left hand, hanging a big, ugly bird at his friend. He could hear laughter behind him. Beans was going down. Ambrose didn't know when, he didn't know how, but he was going down.

When the trees closed around them, hiding them from view of the beach, Fern yanked her hand out of his and ran ahead.

"Fern! Wait."

She kept on running toward the parked cars, and Ambrose wondered why she wouldn't slow, just for a minute. He ran to catch up, reaching her as she clasped the handle on the door of the Sheens' blue van.

"Fern!" He grabbed her arm and she fought free. He grabbed both of her arms and pulled her against him angrily, wanting her to look at him. Her shoulders were shaking, and he realized she was crying. She'd been rushing to get away so he wouldn't see her cry.

"Fern," he breathed, helpless.

"Just let me go! I can't believe you told them. I feel so stupid."

"I told Beans that night, the night he saw us talking in the hallway. I shouldn't have. I'm the stupid one."

"It doesn't matter. High school's over. You're leaving. Beans is leaving. I don't care if I ever see either of you again." Fern wiped at the tears streaming down her face. Ambrose took a step back, shocked by the vehemence in her voice, at the finality in her eyes. And it scared him.

So he kissed her.

It was rough, and it definitely wasn't consensual. He gripped Fern's face between his hands and pressed her back against the door of the old, blue van that she drove to shuttle Bailey around. She was the kind of girl who didn't care about pulling up to a party in a minivan rigged for a wheelchair. The kind of girl who had been giddy to just be asked to play a stupid game. The kind of girl who had come back to say good-bye to him, a boy who had treated her like dirt. And he wished, more desperately than he had ever wished for anything before, that he could change it.

He tried to soften his mouth against hers, tried to tell her he was sorry, but she stayed frozen in his arms, as if she couldn't believe, after everything that had happened, that he thought he could break her heart and take a kiss too.

"I'm so sorry, Fern," Ambrose whispered against her mouth. "I'm so sorry."

Somehow, those words melted the ice that his kiss could not, and Ambrose felt her surrendering sigh against his lips. Fern's hands crept up to his biceps, holding him as he held her, and she opened her mouth beneath his, allowing him in. Gently, afraid he would crush the fragile second chance she'd extended, he moved his lips against hers, touching his tongue to hers softly, letting her seek him. He had never tread so carefully or tried so hard to do it right. And when she pulled away, he let her go. Her eyes were closed, but there were tear-stains on her cheeks and her lips looked bruised where he'd initially pressed too hard, desperate to erase his shame.

Then she opened her eyes. Hurt and confusion flitted across her face for just an instant as she stared him down. Then her jaw tightened and she turned her back on him. Without a word, she climbed into the van and drove away.

9

Be a Good Friend

The doorbell chimed its singsong tune at eight Saturday morning, and the sound meshed so perfectly with Fern's dream that she smiled in her sleep, lifting her face to the handsome man in uniform who had just said, "I do." He lifted her veil and pressed his lips to hers.

"I'm so sorry, Fern," he whispered, just like he had at the lake. "I'm so sorry," he said again.

Fern kissed him frantically, not wanting apologies. She wanted kisses. Lots of them, and hugs too, and somewhere in her subconscious she knew it was all a dream and she would be waking up momentarily, and all opportunities for kissing would melt away into Never-Never-Gonna-Happen Land.

"I'm so sorry, Fern!"

Fern sighed, impatience blurring the fact that it wasn't Ambrose's voice anymore.

"I'm so sorry to wake you up, Fern, but I need to show you something. Are you awake?"

Fern opened her eyes blearily, mournfully accepting the fact that she was not in a church, that no wedding bells had chimed, and Ambrose was hundreds of miles away at Fort Sill.

"Fern?" Rita was standing about a foot from her bed, and without warning she unzipped her pants and wiggled them around her hips, then she lifted her shirt and tucked it in the elastic of her bra so her midsection was exposed. Rita stood akimbo and cried, "See?"

Fern eyed the slim curves and the expanse of bare skin beneath Rita's full breasts sleepily, wishing Rita had waited even a few minutes more to barge into her room and begin undressing. Her eyes were heavy and curvaceous girls didn't rock her boat. She craved a certain man in uniform. She raised questioning eyebrows at Rita and muttered, "Huh?"

"Look, Fern!" Rita pointed with both hands at her lower belly, just below her belly button. "It's huge! I'm not going to be able to hide it anymore. What am I going to do?"

It wasn't huge. It was a softly rounded stomach that protruded gently above a very brief pair of black lace panties. Fern had the same pair that she hid in the back of her drawer and only wore when she had to write a love scene, like the one she'd written last night . . . which had only been a couple hours ago. But Rita wasn't going to leave and let her drift back to dreamland, so Fern raised up on one arm wearily, pushing messy curls out of her eyes so she could get a better perspective on Rita's issue. She tipped her head this way and that, her eyes trained on her friend's tummy.

"Are you pregnant, Rita?" she gasped, the fog of having been suddenly awakened from a deep sleep making her slow to the punch line.

Rita yanked her shirt free from her bra and zipped her pants hastily, as if now that Fern had guessed her secret, she was eager to hide it once more.

"Rita?"

"Yeah. I am." Rita collapsed onto Fern's bed, sitting on Fern's feet in the process. She apologized profusely as Fern yanked her toes free and promptly burst into tears.

"Are you going to get married?" Fern patted her friend's back as she spoke gently, the way her mom did whenever Fern cried.

"Becker doesn't know. Nobody knows! I was going to break up with him, Fern. Now I can't."

"Why? I thought you were crazy about Becker."

"I was. I am. Kind of. But he moves so fast. I feel like I can't keep up. I just wanted to take a little break. Maybe go away to school or something. I even thought about being a nanny . . . maybe even in Europe . . . an au pair. That's what they call them. Isn't that cool? I wanted to be an au pair. Now I can't," Rita repeated and cried harder.

"You've always been really good with kids." Fern struggled to find words that would comfort her friend. "So you'll just have one of your own, now. You may not be able to go to Europe right now. But maybe you could open a little daycare . . . or you could go to school to be a teacher. You would make a great kindergarten teacher. You're so pretty and nice, all the kids would love you."

Fern had thought about leaving town too, maybe going to college, going somewhere where she could start a whole new life, free of old stereotypes. But she couldn't bring herself to leave Bailey. And she wanted to be a writer, a romance writer, and she could do that living in Hannah Lake, living next door to Bailey, as easily as she could do it in Venice, Italy, or Paris, France.

"How did this happen?" Rita wailed.

Fern looked at her blankly. "I know all the words from the *Grease II* song about reproduction. Would you like me to sing it slowly?" Fern asked, trying to make Rita giggle instead of cry.

"Very funny, Fern," Rita said, but she smiled a little as Fern started singing about flowers and stamens in a very enunciated, clear soprano. Rita even joined in for a couple of lines, the lure of corny show tunes irresistible, even in the face of such drama.

"Don't tell Bailey, okay Fern?" Rita said as the song faded and Fern stroked her hair.

"Rita! Why? He's our best friend. He's going to know sooner or later, and then he's going to wonder why you didn't tell him yourself."

"He's always made me feel like I was special . . . you know? So when I screw up and do something stupid, I feel like I'm letting him down. Or maybe I'm just letting myself down and I blame it on him," Rita answered, wiping the tears from her cheeks and taking a deep breath like she was preparing to jump in the pool.

"But that's the cool thing about friendship. It's not about being perfect, or even being deserving. We love you, you love us, so we'll be there for you. Me and Bailey both."

"I do love you, Fern. So much. And Bailey, too. I just hope I don't screw up so bad that I lose you." She hugged Fern fiercely, holding her so tightly Fern couldn't doubt her gratitude or affection. Fern hugged her back and whispered in her ear, "That won't ever happen, Rita."

• • •

1994

"Why don't we have more babies, Mom? Bailey has big sisters. I wish I had a big sister."

"I don't know why, Fern. I tried to have more children, but sometimes we are given something so special, so wonderful, that one is enough."

"Hmm. So one of me is enough?"

"Yes. You've always been enough," Rachel Taylor laughed at her tiny ten-year-old with the wild red hair and the crooked teeth that were too big for her mouth, making her look like she was about to hop away into a forest glade.

"But I need a brother or sister, Mom. I need someone I can take care of and teach stuff to."

"You have Bailey."

"Yeah. I do. But he teaches me stuff more than I teach him stuff. And he's a cousin, not a brother."

"He's not only family, he's a special friend. When Aunt Angie and I found out we were having babies, we were overjoyed together. I didn't think I could have children, and Angie had her two older girls and had always wanted a little boy. Bailey was born before you, but only by a few days. And then you were born. Both of you were little miracle babies, little precious gifts from God."

"I guess having Bailey is almost as good as having a brother." Fern wrinkled her nose thoughtfully.

"Do you know that Jesus had a special friend too? His name was John. John's mother, Elizabeth, was older, like me. She didn't think she could have babies either. After Elizabeth found out she was going to have a baby, Mary, Jesus's mother, came to visit her. They were family too, just like Angie and me. When Elizabeth saw Mary, she felt her baby kick very hard in her stomach. Mary was pregnant with Jesus, and even then, the babies had a special bond, just like you and Bailey."

"John the Baptist, right?" Fern asked. She was well versed in all her Bible stories. Pastor Joshua and Rachel had made sure of that.

"Yes."

"Didn't John get his head cut off?" Fern asked dubiously. Rachel sputtered, laughing. Talk about a story backfiring.

"Yes. He did. But that's not really what my story was about."

"And Jesus got killed too."

"Yes. Yes he did."

"It's a good thing I'm a girl and not a guy named John. And it's a good thing Jesus already came so Bailey doesn't have to save the world. Otherwise, being special friends might not be such a good thing."

Rachel sighed. Leave it to Fern to turn the lesson on its head. With one last attempt at salvaging a teachable moment, she said, "Sometimes being special friends will be hard. Sometimes you will suffer for your friends. Life is not always easy and people can be cruel."

"Like the guys that cut off John's head?"

"Yes. Like that," Rachel said, choking on the inappropriate mirth that clogged her throat. She steeled herself and tried again, wishing for a big finish, wrapping it all in a nice reminder of the Savior's sacrifice. "Good friends are very hard to find. They take care of each other and watch out for each other, and sometimes, they even die for their friends, the way Jesus died for all of us."

Fern nodded her head solemnly, and Rachel breathed a sigh of relief. She wasn't sure who that round went to, or if Fern had learned anything from it. She picked up her laundry basket and headed for the relative safety and quiet of the washing machine. Fern called after her.

"So do you think I will die for Bailey . . . or do you think Bailey will die for me?"

10
Be a Soldier

The high school band played a medley of patriotic songs that Mr. Morgan, the band teacher, had surely drilled into them. Fern knew them all. She wished she was still in high school so she could play along on her clarinet. It would give her something to do besides shiver and huddle with her parents, clapping along with the tinny tunes, watching the pathetic attempt at a parade straggle down Main Street. The whole town was out, but March in Pennsylvania is a terrible time for a parade. The roads had been cleared and the weather had held so far, but the threatening snowstorm made the day fittingly gray for the big send off. The boys had finished basic and AIT—advanced individual training—and their unit had been called up, just like that. They would be among the first soldiers going directly to Iraq.

Fern blew on her icy fingers and her cheeks were as red as her blazing hair. And then the soldiers came. They were dressed in desert camo and lace-up boots with caps snug on their shorn heads. Fern found herself jumping up and down, trying to catch a glimpse of Ambrose. The unit was made up of recruits from the entire southwestern portion on Pennsylvania. The soldiers were making their way through several small towns on convoys made up of a long string of military vehicles, Humvees, and an occasional tank just for the theater of it. Every soldier blended with the next, a swarm of the same, and Fern wondered if that was somehow merciful—take away their individuality so saying good-bye wasn't so personal.

And then Ambrose was there, marching right by her, close enough to touch. His hair was gone. His beautiful hair. But his face was unchanged—strong jaw, perfect lips, smooth skin, dark eyes. After that last night at the lake, she had gone through all the stages. Anger, humiliation, anger again. And then her anger had faded as she'd remembered how it had felt to have her mouth pressed to his.

Ambrose had kissed her. She didn't understand why he had kissed her. She didn't let herself believe it was because he had suddenly fallen in love with her. It hadn't felt that way. It hadn't felt like love. It had felt like an apology. And after weeks of yo-yoing between embarrassment and fury, she'd decided that she could accept his apology. With acceptance came forgiveness, and with forgiveness, all the old feelings she'd harbored for so long crept right back into their familiar places in her heart, and the anger dissipated like an unpleasant dream.

Fern tried to call out, tried to be brave this once, but her voice merely squeaked in a timid cry, his name whisked from her lips as soon as it was released. His eyes stayed straight forward, unaware of her gaze on his face and her attempt to draw his attention. He was taller than the men around him, making him easy to track as he continued down the street.

She didn't see Paulie, Grant, Beans, or Jesse, though she saw Marley, Jesse's pregnant girlfriend, later at the Frosty Freeze, her face blotchy from tears, her belly protruding from the puffy jacket that would no longer close over her midsection. Fern felt a brief flash of jealousy. The drama of being left behind by a handsome soldier was almost delicious in its tragedy, so much so that Fern went home and plotted out a whole new story about two lovers separated by war.

And then they were gone, across the sea, in a world of heat and sand, a world that didn't really exist, not for Fern, at least. And maybe not for the people of Hannah Lake, simply because it was so far away, so far removed from anything they knew. And life went on as it had before. The town prayed and loved and hurt and lived. The yellow ribbons Fern had helped tie around the trees looked jaunty and crisp for about two weeks. But the spring sleet continually raked the cheerful bows with sharp, icy claws, and before long the ribbons surrendered, wind-torn and weary. And the clock ticked quietly.

● ● ●

Six months went by. In that time, Rita delivered a baby boy and Marley Davis had her baby too—a boy she named Jesse after his daddy. Fern added a new chapter in her romance about war-torn lovers and gave them a child, a girl named Jessie. She couldn't help herself. Whenever Marley came into the store, Fern would yearn to hold her baby and could only imagine how Jesse must feel, thousands of miles away. She composed letters to Ambrose, wrote about the goings-on in Hannah Lake, the humorous things she saw, the stats of the high school sports teams, the books she read, her promotion at the grocery store to night manager, the funny things she wanted to say but was never brave enough to utter. And she signed them: Yours, Fern.

Could you belong to someone who didn't want you? Fern decided it was possible, because her heart was his, and whether or not he wanted it didn't seem to make much difference. When she was done writing, she would tuck the letter away in a drawer. Fern wondered what Ambrose would think if she suddenly sent one. He would probably think she was a psycho and regret that apology wrapped in a kiss. He would worry that Fern thought the kiss meant more than it had. He would think she was delusional.

Fern wasn't delusional, she was simply imaginative. But even with her gift for daydreaming and storytelling, she couldn't make herself believe he would ever return her feelings.

She had asked him if she could write—she'd even said she would. But deep down, she didn't really think he wanted her to, and her pride was too fragile to endure another hit. The letters piled up, and she couldn't make herself send them.

• • •

Iraq

"Fern Taylor been writing you any more love notes, Brosey?" Beans said in the darkness of the sleeping tent.

"I think Fern's pretty," Paulie said from his cot. "She looked good at the prom. Did you see her? She can write me letters anytime she wants."

"Fern's not pretty!" Beans said. "She looks like Pippi Longstocking."

"Who the hell is Pippi Longbottom?" Jesse groaned, trying to sleep.

"My sister used to watch a show called *Pippi Longstocking*. She borrowed it from the library and never took it back. Pippi had buck teeth and red hair that stuck out from her head in two braids. She was skinny and awkward and stupid. Just like Fern." Beans was overexaggerating, poking at Ambrose.

"Fern isn't stupid," Ambrose said. He was surprised how much it bugged him, Beans making fun of Fern.

"Okaaaay," Beans laughed. "Like that makes a difference."

"It does." Grant had to get his two cents in. "Who wants a girl you can't talk to?"

"I do!" Beans laughed. "Don't talk, just take off your clothes."

"You're kind of a pig, Beans." Paulie sighed. "It's a good thing we all like ham."

"I hate ham," Jesse growled. "And I hate it when you guys get all chatty-Cathy when it's time to sleep. Shut the hell up."

"Jesse, you really are the Wicked Witch of East." Paulie laughed. "The Wicked Witch of the Middle East." Paulie had written a funny song about Iraq being like the Land of Oz, and before long everyone in their unit had a *Wizard of Oz* nickname.

"And you're the Scarecrow, dumbass. Wasn't he the one who didn't have a brain?"

"Yep. Scarecrow sounds badass, don't you think, Grant?"

"It's better than Dorothy," Grant laughed. He'd made the mistake of wearing his red wrestling shoes to the gym one day and the rest was history. When they weren't on patrol or sleeping, they were working out. There just wasn't much else to do in their down time.

"Why don't you click your heels together, Dorothy, and get us back home?" Paulie said. "Hey, and how come you didn't get a nickname, Beans?"

"Um . . . my name is Connor. I think you just contradicted yourself." Beans was beginning to doze off.

"We should call him Munchkin . . . or maybe Toto. After all he's just a little dog with a big bark," Jesse said.

Beans was alert immediately. "Try it, Jess, and I'll tell Marley about the time you made out with Lori Stringham in the wrestling room." Beans had always been sensitive about his stature. It made for a great 125-pound wrestler, but wasn't especially helpful anywhere else.

"Brosey's the Tin Man because he doesn't have a heart. Poor little Fern Taylor found that out the hard way." Beans tried to turn the attention back to Ambrose, ribbing him once more.

"Brosey's the Tin Man because he's made of metal. Damn, how much did you put up on your bench today, Brosey?" another member of the unit butted into the conversation. "You are a freaking monster! We should call you Iron Man."

"Here we go again," Jesse moaned. "Hercules and now Iron Man." He resented the attention Ambrose always garnered and didn't pretend otherwise.

Ambrose laughed. "I'll let you beat me in an arm wrestle tomorrow, Witchy Poo, okay?"

Jesse chuckled, his irritability more an act than he cared to admit.

The tent quieted down until the occasional snore and sigh was all that was heard in the darkness. But Ambrose couldn't sleep. He kept thinking about what Beans had said. Rita Marsden was beautiful. She'd taken his breath away. He'd thought he was in love with her until he'd figured out he really didn't know her at all. Rita wasn't smart. Not in the way he wanted her to be. He hadn't been able to figure out why she was so appealing in her little notes and then when they were together she was so different. She was beautiful, but after a while, she really wasn't very attractive to him at all. Ambrose wanted the girl in the letters.

His eyes shot open in the dark. The girl in the letters was Fern Taylor. Did he really want Fern Taylor? He laughed a little. Fern was a little bitty thing. They would look ridiculous together. And she wasn't hot. Although she *had* looked pretty good at the prom. Seeing her there in her gold dress, dancing with his stupid friends, had surprised him and ticked him off. Guess he hadn't forgiven her completely for the stunt she and Rita pulled.

He had tried not to think about Fern, about that night at the lake, and he'd all but convinced himself it was just temporary insanity, a last desperate act before leaving home. And she hadn't written like she'd said she would. He couldn't blame her after everything that had happened. But he would have liked to get a letter. She wrote good letters.

Homesickness shot through him. They definitely weren't in Kansas anymore. He wondered what he'd gotten himself into. What he'd gotten them all into. And if he was being honest with himself, he wasn't Hercules and he wasn't the Tin Man. He was the Cowardly Lion. He'd run away from home and brought his friends with him, his security blanket, his very own cheering section. He wondered what the hell he was doing in Oz.

11

Beat Up a Bully

Iraq

"Marley said Rita's getting married," Jesse reported, his eyes on Ambrose. "Your ex is getting hitched, Brosey. How does it feel?"

"She's a fool."

"Whoa!" Jesse cried, surprised by the vehemence from his friend. He thought Ambrose was over Rita. Guess he was wrong.

"You don't still like her, do you, Brose?" Grant asked in surprise.

"No. I don't. But she's a fool to marry Becker Garth."

Beans shrugged. "I've never had a problem with Garth."

"You remember when I got suspended in ninth grade?"

Beans shook his head that he didn't, but Paulie lit up with the memory.

"You smashed Becker's pretty face in! I remember. But you never told us why."

Ambrose adjusted his sunglasses and shifted his weight. They, and about one hundred other soldiers and marines, were on guard duty outside a high-security meeting of the provisional Iraqi government. It was cool to think maybe different factions could come together to form some governing body, that they were making progress, though some days Ambrose wondered. It wasn't the first time he'd played bodyguard, though in Bailey Sheen's case, it had come after the fact.

"I forgot about that!" Grant crowed. "You didn't get to wrestle Lock Haven. Coach was pissed."

"He wouldn't have been quite as mad if he knew why I felt the need to pound Becker," Ambrose said wryly. He supposed enough time and distance had passed for him to share the story without violating confidences.

January 1999

Ambrose knew Becker Garth. Becker was a senior and the girls all seemed to like him and think he was hot. That always made other guys sit up and take notice. Ambrose had noticed him because Becker had started wearing his hair like Ambrose, which Ambrose didn't like. Becker was dark haired too, and when he tossed his chin-length hair back from his brown eyes, he looked too much like Ambrose for comfort.

But that was where the similarities in their appearances ended. Becker was wiry and on the small side, his muscles defined and lean, like a jockey or a runner. He was about five foot eight and big enough that the girls still flocked around him, but Ambrose was much taller, even as a freshman.

Maybe because Becker was smaller than the freshman, or maybe because he was jealous, he liked to poke at Ambrose. Just jabs, innuendos, side comments that made his group of friends snicker and look away. Ambrose ignored it for the most part. He had very little to prove and wasn't bothered too much. His size and strength made him less intimidated and less vulnerable to bullying than the other boys his age. And he comforted himself by imagining Becker in the wrestling room trying to hang with him or any of his friends. But Ambrose wasn't the only one Becker liked to torment.

It was fourth period, right before lunch, and Ambrose asked to be excused from English on the pretext of needing to use the bathroom. Really, he needed to check his weight. He had weigh-ins at 3:00 for the duel against Lock Haven. He was wrestling 160, but that morning he'd been at 162. He could sweat two pounds off, but just getting to 162 had been work. He had started the season at 172, and there wasn't much wiggle room or fat on his big frame to allow for weight loss. And he was still growing. He had a month until district championships and two weeks after that, state. The next six weeks would be brutal, and he would be hungry most of the time. Hungry equated to ornery, and Ambrose was very ornery. When he walked into the locker room and was greeted by darkness, he swore, hoping something wasn't wrong. He needed to see the scale. He felt along the wall, trying to find the switches. A voice rang out in the dark, making him jump.

"Becker?" the voice said nervously.

He found the lights and flipped them, flooding the lockers and benches with light. What he saw made him curse again. In the middle of the tile floor, Bailey Sheen's wheelchair had been tipped over onto its back, and Bailey was hanging helplessly with his thin legs in the air, unable to right himself or do anything but beg for help in the darkness.

"What the hell?" Ambrose said. "Sheen, are you okay?"

Ambrose ran to Bailey, eased the chair back onto its wheels, and sat Bailey up straight in his seat. Bailey's face was flushed and his shoulders shook, and Ambrose wanted to hurt someone. Badly.

"What happened, Sheen?"

"Don't tell anyone, okay, Ambrose?" Bailey begged.

"Why?!" Ambrose was so angry he could feel his pulse pounding behind his eyes.

"Just . . . just don't tell, okay? It's freakin' embarrassing." Bailey gulped and Ambrose could tell he was mortified.

"Who did this?" Ambrose demanded.

Bailey shook his head and wouldn't say. Then Ambrose remembered how Bailey had startled him by calling out a name while Ambrose had been searching for the light.

"Becker?" Ambrose asked, his voice rising in outrage.

"He just pretended he was going to help me out and then he tipped me over. I'm not hurt!" Bailey added, as if being hurt would make him weaker. "Then he turned off the lights and left. I would have been okay. Someone would have come. You came, right?" Bailey tried to smile, but the smile wobbled and he looked down at his hands. "I'm glad it was you and not an entire gym class. It would have been really humiliating."

Ambrose was beyond speech. He just shook his head, the scale forgotten.

"I don't come in here if someone's not with me because I can't open the doors by myself," Bailey offered by way of explanation. "But Becker let me in, and I thought my dad was in here. And I can get out by myself because the door swings out and I can just push it open with my wheelchair."

"Except when someone tips you over and leaves you hanging upside down," Ambrose said, anger dripping from his comment.

"Yeah. Except then," Bailey said softly. "Why do you think he did that?" Bailey looked at Ambrose, his face troubled.

"I don't know, Sheen. Because he's an asshole with a little pecker," Ambrose grumbled. "He thinks picking on people who can't or won't fight back will make his pecker bigger. But it just gets smaller and smaller and he just gets meaner and meaner."

Bailey howled with laughter, and Ambrose smiled, glad that Bailey wasn't shaking anymore.

"You promise you won't tell anyone?" Bailey insisted again.

Ambrose nodded. But he didn't promise not to make Becker pay.

When Ambrose entered the lunchroom, he found Becker seated at a corner table, surrounded by a group of other seniors and several pretty girls that Ambrose wouldn't mind talking to under different circumstances. Ambrose gritted his teeth and walked to the table. He hadn't told his friends what was up. His friends were wrestlers, and Ambrose was probably going to get suspended for what he was about to do. He didn't want them getting in trouble with him and hurting the team's chances against Lock Haven. He probably wouldn't be wrestling tonight. Guess it was okay that he was a couple of pounds over his weight.

Ambrose brought his fists down on the table as hard as he could, spilling people's drinks and making an empty tray clatter to the floor. Becker looked up in surprise, his curse ringing out above the din in the lunchroom as milk splashed in his lap.

"Stand up," Ambrose demanded quietly.

"Get lost, gorilla boy." Becker sneered, wiping at the milk. "Unless you want to get the shit beat out of you."

Ambrose leaned over the table and shot his right hand out toward Becker's face. His flat palm connected squarely with Becker's forehead, thumping his head back against the wall behind him.

"Stand up!" Ambrose wasn't quiet anymore.

Becker came out from around the table and lunged wildly for Ambrose, his sharp fist catching Ambrose across the bridge of his nose, making his eyes smart and the blood start to stream from his left nostril. Ambrose swung back, catching Becker across the mouth, then again in his right eye. Becker howled and went down in a snarling heap. Ambrose grabbed the collar of his shirt and the back of his jeans and stood him up again. Becker swayed. Ambrose had hit him hard.

"That's for Bailey Sheen," he whispered in Becker's ear, honoring his promise to Bailey that no one would know what Becker had done. Then he released Becker and turned away, wiping his nose on his ruined white shirt.

Coach Sheen was striding toward him, his face red with anger. Apparently, it was his turn at lunchroom duty. Damn Ambrose's luck. Ambrose followed him meekly, willing to take whatever punishment was his, and true to his word, he didn't utter Bailey Sheen's name even once.

● ● ●

"I'm getting married, Fern." Rita shoved her hand beneath Fern's nose, an impressive diamond on her left ring finger.

"It's beautiful," Fern said honestly and tried to smile, tried to give her friend the reaction she obviously wanted, but she felt a little sick inside. Becker was very handsome and he and Rita looked so good together. And Ty, Rita and Becker's baby, would have both his parents under one roof. But Becker scared Fern. Fern wondered why he didn't scare Rita. Or maybe he did. Some girls were drawn to that.

"We want to be married next month. I know it's soon, but do you think your dad would marry us? He's always been so nice to me. Your mom, too. We're just going to have a little party afterward. Maybe I can get a DJ and we can dance. Becker's a good dancer."

Fern remembered Rita and Becker dancing at the prom, Rita glowing with new love, Becker trying to control his temper when Bailey had interrupted and stolen a couple of dances.

"Sure. Dad would love to. Pastors like nothing better than a wedding. Maybe you could have your reception under the church pavilion. There's power and tables. We can get flowers and refreshments and you can wear a beautiful dress. I'll help."

And she did. They planned frantically for a month, finding Rita a dress that made Sarah Marsden, Rita's mother, cry and dance around her lovely daughter. They sent out invitations, hired a photographer, ordered flowers, made mints, cream puffs, and homemade chocolates, and filled the Taylors' garage freezer to overflowing with their efforts.

The morning of the big day, they wrapped white twinkle lights around each column of the pavilion and moved the tables covered in white lace out onto the lawn, lining the pavilion so the concrete floor beneath the pavilion could serve as the dance floor. They filled yellow vases with daisies for centerpieces and tied yellow balloons to every chair.

They put daisies in the church, too. Fern was the maid of honor, and Rita had let her pick her own dress in whatever shade of yellow she wished. Fern found Bailey a yellow tie to match and he escorted her down the aisle in his wheelchair. Fern carried a bouquet of the cheerful flowers, and Bailey had a daisy pinned to his black suit coat.

Becker wore black as well, a yellow rose pinned to his lapel that matched the roses in Rita's bouquet. His hair was swept back from his high-cheekboned face, reminding Fern of Ambrose and the way his hair had fallen to his shoulders like a young Adonis. Ambrose's long hair was gone now, and Ambrose was gone too.

She still thought about him more than she should. He'd been in Iraq for a year. In fact, it had been eighteen months since he first left for basic training. Marley Davis, Jesse's girlfriend, attended the wedding, and she told Fern the boys had only six months left on their tour. Marley said Jesse had asked her to marry him when he got home. She seemed thrilled at the prospect. Jesse Jr. was the same age as Rita's baby, Tyler. But where Ty favored his mother, baby Jesse favored his daddy, his brown skin and kinky black hair making him a little replica of his father. He was adorable, happy and healthy, and already a handful for his young mother.

When Rita walked down the aisle and made her solemn vows to Becker Garth and he repeated them in return, both sacred and sweet, Fern felt her heart swell in hope for her friend. Maybe it would be okay. Maybe Becker loved her like he said he did. And maybe love would be enough. Maybe the promises he was making would inspire him to be a better man.

From the look on Bailey's face, he didn't hold out much hope. Bailey sat beside Fern in the front row, his wheelchair parked at the end of the long pew, his expression as wooden as the bench. After all, he and Rita were friends too, and he worried just like Fern. Bailey had been subdued since Rita's announcement. Fern knew he had feelings for Rita. But she thought he'd moved beyond them, sort of the way she'd outgrown her infatuation with Ambrose Young. And maybe that was his problem . . . because Fern really hadn't outgrown anything. But Rita was a mother now, tied to Becker in a way that was permanent and final. Still, old feelings had a way of resurfacing just when you thought they were gone forever.

"'Til death do us part," Rita promised, her face lovely in its sincerity.

When Becker kissed her smiling lips, sealing the deal, Bailey closed his eyes, and Fern reached for his hand.

12

Build a Hideaway

It only took about three months before Rita drifted out of sight. The occasions she was seen in public with her husband, she kept her eyes carefully averted and other times wore sunglasses even when it was raining. Fern called regularly and even stopped by Rita's duplex a few times. But her visits seemed to make Rita nervous. Once Fern swore she saw Rita pull into her garage just before Fern arrived, yet Rita didn't answer the door when she knocked.

Things improved slightly when Becker got a job where he traveled for several days at a time. Rita even called and took Fern to lunch on her birthday. They ate enchiladas at Mi Cocina, and Rita smiled brightly and reassured Fern that everything was just fine when Fern asked gently if she was okay. According to Rita, everything was just wonderful—perfect. But Fern didn't believe her.

Fern didn't tell Bailey about her fears for Rita. She didn't want to upset him, and what could he do? Fern saw Becker every once in a while at the store, and though he was polite and always greeted her with a smile, Fern didn't like him. And he seemed to know it. He was always perfectly groomed, every dark hair in place, his handsome face clean-shaven, his clothes crisp and stylish. But it was all packaging. And Fern was reminded of the analogy of the grease her father had shared with Elliott Young once upon a time. Fern couldn't have been more than fourteen, but the lesson had stuck.

Elliott Young looked nothing like his son. He was short, maybe five foot eight at the most. His blond hair had thinned until he'd finally shaved it off. His eyes were a soft blue, his nose a little flat, his smile always at the ready. Today he wasn't smiling, and his eyes were heavily ringed, like he hadn't slept well in a long time.

"Hi, Mr. Young," Fern said, a question in her voice.

"Hi, Fern. Is your dad home?" Elliott didn't make a move to enter even though Fern held the screen door wide in welcome.

"Dad?" Fern called toward her dad's office. "Elliott Young is here to see you."

"Invite him in Fern!" Joshua Taylor called from the recesses of the room.

"Please come in, Mr. Young," Fern said.

Elliott Young shoved his hands in his pockets and let Fern lead him into her father's office. There are various churches and denominations in Pennsylvania. Some say it's a state where God still has a foothold. There are lots of Catholics, lots of Methodists, lots of Presbyterians, lots of Baptists, lots of everything. But in Hannah Lake, Joshua Taylor ran his little church with such care and commitment to the community that it didn't matter to him what you called yourself, he was still your pastor. If you didn't sit in his pews each Sunday, it really made no difference to him. He preached from the Bible, kept his message simple, kept his sermons universal, and for forty years he had labored with one goal: love and serve—the rest would take care of itself. Everyone called him Pastor Joshua, whether he was their pastor or not. And more often than not, when someone was soul-searching, they found themselves at Pastor Joshua's church.

"Elliott!" Joshua Taylor stood from his desk as Fern led Elliott Young into the room. "How are you? I haven't seen you in a while. What can I do for you?"

Fern pulled the French doors shut behind her and walked into the kitchen, wishing desperately to hear the rest of the conversation. Elliott was Ambrose's dad. Rumors were, he and Ambrose's mother were splitting up, that Lily Young was leaving town. Fern wondered if that meant Ambrose would leave too.

Fern knew she shouldn't do it, but she did. She sneaked into the pantry and positioned herself on a sack of flour. Sitting in the pantry was almost as good as sitting in her father's office. Whoever had framed up the house must have scrimped on the wall that divided the back of the pantry from the little room her father used for his office, because if Fern wedged herself into the corner, not only could she hear perfectly, she could even see into the room where the sheet rock didn't quite reach the corner. Her mother was at the grocery store. She was safe to listen without getting caught, and if her mother suddenly came home, she could swoop up the full trash and pretend like she was just doing her chores.

". . . she's never been happy. She's tried, I think. But these last few years . . . she's just been hiding out." Elliott Young was talking. "I love her so much. I thought if I just kept loving her, she would love me back. I thought I had enough love for both of us. For all three of us."

"Is she determined to leave?" Fern's father asked softly.

"Yes. She wants to take Ambrose with her. I haven't said anything. But that's the hardest part. I love that boy. If she takes him, Pastor, I don't think I will survive. I don't think I'm strong enough." Elliott Young wept openly and Fern felt sympathetic tears well in her own eyes. "I know he's not mine. Not biologically. But he's my son, Pastor. He's my son!"

"Does Ambrose know?"

"Not everything. But he's fourteen, not five. He knows enough."

"Does Lily know you want the boy to stay, even if she leaves?"

"He is legally my son. I adopted him. I gave him my name. I have rights like any father would. I don't think she would fight it if Ambrose wanted to stay, but I haven't said anything to Brosey. I guess I keep hoping Lily will change her mind."

"Talk to your son. Tell him what is happening. Just the facts—no blame, no condemnation, just the fact that his mother is leaving. Tell him you love him. Tell him that he is your son and that nothing will change that. Don't for one minute let him believe that he doesn't have a choice because of blood. Let him know he can go with his mother if that is his wish, but that you love him and want him to stay with you if that is what he wants."

Elliott was quiet for several long minutes, Joshua Taylor too, and Fern wondered if that was all that was going to be said. Then Joshua Taylor asked softly, "Is that all that's bothering you, Elliott? Is there something else you want to talk about?"

"I keep thinking that if I just looked different, if I looked more like him, none of this would be happening. I know I'm not the best-looking guy in the world. I know I'm a little on the homely side. But I exercise and I keep myself trim and I dress nice and wear cologne . . ." Elliott Young sounded embarrassed, and his voice drifted off.

"Looked more like who?" Joshua Taylor asked gently.

"Ambrose's father. The man Lily can't seem to get out of her system. He wasn't nice to her, Pastor. He was selfish and mean. He pushed her away when he found out she was pregnant. He told her he wanted nothing to do with her. But he was handsome. I've seen pictures. Looks just like Brosey." Elliott's voice broke when he said his son's name.

"I've often thought that beauty can be a deterrent to love," Fern's father mused.

"Why?"

"Because sometimes we fall in love with a face and not what's behind it. My mother used to pour the grease off the meat when she cooked, and she stored it in a tin in the cupboard. For a while, she used a tin that had once held those long, praline-covered cookies with hazelnut crème inside. The expensive ones? More than once I got that tin down thinking I'd found my mom's secret stash, only to take off the lid and see smelly mounds of grease."

Elliott laughed, getting the point. "The container didn't matter much at that point, huh?"

"That's right. It made me want cookies, but that container was major false advertising. I think sometimes a beautiful face is false advertising too, and too many of us don't take the time to look beneath the lid. Funny, this reminds me of a sermon I gave a few weeks back. Did you hear it?"

"I'm sorry, Pastor. I work nights at the bakery, you know. Sometimes Sunday morning I'm just too tired," Elliott said, his guilt over missing church evident, even through the pantry wall.

"It's okay, Elliott." Joshua laughed. "I'm not taking roll. I just wanted to know if you'd heard it so I wouldn't bore you silly." Fern heard her father turning pages. She smiled a little. He always brought everything back to the scriptures.

"In Isaiah 53:2 it says, 'For he shall grow up before him as a tender plant, and as a root out of a dry ground: he hath no form nor comeliness; and when we shall see him, there is no beauty that we should desire him.'"

"I remember that verse," Elliott said softly. "It always struck me that Jesus wasn't handsome. Why wouldn't God make his outside match his inside?"

"For the same reason He was born in a lowly manger, born to an oppressed people. If He had been beautiful or powerful, people would have followed him for that alone—they would have been drawn to him for all the wrong reasons."

"That makes sense," Elliott said.

Fern found herself nodding in agreement, sitting there on a sack of flour in the corner of the pantry. It made sense to her too. She wondered how she had missed this particular sermon. It must have come when she sneaked her romance novel in between the pages of the hymnal a few weeks ago. She felt a twinge of remorse. Her father was so wise. Maybe she should pay more attention.

"There's nothing wrong with your face, Elliott," Joshua said gently. "There's nothing wrong with you. You are a good man with a beautiful heart. And God looks on the heart, doesn't he?"

"Yeah." Elliott Young sounded close to tears once more. "He does. Thanks, Pastor."

After Elliott Young left, Fern sat in deep contemplation in the pantry, her hands clasped around her knees. Then she went upstairs and began writing a love story about a blind girl searching for a soul mate and an ugly prince with a heart of gold.

● ● ●

Iraq

"I would really like to see a woman that wasn't wearing a tent over her head. Just once! And I would appreciate it if she was blonde or, even better, redheaded!" Beans moaned one afternoon after guarding a lonely checkpoint for several hours with only a handful of women clad in burkas and children coming through to make them feel useful. Maybe it was ironic that Beans longed for a blonde when he was Hispanic. But he was American, and America had the most diverse population in the world. A little diversity right now would be welcome.

"I'd be happy to never see another burka again." Grant wiped the sweat and dust from his nose and flinched up at the sun, wishing it would take a break.

"I heard that some guys, especially in places like Afghanistan, don't see their wives at all until after they are married. Can you imagine? Surprise, sweetie!" Jesse batted his eyelashes as he made a hideous face. "What's wrong? Don't you think I'm pretty?" he said in a high falsetto and contorted his face even more.

"So how do they even know who it is they're marrying?" Paulie asked, flummoxed.

"Handwriting," Beans said seriously. But his nostrils flared slightly, and Ambrose rolled his eyes, knowing that Beans was telling a tale.

"Really?" Paulie gasped, falling like a brick. It wasn't his fault he was so gullible. It came with the sweet temperament.

"Yeah. They write letters back and forth for a year or more. Then at the ceremony, she signs her name along with a promise that she'll always wear her burka in front of other men. He recognizes her handwriting and that's how he knows it's her beneath her veil."

Grant was scowling. "I've never heard anything like that. Handwriting?"

Jesse had caught on and was trying not to laugh. "Yeah. Just think, if Ambrose and Fern had lived in Iraq, he never woulda figured out that it was Fern writing him those letters instead of Rita. Fern could have roped him into marriage. Ambrose would have seen her handwriting at the wedding and said, 'Yep, it's Rita, all right!'"

Ambrose's friends howled with laughter, even Paulie, who had finally figured out that it was just a setup to rib Ambrose about Fern. Again.

Ambrose sighed, his lips twitching. It was pretty funny. Beans was laughing so hard he was wheezing, and he and Jesse were making each other laugh even harder as they reenacted the moment the burka was removed and Fern stood beneath it instead of the buxom blonde, Rita.

Ambrose wondered what his friends would think if they knew he'd kissed Fern. Really kissed her. Knowing full well who he was kissing. No need of subterfuge. Or burkas. He wondered absentmindedly if the burka was such a bad idea. Maybe more guys would make better decisions if they weren't distracted by the packaging. For that matter, maybe guys should wear them too. 'Course, his packaging had always worked in his favor.

He pondered whether Fern would have even wanted him if he was packaged differently. He knew Rita wouldn't have. Not because she wasn't a nice enough girl, but because they had nothing in common. Take away the mutual physical attraction, and they had nothing.

With Fern, there was a possibility of a lot more. At least, the letters made him think there could be more. The tour was up in two months. He decided when he got home, he would find out. And his friends would never let him hear the end of it. They would torment him for the rest of his life. He sighed and checked his weapon for the umpteenth time, wishing the day would end.

13

Live

It was just a routine patrol—five army vehicles taking a turn around the southern part of the city. Ambrose was at the wheel of the last Humvee, Paulie in the passenger seat beside him. Grant was driving the vehicle in front of Ambrose, Jesse riding shotgun, Beans in the turret—the last two vehicles in the small convoy of five.

Just out for a routine patrol. Out for an hour, back to base. Up and down the crumbling, embattled streets of Baghdad along the assigned route. Paulie was singing the song he'd made up about Oz. "Iraq may not have munchkins, but it sure as hell has sand. I haven't got my girlfriend, but I've still got my hand . . ."

Suddenly, a group of kids were running along the side of the road, shrieking and running their fingers across their throats. Little boys and girls of various ages, shoeless, limbs slim and brown, clothing leached of color in the simmering heat. Running, yelling. At least six of them.

"What are they doing?" Ambrose grunted, confused. "Are they doing what I think they're doing? Do you think they hate us that much? They want our throats slashed? They're just kids!"

"I don't think that's what they're doing." Paulie turned, watching the kids fall back as the convoy passed. "I think they were warning us." He had stopped singing, and his face was still, contemplative.

Ambrose checked his rearview mirror. The kids had stopped running and stood in the road unmoving. They grew smaller as the convoy continued down the road, but they remained in the street, watching. Ambrose turned his attention back to the road in front of them. Except for the convoy, it was completely empty, abandoned. Not a single soul in sight. They would turn the corner on the next street, circle around the block, and head back to base.

"Brosey . . . do you feel that?"

Paul's face was tipped as if he was hearing something in the distance, something Ambrose couldn't hear, something he definitely couldn't feel. It reminded Ambrose of the way Paulie had looked when they made their clandestine visit to the memorial of Flight 93, when he'd asked the very same question. It had been almost too still that night at the memorial, as if the world had bowed its head for a moment of silence and never lifted it up again. It was too still now. The hair rose on Ambrose's neck.

And then hell shoved a gnarled hand up through the hard packed road and unleashed fire and flying shards of metal beneath the wheels of the Humvee in front of Ambrose and Paulie, the Humvee that carried Grant, Jesse, and Beans—three boys, three friends, three soldiers from Hannah Lake, Pennsylvania. And that was the last thing Ambrose Young remembered, the very last piece of Before.

• • •

When the phone rang early Monday morning, the Taylor family looked at each other with bleary eyes. Fern had stayed up all night writing and was looking forward to crawling back into bed after she ate her Cheerios. Joshua and Rachel had plans to head to Lock Haven College for a symposium for the next couple of days and wanted to get an early start. Fern couldn't wait to have the house to herself for a few days.

"It's only six thirty! I wonder who that is?" Rachel said, puzzled.

As the local pastor, calls at odd hours weren't unusual—but the odd hours tended to be from midnight to three am. People were usually too tired at six thirty in the morning to get in trouble or bother their pastor.

Fern jumped up and grabbed the receiver and chirped a cheerful hello, her curiosity getting the best of her.

An official-sounding voice asked for Pastor Taylor, and Fern handed her father the phone with a shrug. "They want Pastor Taylor," she said.

"This is Joshua Taylor. How can I help you?" Fern's father said briskly, standing up and moving to the side so that he didn't have to stretch the curly cord across the table. The Taylors hadn't invested in anything as sophisticated as a cordless phone.

He listened for all of ten seconds before he sat down again.

"Oh. Oh, dear God." He groaned and closed his eyes like a child trying to hide.

Rachel and Fern looked at each other in alarm, breakfast forgotten.

"All of them? How?"

Another silence.

"I see. Yes. Yes. I'll be ready."

Joshua Taylor stood once more and walked to the wall unit, hanging up the ancient phone with a finality that made Fern's heart quake in her chest. When he turned toward the table, Joshua Taylor's face was sickly gray and his eyes bleak.

"That was a man named Peter Gary. He's an army chaplain assigned to casualty assistance. Connor O'Toole, Paul Kimball, Grant Nielson, and Jesse Jordan were killed by a roadside bomb in Iraq yesterday."

"Oh, no! Oh, Joshua," Rachel's voice was shrill and she covered her mouth, as if to push the words back in, but they reverberated throughout the kitchen.

"They're dead?" Fern cried in disbelief.

"Yes, Fern. They are." Joshua looked at his only daughter and his hand shook as he reached for her, wanting to touch her, wanting to console her, wanting to fall to his knees and pray for the parents who had lost their sons. Parents he was going to have to notify in less than an hour's time.

"They contacted me because I am the local clergy. They want me to go with the officers assigned to the team to tell the families. They will have a vehicle here in half an hour to pick me up. I have to change," he said helplessly, looking down at his jeans and favorite T-shirt that asked, "What Would Jesus Do?"

"But they were scheduled to come home next month! I just saw Jamie Kimball in the store yesterday. She's been counting down the days!" Fern said, as if the news couldn't possibly be true for that reason. "And Marley! Marley's been planning her wedding. She and Jesse are getting married!"

"They're gone, Fernie."

The tears had started to fall, the initial shock turning into teary devastation. Pastor Taylor's eyes swam with grief, Rachel was weeping quietly, but Fern sat in stunned silence, unable to feel anything but sheer disbelief. She looked up suddenly, horrified as a new question exploded into her mind.

"Dad? What about Ambrose Young?"

"I didn't ask, Fern. I didn't think. They didn't mention Ambrose. He must be okay."

Fern shuddered with relief and immediately felt remorse that his life was more important to her than the others. But at least Ambrose was alive. At least Ambrose was okay.

• • •

Half an hour later, a black Ford Taurus pulled up to the Taylor residence. Three officers in full uniform stepped from the inauspicious vehicle and walked up the walk. Joshua Taylor was in a suit and tie, freshly showered and pressed into his most respectful attire, and he opened the door to the three men. Rachel and Fern hovered in the kitchen, listening to the surreal conversation in the next room.

One man, whom Fern assumed was the chaplain who had called her father, briefed the pastor on the procedure, giving him the information that he knew, asking advice on whom to inform first, on who might have family that they would need to gather from distances, who would need the most support. Fifteen minutes later the four men, including Pastor Taylor, drove off.

Jamie Kimball was the first to receive the news that her son, Paul, was dead. Then Grant Nielson's family was delivered the news that their twenty-year-old son, their big brother, the kid with good grades and perfect attendance would be coming home in a casket. Jesse Jordan's estranged parents were notified and then had the unenviable task of escorting the officers to the home of their little grandson and telling Marley Davis there would be no wedding in the fall. Luisa O'Toole ran from her house shrieking when the noncommissioned officer who spoke fluent Spanish extended his heartfelt condolences. Seamus O'Toole wept and clung to Pastor Taylor.

The news spread through the town like wildfire—early morning joggers and dog walkers saw the black car with the uniformed men inside and gossip and speculation tumbled out of mouths and into ears before the truth made its way on slower legs through the devastated town. Elliott Young was at the bakery when early word reached him that Paul Kimball and Grant Nielson were dead and that the black car was still parked outside the O'Tooles' home. He hid in the bakery's freezer for half an hour, praying for his son's life, praying the uniformed men wouldn't find him . . . surely if they couldn't find him, then they couldn't tell him his son was dead too.

But they did find him. Mr. Morgan, the grocery store owner, opened the freezer to tell him the officers were there. Elliott Young shook from cold and terror as he received the news. And he collapsed into the arms of Joshua Taylor when he heard his son was alive. Alive, but gravely injured. He had been flown to Ramstein Air Base in Germany, where he would stay until he was stable enough to bring back to the United States. If he lived that long.

• • •

The roles of a pastor and his family in a community are to love and serve first. That was Pastor Joshua's philosophy. So that's what he did. And Rachel and Fern did their utmost to do the same. The whole township was in a state of shock and mourning, leveled by the loss. It was a state of emergency and there was no relief in sight. There would be no federal funds to rebuild. It was death. It was permanent. So there was a lot to do.

The bodies of the four boys were flown home to their families. Funeral services were organized and held, four days in a row, four days of unimaginable grief. The surrounding counties pitched in and raised several thousand dollars for a memorial. The boys wouldn't be buried in the town cemetery, but on a little hill overlooking the high school. Luisa O'Toole had protested initially, wanting to have her son buried in some remote border town in Mexico where her parents were buried. But for once, Seamus O'Toole stood up to his fiery spouse and insisted that his son be buried in the country he had died serving, in the town that mourned his loss, with the friends who had lost their lives beside him.

Ambrose Young was flown to Walter Reed Medical Center and Elliott Young closed his bakery to be with him, only to have the townsfolk pitch in and reopen it, keeping it running for him while he was away. Everyone knew Elliott couldn't afford to lose the business or the income.

Ambrose's name graced the marquee again. Only this time it simply said, "Pray for Ambrose." And they did, as he had surgery after surgery to repair his damaged face. Rumors circulated that he was horribly disfigured. Some said he was blind. Some claimed he could no longer speak. He would never wrestle again. What a waste. What a tragedy.

But eventually the plea for prayers was taken down, the flags in the windows were removed, and life in Hannah Lake resumed. The townsfolk were battered. Their hearts were broken. Luisa O'Toole boycotted the bakery because she claimed it was Ambrose's fault her son was dead. It was his fault they were all dead. She spat whenever someone said his name. People tsked and hemmed. But some secretly agreed with her. Deep down they wondered why he hadn't just stayed home. Why hadn't they all stayed home?

Elliott Young returned to work eventually, after taking out a second mortgage on his home and selling everything he owned of any value. But he still had his son, unlike the others, and he didn't complain about the financial hardship. Ambrose's mother and Elliott took turns at Ambrose's side, and six months after he'd been flown out of Iraq, Ambrose came home to Hannah Lake.

For weeks, talk was thick and curiosity ran rampant. There was talk of a parade or a ceremony of some sort to celebrate Ambrose's homecoming. But Elliott made excuses and apologies. Ambrose didn't feel up to a celebration of any kind. People accepted that, albeit reluctantly. And they waited a little longer before they started asking again. More months went by. Nobody saw him. Rumors started up again about his injuries, and some asked the question, if he was truly that disfigured, what kind of life could he really have? Some people wondered if it wouldn't have been better if he had just died with his friends. Coach Sheen and Bailey tried to see him many times but were turned away . . . many times.

Fern grieved for the boy she had always loved. She wondered how it would feel to be beautiful and have it taken away. How much harder would it be than never knowing what it felt like in the first place? Angie often remarked that Bailey's illness was merciful in one regard: it happened slowly through early childhood, robbing the child of his independence before he'd really gained it. So different from those who are paralyzed in an accident and confined to a wheelchair as adults, knowing full well what they have lost, what independence felt like.

Ambrose knew what it felt like to be whole, to be perfect, to be Hercules. How cruel to suddenly fall from such heights. Life had given Ambrose another face and Fern wondered if he would ever be able to accept it.

14
Solve a Mystery

Riding home on her bike after work was as second nature as finding her way through the hallways of her home in the dark. Fern had done it a hundred times, finding her way home around midnight without noticing the familiar houses and streets around her, her mind often somewhere else completely. She was the night manager at Jolley's Supermarket. She'd started at Jolley's her sophomore year in high school, bagging groceries, sweeping floors. She eventually worked her way into a cashier position and finally, last year, Mr. Morgan had given her a title, a small raise, and the keys to the store so she could close it up five nights a week.

She was probably riding too fast. She could admit that now, but she hadn't expected a giant grizzly bear running on his hind legs to come around the corner as she turned onto her street. She yelped, yanking her handlebars to the left to avoid a collision. Her bike flew over the curb and up onto the grass before it struck a fire hydrant and she was propelled over the handle bars onto the Wallaces' well-kept front lawn. She lay there for a minute, gasping to recapture the air that had been forcibly expelled from her chest. Then she remembered the bear. She scrambled to her feet, wincing, and turned to retrieve her bike.

"Are you okay?" the bear growled behind her.

Fern yelped again and jerked around, finding herself about ten feet from Ambrose Young. Her heart dropped like a two-ton anchor and rooted her to the spot. He was holding her bike up, which looked a bit mangled from the impact with the fire hydrant. He wore a snug, black sweat shirt with a hood that hung low on his forehead. He kept his face averted as he spoke to her and the streetlight cast his face in partial shadow. But it was Ambrose Young, no doubt about it. He didn't look wounded. He was still huge, the width of his shoulders and length of his arms and legs still impressively muscled, at least as far as she could tell. He had on a pair of fitted black knit pants and black running shoes, which was obviously what he had been doing when she mistook him for a bear running down the middle of the road.

"I think so," she answered breathlessly, not believing her eyes. Ambrose was standing there, whole, strong, alive. "Are you? I just about ran you over. I wasn't paying attention. I'm so sorry."

His eyes darted to her face and away again, and he kept his face angled to the side, like he couldn't wait to be on his way.

"We went to school together, didn't we?" he asked quietly and shifted his weight from one foot to the other, the way an athlete does when they are preparing for an event. He seemed nervous, jittery even.

Fern felt a stab of pain—the hurt that comes when a lifelong crush acknowledges that you look vaguely familiar, but nothing more.

"Ambrose, it's me. Fern?" Fern said hesitantly. "Bailey's cousin, Couch Sheen's niece . . . Rita's friend?"

Ambrose Young's gaze shot to her face again and held. He was staring at her from the corner of his eye, keeping one side of his face in the shadows, and Fern wondered if his neck was hurt, making turning his head painful.

"Fern?" he repeated hesitantly.

"Uh, yeah." Now it was Fern's turn to look away. She wondered if he too was remembering the love notes and the kiss at the lake.

"You don't look the same," Ambrose said bluntly.

"Um, thank you. That's kind of a relief," Fern said honestly. Ambrose looked surprised and his mouth quirked ever so slightly. Fern felt herself smiling along with him.

"The frame is a little bent. You should try it. See if you can make it home." Ambrose pushed the bike toward her, and Fern grasped the handles, taking it from his hands. For a second, the light from the streetlight hit him squarely in the face. Fern felt her eyes widen, the breath catching in her throat. Ambrose must have heard the swift intake of breath, because his gaze locked on hers for a heartbeat before he pulled back. Then he turned and was running swiftly in smooth strides down the road, the black of his clothing melding with the darkness and obscuring him from view almost immediately. Fern watched him go, frozen in place. She wasn't the only one who didn't look the same.

● ● ●

August 2004

"Why won't anyone let me see a mirror, Dad?"

"Because right now it looks worse than it really is."

"Have you seen what I look like . . . underneath?"

"Yes." Elliott whispered.

"Has Mom?"

"No."

"She still doesn't like to look at me, even all bandaged up."

"It hurts her."

"No. It scares her."

Elliott looked at his son, at the gauze-wrapped face. Ambrose had seen himself in the bandages and he tried to picture himself from his father's perspective. There wasn't much to see. Even Ambrose's right eye was swathed. His left eye looked almost alien in the sea of white, like a Halloween mummy with removable parts. He sounded like one too—his mouth was wired shut, forcing him to mumble through his teeth, but Elliott understood him if he listened closely enough.

"She's not afraid of you, Ambrose," Elliott said lightly, trying to smile.

"Yes she is. Being ugly scares her more than anything else." Ambrose closed his eye, shutting out his father's haggard face and the room around him. When he wasn't in pain, he was in a fog from the painkillers. The fog was a relief, but it frightened him too, because lurking in the fog was reality. And reality was a monster with gleaming red eyes and long arms that pulled him toward the yawning black hole that made up its body. His friends had been devoured by that hole. He thought he remembered their screams and the smell of flesh burning, but he wondered if it was just his mind filling in the blanks between then and now. So much had changed that his life was as unrecognizable as his face.

"What scares you the most, son?" his father asked quietly.

Ambrose wanted to laugh. He wasn't afraid of anything. Not anymore. "Not a damn thing, Dad. I used to be afraid of going to hell. But now that I'm here, hell doesn't seem so bad." Ambrose's voice had become slurred and he felt himself slipping away. But he needed to ask one more question.

"My right eye . . . it's done . . . isn't it? I'm not going to see again."

"No, son. The doc says no."

"Huh. Well. That's good I guess." Ambrose knew he wasn't making sense, but he was too far gone to explain himself. In the back of his mind, he thought it only fair that if his friends had lost their lives, he should lose something as well.

"My ear's gone, too."

"Yeah. It is." Elliott's voice sounded far off.

Ambrose slept for a while, and when he awoke, his dad no longer sat in the chair beside his bed. He didn't leave often. He must be finding something to eat or getting some sleep. The little window in his hospital room looked out on a black night. It must be late. The hospital slumbered, though it was never completely quiet on his floor. Ambrose levered himself up, and before he could let himself reconsider, he started unraveling the long layers of gauze from his face. Round and round, one after the other, making a pile of medicine-stained bandages on his lap. When he pulled the last one free, he staggered from his bed, holding onto the rolling rack that held the bags of antibiotics, fluids, and painkillers they were pumping into his body. He'd been up a few times and knew he could walk. His body was virtually unscathed. Just some shrapnel in his right shoulder and thigh. Not even a broken bone.

There wasn't a mirror in the room. There wasn't a mirror in the bathroom. But the window, with its thin blinds, would work almost as well. Ambrose reached for it, pushing the blinds upward with his left hand, clinging to the metal pole with his right, freeing the glass so he could stare at his face for the first time. At first he couldn't see anything but the dim streetlights far below. The room was too dark to reflect his image off the glass.

Then Elliott walked through the door and saw his son standing at the window, clenching the blinds like he wanted to rip them from the wall.

"Ambrose?" His voice rose in dismay. And then he flipped on the light. Ambrose stared and Elliott froze, realizing instantly what he had done.

Three faces stared back at Ambrose from the glass. He registered his father's face first, a mask of despair just behind his right shoulder, and then he saw his own face, gaunt and swollen, but still recognizable. But merged with the recognizable half of his reflection was a pulpy, misshapen mess of ruined skin, Frankenstein stitching, and missing parts—someone Ambrose didn't know at all.

● ● ●

When Fern told Bailey she had seen Ambrose, Bailey's eyes grew wide with excitement.

"He was running? That's good news! He's refused to see every-body, as far as I know. That's definite progress. How did he look?"

"At first I couldn't see any change," Fern answered honestly.

Bailey's look grew pensive. "And?" he pressed.

"One side of his face is very scarred," she said softly. "I only saw it for a second. Then he just turned and started running again."

Bailey nodded. "But he was running," he repeated. "That's very good news."

But good news or not, a month passed and then one more, and Fern didn't see Ambrose again. She kept her eyes peeled as she ped-aled home from work each night, hoping to see him running up and down the darkened streets, but she never did.

Imagine her surprise then, when one night she stayed later than usual at the store and caught sight of him behind the swinging bakery doors. He must have seen her too, because he ducked out of sight immediately and Fern was left gaping in the hallway.

Ambrose had worked in the bakery with his father all through high school. It was a family business after all, started by Elliott's grandfather almost eighty years before when he partnered with John Jolley, the original owner of the town's only grocery store.

Fern had always liked the contradiction of big, strong Ambrose Young working in a kitchen. In high school, he'd worked during the summers and on the weekends when he wasn't wrestling. But the night shift, the shift when the majority of the baking was done, was the kind of job where he wouldn't ever be seen if he chose not to be, working from 10:00 when the store was just closing, until 6:00 a.m., an hour before it opened again. The hours obviously suited him just fine. Fern wondered how long he had been back at the bakery and how many nights she'd barely missed him or just not realized he was there at all.

The next night the registers were off, and Fern couldn't seem to get the books to balance. At midnight, as she was finally finishing up, the aroma of wonderful things started to curl from the bakery, wafting around the corner to the little office where she labored. She logged out of the computer and crept down the hallway, positioning herself so that she could see through the swinging doors that led into the kitchen. Ambrose had his back to her, and his plain white T-shirt and jeans were partially covered by a white apron, "Young's Bakery" splashed across in bright red print. Elliott Young had worn the same apron for as long as Fern could remember. But somehow on Ambrose it looked totally different.

Fern could see now that his long hair had not grown back. She had half expected to see it brushing his shoulders. From what she could see, he had no hair whatsoever. His head was covered with a red bandana tied tightly in the back like he had just climbed off a Harley and decided to whip up a batch of brownies. Fern giggled to herself at the mental image of a biker making brownies, and winced when the giggle was louder than she'd intended. Ambrose turned, giving her a view of the right side of his face, a view she'd only seen briefly in the dark. Fern darted back around the corner, worried that he would hear her and misunderstand her laughter, but after a minute couldn't resist moving back where she could watch him while he worked.

His radio was turned up loud enough to drown out the canned music that played all day, every day, at Jolley's market. His mouth moved with the lyrics, and for a minute Fern watched his lips in fascination. The skin on the right side of his face was rippled, the way the sand looks when the wind blows across it and creates waves. Where there weren't ripples, there were pock marks, and the right side of his face and neck was spotted with black marks, like a prankster had taken a felt tip marker to his cheek while he slept. As she watched, he reached a hand to his face and rubbed at the marks that marred his skin, scratching as if they bothered him.

A long, thick scar ran from the corner of his mouth and up the side of his face, disappearing into the bandana on his head. His right eye was glassy and fixed, and a scar ran vertically through his eyelid, extending above his eye through his eyebrow and below his eye in a straight line with his nose intersecting the scar that started at the corner of his mouth.

Ambrose was still imposing, tall and straight, and his wide shoulders and long arms were still corded with muscles. But he was leaner, even leaner than he'd been during wrestling season, when the boys were so lean their cheeks were hollow and their eyes sunken in their faces. He'd been running the night Fern had first seen him. She wondered briefly if he was trying to get back in shape, and if so . . . why? Fern didn't love exercise, so it was hard to imagine him running for the joy of it, although she was sure that was a possibility. Her idea of exercise was to turn on the radio and dance around her room, shaking her little body until she worked up a good sweat. It had served her well enough. She definitely wasn't fat.

Fern wished she dared approach him, dared talk to him. But she didn't know how. Didn't know if he would want her to, so she stayed hidden for several moments more before she made her way to the exit and headed for home.

15

Make Friends with a Monster

A small whiteboard was mounted just outside the bakery door in the hallway that led to Mr. Morgan's office and the employee break-room. It had been there forever, and it had never had anything written on it, as far as Fern could tell. Maybe Elliott Young had thought it would make a good place to write schedules or reminders, but he'd never gotten around to it. Fern decided it would be perfect. She wouldn't be able to put anything too suggestive there . . . but suggestive wasn't really her style, after all. If she wrote on the board at about eight o'clock, after the bakery was officially closed for the night and before Ambrose arrived to start his preparations in the kitchen, he would be the only one to see what was written on the board. And he could erase it if he didn't want anyone else to see it.

The key was to write something that would make him smile—something that he would know was meant for him—without cluing anyone else in and without making herself feel like an idiot. She struggled with the words for two days. Everything from "Hi. Glad you're back!" to "I couldn't care less if your face isn't perfect, I still want to have your babies." Neither seemed quite right. And then she knew what she would do.

In big black letters she wrote KITES OR BALLOONS across the whiteboard, and she taped a red balloon, his favorite color, to the side. He would know it was Fern. Once upon a time, they had asked each other a million questions just like this. In fact, Ambrose had been the first to ask this particular question. *Kites or Balloons?* Fern had said *kites* because if she were a kite she could fly, but someone would always be holding onto her. Ambrose had said *balloons*: "I like the idea of flying away and letting the wind take me. I don't think I want anyone holding onto me." Fern wondered if his response would be the same now as it had been then.

When Ambrose had discovered she was writing the letters instead of Rita, and the correspondence had come to a screeching halt, Fern had missed questions like these the very most. In his responses, sometimes with only a word or a funny one-liner, she had started to know Ambrose and had begun to reveal herself as well. And she had revealed Fern, not Rita.

Fern watched the white board for two days, but the words stayed there, unacknowledged, unanswered. So she erased them and tried again. SHAKESPEARE OR EMINEM, she wrote. He had to remember that one. Back then, she thought for sure he would share her secret fascination with the rhyming ability of the white rapper. Ambrose's response had been, surprisingly, Shakespeare. Ambrose had then sent her some of Shakespeare's sonnets, and told her Shakespeare would have been an incredible rapper. She had also discovered that Ambrose was much more than a pretty face. He was a jock with a poet's soul, and the heroes in Fern's novels had nothing on him. Nothing.

The following day the whiteboard also had nothing on it. Nothing. Strike two. Time to get a little more blunt. She erased SHAKE-SPEARE OR EMINEM and wrote HIDE OR SEEK? He'd been the one to ask that one the first time around. And she had circled seek . . . because wasn't that what she had been doing? Seeking him out, discovering him?

Fern wondered if she should pick a different either/or, since he was so obviously hiding. But maybe it would provoke a response. When she arrived at three the next afternoon she glanced at the board as she walked by, not hoping for much, and came to a screeching halt. Ambrose had erased her question and written one of his own.

DEAF OR BLIND?

This was a question she had asked him before. At the time, he had chosen deaf. She had agreed, but had listed all her favorite songs in response, indicating what she would have to give up in exchange for her eyesight. Her list of songs had prompted questions about country or classical, rock or pop, show tunes or a bullet to the brain. Ambrose had claimed he would rather take the bullet, which inspired a slew of either/or questions about ways to die. Fern didn't think she would be using any of those questions in the present situation.

She circled DEAF, just as she had back then. The next day when she checked the board Ambrose had circled both words. Both deaf and blind. She had wondered about his right eye, now she knew. Was he deaf in his right ear as well as blind in his right eye? She knew he wasn't deaf in both ears because of their brief conversation the night she almost hit him on her bike. Below the circled words there was a new question. He'd written, LEFT OR RIGHT?

This wasn't one they had asked before, and Fern had a sneaking suspicion Ambrose was referring to his face. Left side or right? She responded by circling both left and right, just as he had done with deaf or blind.

The next day everything was erased.

● ● ●

Two days went by and Fern decided on a new tactic. She wrote in careful letters:

> *"Love is not love*
> *Which alters when alteration finds,*
> *Or bends with the remover to remove:*
> *Oh, no! It is an ever-fixèd mark,*
> *That looks on tempests and is never shaken."*

Shakespeare. Ambrose would know why she wrote it. It was one of the sonnets he had said was his favorite. Let him make of it what he would. He might groan and roll his eyes, worried that she would follow him around with her tongue hanging out, but maybe he would understand what she was trying to say. The people who cared about him still cared about him, and their love or affection wouldn't change just because his appearance had. It might just bring him comfort to know that some things stayed the same.

Fern left her shift that night without seeing him, closing the store without a glimpse. When she arrived the next day the board had been wiped clean. Embarrassment rose in her chest but she tamped it down. This wasn't about her. At least Ambrose knew somebody cared. So she tried again, continuing with Sonnet 116, which had also been her favorite since Lady Jezebel had included it in a letter to Captain Jack Cavendish in one of Fern's first novels, *Lady and the Pirate*. She used a red marker this time, writing the words in her best cursive.

> *"Love's not Time's fool,*
> *though rosy lips and cheeks*
> *Within his bending sickle's compass come;*
> *Love alters not with his brief hours and weeks,*
> *But bears it out even to the edge of doom."*

• • •

"THEY DO NOT LOVE THAT DO NOT SHOW THEIR LOVE"—Hamlet was scrolled across the whiteboard in block letters the following afternoon.

Fern pondered that one all day. Obviously, Ambrose hadn't felt welcomed home with outstretched arms. She wondered why. People had wanted to throw him a parade, hadn't they? And Coach Sheen and Bailey had gone to see him and been turned away. Maybe people wanted to see him . . . but maybe they were afraid. Or maybe it hurt too much. The town had been rocked. Ambrose hadn't seen the devastation after the news had hit Hannah Lake. A writhing tornado had whipped its way up and down the streets, leaving families and friends leveled. Maybe no one had been with him in his darkest hours because they were stumbling around in their own.

Fern spent her half-hour dinner break finding a suitable response. Was he talking about her? Surely he hadn't wanted to see her. The possibility that he might be referring to her gave her the courage to be bold in her reply. He could doubt the town, but he wouldn't be able to claim that she didn't care. It was a little over the top, but it *was* Shakespeare.

> *"Doubt thou the stars are fire,*
> *Doubt the sun doth move,*
> *Doubt truth to be a liar*
> *But never doubt I love."*

And his response?

"DO YOU THINK I AM EASIER TO
BE PLAYED ON THAN A PIPE?"

"Shakespeare didn't say that." Fern scowled, talking to herself and staring at the flippant response. But when she typed the quote into the search engine, she found he had. The quote was from Hamlet again. Big surprise. This wasn't quite what she'd had in mind when she'd started writing messages. Not at all. Squaring her shoulders she tried again. And she hoped he would understand.

> *"Our doubts are traitors,*
> *And make us lose the good we oft might win*
> *By fearing to attempt."*

She watched for him that night, wondering if he would respond right away. She checked the board before she left for the night. He'd responded all right.

NAIVE OR STUPID?

Fern felt the tears flood her eyes and spill out onto her cheeks. With a straight back and chin held high she walked to her register, picked up her purse from beneath the counter and walked out of the store. He might be hiding but she was through seeking Ambrose Young.

● ● ●

Ambrose watched Fern go, and he felt like an asshole. He'd made her cry. Awesome. She was trying to be nice. He knew that. But he didn't want nice. He didn't want to be encouraged and he sure as hell didn't want to keep finding Shakespeare quotes to write on that damn whiteboard. Better that he run her off right away. Period.

He scratched at his cheek. The shrapnel still buried in his skin drove him crazy. It itched, and he could feel the pieces working their way out. The doctors told him some of the shrapnel, the pieces buried deep in his right arm and shoulder, and some of the pieces in his skull would probably never work themselves out. He wouldn't be going through any metal detectors without setting them clanging. That was fine, but the shrapnel in his face, the pieces that he could feel, they bothered him, and he had a hard time not touching them.

His thoughts flew back to Fern. He worried that if he let her get too close, he might have a hard time not touching her, too. And he was pretty sure she didn't want that. He had started back at the bakery full time a month ago. He'd been working a few hours in the early morning with his dad for longer than that, but it had only been a month since he had completely taken over the night shift, the most important shift for the bakery. He made pies, cakes, cookies, donuts, rolls, and bread. His dad had taught him well over the years, and it was work he knew how to do. The work was comforting and quiet—safe. His dad would do the cake decorating and the specialty orders when he came in at four and they would work together for an hour or two before the bakery opened. Ambrose would slip out when it was still dark and head home without being seen, just the way he liked it.

For a long time, no one had known he was working at the bakery again. But Fern closed the store five nights a week, and for an hour or two after he came into work most nights, Ambrose and Fern were alone in the store. There was the random customer coming for a last-minute gallon of milk or a late-night grocery run, but from about nine to eleven it was quiet and slow. Before long, Fern had seen him in the kitchen, though he had tried to stay out of sight.

He'd been watching her long before she'd realized he was there. She was a quiet girl; her hair was the loudest thing about her, a fiery, riotous crown on an otherwise demure face. She had let it grow since he'd seen her last and it hung in long curls halfway down her back. And she no longer wore glasses. The long hair and the missing glasses had thrown him that night, the night he'd made her crash her bike. And of course he'd been trying not to look directly at her so she wouldn't look directly at him.

Her eyes were a deep, soft brown and a sprinkling of freckles speckled her small nose. Her mouth was slightly disproportionate to the rest of her face. In high school, when she wore braces, her top lip had looked almost comical, like a duck bill stretched over her protruding teeth. Now her mouth was almost sensual, her teeth straight and white, her smile wide and unpretentious. She was quietly lovely, unassumingly pretty, completely unaware that at some point between awkwardness and adulthood she had grown so appealing. And because she was unaware, she became more appealing still.

Ambrose had watched her, night after night, positioning himself where he could gaze at her unobtrusively. And he wondered more than once how he could have so easily dismissed her before. Moments like these made him long for the face that he used to see when he looked in the mirror, a face that he'd taken for granted. A face that had smoothed his way more than once with a pretty girl that caught his eye. It was a face that would surely attract her to him, the way she'd been attracted to him before. But it was a face he would never have again, and he found he was lost without it. So he just watched.

She always had a paperback tucked to the side of the cash register, and she would pull her long curls around her left shoulder, twining them around her fingers as she read, the lateness of the hour making shoppers few and far between, giving her long stretches where she manned her register with little to do but flip pages and twirl her red locks.

Now she was writing him notes using word games and Shakespeare, just like she'd done senior year, posing as Rita. He had been so angry when he'd found out. But then she'd been so sweet and so obviously sorry when she'd offered her apology. It hadn't been difficult to see she had a huge crush on him. It's hard to stay angry with someone who loves you. And now she was at it again. But he didn't think for a minute that she actually liked him. She still liked the old

Ambrose. Had she even looked at him? Really looked at him? It had been dark the night she practically ran over him on her bike. She'd gasped when she saw his face. He'd heard her, loud and clear. So what was she up to now? Thinking about it just made him angry all over again. But before the night was out he was back to feeling like a jerk. So he walked to the white board and scribbled the words.

ASSHOLE OR JERK?

He thought his dad might object to the word "asshole" being written on the bakery whiteboard, but didn't think any other word would do. Shakespeare wasn't going to cut it this time around. Plus, he had no idea if Shakespeare's characters ever begged for forgiveness from pretty redheads with hearts that were too soft for their own good. He went home in a sour mood that soured his stomach and made the maple bars he'd eaten feel like rocks in his gut. When he arrived at work at ten o'clock the following night, the board had been wiped clean and no new message had been added. Good. He was relieved. Kind of.

16

Kiss Rita

Ambrose sneaked little peeks through the opening that separated the bakery display cases and front counter from the working part of the kitchen, trying to catch a glimpse of Fern, wondering if she had finally decided he wasn't worth her time. She had already been gone by the time he arrived at work the last few nights. He had started coming in earlier and earlier so he could see her—even from behind the bakery window—before she left work for the night. He made excuses to Elliott about things that needed to be done at the bakery, but his dad never questioned it. He was probably glad to see Ambrose out of the house and out of his childhood room, although he would never say so. It was exactly what the doctor ordered.

His psychologist, the one the army made sure he had, told Ambrose that he needed to learn to adjust to his "new reality," to "come to terms with what had happened to him," to "find new pursuits and associations." The job was a start. Ambrose hated to admit that it was actually helping, and he'd been running and lifting weights too. Exercise was the only thing that made him feel something besides despair. So he exercised a lot. Ambrose wondered suddenly if spying would qualify as a "new pursuit."

He felt like a creep, spying on Fern, but he spied anyway. Tonight, Fern was sweeping the floor singing along with "The Wind Beneath my Wings," using the broom handle as a microphone. He hated the song, but he found himself smiling as he watched her swaying back and forth, singing in a slightly off-key but not-unpleasant soprano. She moved her pile of dirt until she was directly in front of the bakery counter. She saw him standing in full view and stopped, staring back at him as the last words rang through the empty store. She smiled tentatively, as if he hadn't made her cry just a few nights before, and Ambrose felt the newly acquired fight-or-flight reaction that flooded him anytime someone looked directly at him.

Fern had turned up the music that trickled out of the store's sound system until it felt more like a skating rink than a grocery store. The tunes were a benign mix of soft hits designed to put shoppers in a coma as they perused the aisles for items they could probably do without. Ambrose suddenly longed for a little Def Leppard, complete with full-throated wailing and high-powered choruses.

Suddenly, Fern dropped the broom and ran for the front doors. Ambrose stepped out from the kitchen, rounding the counter, slightly alarmed that something was wrong. Fern was unlocking the sliding doors and pushing one aside to allow Bailey Sheen to roll through in his wheelchair. Then she pulled it back and relocked it, chattering with Bailey as she did.

Ambrose tried not to smile. Really he did. But Bailey was wearing a head lamp on his head, a giant one, with thick elastic bands that wrapped around his head like one of those old-fashioned retainers. It was the kind of head lamp he imagined miners would wear as they tunneled into the earth. It was so bright Ambrose winced, covering his good eye and turning away.

"What the hell are you wearing, Sheen?"

Fern's head whipped around, obviously surprised that he had ventured out from the confines of the bakery.

Bailey wheeled past Fern and kept rolling toward Ambrose. Bailey didn't act surprised to see him there, and though his eyes were locked on Ambrose's face, he didn't react at all to the changes in Ambrose's appearance. Instead, he rolled his eyes and wrinkled his brow, trying to look up at the klieg light strapped to his forehead.

"Help me out, man. My mom makes me wear this damn thing whenever I'm out at night. She's convinced I'm going to get run over. I can't take it off by myself."

Ambrose reached out, still grimacing at the blazing bluish-white light. He pulled the lamp from Bailey's head and snapped the light off. Bailey's hair stood up on end, and Fern smoothed it down absentmindedly as she walked up behind him. It was a touching gesture, maternal even. She patted Bailey's hair into place as if she had done it a thousand times before, and Ambrose realized suddenly that she probably had. Fern and Bailey had been friends for as long as he could remember. Obviously, Fern had become accustomed to doing things for Bailey that he couldn't do for himself, without him asking or even realizing what she was doing.

"What are you doing here?" he asked Bailey, surprised that Bailey was roaming the streets in his wheelchair at eleven o'clock.

"Karaoke, baby."

"Karaoke?"

"Yep. Haven't done it in a while, and we've been getting complaints from the produce section. Seems the carrots have formed a Bailey Sheen fan club. Tonight is for the fans. Fern's got quite a following in the frozen foods."

"Karaoke . . . here?" Ambrose didn't even crack a smile . . . but he wanted to.

"Yep. Closing time means we have free rein of the place. We take over the store's sound system, use the intercom for a microphone, plug in our CDs, and rock Jolley's Supermarket. It's awesome. You should join us. I should warn you, though, I'm amazing, and I'm also a mic hog."

Fern giggled, but looked at Ambrose hopefully. Oh, hell, no. He wasn't singing karaoke. Not even to please Fern Taylor, which he actually wanted to do, surprisingly enough.

Ambrose stammered something about cakes in the oven and made a hasty beeline for the kitchen. It was only a few minutes before the store was filled with karaoke tracks and Bailey was doing a very poor Neil Diamond impression. Ambrose listened as he worked. He really had no choice. It was loud, and Bailey was definitely a mic hog. Fern only jumped in occasionally, sounding like a kindergarten teacher trying to be a pop star, her sweet voice completely at odds with the songs she chose. When she broke into Madonna's "Like a Virgin" he found himself laughing out loud, and stopped abruptly, surprised at the way the laughter felt rumbling in his chest and spilling out his mouth. He thought back, his mind racing over the last year, since the day his life had been thrown into a black hole. He didn't think he had laughed. Not once in an entire year. No wonder it felt like engaging the gears on a fifty-year-old truck.

They sang a duet next. And it was a stunner. "Summer Nights" from *Grease*. *Wella wella wella oomph* poured from the speakers and the Pink Ladies begged to be told more as Bailey and Fern sang their lines with gusto, Bailey growling on all the suggestive parts and Fern snickering and flubbing her words, making up new ones as she went along. Ambrose laughed through the next hour, enjoying himself thoroughly, wondering whether Bailey and Fern had ever considered doing comic relief. They were hysterical. He had just finished rolling out a batch of cinnamon rolls when he heard his name echoing throughout the store.

"Ambrose Young? I know you can sing. How about you come out here and quit pretending we can't see you back there, spying on us.

We can, you know. You aren't as sneaky as you think. I know you want to sing this next song. Wait! It's the Righteous Brothers! You have to sing this one. I won't be able to do it justice. Come on. Fern's been dying to hear you sing again ever since senior year when we heard you nail 'The National Anthem' at that pep rally."

Had she really? Ambrose thought, rather pleased.

"AAAAAMMMMMBRRRROOOOSE YOUUUNG!" Bailey thundered, obviously enjoying the intercom way too much. Ambrose ignored him. He was not going to sing. Bailey called him several more times, changing his tactics until finally the lure of the karaoke track distracted him. Ambrose continued working as Bailey informed him that he'd lost that loving feeling.

Yeah. He had. A year ago in Iraq. That loving feeling had been completely decimated.

• • •

Rita's left eye was swollen shut and her lip was puffy and split down the middle. Fern sat by her side and held the ice to her face, wondering how many other times Rita had looked this way and hid it from her friends.

"I called the cops. Becker's uncle Barry showed up and took Becker in, but I don't think they're going to charge him," Rita said dully. At that moment she looked like she was forty years old. Her long, blonde hair lay limp on her shoulders and the fatigue in her face created shadows and valleys that wouldn't otherwise be there.

"Do you want to come to my house? Mom and Dad would let you and Ty stay as long as you wanted." Sadly, Rita had come and stayed before, but always went back to Becker.

"I'm not leaving this time. Becker can leave. I didn't do anything wrong." Rita stuck out her bottom lip in defiance, but her eyes filled with tears, contradicting her brave words.

"But . . . but he's dangerous," Fern argued gently.

"He'll be nice for a while. He'll be super sorry and be on his best behavior. And I'll start making plans. I've been saving up. Mom and I are going to take little Ty guy and run away. Soon. And Becker can go to hell."

Ty whimpered in his sleep and snuggled his face into his mother's breast. He was small for a two-year-old. It was a good thing, because Rita packed him everywhere, as if she was afraid to set him down.

"I'm only twenty-one years old, Fern! How did I get myself in this situation? How did I make such a terrible choice?" Not for the first time, Fern was grateful she had been a late bloomer—small, plain, ignored. In some ways, her ugly duckling status had been like a force field, keeping the world at bay so she could grow, come into her own, and figure out that there was more to her than the way she looked. Rita continued on, not really expecting Fern to answer.

"Do you know that I used to dream about Bailey? About them finding a cure so he could walk? Then he and I would get married and live happily ever after. My mom worked her fingers to the bone taking care of my dad after his accident. And he was so miserable. He hurt all the time, and the pain made him mean. I knew I wasn't that strong. So even though I loved Bailey, I knew I wasn't strong enough to love him if he couldn't walk. So I prayed that he would just magically be healed. I kissed him once, you know."

Fern felt her jaw drop. "You did?"

"Yep. I had to see if there was any heat."

"And was there?"

"Well . . . yeah. There was. I mean, he had no clue what he was doing. And I took him by surprise, I think. But yeah. There was heat. Enough heat that I considered maybe just being able to kiss him was enough. Maybe being with someone I loved who would love me back was enough. But I got scared. I wasn't strong enough, Fern."

"When? When did this happen?" Fern gasped.

"Junior year. Christmas break. We were watching movies at Bailey's, remember? You felt sick and walked home before the movie was over. Bailey's dad had helped Bailey out of his wheelchair so he was sitting on the couch. We were talking and laughing and . . . then I held his hand. And before the night was over . . . I kissed him too."

Fern was stunned. Bailey had never told her. Never said a word. Her thoughts spun round and round like a mouse in a wheel, running in circles and never getting anywhere.

"Was that the only time?" Fern asked.

"Yes. I went home that night and when I saw Bailey after Christmas break, he acted like it never happened. I thought I'd ruined everything. I thought he would expect me to be his girlfriend, even though I kind of wanted to be. But I was afraid too."

"Afraid of what?"

"Afraid that I would hurt him, or that I would make promises that I couldn't keep."

Fern nodded. She understood, but her heart ached for Bailey. If she knew Bailey, which she did, the kiss had been a defining moment. Maybe to protect Rita, maybe to protect himself, he had kept it to himself.

"Then Becker came along. He was so persistent. And he was older and I just kind of . . . got swept away, I guess."

"So you and Bailey never even talked about it again?"

"The night before I married Becker, Bailey called me. He told me not to do it."

"He did?" Fern asked. This night was just full of surprises.

"Yeah. But I told him it was too late. Bailey's too good for me anyway."

"That's crap, Rita," Fern blurted out.

Rita jerked like Fern had slapped her face.

"I'm sorry. But that's just an excuse not to do the hard thing," Fern said bluntly.

"Oh, really?" Rita snapped. "Look who's talking. You've been in love with Ambrose Young your whole life. Now he's home with a messed-up face and a messed-up life and I don't see you doing the hard thing!"

Fern didn't know what to say. Rita was wrong. Ambrose's face wasn't keeping her away. But did it matter what the reason was?

"I'm sorry, Fern." Rita sighed tearfully. "You're right. It's crap. My whole life is crap. But I'm going to try to change it. I'm going to be better. You'll see. No more bad choices. Ty deserves better. I just wish Bailey . . . I wish things were different, you know?"

Fern began to nod, but then thought better of it, and shook her head in disagreement.

"If Bailey had been born without MD, he wouldn't be Bailey. The Bailey who is smart and sensitive, and seems to understand so many things we don't. You might have looked right past Bailey if he'd grown up healthy, wrestling on his dad's team, acting like every other guy you've ever known. A big part of the reason Bailey is so special is because life has sculpted him into something amazing . . . maybe not on the outside, but on the inside. On the inside, Bailey looks like Michelangelo's *David*. And when I look at him, and when you look at him, that's what we see."

17

Take a Stand

Two days later, Becker Garth came strolling into Jolley's like his wife wasn't still bruised and his shirt didn't still smell like the slammer. Apparently, his connections on the Hannah Lake police force were coming in handy. He smiled cheekily at Fern as he strutted by her register.

"You're looking pretty today, Fern." His eyes slid to her chest and back up again. He winked and popped his gum. Fern had always thought Becker was a handsome guy. But the handsome didn't quite cover the scum beneath, and sometimes the scum seeped through and oozed out around the edges. Like it was doing now.

He obviously didn't expect her to respond because he walked on, calling over his shoulder, "Rita says you came by. Thanks for the money. I needed some beer." He held up the twenty-dollar bill Fern had left on the counter for Rita and waved it in the air. Becker sauntered toward the aisle where the alcohol was shelved and disappeared from sight. And Fern saw red. She wasn't a girl prone to anger or rash acts. Until now. She was amazed at the steadiness of her voice as she spoke into the intercom.

"Attention Jolley's shoppers, today at Jolley's Supermarket we have some wonderful specials going on. Bananas are on sale for thirty-nine cents a pound. Juice boxes are ten for a dollar, and our bakery has a dozen sugar cookies for $3.99," Fern paused and gritted her teeth, finding she was unable to stay quiet. "I would also like to draw your attention to the giant asshole in aisle ten. I promise you have never seen a bigger asshole than this one, shoppers. He regularly hits his wife and tells her she's ugly and fat even though she's the most beautiful girl in town. He also likes to make his baby cry and can't hold down a steady job. Why? You guessed it! Because Becker Garth is a big, ugly, giant butt . . ."

"You bitch!" Becker came roaring down aisle ten, screaming, a twelve pack of beer under his arm and rage in his eyes.

Fern held the phone in front of her, as if the intercom would provide a buffer between her and the man she'd publicly insulted. Patrons were gaping, some laughing at Fern's audacious display, others frowning in confusion. Becker threw down the twelve pack and several punctured cans shot out of the broken box, spraying beer in a wide swath. He ran toward Fern and snatched the phone from her hands, pulling on its curly cord until it sprang free, whipping past Fern's face. She ducked reflexively, certain that Becker was going to swing the phone like a nunchuk, striking everything in its path.

Suddenly, Ambrose was there, grabbing Becker by the arm and the back of his shirt, twisting the fabric in his hands until he lifted Becker completely off his feet, his legs flailing helplessly, his tongue hanging out, strangled by his own T-shirt. Then Ambrose threw him. Just tossed him away, like Becker weighed little more than a child. Becker landed on his hands and feet, twisting like a cat as he fell, and he stood up as if he'd meant to be flung ten feet, pushing his chest out like a rooster among his hens.

"Ambrose Young! You look like shit, man! Better run before the townsfolk mistake you for an ogre and come after you with pitchforks!" Becker spat, smoothing down his T-shirt and prancing like a boxer ready to enter the ring.

Ambrose's head was covered with a red bandana, making him look like a huge pirate, the way he always wore it when he was working in the bakery, away from curious eyes. His apron was still wrapped tightly around his lean torso and his hands were fisted at his sides, his eyes on Becker. Fern wanted to hurl herself over the counter and tackle Becker to the ground, but her brief impetuosity had created this situation, and she didn't want to make it worse—for Ambrose especially.

Fern noticed how the patrons of the store were frozen in place, their eyes glued on Ambrose's face. Fern realized that none of them had probably seen him, not since he'd left for Iraq two and a half years before. There had been rumors, as there always were in small towns with big tragedies. And the rumors had been exaggerated, making Ambrose out to be horrifically wounded, grotesque even, but many of the faces registered surprise and sadness, but not revulsion.

Jamie Kimball, Paul Kimball's mother, stood in line at another register, her face pale and grief-stricken as her eyes clung to Ambrose's scarred cheek. Hadn't she seen Ambrose since he returned? Had none of the parents of the fallen boys gone to visit him? Or maybe he hadn't allowed them entrance. Maybe it was more than any of them could bear.

"You need to leave, Becker," Ambrose said, his voice a soft rumble in the shocked silence of the grocery store. An instrumental version of "What a Wonderful World" serenaded Jolley's shoppers as if all was well in Hannah Lake when it decidedly was not. Ambrose continued, "If you decide to stay, I'll pound you like I did in ninth grade, and this time I'll blacken both your eyes and you'll lose more than just one tooth. Don't let my ugly mug fool you; there isn't anything wrong with my fists."

Becker sputtered and turned away, glaring at Fern and pointing at her face, issuing his own warning. "You're a bitch, Fern. Stay away from Rita. You come around my house, and I'll call the cops." Becker turned his venom back on Fern, ignoring Ambrose, saving face by turning on a weaker opponent, the way he always did.

Ambrose shot forward, grabbing Becker by the shirt once more and propelling him toward the sliding doors at the front of the store. The doors slid open in accommodation, and Ambrose hissed a warning into Becker's ear.

"You call Fern Taylor a bitch again or threaten her in any way, and I will rip your tongue out of your mouth and feed it to that ugly dog you keep chained and hungry in your backyard. The one that barks at me whenever I run by. And if you so much as harm a hair on Fern's head or lift your hand to your wife or child, I will find you and I will hurt you." Ambrose gave a shove and sent Becker sprawling out onto the crumbling blacktop in front of the store.

● ● ●

Two hours later, when the store was empty, the beer mess cleaned up, and the doors locked, Fern made her way to the bakery. The yeasty smell of bread, the warm sweetness of melted butter, and the heavy sugar scent of icing greeted her as she pushed through the swinging door that separated Ambrose from the rest of the world. Ambrose started when he saw her, but continued pounding and kneading the giant mound of dough on a floured surface, positioning himself so that his left side, his beautiful side, was facing her. A radio in the corner spilled out eighties rock and Whitesnake asked, "Is This Love?" Fern thought it might be.

The muscles in Ambrose's arms tensed and released, bunching as he rolled the dough into a wide circle and began stamping circles with a giant, eight-section cookie cutter. Fern watched him, his motions smooth and sure, and decided she liked the looks of a man in the kitchen.

"Thank you," she said at last.

Ambrose looked up briefly and shrugged, grunting something unintelligible.

"Did you really beat him up in ninth grade? He was a senior then."

Another grunt.

"He's a bad man . . . if you can call him a man. Maybe he's not grown up yet. Maybe that's his problem. Maybe he'll be better when he is. I guess we can hope."

"He's old enough to know better. Age isn't an excuse. Eighteen-year-old kids are considered old enough to fight for their country. Fight and die for their country. So a twenty-five-year-old piece of shit like Becker can't hide behind that excuse."

"Did you do it for Rita?"

"What?" His eyes shot to her face in surprise.

"I mean . . . you used to like her, right? Did you throw him out of the store tonight because of Rita?"

"I did it because it needed to be done," Ambrose said briefly. At least he wasn't grunting anymore. "And I didn't like him getting in your face." Ambrose met her eyes briefly again before he turned to pull an enormous tray of sugar cookies from the oven. "Even though you did taunt him . . . just a little bit."

Was that a grin? It was! Fern smiled in delight. Ambrose's lips quirked on one side, just for a second, before he started the process of rolling the dough all over again.

When Ambrose smiled, one side of his mouth, the side damaged by the blast, didn't turn up as much, giving him a crooked grin. Fern thought it was endearing, but judging from the infrequency of his smile, Ambrose probably didn't think so.

"I did taunt him. I don't think I've ever taunted anyone before. It was . . . fun," Fern said seriously, honestly.

Ambrose burst out laughing and set down his rolling pin, looking at her and shaking his head. And this time he didn't duck his head and turn away.

"Never taunted anyone, huh? I seem to remember you making faces at Bailey Sheen at a big wrestling tournament. He was supposed to be taking stats, but you were making him laugh. Coach Sheen got after him, which hardly ever happened. I think that qualifies as taunting."

"I remember that tournament! Bailey and I were playing a game we made up. You saw that?"

"Yeah. You two looked like you were having fun . . . and I remember wishing I could trade places with the two of you . . . just for an afternoon. I was jealous."

"Jealous? Why?"

"The coach from Iowa was at that tournament. I was so nervous I was sick. I was throwing up between matches."

"You were nervous? You won every match. I never saw you lose. What did you have to be nervous about?"

"Being undefeated was a lot of pressure. I didn't want to disappoint anybody." Ambrose shrugged. "So tell me about this game." Ambrose smoothly moved the conversation away from himself. Fern tucked away the information he had revealed for later perusal.

"It's a game Bailey and I play. It's our version of charades. Bailey can't really act anything out, for obvious reasons, so we play this game we call Making Faces. It's stupid, but . . . fun. The idea is to communicate strictly through facial expressions. Here. I'll show you. I'll make a face and you tell me what I'm feeling."

Fern dropped her jaw and widened her eyes theatrically.

"Surprise?"

Fern nodded, smiling. Then she flared her nostrils and wrinkled her forehead, screwing her mouth up in disgust. Ambrose chortled.

"Something smells bad?"

Fern giggled and immediately changed faces. Her lower lip quivered and her chin puckered and shook and her eyes filled with tears.

"Oh, man, you are way too good at that!" Ambrose was laughing full-out now, the dough forgotten as she entertained him.

"Do you want to try?" Fern was laughing too, wiping away the tears she had manufactured to create her "sad" face.

"Nah. I don't know if my face would cooperate," Ambrose said quietly, but there was no self-consciousness in his voice, no defensiveness, and Fern let it go with a quiet "okay."

They visited for a few minutes more and then Fern thanked him again and said good night. And it had been a good night, in spite of Becker Garth. Ambrose had talked to her. He'd even laughed with her. And Fern felt a glimmer of hope flicker in her heart.

• • •

The following day when Fern arrived at work there was a quote on the whiteboard.

"God has given you one face and you
make yourself another."—Hamlet

Shakespeare again. Hamlet again. Ambrose seemed to have a thing for the tortured character. Maybe because he was a tortured character. But she had made him laugh. Fern smiled, remembering the invention of the Making Faces game.

2001

"Why are you making that face, Fern?" Bailey asked.

"What face?"

"That face that looks like you can't figure something out. Your eyebrows are pushed down and your forehead is wrinkled. And you're frowning."

Fern smoothed out her face, realizing she was doing exactly what Bailey said she was doing. "I was thinking about a story I've been writing. I can't figure out how to end it. What do you think this face means?" Fern gave herself an underbite and crossed her eyes.

"You look like a brain-dead cartoon character," Bailey answered, snickering.

"What about this one?" Fern pursed her lips and raised her eyebrows while wincing.

"You're eating something super sour!" Bailey cried. "Let me try one." Bailey thought for a minute and then he made his mouth go slack and opened his eyes as wide as they could go. His tongue lolled out the side of his mouth like a big dog's.

"You're looking at something delicious," Fern guessed.

"Be more specific," Bailey said and made the face once more.

"Hmm. You're looking at a huge ice-cream sundae," Fern tried again. Bailey pulled his tongue back into his mouth and grinned cheekily.

"Nope. That's the face you make every time you see Ambrose Young."

Fern swatted Bailey with the cheap stuffed bear she'd won at the school carnival in fourth grade. The arm flew off and ratty stuffing flew in all directions. Fern tossed it aside.

"Oh, yeah? What about you? This is the face you make whenever Rita comes over." Fern lowered one eyebrow and smirked, trying to replicate Rhett Butler's smolder in Gone with the Wind.

"I look constipated whenever I see Rita?" Bailey asked, dumbfounded.

Fern snorted, laughter exploding from her nose, making her grab for a tissue so she didn't gross herself out too much.

"I don't blame you for liking Ambrose," Bailey said, suddenly serious. "He is the coolest guy I know. If I could be anyone in the whole world, I'd be Ambrose Young. Who would you be?"

Fern shrugged, wondering as she always did what it would be like to be beautiful. "I wouldn't mind looking like Rita," she answered honestly. "But I think I would still like to be me on the inside. Wouldn't you?"

Bailey thought for a minute. "Yeah. I am pretty awesome. But so is Ambrose. I'd still trade places."

"I'd just trade faces," Fern said.

"But God gave you that face," Rachel Taylor said from the kitchen. Fern rolled her eyes. Her mother had the hearing of a bat; even at sixty-two years old she didn't miss trick.

"Well, if I could, I'd make myself another," Fern retorted. "Then maybe Ambrose Young wouldn't be too beautiful to even look at me."

She hadn't even meant to quote Shakespeare then, but Ambrose *had* been too beautiful to even look at her.

Fern wondered at Ambrose's choice in quotes until she saw the display cases in front of the bakery. She shrieked like an excited little girl seeing her favorite pop star, and then began laughing out loud. The cases were filled with dozens of round sugar cookies iced in cheerful pastels. Each cookie had a simple face. Squiggles and lines in black icing created a different expression on each one—frowns and smiles and scowls, edible emoticons.

Fern bought a dozen of her favorite ones and wondered how in the world she would ever be able to eat them, or let anyone else eat them. She wanted to save them forever and remember the night she made Ambrose Young laugh. Maybe having a funny face wasn't such a bad thing after all.

Fern found a marker and wrote *Making cookies or Making faces* beneath Ambrose's message on the board. Then she circled Making cookies, so he would know she had seen his offering. And she added a little smiley face.

18
Eat Pancakes Every Day

The next night when Ambrose came to work, there was another message on the board: *Pancakes or Waffles?*

Ambrose circled pancakes. About an hour later, Fern stood in the doorway of the bakery. Her hair hung in curly disarray down her back and she was wearing a pale-pink T-shirt with white jeans and sandals. She'd taken off her bright-blue Jolley's Supermarket apron and had slicked some gloss on her lips. Ambrose wondered if it was the flavored kind and looked away.

"Hi. So . . . I like pancakes too." Fern grimaced like she had said something incredibly embarrassing or stupid. He realized she was still a little afraid to talk to him. He didn't blame her. He hadn't been terribly friendly, and he was pretty scary looking.

"You aren't working tomorrow night, right? Doesn't Mrs. Luebke come in on Saturday and Sunday nights?" she rushed, the words tumbling out as if she had practiced them.

He nodded, waiting.

"Would you want to come with me and Bailey for pancakes? We go to Larry's at midnight sometimes. It makes us feel like grown-ups to have pancakes past our bedtimes." Fern smiled winsomely, that part obviously wasn't rehearsed, and Ambrose realized she had a dimple in her right cheek. He couldn't look away from that little dent in her creamy skin. It disappeared as her smile faltered.

"Uh, sure," Ambrose said hastily, realizing he'd waited too long to respond. He instantly regretted his words. He didn't want to go to Larry's. Someone would see him and it would be awkward.

The dimple was back. Fern beamed and rocked back and forth onto her toes. "Okay. Um, I'll pick you up at midnight, okay? We have to take Bailey's mom's van because, well, you know . . . the wheelchair. Okay, bye." Fern turned and stumbled out the door and Ambrose smiled at her retreating form. She was extremely cute. And he felt like he was thirteen, going on his first date to the bowling alley.

• • •

There is something so comforting about pancakes at midnight. The smell of warm butter, maple syrup, and blueberries hit him like a gale force wind and Ambrose moaned at the simple pleasure of unhealthy food at an ungodly hour. It was almost enough to take away his fear of curious stares and the attempts people made to act like there was nothing wrong with his appearance. Bailey led the way into the sleepy dining room and motored to a booth in the corner that obviously worked for his wheelchair. Fern followed him and Ambrose brought up the rear, refusing to look left or right or count the number of patrons in the place. The tables around them were empty at least. Fern paused, letting Ambrose choose his seat, and he slid gratefully onto the bench that allowed his left side to face the room. Fern slid across from him and bounced a little, the way a kid automatically does when sitting on something with some spring in it. His legs were too long and crowded hers beneath the table, and he shifted, feeling the warmth of her slim calf against his. She didn't move away.

Bailey maneuvered his chair right up to the end of the table. It hit him at chest level, which he claimed was perfect. Fern carefully propped his arms on the table so that when his food came, he could lean forward against the edge and kind of shovel the food into his mouth. She ordered for the two of them, Bailey obviously trusting her to know what he wanted.

The waitress seemed to take the three of them in stride. They were definitely an odd trio, Ambrose realized. It was midnight and the joint was almost empty, just as Fern had promised, but he could see their reflection in the windows that surrounded their booth, and the picture they made was comical.

Ambrose had covered his head with a black, knit stocking cap. His T-shirt was also black. Combined with his size and his messed up face, he looked more than a little scary, and if he hadn't been accompanied by a kid in a wheelchair and a little redhead in pigtails, he could have passed as someone from a slasher movie.

Bailey's wheelchair sat lower than the benches of the booth, and it made him look small and hunched, younger than his twenty-one years. He wore a Hoosiers jersey and a backward baseball cap over his light-brown hair. Fern was wearing her hair in two loose ponytails that hung over her shoulders and curled against her breasts. Her lemon-yellow T-shirt was snug and claimed that she wasn't short, she was fun-sized. Ambrose found himself agreeing wholeheartedly with the T-shirt, and wondered briefly just how fun it would be to kiss her smiling mouth and wrap his arms around her little body. She looked like Mary Ann on *Gilligan's Island*, except with Ginger's hair color. It was a very appealing combination. Ambrose gave himself a mental slap and pushed the thought away. They were eating pancakes with Bailey. This was not a date. There would be no goodnight kiss at the end of it. Not now. Not ever.

"I can't wait to eat." Fern sighed, smiling happily after the waitress left with their orders. "I'm starving." The soft lighting swinging above his head wasn't going to allow him to hide anything from Fern, who now faced him, but there was nothing he could do about that. He could spend the meal staring out the window, giving her a view of his unscathed cheek. But he was hungry too . . . and he was weary of giving a damn.

Ambrose hadn't been to Larry's since the night after he'd taken state, senior year. That night he'd been surrounded by his friends and they had eaten themselves sick. Any wrestler knows that nothing feels as good as eating without fear of the morning scales. The season was officially over and most of them would never weigh in again. The reality of the end would hit soon enough, but that night they celebrated. Like Bailey, he didn't need to look at the menu.

When his pancakes came he toasted his friends silently, letting the thick syrup baptize the memory. The butter followed the syrup over the side, and he scooped it up and placed it back on top of the stack, watching it lose its shape and cascade down the sides once more. He ate without contributing to the conversation, but Bailey spoke enough for the three of them, and Fern seemed content to carry her end when Bailey had to swallow. Bailey did pretty well feeding himself, although his arms would slip now and again and Fern would have to prop them back up. When he was finished, Fern helped him place his hands back on the armrests of his chair, only to be informed of a new problem.

"Fern, my nose itches something fierce." Bailey was trying to wiggle his nose to alleviate his discomfort.

Fern lifted Bailey's arm, supporting his elbow and placing his hand on his nose so that he could scratch to his heart's content. Then she placed his hand back in his lap.

She caught Ambrose watching and explained needlessly, "If I scratch it for him, I never seem to get it. It's better if I just help him do it himself."

"Yep. It's our version of 'a hand up not a handout,'" Bailey said.

"I must have had syrup on my fingers. Now my nose is sticky!" Bailey laughed and Fern rolled her eyes. She wetted the tip of her napkin in her water glass and dabbed at his nose. "Better?"

Bailey wiggled it, testing for syrup residue. "I think you got it. Ambrose, I've been trying for many years to lick my nose, but I was not blessed with a particularly long tongue." Bailey proceeded to show Ambrose how close he could come to sticking the tip of his tongue in his left nostril. Ambrose found himself smiling at Bailey's efforts and the way his eyes crossed as he focused his attention on his nose.

"So Ambrose, you coming with us tomorrow? We're going to head over to Seely to hit the double feature at the drive-in. Fern will bring the lawn chairs and snacks and I'll bring my adorable self. Whaddaya say?"

Seely had an old drive-in movie theater that was still a main attraction in the summertime. People drove a couple of hours just to enjoy a movie lying in the backs of their trucks or sitting in the front seats of their cars.

It would be dark. Nobody would see him. It sounded . . . fun. He could just hear the guys laughing at him. He was hanging out with Bailey and Fern. Oh, how the mighty had fallen.

● ● ●

Ambrose found he couldn't keep his attention on the screen. The sound was tinny and the speaker was closer to his bad ear, making it hard for him to tell what was being said. He should have spoken up when they'd arranged the chairs, but he had wanted to sit to Fern's right so his left side would be facing her, and he'd said nothing. She sat between him and Bailey and made sure Bailey had everything he needed, holding his drink up to his mouth so he could sip through the straw, and keeping a steady stream of popcorn coming. Ambrose finally gave up on the movie and just focused on the way it felt to sit outside, the wind ruffling Fern's hair, the smell of popcorn wafting around him, summer in the air. Last summer he'd been in the hospital. The summer before that, Iraq. He didn't want to think about

Iraq. Not now. He pushed the thought away and focused on the pair beside him.

Bailey and Fern enjoyed themselves thoroughly, laughing and listening intently. Ambrose marveled at their innocence and their simple appreciation of the littlest things. Fern got laughing so hard at one part that she snorted. Bailey howled, snorting every once in a while throughout the rest of the film just to tease her. She turned to Ambrose and grimaced, rolling her eyes as if she needed moral support to combat the lunatic to her left.

The clouds rolled in toward the end of the first show and the second feature was canceled due to the gathering storm. Fern rushed around picking up chairs and trash, pushing Bailey up the ramp into the vehicle as the thunder cracked and the first drops plopped heavily against the windshield.

They pulled into a gas station on the outskirts of Hannah Lake after midnight, and before Ambrose could offer, Fern was jumping out of the van and slamming the door against the driving rain, running inside to pay for the gas. She was a bundle of efficiency, and Ambrose wondered if Fern thought she needed to take care of him like she took care of Bailey. The thought made him feel sick. Was that the image he projected?

"Fern has Ugly Girl Syndrome," Bailey said, out of the blue. "Also known as UGS."

"Fern's not ugly," Ambrose said, his eyebrows sinking low over his dark eyes, distracted momentarily from his depressing thoughts.

"Not now. But she was," Bailey said matter-of-factly. "She had those gnarly teeth and those inch-thick glasses. And she was always so skinny and pasty. Not good-looking. At all."

Ambrose shot a look of disgust over his shoulder at Fern's cousin and Bailey surprised him by laughing.

"You can't punch a man in a wheelchair, Ambrose. And I'm kidding. I just wanted to see what you'd say. She wasn't that bad. But she grew up thinking she was ugly. She doesn't realize that she shed the ugly a long time ago. She's beautiful now. And she's just as pretty on the inside, which is a side benny of UGS. See, ugly girls actually have to work on their personalities and their brains because they can't get by on their looks, not like you and me, you know, the beautiful people." Bailey smiled impishly and waggled his eyebrows.

"Fern doesn't have a clue how pretty she is. That makes her priceless. Make sure you snatch her up before she clues in to her good looks, Brosey."

Ambrose eyed Bailey balefully. Ambrose wasn't interested in being manipulated, even by Bailey Sheen. He stepped out of the van without responding to Bailey's commentary and rounded the vehicle to the side with the gas tank, not wanting Fern to stand out in the rain putting gas in the car while he sat in the passenger seat being waited on. It was early June and the rain wasn't cold, but it was coming down hard, and he was soaked almost instantly. Fern ran out of the station and saw him waiting by the pumps.

"I can do it, Ambrose. Get back in! You're getting soaked!" She squealed, dodging puddles as she made her way back to him.

He saw the credit appear on the gas tank display and immediately removed the gas cap and shoved the nozzle home. Fern huddled nearby, water streaming down her face, obviously not wanting to let him get wet alone. Unfortunately, with Bailey's condition, she was obviously used to being the one who did the grunt work. But he wasn't Bailey.

"Get in the van, Fern. I know how to pump gas," he growled. Her shirt was sticking to her, and Ambrose was getting a delightful eyeful. He gritted his teeth and squeezed the nozzle tighter. It felt like whenever he was close to her he spent all his time trying not to look at her.

An old truck slid up to the other side of the pump, and Ambrose ducked his head instinctively. A door slammed and a familiar voice spoke up behind him.

"Ambrose Young. That you?"

Ambrose turned reluctantly.

"It is you! Well, I'll be damned. How ya doin' lad?" It was Seamus O'Toole, Beans's dad.

"Mr. O'Toole." Ambrose nodded stiffly, extending the hand that wasn't pumping gas.

Seamus O'Toole clasped his hand and his eyes roamed over Ambrose's face, wincing slightly at what he saw. After all, Ambrose's face was also a casualty of the bomb that took his son. His lips trembled and he released Ambrose's hand. Turning, he leaned into his vehicle and spoke to the woman sitting in the passenger seat. The nozzle snapped, indicating the tank was full, and Ambrose wished he could turn and make a break for it while Seamus's back was turned.

Luisa O'Toole stepped out into the rain and walked over to Ambrose, who had replaced the nozzle and was waiting with his hands shoved in his pockets. She was a tiny woman, smaller than Fern by a couple of inches, maybe five feet at the most. Beans got his height, or lack of it, from her. He was there in her fine features, as well, and Ambrose felt nausea roil in his belly. He should have just stayed home. Luisa O'Toole was as fiery as her husband was meek. Beans said his mom was the reason his dad drank himself into a better mood every night. It was the only way to deal with her.

Luisa walked past the pump and stopped in front of Ambrose, lifting her face to the rain so she could gaze up at him. She didn't speak and neither did Ambrose. Fern and Seamus looked on, not knowing what to say or do.

"I blame you," Luisa said finally, her accented English broken and bleak. "I blame you for this. I tell him no go. He go. For you. Now he dead."

Seamus sputtered and apologized, taking his wife by the arm. But she shook him off and turned toward the truck, not looking back at Ambrose as she climbed in and shut the door firmly behind her.

"She's just sad, lad. She just misses him. She doesn't mean it," Seamus offered gently. But they both knew he lied. He patted Ambrose's hand and tipped his head to Fern. Then he returned to his truck and drove away without filling his tank.

Ambrose stood frozen in place, his T-shirt soaked through, his black knit cap plastered against his head. He pulled it off and threw it, sending it flying across the parking lot, a soggy, pathetic substitute for the things he wanted to do, for the rage he needed to expend. He turned and started walking, away from Fern, away from the terrible scene that had just transpired.

Fern ran after him, slipping and sliding, calling for him to wait. But he walked, ignoring her, needing to escape. He knew she wouldn't follow. Bailey was sitting in the van at the pumps, unable to get home on his own.

19

Finish a Thousand-Piece Puzzle

Ambrose had been walking for about half an hour, walking toward home with his back to the rain letting it trickle down the back of his shirt and soak his jeans. His feet squished in his boots with each step. He wished he hadn't chucked his hat. The occasional streetlight shone down on his smooth head, and he felt exposed and vulnerable, unable to cover himself. His bald head bothered him almost more than his face, made him feel more like a freak than the ridges and scars, so when car lights drew up behind him and slowed to a crawl, he ignored them, hoping his appearance would scare them off and make them think twice about messing with him, or worse, offering him a ride.

"Ambrose!" It was Fern, and she sounded scared and upset. "Ambrose? I took Bailey home. Please get in. I'll take you wherever you want to go . . . okay?"

She'd obviously switched cars after she took Bailey home. She was driving an old sedan that belonged to her father. Ambrose had seen that car parked at the church for as long as he could remember.

"Ambrose? I'm not leaving you. I will follow you all night if I have to!"

Ambrose sighed and looked at her. She was leaning across the seat so she could peer out the passenger side window as she inched along beside him. Her face was pale and she had mascara under her eyes. Her hair was plastered against her head and her shirt still stuck to her pretty breasts. She hadn't even taken a second to change her wet clothes before she'd come after him.

Something in his face must have told her she'd won, because she slowed to a stop and hit the door locks as he reached for the handle. The warmth that blasted from the heaters felt like an electric blanket against his skin and he shivered involuntarily. Fern reached over and rubbed his arms briskly as if he was Bailey and she had rescued him from a blizzard and wasn't soaking wet herself. She shoved the car into park and leaned over the seat, reaching for something in the back.

"Here. Wrap this around yourself!" she said, dropping a towel in his lap. "I grabbed it when I switched cars."

"Fern. Stop. I'm fine."

"You're not fine! She should never have said those things to you! I hate her! I am going to throw rocks at her house and break all her windows!" Fern's voice broke, and he could see she was close to tears.

"She lost her son, Fern," Ambrose said softly. His own anger dissipated as he spoke the simple truth. He took the towel from Fern's hands and used it on her hair, wrapping and squeezing, absorbing the moisture, the way he used to do on his own. She stilled, obviously not used to a man's hands in her hair. He continued his ministrations, and she sat quietly, her head lolling to the side, letting him.

"I haven't seen any of them. Not Grant's family. Not Jesse's. I haven't seen Marley or Jesse's little boy. Paulie's mom sent me a basket of stuff when I was in the hospital. But my jaw was wired shut and I gave most of it away. She sent a card too. Told me to get well. She's like Paulie, I think. Sweet. Forgiving. But I haven't seen her since I've been back either, even though she works the front counter at the bakery. Tonight was the first time I've had any contact with any of the families. It went about like I expected. And frankly, it was what I deserved."

Fern didn't argue with him. He got the feeling she wanted to, but then she sighed and wrapped her hands around his wrists, pulling his hands from her hair. "Why did you go, Ambrose? Didn't you have a big scholarship? I mean . . . I understand patriotism and wanting to serve your country, but . . . didn't you want to wrestle?"

He had never spoken about this to anyone, never verbalized the feelings he'd had back then. He decided to start at the beginning.

"We sat at the back of the auditorium—Beans, Grant, Jesse, Paulie, and me. They laughed and made jokes during the army recruiter's whole presentation. It wasn't out of disrespect . . . not at all. Mostly it was because they knew that nothing the army could throw at us could possibly be any worse than Coach Sheen's wrestling practices. Any wrestler knows that there is nothing worse than being hungry, tired, sore, and being told at the end of a brutal practice that it's time to run halls. And knowing if you don't bust your ass, you'll be letting your teammates down, 'cause Coach will make everyone run 'em again if you aren't pushing the whole time. Joining the army couldn't be harder than wrestling season. No way.

"It didn't scare us, signing up. Not the way I imagine it scares most guys. For me it felt like a chance to get away, to be with the guys just a little longer. I didn't really want to go to college. Not yet. I felt like the whole town was depending on me, and if I screwed up or didn't perform well at Penn State, I was going to let everyone down. I liked the idea of being a different kind of hero. I always wanted to be a soldier, I just never told anyone. And after 9/11, it just felt like the right thing to do. So I convinced the guys to sign up.

"Beans was actually the easiest to persuade. Then he just kept working on everyone. Paulie was the last one to sign on. He'd spent four years wrestling, doing what we wanted. See, wrestling was never really his passion. He was just damn good at it, and he didn't have a dad around; Coach Sheen kind of filled that role for him.

"He wanted to be a musician and tour the world with his guitar. But he was a good friend. He loved us. So in the end he came along, just like he always did." Ambrose's voice shook and he rubbed at his cheek viciously, as if trying to erase the end of his tale, to change what happened next.

"So we all went. My dad cried, and I was embarrassed. Jesse got wasted the night before we left for basic training and got Marley pregnant. Jesse never met his baby boy. I really should go see Marley, but I can't. Grant was the only one who seemed to take it all seriously. He told me he never prayed so hard as he prayed the night before we left for Iraq. And that kid was always praying. Which is why I don't ever pray anymore. 'Cause if Grant prayed that hard and still died, then I'm not wasting my time."

"God spared your life," Fern said, a pastor's daughter through and through.

"You think God saved my life?" Ambrose struck back, his face incredulous. "How in the hell do you think that makes Paul Kimball's mother feel? Or Grant's parents? Or Jesse's girl, or his baby boy, when he's old enough to realize he had a daddy who he'll never meet? We know how Luisa O'Toole feels about it. If God saved my life, why didn't he save their lives? Is my life so much more valuable? So I'm special . . . and they're not?"

"Of course not," Fern protested, her voice rising slightly in response to his vehemence.

"Don't you get it, Fern? It's so much easier to take if God had nothing to do with it. If God has nothing to do with it, then I can accept that it's just life. Nobody is special, but nobody *isn't special*, either. You know what I mean? I can come to terms with that. But I can't accept that your prayers are answered and theirs aren't. That makes me angry and hopeless—desperate even! And I can't live that way."

Fern nodded and let his words settle around them in the steamy interior of the car. She didn't argue with him, but after a moment she spoke up.

"My dad always quotes this scripture. It's always his answer when he doesn't understand something. I've heard it so often in my life, it's become kind of like a mantra," Fern said. "'For my thoughts are not your thoughts, neither are your ways my ways, declares the Lord. For as the heavens are higher than the earth, so are my ways higher than your ways, and my thoughts than your thoughts.'"

"What does that even mean, Fern?" Ambrose sighed, but his fervor had dimmed.

"I guess it means we don't understand everything, and we're not going to. Maybe the whys aren't answered here. Not because there aren't answers, but because we wouldn't understand the answers if we had them."

Ambrose raised his eyebrows, waiting.

"Maybe there is a bigger purpose, a bigger picture that we only contribute a very small piece to. You know, like one of those thousand-piece puzzles? There's no way you can tell by looking at one piece of the puzzle what the puzzle is going to look like in the end. And we don't have the picture on the outside of the puzzle box to guide us." Fern smiled tentatively, hesitating, wondering if she was making any sense. When Ambrose just waited, she continued.

"Maybe everyone represents a piece of the puzzle. We all fit together to create this experience we call life. None of us can see the part we play or the way it all turns out. Maybe the miracles that we see are just the tip of the iceberg. And maybe we just don't recognize the blessings that come as a result of terrible things."

"You're kind of a strange girl, Fern Taylor," Ambrose said softly, his eyes on hers, his right eye sightless, his left eye trying to see beneath the surface. "I've seen those books you read. The ones with the girls on the front with their boobs falling out and the guys with the torn shirts. You read smutty romance novels and quote scripture. I'm not quite sure I have you figured out."

"Scripture comforts me, and romance novels give me hope."

"Oh, yeah? Hope for what?"

"Hope that I'll be doing more than quoting scripture with Ambrose Young in the very near future." Fern blushed furiously and looked at her hands.

Ambrose didn't know what to say. After a tense silence, Fern put the car into drive and eased it back onto the wet road.

Ambrose thought about what Bailey had said, how Fern had Ugly Girl Syndrome. UGS. Maybe Fern was only hitting on him because he was ugly and she thought, because of her UGS, that he was the best she could do. Maybe he had developed Ugly Guy Syndrome and was willing to peck up any crumbs a pretty girl tossed his way. But Fern hadn't tossed him a crumb. She'd tossed him an entire cookie and was waiting for him to take a bite.

"Why?" he whispered, his eyes locked straight ahead.

"Why what?" her voice was light, but he sensed a little embarrassment. She obviously wasn't used to tossing cookies to men, ugly or otherwise.

"Why do you act like I'm the old Ambrose? You act like you want me to kiss you. Like nothing's changed since high school."

"Some things haven't changed," Fern said quietly.

"News flash, Fern Taylor!" Ambrose barked, slamming his hand against the dashboard, making Fern jump. "Everything has changed! You are beautiful, I am hideous, you don't need me anymore, but I sure as hell need you!"

"You act like beauty is the only thing that makes us worthy of love," Fern snapped. "I didn't just l-love you because you were beautiful!" She'd said the L word, right out loud, though she'd tripped over it.

She swung the car in front of Ambrose's house and slammed it into park before it had come to a complete stop, making the car jerk and sputter.

Ambrose shook his head like he didn't believe her. He searched for the door handle and Fern's temper broke, the rush of anger obviously giving her the courage to reveal the things she would otherwise never say. She grabbed Ambrose's arm and demanded that he meet her gaze.

"I've been in love with you since you helped me bury that spider in my garden, and you sang with me like we were singing 'Amazing Grace' instead of 'The Itsy, Bitsy Spider.' I've loved you since you quoted Hamlet like you understood him, since you said you loved Ferris wheels more than roller coasters because life shouldn't be lived at full speed, but in anticipation and appreciation. I read and reread your letters to Rita because I felt like you'd opened up a little window into your soul, and the light was pouring out with every word. They weren't even for me, but it didn't matter. I loved every word, every thought, and I loved you . . . so much."

Ambrose had been holding his breath, and he released it in a hiss, his eyes locked on Fern's. She continued, her voice dropping to a whisper.

"When we heard the news . . . about the IED in Iraq . . . did you know they called my dad first? He went with the officers to inform the families."

Ambrose shook his head. He hadn't known. He'd never let himself think about that day, the day the families had heard the news.

"All I could think about was you." Fern was holding back tears and her sorrow made the grief well up inside his own chest. "I was heartbroken for the others . . . especially Paulie. But all I could think about was you. We didn't know immediately what had happened to you. I promised myself that if you came home, I wouldn't be afraid to tell you how I felt. But I'm still afraid. Because I can't make you love me back."

Ambrose reached for her then and pulled her into his arms. The embrace was awkward, the gear shift sticking up between them, but Fern laid her head on his shoulder and Ambrose smoothed her hair, amazed at how much better if felt to give comfort than receive it. He'd been on the receiving end of care and comfort from Elliott and his mother, as well as his hospital staff, for many long months. But since the attack, he had never given comfort, never offered a shoulder to cry on, never burdened himself with the weight of someone else's grief.

After a while, Fern pulled away, wiping her eyes. Ambrose hadn't spoken, hadn't revealed his own feelings or responded to her professions of love. He hoped she didn't expect it. He had no idea how he felt. Right now, he was tied up in a million knots, and he couldn't say things he didn't mean, just to make the moment easier. But he marveled at her courage to speak, and beneath his confusion and despair, he believed her. He believed she did love him. And that humbled him. Maybe someday, as the knots became unraveled, this moment would wrap around him, tying him to her. Or maybe her love would simply loosen the strings, freeing him to walk away.

20
Get a Pet

Strangely, with Fern's confession, a new peace settled between them. Ambrose didn't constantly try to hide his face or cower in the kitchen. He smiled more. He laughed. And Fern found that he was a bit of a tease. There were even some nights, after the store closed, when he would seek her out. One night he found her still at her register, immersed in a love scene.

Fern had been reading romances since she was thirteen years old. She had fallen in love with Gilbert Blythe from *Anne of Green Gables* and was hungry to fall in love like that over and over again. And then she discovered Harlequin. Her mother would have croaked face first into her herbal mint tea if she'd known how many forbidden romances Fern consumed the summer before eighth grade, and Fern had had a million book boyfriends since then.

Ambrose grabbed Fern's book from her hands and immediately opened it to where Fern was reading. She grabbed at him, mortification flooding her, not wanting him to see what had so captured her attention. He just held the book up in front of his face and wrapped one arm around her, effectively pinning her as if she were five years old. He was like a big ox, immovable and brawny, and all Fern's squirming to free her arms and retrieve the book was entirely useless. Fern gave up and hung her head in dejection. The heat from her cheeks radiated out around her face and she held her breath, waiting for him to howl in laughter. Ambrose read in silence for several minutes.

"Huh." Ambrose sounded a little flummoxed. "So . . . that was interesting." His arm loosened slightly, and Fern ducked out beneath it, tucking a stray curl behind her ear and busily looking at everything except Ambrose.

"What's interesting?" she asked breezily, as if she hadn't been wracked with embarrassment only seconds before.

"Do you read a lot of this kind of thing?" Ambrose countered with a question of his own.

"Hey, don't knock it 'til you've tried it!" Fern said meekly and shrugged as if she wasn't dying inside.

"But that's just it." Ambrose poked Fern in the side with one long finger. She squirmed again and slapped at his hand. "You haven't tried it, any of it . . . have you?"

Fern's eyes shot to his and her lips parted on a gasp.

"Have you?" Ambrose asked, his eyes locked on hers.

"Tried what?" Fern's voice was a shocked hiss.

"Well, let me see." Ambrose thumbed through a couple of pages. "How about this?" He started reading slowly, his deep voice rumbling in his chest, the sound making Fern's heart pound like a frantic drummer.

". . . he pushed her back against the pillows, and ran his hands along her bare skin, his eyes following where his hands had been. Her breasts rose in fevered anticipation . . ."

Fern swatted at the book desperately and managed to dislodge it this time, sending the book careening across several registers and landing in the back of a shopping cart.

"You've tried that?" Ambrose's expression was deadly serious, the corners of his mouth flattened in consternation. But his good eye gleamed, and Fern knew he was silently laughing at her.

"Yes!" Fern blustered, "I have! Many times, actually. It's . . . it's wonderful! I love it!" She grabbed a spray bottle and a rag from beneath the counter by her register and immediately started squirting and scrubbing away at her already pristine workspace.

Ambrose drew close and whispered in her ear, making the tendrils that had escaped from her ponytail tickle her cheeks as he spoke. "With who?"

Fern stopped scrubbing and looked up furiously, her face only inches from his.

"Stop it, Ambrose! You're embarrassing me."

"I know, Fern." Ambrose chuckled, revealing his endearingly lopsided grin. "And I can't help it. You're just so damn cute."

The moment the words left his lips, Ambrose straightened as if his flirtatious comment had surprised him, and he turned away, suddenly embarrassed, too. The canned music overhead morphed into something by Barry Manilow, and Fern instantly wished she hadn't reprimanded Ambrose. She should have just let him tease her. For a moment, he'd been so lighthearted, so young, and now he was rigid again, his back to her, hiding his face once more. Without another word, he started moving back toward the bakery.

"Don't go, Ambrose," Fern called out. "I'm sorry. You're right. I haven't tried any of those things. You're the only guy who's ever kissed me. And you were kind of drunk, so you can tease me all you want."

Ambrose paused and turned slightly. He pondered what she had said for several seconds and then asked, "How does a girl like you . . . a girl who loves romance novels and writes amazing love letters," Fern's heart ceased beating, "how does a girl like you manage to sneak through high school without ever being kissed?"

Fern swallowed and her heart resumed its cadence with a lurch. Ambrose watched her, obviously waiting for a response.

"It's easy when you have flaming red hair, you're not much bigger than a twelve-year-old, and you wear glasses and braces until senior year," Fern said wryly, confessing the truth easily, as long as it took the look of desolation from his eyes. He smiled again, and his posture eased slightly.

"So that kiss up at the lake, that was your first?" Ambrose asked hesitantly.

"Yep. I got my first kiss from the one and only Ambrose Young." Fern grinned and waggled her eyebrows.

But Ambrose didn't laugh. He didn't smile. His eyes searched Fern's face for a long moment.

"Are you mocking me, Fern?"

Fern shook her head desperately, wondering why she couldn't seem to ever say the right thing. "No! I was just . . . being . . . silly. I just wanted you to laugh again!"

"I guess it is pretty funny," Ambrose said. "The one and only Ambrose Young . . . yeah. Wouldn't that be something to brag about? A kiss from an ugly son of a bitch that half the town can't stand to look at." Ambrose turned and walked into the bakery without a backward glance. Barry Manilow cried for a girl named Mandy, and Fern felt like crying along with him.

● ● ●

Fern closed the store at midnight, just as she always did, Monday through Friday night. She had never had reason to feel nervous or even think twice about locking the store at midnight and riding home on her bike that she left chained by the employee entrance. She didn't even look sideways as she pushed through the heavy exit door and locked it, her mind already on her ride home and the manuscript that waited.

"Fern?" his voice came from her left and Fern had no chance to react before she was being pushed back against the side of the building. Her head banged against the block wall and she winced as her eyes flew to her assailant's face.

The parking lot was poorly lit out front, but the lighting on the employee side of the building was nonexistent. Fern had never even thought to complain. What little moonlight there was did little to illuminate her surroundings, but she could make out Ambrose's broad shoulders and shadowed face.

"Ambrose?"

His hands cupped the back of her head, his fingers soothing the hurt he'd caused when her head had connected with the wall behind her. Her head barely reached his shoulder and she pressed her head back into his hands, lifting her chin to try to discern his expression. But the darkness kept his motives hidden, and Fern wondered briefly if Ambrose was dangerous and if his injuries were more than skin deep. But the thought had no time to simmer as Ambrose bent his head and lightly touched his lips to Fern's.

Shock and surprise bloomed in her chest, crowding out the brief moment of fear, and Fern's attention narrowed instantly to the sensation of the brush of Ambrose's mouth against her own. She catalogued the prickle of stubble on his left cheek, the whisper of his exhale, the warmth of smooth lips, and the hint of cinnamon and sugar, as if he had sampled something he'd baked. He was hesitant, his gentleness at odds with his aggressive display. Maybe he thought she would push him away. When she didn't, she felt his sigh tickle her lips and the hands that held her head relaxed and slid to her shoulders, pulling her into him as he pressed his lips more firmly against hers.

Something unfurled itself low in Fern's belly, a shaky heat that curled and twisted its way through her stunned limbs and clenched hands. She recognized it immediately. It was desire. Longing. Lust? She had never experienced lust. She'd read about it enough. But feeling it firsthand was a whole new experience. She stretched up and held Ambrose's face between her palms, holding him to her, hoping he wouldn't come to his senses any time soon. She registered the contrast between his left cheek and his right, but the ridges and bumps that marked the right side of his face were of little consequence when his beautiful mouth was exploring her own.

He stopped abruptly, pulling his face from her palms and man-acling her wrists with his big hands. Fern searched his face in the darkness.

"There. That was much better than the first one," he murmured, his hands still locked around hers.

Fern was dizzy from the contact, drunk on sensation, and at a complete loss for words. Ambrose released her wrists and he stepped back and walked to the bakery entrance without so much as a "see you later." Fern watched him go, saw the door swing shut behind him, and felt her heart skip along after him like a lovesick puppy. One kiss wasn't going to be nearly enough.

● ● ●

The very next night, Bailey Sheen rolled into the bakery at midnight like he owned the place. Fern had obviously let him in, but she wasn't tagging along behind him. Ambrose told himself he wasn't disap-pointed. Bailey did have a cat though. It scampered along beside him like a co-owner.

"You can't have an animal in here, Sheen."

"I'm in wheelchair, man. You gonna tell me I can't have my seeing-eye cat with me? Actually, it can be your seeing-eye cat, since you're blind and all. One of the perks to being a pathetic figure is that I tend to get what I want. Did you hear that, Dan Gable? He called you an animal. Go get him, boy. Sic him!"

The cat sniffed at one of the tall metal shelves, ignoring Bailey.

"You named your cat Dan Gable?"

"Yep. Dan Gable Sheen. Had him ever since I was thirteen. My mom took us to this farm for my birthday and Fern and I each got to pick one from the litter. I named mine Dan Gable and Fern named hers Nora Roberts."

"Nora Roberts?"

"Yep. Apparently she's some writer. Fern loves her. Unfortunately for Nora Roberts, she got knocked up and died giving birth."

"The writer?"

"No! The cat. Fern's never had very good luck with animals. She smothers them with affection and care and they thank her by croaking. Fern hasn't figured out how to play hard to get."

Ambrose liked that about her. There wasn't any pretense with Fern. But he wasn't going to tell Bailey that.

"I've been trying to teach Dan Gable a few wrestling moves, in honor of his namesake, but so far all he can do is sprawl. But hey, sprawling is one of the basics—and it's more than I can do," Bailey said with a chuckle.

Dan Gable was a wrestler who had won an Olympic gold medal. In fact, he didn't surrender a single point during the whole Olympic games. He graduated from Iowa State with only one loss, coached the Iowa Hawkeyes, and was a legend in the sport. But Ambrose didn't think he would be especially honored to know a cat had been named for him.

Dan Gable, the cat, rubbed himself against Ambrose's leg but abandoned him immediately when Bailey patted his knees with the tips of his fingers. The cat jumped up on Bailey's lap and was rewarded with stroking and praise.

"Animals are supposed to be good therapy. Actually, I was supposed to get a puppy. You know, man's best friend, a dog to love only me, the kid who couldn't walk. Cue the violins. But Mom said no. She sat down at the kitchen table and cried when I asked her."

"Why?" Ambrose asked, surprised. Angie Sheen was a damn good mom, as far as he could tell. It seemed a little out of character for her to refuse a dog to the kid who couldn't walk, who needed a loyal companion . . . cue the soft lighting and the farmhouse on Christmas morning.

"Do you know that I can't wipe my own ass?" Bailey said, looking Ambrose straight in the eye. He wasn't smiling.

"Um. Okay," Ambrose said uncomfortably.

"Do you know that if I lean down too far to get something, I can't sit back up? I got caught once for a half hour just hanging limp over my knees until my mom came back from running errands and sat me back up again."

Ambrose was silent.

"Do you know that my 120-pound mother can pick me up under the arms and move me into the chair in my shower? She washes me, dresses me, brushes my teeth, combs my hair. All of it. At night, she and my dad take shifts coming in and turning me throughout the night because I can't roll over, and I get sore if I lay in one spot. They've done that since I was about fourteen, night after night."

Ambrose felt a lump forming in his throat, but Bailey carried on.

"So when I said I wanted a puppy, I think something kind of broke in her. She just couldn't take care of anyone else. So we compromised. Cats are low maintenance, you know? There's cat food and a litter box in the garage. Most of the time Fern is the one who feeds Dan Gable and changes his litter. I think she made a deal with my mom when we got the kittens, though I can't pin either one of them down on it."

"Shit." Ambrose ran his hands over his bald head, agitated and distraught. He didn't know what to say.

"When are you going to start wrestling again, Brosey?" Bailey used the name the guys had called him. Ambrose had a feeling he did it on purpose. "I want to see you wrestle again. Having a cat named Dan Gable just doesn't cut it." Dan Gable meowed and hopped off Bailey's lap as if he didn't appreciate Bailey's comments.

"And just like that, he abandons the cripple." Bailey sighed tragically.

"I can't hear or see on my right side, Bailey. I can't see anyone coming! Hell, my legs would be tied up so fast I wouldn't know what hit me. Add to that, my balance sucks. The hearing loss has thrown it all out of whack, and I would really rather not have an entire arena of people looking at me."

"So you're just going to make cupcakes?"

Ambrose glared at Bailey, and Bailey grinned back.

"How much can you bench, Brosey?"

"Will you quit calling me that?"

Bailey looked genuinely confused. "Why?"

"Because it . . . it . . . just . . . call me Ambrose."

"So four hundred, five hundred pounds? How much?"

Ambrose was glaring again.

"You can't tell me you haven't been lifting," Bailey said. "I can tell. You may have a naturally good physique, but you're shredded. You've got serious size and you're hardened down."

This coming from a kid who'd never lifted a weight in his life, Ambrose thought, shaking his head and pushing another tray of cupcakes into the oven. Yeah, cupcakes.

"So what's the point? I mean, you've got this amazing body—big, strong. You just going to keep it to yourself? You gotta share it with the world, man."

"If I didn't know better, I would think you were hitting on me," Ambrose said.

"Do you stand naked in front of the mirror and flex every night? I mean, really, at least go into the adult film industry. At least it won't go completely to waste."

"There you go again . . . talking about things you know nothing about," Ambrose said. "Fern reads romance novels and you are suddenly Hugh Hefner. I don't think either of you has room to lecture me about anything."

"Fern's been lecturing?" Bailey sounded surprised and not at all offended that Ambrose had basically told him he didn't know jack crap because he was in a wheelchair.

"Fern's been leaving inspirational quotes," Ambrose said.

"Ahhh. That sounds more like Fern. Like what? Just believe? Dream big? Marry me?"

Ambrose choked and then found himself laughing, in spite of everything.

"Come on, Bros—Ambrose," Bailey amended, his tone conciliatory, his face serious. "Don't you even think about it? Coming back? My dad unlocks the wrestling room for open use in the summer. He would work with you. Hell, he'd wet himself if you told him you wanted to drill some shots. You think all this hasn't been hard on him? He loved you guys! When he heard the news . . . Jesse, Beans, Grant . . . Paulie. They were his too. They weren't just yours, man. They were his boys. He loved them too! I loved them too," Bailey said, vehemence making his voice shake. "Did you ever think about that? You aren't the only one who lost them."

"Don't you think I know that? I get it!" Ambrose said, incredulous. "That's the problem, Sheen. If I was the only one who had lost . . . if I was the only one in pain, it would be easier . . ."

"But we didn't just lose them!" Bailey interrupted. "We lost you! Don't you think this whole damn town mourns for you?"

"They mourn for the superstar. Hercules. I'm not him. I don't think I can wrestle anymore, Bailey. They want the guy that wins every match and has Olympic prospects. They don't want the bald freak that can't hear the damn whistle being blown if it's on his bad side."

"I just explained to you how I can't go to bathroom by myself. I have to depend on my mother to pull down my pants, blow my freakin' nose, put deodorant on my armpits. And to make matters worse, when I went to school, I had to rely on someone to help me there too, with almost every damn thing. It was embarrassing. It was frustrating. But it was necessary!

"I have no pride left, Ambrose!" Bailey said. "No pride. But it was my pride or my life. I had to choose. So do you. You can have your pride and sit here and make cupcakes and get old and fat and nobody will give a damn after a while. Or you can trade that pride in for a little humility and take your life back."

21
Climb the Rope

Bailey said he'd never been to the memorial for Paulie, Jesse, Beans, and Grant. Ambrose could see why. It involved a bit of a climb up a little dirt road that was far too steep going both up and down for a wheelchair to traverse. Elliott told Ambrose the city was working on having the road paved, but it hadn't happened yet.

When Bailey told him about the spot, Ambrose could see how much Bailey wanted to go, and Ambrose told himself he would take him. But not yet. This time, this first time, Ambrose needed to go by himself. He had avoided it since coming home to Hannah Lake almost six months before. But talk of cupcakes and humility and Bailey's lack of pride had convinced Ambrose that maybe it was time for small steps. And so he put one foot in front of the other and climbed the hill that led to the pretty overlook where his four friends were buried.

They stood in a straight line, four white headstones looking out over the high school where they had all wrestled and played football, where they had grown to maturity. There was a little stone bench situated near the graves where family or friends could sit for a while and the trees were thick beyond the clearing. It was a good spot, quiet and peaceful. There were flowers and a few notes and stuffed animals placed around the graves, and Ambrose was happy to see that others had frequently visited, though he hoped no one would visit today. He needed some time alone with his friends.

Paulie and Grant were in the middle, Beans and Jesse on each side. Funny. That was kind of how it had been in life. Paulie and Grant were the glue, the steady ones, Beans and Jesse the protectors, the wild men. The two that would bitch and moan about you to your face but who, in the end, always had your back. Ambrose crouched next to each grave and read the words carved into the stones.

Connor Lorenzo "Beans" O'Toole
May 8, 1984–July 2, 2004
Mi hijo, Mi corazón

Paul Austin Kimball
June 29, 1984–July 2, 2004
Beloved friend, brother, and son

Grant Craig Nielson
November 1, 1983–July 2, 2004
Forever in our Hearts

Jesse Brooks Jordan
October 24, 1983–July 2, 2004
Father, Son, Soldier, Friend

Victory is in the Battle was written on the stone bench. Ambrose traced the words. It was something Coach Sheen always said. Something Coach Sheen always yelled from the side of the mat. It was never about the end result with Coach. It was always about fighting to the whistle.

Ambrose sat down on the bench and looked out over the valley below, at the town where he'd lived every day of his life, every day except the years where everything had changed. And he talked to his friends. Not because he believed they could hear him, but because there were things he knew he needed to say.

He told them about what Bailey had said. About taking his life back. He wasn't sure what that meant. Sometimes you can't take your life back. Sometimes it's dead and buried and you can only make a new life. Ambrose didn't know what that new life would look like.

Fern's face floated in his mind. Maybe Fern would be part of a new life, but strangely enough, Ambrose didn't want to talk to the guys about Fern. It felt too soon. And he discovered he wanted to protect her, even from the ghosts of his closest friends. They'd all laughed too often at the little redhead, told too many jokes at her expense, poked too many holes, and taunted one too many times. So Ambrose kept Fern to himself, safe inside a rapidly expanding corner of his heart, where only he knew she belonged.

When the sun started to wane and dip below the trees, Ambrose rose and found his way back down the hill, relieved that he'd finally found the strength to climb it.

• • •

The wrestling room smelled like sweat and bleach and memories. Good memories. Two long ropes hung in the corners, ropes he'd climbed and swung from a thousand times. The mats were unrolled, thick red slabs of rubber with the circle that marked inbounds and the lines in the center where the action began. Coach Sheen was mopping down the mats, something he'd probably done more than a thousand times. In a thirty-year coaching career, it had to be more.

"Hey, Coach," Ambrose said softly, his mind on all the times he'd turned Coach away when he first returned home.

Coach Sheen looked up in surprise, startled from his own thoughts, not expecting company.

"Ambrose!" His face wore such an expression of sheer joy that Ambrose gulped, wondering why he'd kept his old coach at arm's length for so long.

Coach Sheen stopped mopping and folded his hands on the handle. "How are ya, soldier?"

Ambrose winced at the address. Guilt and grief hung like heavy chains around the word. His pride in being a soldier had been decimated by the loss of his friends and the responsibility he felt for their deaths. Let heroes wear the word. He felt unworthy of the title.

Mike Sheen's eyes narrowed on Ambrose's face, not missing the way Ambrose flinched at his greeting or the way his mouth tightened like he had something to say, but wouldn't say it. Coach Sheen felt his heart quake in his chest. Ambrose Young had been a phenom, an absolute monster in the sport. He was the kind of kid every coach dreamed of coaching, not because of the glory it would bring to him, but because of the thrill of being part of something truly inspiring and watching history unfold before your eyes. Ambrose Young was that kind of an athlete. Still could be, maybe. But as he hovered by the door, his face a web of scars, his youth gone, his hair gone too, Mike Sheen had his doubts.

The irony that his hair was gone did not escape Coach Sheen. Ambrose Young had been absolutely teachable and obedient in the wrestling room, except for when it came to his hair. He had flatly refused to cut it. Coach liked his boys clean-cut and military short. It showed respect and a willingness to sacrifice. But Ambrose had calmly, in private, told Coach he would wear it in a tight ponytail off his face when he was in practice and when he wrestled, but he wouldn't cut it.

Coach Sheen had told Ambrose that he would allow it if Ambrose would lead in every other way. Meaning, if the team all started growing their hair out, taking practice lightly, or disrespecting the team or the coaching staff in any way, he would hold Ambrose personally responsible, and Ambrose would cut his hair. Ambrose had held to his end of the deal. He led the team. On match days, he wore slacks, a dress shirt, and a tie to school, and made sure all the other boys did too. He was the first to practice, the last to leave, the hardest worker, the consistent leader. Coach Sheen had considered it the best deal he'd ever made.

Now Ambrose's hair was gone. So was his sense of direction, his confidence, the light in his eyes. One eye was permanently dimmed, and the other roved the room nervously. Coach Sheen wondered if there really were such things as second chances. It wasn't the physical stuff that worried him. It was the emotional toll.

Ambrose walked toward his old coach, clutching his gear, feeling like an intruder in a place he used to love more than any place on earth. "I talked to Bailey. He said you would be here."

"Yeah? I'm here. You wanna work out? Shake the rust off?" Mike Sheen held his breath.

Ambrose nodded, just once, and Coach Sheen released the air in his lungs.

"All right. Let's drill a little."

• • •

"You could sign up for some ballet or some gymnastics," Coach Sheen suggested after Ambrose lost his balance and fell to the mat for the tenth time. "That's what we used to have some of the football players do when they needed to work on balance, but I'm guessing you'd look hideous in a tutu and the little girls would think it was a reenactment of *Beauty and the Beast*."

Ambrose was a little stunned by the blunt assessment of his lack of beauty. Leave it to Coach Sheen not to pull any punches. Bailey was just like him.

Coach Sheen continued, "The only way your balance is going to come back is if you just keep drilling. It's muscle memory. Your body knows what to do. You're just second-guessing yourself. Hell, stick an earplug in the other ear and see if it helps to be deaf in both."

The next night, Ambrose tried it. Not being able to hear at all actually evened things out a bit. The eyesight wasn't as big an impediment. Ambrose had always been a hands-on wrestler—constant contact, hands on your opponent at all times. There were blind wrestlers in the world. Deaf ones, too. There were wrestlers without legs, for that matter. There were no allowances made, but no one was excluded either. If you could compete, you were allowed on the mat—may the best wrestler win. It was the kind of sport that celebrated the individual. Come as you are, turn your weaknesses into advantages, dominate your opponent. Period.

But Ambrose hadn't ever had weaknesses on the mat. Not like this. This was all new. Coach Sheen had him shooting single legs, double legs, high-C's, ankle picks, and duck-unders until his legs shook, and then he had him do it from the other side. Then he was pulling his big body up the rope. It was one thing to climb a rope if you were a wiry five foot five 125-pounder. It was a completely different matter when you were six foot three and over two hundred pounds. He hated the rope climb. But he made it to the top. And then he made it again the next night. And the next.

22

Make Fireworks

FIREWORKS OR PARADES?

"You think Sheen wants to come with us?" Ambrose asked when Fern stepped out onto her front steps. He'd been relieved when Fern had circled *fireworks* on the whiteboard. Parades were boring and they usually involved lots of glaring sunlight and lots of staring people. Plus, it was the Fourth of July and Hannah Lake Township always had a pretty good fireworks display on the football field at the high school. Fern had seemed excited when he'd asked her if she wanted to go.

"Bailey's in Philadelphia."

Ambrose tamped down the jubilant leap of his heart. He loved Sheen, but he really wanted to be alone with Fern.

"Should we walk?" Fern suggested. "It's nice out, and the field isn't far."

Ambrose agreed, and he and Fern cut across the lawn and headed toward the high school.

"What's Bailey doing in Philly?" he asked after they'd walked a ways.

"Every year, Bailey, Angie, and Mike head to Philadelphia for the Fourth of July. They visit the Museum of Art, and Mike carries

Bailey up those seventy-two steps and they do the Rocky reenactment. Angie helps Bailey raise his arms and they all yell, 'One more
year!' Bailey loves Rocky. Does that surprise you?"

"No. It doesn't," Ambrose said with a wry twist of his lips.

"They first went on a family vacation to Philadelphia when Bailey
was eight. He climbed the steps himself. They have a picture of him
in their family room with his arms up, dancing around."

"I've seen it," Ambrose said, now understanding the significance
of the picture he'd seen in a place of prominence in the Sheen home.

"They had such a good time, they went back the next year, and
Bailey made it up the steps again. It became more and more signifi-
cant every year. The summer Bailey was eleven, he couldn't make it
up the steps, not even a few of them. So Uncle Mike carried him."

"One more year?"

"Yep. Bailey's already defying the odds. Most kids with Duchenne
muscular dystrophy don't reach his age. And if they're still around,
they don't look like Bailey. They aren't nearly as healthy. Twenty-
one has always been a bit of a battle cry for Bailey. When he turned
twenty-one this year, we had a huge party. We're all convinced he's
going to set records."

Ambrose spread the blanket out on the edge of the grass, far
away from the other folks that had gathered to watch the display.
Fern settled beside him and it wasn't long before the first fireworks were being shot into the sky. Ambrose lay back, stretching
out so he could see without straining his neck. Fern eased herself
back self-consciously. She had never lain on a blanket with a boy.
She could sense the hard length of Ambrose along her right side,
his big body taking up more than half of the small blanket. He
had chosen the right side of the blanket so the right side of his
face was turned away from her, as usual. She and Ambrose didn't
link hands, and she didn't lay her head on his shoulder. But she
wanted to.

Fern felt like she'd spent most of her life wanting Ambrose in some way or another, wanting him to see her . . . really see her. Not the red hair or the freckles on her nose. Not the glasses that made her brown eyes look like MoonPies. Not the braces on her teeth or the boyishness of her figure.

When those things morphed and eventually disappeared—well, all except for the freckles—she wished he *would* notice. She wished he *would* see her brown eyes, free of glasses. She wished he *would* see that her figure had finally rounded and filled out, see her teeth that were white and straight. But whether she was homely or pretty, she still found herself wishing.

Fern's yearning for Ambrose was something that had been so much a part of her, that as the patriotic songs accompanying the display rang across the football field, Fern felt incredibly grateful, grateful that in that moment, Ambrose Young lay by her side. That he knew her. Seemingly liked her, and had returned to her, to the town, to himself.

The gratitude made her weepy, and moisture leaked out the sides of her eyes and made warm rivers on her cheeks. She didn't want to wipe them away because that would draw attention to them. So she let them flow, watching the burst of colors crackle and boom in the air, feeling the aftershocks ring in her head.

Fern wondered suddenly if the sound was reminiscent of war and hoped that Ambrose was in the moment with her and not somewhere in Iraq, his mind on roadside bombs and the friends who didn't come home. Afraid that he might need someone to hold him there, hold him to the celebration, she reached out and slipped her hand in his. His hand tightened around hers.

He didn't interlock his fingers the way couples do as they walk. Instead he held her hand inside his, like an injured bird in his palm. And they watched the display to its conclusion, not speaking, their heads tilted toward the light, only their hands touching. Fern sneaked a look at his profile, noting that in the darkness, in the space between bursts of cascading light, his face was beautiful, as beautiful as it had ever been. Even the smoothness of his bald head did not detract from the strength of his features. Somehow it made them more stark, more memorable.

With the last crack of the manic finale, families and couples started to stand and make their way off the field. Nobody had noticed Fern and Ambrose there on the far edge, beyond the circle of the track, behind the goal post. As the field lost its occupants and the smoky residue of revelry left the air, the sounds of night resumed. Crickets chirped, the wind whispered softly in the trees that edged the field, and Fern and Ambrose lay still, neither of them wishing to break the silence or the sense of pause that surrounded them.

"You are still beautiful," Fern said softly, her face turned to his. He was quiet for a moment, but he didn't pull away or groan or deny what she'd said.

"I think that statement is more a reflection of your beauty than mine," Ambrose said eventually, turning his head so he could look down at her. Fern's face was touched with moonglow, the color of her eyes and the red of her hair undecipherable in the wash of pale light. But her features were clear—the dark pools of expressive eyes, the small nose and soft mouth, the earnest slant of her brow that indicated she didn't understand his response.

"You know that thing people always say, about beauty being in the eye of the beholder?"

"Yes?"

"I always thought it meant we all have different tastes, different preferences . . . you know? Some guys focus on the legs, some guys prefer blondes, some men like girls with long hair, that kind of thing. I never thought about it really, not before this moment. But maybe you see beauty in me because *you* are beautiful, not because I am."

"Beautiful on the inside?"

"Yes."

Fern was silent, thinking about what he'd said. Then, in a small voice she whispered, "I understand what you're saying . . . and I appreciate it. I do. But I would really like it if, just for once, I could be beautiful to you on the outside."

Ambrose chuckled and then stopped. The expression on her face made him think she wasn't kidding, wasn't being flirtatious. Ahh. Ugly Girl Syndrome again. She didn't think he thought she was pretty.

He didn't know how to make her understand that she was so much more than just pretty. So he leaned forward and pressed his mouth to hers. Very carefully. Not like the other night, when he'd been scared and impulsive and had smacked her head against the wall in his attempt to kiss her. He kissed her now to tell her how he felt. He pulled away almost immediately, not giving himself a chance to linger and lose his head. He wanted to show her he valued her, not that he wanted to rip her clothes off. And he wasn't sure, when it came right down to it, that she wanted to be kissed by an ugly SOB. She was the kind of girl that would kiss him because she didn't want to hurt his feelings. The thought filled him with despair.

She let out a frustrated sigh and sat up, running her hands through her hair. It flowed through her fingers and down her back, and he wished he could bury his own hands in it, bury his face in the heavy locks and breathe her in. But he'd obviously upset her.

"I'm sorry, Fern. I shouldn't have done that."

"Why?" she snapped, startling him enough that he winced. "Why are you sorry?"

"Because you're upset."

"I'm upset because you pulled away! You're so careful. And it's frustrating!"

Ambrose was taken back by her honesty, and he smiled, instantly flattered. But the smile faded as he tried to explain himself.

"You're so small, Fern. Delicate. And all of this is new to you. I'm afraid I'm going to come on too strong. And if I break you or hurt you, I won't survive that, Fern. I won't survive it." That thought was worse than walking away from her, and he shuddered inwardly. He wouldn't survive it. He had already hurt too many. Lost too many.

Fern knelt in front of him, and her chin wobbled and her eyes were wide with emotion. Her voice was adamant as she held his face between her hands, and when he tried to pull away so she wouldn't feel his scars, she hung on, forcing his gaze.

"Ambrose Young! I have waited my whole life for you to want me. If you don't hold me tight, I won't believe you mean it, and that's worse than never being held at all. You'd better make me believe you mean it, Ambrose, or you will most definitely break me."

"I don't want to hurt you, Fern," he whispered hoarsely.

"Then don't," she whispered back, trusting him. But there were lots of ways to cause pain. And Ambrose knew he was capable of hurting her in a thousand ways.

Ambrose stopped trying to pull his face away, surrendering to the way it felt to be touched. He hadn't allowed anyone to touch him for a long time. Her hands were small, like the rest of her, but the emotions they stirred in him were enormous, gigantic, all-consuming. She made him shake, made him quake inside, made him vibrate like the tracks under an oncoming train.

Her hands left his face and traveled down the sides of his neck. One side smooth, the other riddled with divots and scars and rippled where the skin had been damaged. She didn't pull away, but felt each mark, memorized each wound. And then she leaned forward and pressed her lips to his neck, just below his jaw. And then again on the other side, on the side that bore no scars, letting him know that the kiss wasn't about sympathy, but desire. It was a caress. And his control broke.

She was on her back on the blanket, his big body pressing into hers, her face between his hands as his mouth took hers without finesse, without restraint, and without thought. He simply took. And she gave, opening for him, welcoming the slide of his tongue against hers, the grip of his hands on her face and in her hair and on her hips. He felt her hands slide beneath his shirt and tiptoe up his back, and it felt so good he caught his breath, losing contact with her mouth for a heartbeat as his eyes fell closed and his head dropped to nuzzle the sweetness of her neck. Her chest rose and fell rapidly, as if she too had lost control. She kissed his head, the way a mother soothes a child, and stroked the bare skin as he fought for control and lost once more, his hand sliding up to cradle her breast in his palm, his thumb caressing the full underside that made him long to pull her shirt over her head and see if she looked as good as she felt.

But she was a girl who had hardly been kissed, and she needed many more kisses, deserved many more. And so with regret, he slid his hand back to her waist. She arched against him and protested the loss sweetly with a sigh that made his blood boil and his heart knock against his ribs. So he kissed her again, communicating his own need. Her lips welcomed his, moving softly, seeking, savoring, and Ambrose Young felt himself slip and slide, falling helplessly—with very little resistance—in love with Fern Taylor.

● ● ●

"Look who's here!" Bailey crowed as he cruised through the sliding doors into the store. Rita followed behind him, her little son on her hip and a big smile on her face. Fern squealed and ran to her friend, taking the towheaded toddler from her arms and smothering his little face with kisses. Apparently, Becker was out of town and Rita had been driving home from her mother's when she'd seen Bailey motoring down the street on his way to the store. He'd convinced her that karaoke and dancing were just what she needed.

Before long, Bailey had the music blaring and Rita's son, Ty, in his lap, cruising up and down the aisles, making the little boy shriek with glee. Rita ran along beside them, her face wreathed in smiles at her son's happiness. Like Fern, Rita had changed since high school. Ambrose wondered how just a few years could alter each of them so drastically, though from what he'd seen of Becker Garth, he hadn't changed at all. He was still a bully, and his wife was now his main target. Rita was still beautiful, but she looked beaten down and skittish and didn't seem comfortable looking at him, so he retreated to the bakery not long after she and Bailey arrived.

"Ambrose?" Fern was smiling at him from the doorway and he smiled back, liking the way she looked at him, as if there was nothing wrong with his face, as if his very presence made her happy. "You have to come out, just for a minute."

"Yeah? I think I like it in here better," he said mildly.

"We're playing the Sheen/Taylor Greatest Hits CD, all our favorite dance songs, and I want to dance with you."

Ambrose groaned and laughed simultaneously. Leave it to Bailey and Fern. They would have a greatest hits CD. And he would be happy to dance with Fern—he would be happy to do almost anything with Fern—but he would rather stay in the kitchen and dance where no one was watching.

Fern started pulling on his hand, wrapping both of hers around his, smiling and cajoling as she drew him from his cave. "The next song is my favorite song of all time."

Ambrose sighed and let her have her way. Plus, he wanted to hear what her favorite song of all time was. He found he wanted to know everything about her.

"I've told Bailey if I indeed die before he does . . . which was his greatest wish when we were ten, that he better make sure they play it at my funeral. And I want everyone to dance. Listen! Tell me you don't just immediately feel better when you hear it."

She waited in anticipation and Ambrose listened intently. The first bars of the song rang through the store and Bailey and Fern moaned in unison, right along with Prince, and launched into frenzied dancing. Rita laughed and whooped and joined them immediately, Tyler on her hip. Ambrose didn't dance . . . but he enjoyed the show.

Fern had no rhythm. Bailey wasn't much better. But his lack of skill wasn't exactly his fault. He moved his chair forward and back in a parody of the simple step-touch move everyone resorted to at a school dance. He bobbed his head in time with the music and his face wore an expression that said "Hell, yeah," even though his body said "No way." Rita danced around Bailey's chair, but her moves were too self-conscious, too self-aware, to allow her to truly enjoy herself, or for anyone to enjoy watching her. Fern shook her butt and did chicken arms and clapped and snapped randomly, but there was such uninhibited joy, such wild abandon, such pleasure in the act, that although he was laughing at her—yes, laughing *at* her—she was laughing, too.

She danced anyway, knowing she was horrible, knowing there was nothing about her performance that would lure him in or make him want her, and doing it anyway, just for the fun of it. And somehow, suddenly, he did. He did want her. Desperately. Her light, her loveliness, her enthusiasm for simple things. All of her. Everything. He wanted to pick her up, right off of her dancing feet, her legs dangling above the ground, and kiss her until they were breathless with passion instead of laughter.

"And your kiss!" Fern sang out the final words and struck an awkward pose, breathing hard and giggling. "The. Most. Awesome. Song. Ever." She sighed, throwing her arms wide, ignoring the next song on the Taylor/Sheen hits CD.

"You need to come with me for just a minute. I need to show you something in the, um, kitchen," Ambrose said firmly, grabbing Fern by the hand and pulling her along behind him like she'd just done to him minutes before. Bailey and Rita were dancing again, Queen and David Bowie's *Under Pressure* picking up where Prince had left off.

"Wh-what? But there's a slow song coming up after this, and I really, really want to slow dance with you," Fern protested, resisting, pulling against his arm. So Ambrose swept her up, right off her feet, just like he'd imagined and barreled through the swinging kitchen doors without missing a step. He flipped off the bakery lights so the room was swathed in darkness and then he swallowed Fern's gasp, his mouth crashing down on hers, one hand sliding under her butt to anchor her to him as his other hand cradled the back of her head, controlling the angle of the kiss. And all resistance ceased.

23

Find the Silver Lining

Bailey was heavier than Ambrose had anticipated, lankier, and harder to hold onto. But he swept him up in his arms and walked steadily up the well-worn trail, placing his feet carefully, not hurrying. He had run miles in full uniform with 150 pounds on his back many times, and he could carry Bailey up the hill and back again.

They were on their way to visit the graves of the four fallen soldiers, Ambrose for the second time, Bailey for the first. The path was steep and narrow, and getting Bailey's wheelchair to the top with him in it would be harder than carrying him, but carrying him was too much for Mike Sheen or anyone else in Bailey's inner circle, so Bailey had been unable to visit the resting place of his friends. When Ambrose had discovered this, he told Bailey he would carry him to the top, and had shown up unannounced that afternoon, ready to fulfill his promise.

Angie Sheen volunteered to let him take the van, but Ambrose had declined, scooping Bailey up in his arms and depositing him on the passenger side of his old truck and buckling him in snugly. Bailey started to list to the side, unable to keep himself upright without the support of his chair, but Ambrose wedged a pillow between the seat and the door so he could lean against it.

He could tell Angie was a little worried about letting them go without the wheelchair, but she waved them off with a tight smile, and Ambrose took the corners carefully. They didn't have far to go, but Bailey seemed to enjoy riding shotgun and insisted Ambrose crank up the radio and roll down the windows.

When they reached the top of the hill, Ambrose sat Bailey carefully on the stone bench, then sat close beside him, propping him up against his side, making sure he wouldn't tip over.

They sat in reverence for a while, Bailey reading the words on each headstone, Ambrose looking beyond the graves, his mind heavy with memories that he wished he could extinguish.

"I wish I could be buried up here with them. I know it's a war memorial. But they could bury me over here by the bench. Put a little asterisk on my tombstone."

Ambrose laughed, just like Bailey expected him to, but Bailey's glib acceptance of his own demise bothered him.

"But I'm going to be buried in the town cemetery. My grandparents are there and a few other Sheens from generations back. I've got my spot all picked out," Bailey said easily, comfortably even, and Ambrose could hold his tongue no longer.

"How do you stand it, Bailey? Looking death in the face for so long?"

Bailey shrugged and glanced at him curiously. "You act like death is the worst thing."

"Isn't it?" Ambrose could think of nothing worse than losing his friends.

"I don't think so. Death is easy. Living is the hard part. Remember that little girl over in Clairemont County who was kidnapped about ten years ago when her family was camping?" Bailey asked, his eyes narrowed on Ambrose's face. "Fern's parents and my parents volunteered with the search. They thought she might have fallen in the creek or just wandered off. But there were enough other campers there that weekend that there was also the possibility that someone had just taken her. By the fourth day, my mom said the mother of the little girl was praying that they would find the child's body. She wasn't praying they would discover her alive. She was praying that her baby had died quickly and accidentally, because the alternative was a lot more terrible. Can you imagine knowing your child was somewhere suffering horribly and you couldn't do anything about it?"

Ambrose stared at Bailey, turmoil in his eyes.

"You feel guilty because you lived and they died." Bailey tipped his head toward the four headstones. "Maybe Beans and Jesse and Grant and Paulie are looking down on you shaking their heads, saying 'Poor Brosey. Why did he have to stay?'"

"Mr. Hildy told me the lucky ones are the ones who don't come back," Ambrose remembered, his eyes on the graves of his friends. "But I don't think the guys are looking down on me from some heavenly paradise. They're dead. Gone. And I'm here. Period."

"I think deep down you don't really believe that," Bailey said quietly.

"Why me, Bailey?" Ambrose shot back, his voice too loud for the sober setting.

"Why *not* you, Ambrose?" Bailey bit back immediately, making Ambrose start as if Bailey had convicted him of a crime. "Why me? Why am I in a flipping wheelchair?"

"And why Paulie and Grant? Why Jesse and Beans? Why do terrible things happen to such good people?" Ambrose asked.

"Because terrible things happen to everyone, Brosey. We're all just so caught up in our own crap that we don't see the shit everyone else is wading through."

Ambrose had no answer for that and Bailey seemed content to let him wrangle with his thoughts for a time. But eventually, Bailey spoke again, unable to sit in silence for too long.

"You like Fern, don't you, Brosey?" Bailey's gaze was apprehensive, his voice grave.

"Yeah. I like Fern." Ambrose nodded absently, his thoughts still on his friends.

"Why?" Bailey demanded immediately.

"Why what?" Ambrose was confused by Bailey's tone.

"Why do you like Fern?"

Ambrose sputtered a little, not sure what Bailey was getting at, and a little pissed that Bailey thought he was entitled to have it spelled out.

Bailey jumped in. "It's just that she isn't really the kind of girl you used to go for. She and I were talking the other day. She seems to think she's not good enough for you . . . that you are tolerating her because, in her words, she's 'thrown herself at you.' I can't quite imagine Fern throwing herself at anyone. She's always been pretty shy when it comes to guys."

Ambrose thought of the night of the fireworks when she'd kissed his eyelids, his neck, his mouth and slid her hands beneath his shirt. She hadn't been shy then, but he thought he'd keep that to himself.

Bailey continued: "I think that's why Fern has always liked to read so much. Books allow you to be whoever you want to be, to escape yourself for a while. You know how Fern loves to read those romance novels?"

Ambrose nodded and smiled, remembering how embarrassed Fern had been when he'd read a passage from her book out loud. He wondered briefly if the romance novels were what made Fern so passionate and responsive. Just thinking about her made him long for her, and he tamped down the desire immediately.

"Do you know she writes them too?"

Ambrose jerked his head around to meet Bailey's smirk. "Really?"

"Yep. I think she must be on her sixth novel. She's been sending her books out to publishers since she was sixteen. So far, she hasn't gotten a deal, but she will eventually. They're actually pretty good. A little sappy and sweet for my taste, but that's Fern. She writes under a fake name. Her parents don't even know."

"A fake name? What is it?"

"Nah. You'll have to get that info from her. She's going to kill me for telling you about the books."

Ambrose nodded, his attention riveted on exactly how he was going to coax little Fern to tell him all her secrets. The desire for her rose again, and he almost groaned out loud.

"I've always liked to read. But I prefer a little different kind of book. Romance is just torture for me, you know?" Bailey added.

Ambrose nodded, his mind on the fireworks, the way it felt to lay next to Fern as light exploded above them, her sweetness, the smell of her skin and the soft sweep of her hair. He understood torture.

"So let's hear it, man. What's the deal? I can't kick your ass, but I will definitely know if you're lying to me. Is Fern right? Are you just taking what's available?"

"Hell, Bailey! You remind me of Beans—" Ambrose winced at the pain that lanced through him, like he'd pressed his fingers into a fresh wound, the sharp sting silencing him immediately. But his silence only fed Bailey's fears.

"If you are stringing my cousin along and you aren't head over heels in love with her, I will find a way to kick your ass!" Bailey was getting agitated, and Ambrose laid a hand on his shoulder, soothing him.

"I do love Fern," Ambrose admitted, his voice hushed, his gaze heavy with confession, and felt a frisson of shock at the truth. He did love her. "I think about her all the time. When I'm not with her I'm miserable . . . but when I'm with her I'm miserable too, because I know it's Fern that's settling. Look at me, Bailey! Fern could have anyone she wanted. Me? Not so much."

Bailey laughed and groaned loudly. "Boo, freakin' hoo! Waaa! You big baby! Do you expect me to feel sorry for you, Ambrose? 'Cause I don't. It reminds me of a book I just read for this online English course I'm taking. This guy, Cyrano de Bergerac, was born with a big nose. Who the hell cares? So Cyrano never got with the girl he loved because he was ugly. That's the stupidest thing I've ever heard in my life! He let his big honker keep him away?"

"That Cyrano guy? Wasn't he the one that wrote love notes for the good-looking guy? Didn't they make a movie out of that?"

"That's the one. Remind you of anyone? I seem to remember someone writing you love notes and signing them Rita. Just like Cyrano. Kind of ironic, isn't it? Fern didn't think she was good enough for you then, and you don't think you're good enough for her now. And both of you are wrong . . . and so stupid! Stuuupiiiid!" Bailey dragged the word out in disgust. "I'm ugly! I'm not worthy of love, waaa!" Bailey mimicked them in a whiny, high-pitched voice, and then he shook his head as if he was thoroughly disappointed. He paused a moment, gearing up for a new rant.

"Now you're telling me that you are afraid to love Fern because you don't look like a movie star anymore? Shoot, man! You still look like a movie star . . . just one that's been through a war zone is all. Chicks dig that! I keep thinking that maybe you and I could take a road trip and tell all the girls we meet along the way that we're both vets. You've got a messed up face and my war wounds have put me in this chair. You think they'd believe it? Maybe then I could get some action. Problem is, how am I going to get a handful of tit if I can't lift my arms?"

Ambrose choked, laughing at Bailey's irreverence, but Bailey just continued, unfazed.

"I would give anything to do one of those *Freaky Friday* switcha-roo things with you, Ambrose. Just for one day I want to trade bodies with you. I wouldn't waste one second. I'd be knocking on Rita's door. I'd pummel Becker a few times, throw Rita over my shoulder, and I wouldn't come up for air until neither of us could move. That's what I would do."

"Rita? You like Rita?"

"I love Rita. Always have. And she's married to a dick, which is actually comforting in a very selfish way. If she was married to a cool, nice, awesome guy, I would be more miserable."

Ambrose found himself laughing again. "You are something else, Bailey! Your logic is priceless."

"It is kinda funny. Funny ironic, I mean. Fern always said Rita has spent her whole life being chased by boys. Because of that, she never had a chance to stop running long enough to figure out who she was and what kind of guy she should let catch her. It's kinda ironic that Rita and I are friends, seeing as I've never been able to chase her. Maybe that's the silver lining. I couldn't chase her, so she never had to run."

After a time, Ambrose picked Bailey up in his arms once more, and together they descended the hill from the memorial, lost in their own thoughts of life and death and silver linings.

24

Make Something Disappear

Uncle Mike looked surprised when he saw Fern slip into the wrestling room with Bailey Saturday night. He did a double take, then seemed confused, and then he looked at Fern again, frowning a little. But when Ambrose noticed her sitting on a rolled-up mat next to Bailey's chair, he smiled, and his smile negated Uncle Mike's frown.

Bailey was transfixed by the action in the center of the room. Fern was too, although not for the same reasons. For Bailey it was the smell of the mats, the movement, the wrestler who might just make a comeback. For Fern it was the smell of the man, his movements, the wrestler who had finally come back. Bailey had been crashing some of the drill sessions between his dad and Ambrose for the last few weeks, but tonight was a first for Fern. She tried not to chew on her nails—a habit she forbade herself, especially since she'd just painted them that morning—and looked on, hoping it was really okay that she was there.

Ambrose was dripping with sweat. His gray shirt was soaked through on his chest and down his back, and he mopped at his bare head with a hand towel. Mike Sheen challenged him through another series of drills, encouraging, correcting, but when Ambrose flopped on the mat at the end of the workout, the coach's brow was furrowed and he kept biting his lip, chewing over an obvious concern.

"You need a partner. You need some guys to beat up on, to beat up on you . . . drilling shots is one thing. But you gotta do some live wrestling or you aren't going to get back into the kind of shape you need to be in . . . not wrestling shape, anyway.

"Remember how gassed Beans got when he couldn't compete until halfway through the season his junior year? He'd been in the room, practicing with the team, but he hadn't been in a real live match, and he about died those first couple meets after he came back. Heck, Grant pinned him in the Big East tourney, and Grant had never pinned Beans before. Remember how tickled he was?"

Coach Sheen's words rang through the room, the mention of Grant and Beans, the mention of death in any context, creating an odd echo that kept ricocheting off the walls. Ambrose stiffened, Bailey hung his head, and Fern gave in and gnawed her fingernail. Mike Sheen realized what he'd said and ran a hand over his cropped hair. He continued on as if the words hadn't been spoken.

"We'll get some guys in here, Brose. I've got a couple bigger guys on the high school team that you could work over. It'd be good for them and helpful to you."

"No. Don't do that." Ambrose shook his head, his voice a low rumble as he stood and started shoving his gear into a gym bag. "I'm not here for that, Coach. I don't want you thinking I am. I missed the room. That's all. I just missed the room. But I'm not wrestling . . . not anymore."

Mike Sheen's face fell and Bailey sighed beside Fern. Fern just waited, watching Ambrose, noticing the way his hands shook as he untied his wrestling shoes, the way he had turned away from his old coach so he couldn't see Mike Sheen's reaction to his firm refusal.

"All right," Coach Sheen said gently. "Are we done for today?"

Ambrose nodded, not looking up from his shoes, and Mike Sheen jangled the keys in his pocket. "You going home with Fern, Bailey?" he said to his son, noting the dejection in Bailey's posture.

"We walked and rolled, Dad," Bailey quipped, trying as he always did to ease an uncomfortable situation with humor. "But I'll come home with you, if you don't mind . . . you got the van, right?"

"I'll take Fern," Ambrose spoke up keeping his gaze on his laces. He hadn't moved from where he was crouched by his bag, and he didn't look up at the three people who were all focused on him. He seemed tense and eager to be left alone, and Fern wondered why he wanted her to remain behind. But she said nothing, letting her uncle and Bailey leave without her.

"Make sure the lights are off and the doors are all locked," Coach Sheen said quietly, and held the door open for Bailey to wheel through. Then the heavy door swung shut and Fern and Ambrose were alone.

Ambrose took a long draw from a bottle of water, his throat working as he swallowed greedily. He splashed a little on his face and head and wiped it off with his towel, but still made no move to get up. He pulled his wet shirt over his head, grabbing the back of the neck with one hand and yanking it over his head the way guys always do and girls never do. He didn't pause to let her look at him, though her eyes raced over his skin, trying to soak in every detail. Showing off wasn't his intent, and a clean blue T-shirt replaced his soiled gray one almost instantly. He slipped his running shoes on and laced them up, but still he sat, his arms looped around his knees, his head bent against the glare of the fluorescent lights overhead.

"Will you turn off the light, Fern?" His voice was so soft she wasn't sure she heard him right, but she turned and walked toward the door and the light switches that were lined up to the right of it, expecting him to follow her.

"Are you coming?" she asked, her hand poised on the switch.

"Just . . . turn it off."

Fern did as he asked, and the wrestling room vanished before her eyes, disappearing in the darkness. Fern paused uncertainly, wondering if he wanted her to leave him there in the dark. But why then had he said he would take her home?

"Do you want me to go? I can walk . . . it's not that far."

"Stay. Please."

The door thumped shut and Fern stood next to it, wondering how she was going to find her way back to him. He was acting so strange, so forlorn and aloof. But he wanted her to stay. That was enough for Fern. She walked toward the middle of the room, carefully placing one foot in front of the other.

"Fern?" Just a little to the left. Fern sank to her hands and knees and crawled toward the sound of his voice.

"Fern?" He must have heard her coming, because his voice was soft, more welcome than question. She stopped and, reaching out, felt her fingers graze his upraised knee. He clasped her fingers immediately and then slid his hand up her arm, pulling her into him and then down to the mat, where he stretched out beside her, his length creating a wall of heat on her left side.

It was a strange sensation, feeling his touch in the dark. The wrestling room had no windows, and the darkness was absolute. Her senses were heightened by her lack of sight, the sound of his breathing both erotic and chaste—erotic because she didn't know what would come next, chaste because he was simply breathing, in and out, a flutter of warmth against her cheek. Then his mouth descended and the warmth became heat that singed her parted lips. And the heat became pressure as his mouth sank into hers.

He kissed Fern like he was drowning, like she was air, like she was land beneath his feet, and maybe that was simply how he kissed, how he had always kissed, whenever he kissed whomever he kissed. Maybe that was the way he had kissed Rita. But Fern had only been kissed by Ambrose and had nothing to compare it to, no informed analysis of what was good or bad, skilled or unschooled. All she knew was that when Ambrose kissed her, he made her feel like she was going to implode, implode like one of those controlled demolitions where the building simply collapses into a neat pile of rubble, disturbing nothing and no one around it.

Nothing around Fern would collapse. The room would not burst into flame, the mats would not melt beneath her, but when Ambrose was done with her, she would be a smoldering pile of what used to be Fern Taylor all the same, and there was no way she could go back. She would be unalterably changed, ruined for anyone else. And she knew it as surely as if she'd been kissed by a thousand men.

She moaned into his mouth, the sigh wrenched from the hungry little beast inside her that longed to tear at his clothing and sink her tiny claws into him just to make sure she wouldn't be hungry for long, just to make sure he was absolutely real and absolutely hers, even if it was just for this moment. She pressed herself against him, breathing in the clean sweat that tangled with the scent of the freshly laundered cotton of his clean shirt. She licked and kissed at the salt on his skin, the ripples of his scarred cheek a contrast to the sandpapery line of his jaw. And then, just like that, a thought slid into her fevered brain, a venomous sliver of self-doubt wrapped in a moment of truth.

"Why do you only kiss me in the dark?" she whispered, her lips hovering above his.

Ambrose's hands moved restlessly, circling her hips, sliding up the slim curve of her waist and brushing by the places he most wanted to explore, and Fern trembled, straddling the need to continue and the need to be reassured.

"Are you afraid someone will see us?" she breathed, her head falling to his chest, her hair tickling his mouth and neck and wrapping around his arms.

His silence felt like ice dribbled down her back, and Fern pulled herself from him, moving away in the darkness.

"Fern?" He sounded lost.

"Why do you only kiss me in the dark?" Fern repeated, her voice small and tight, as if she were trying to prevent her feelings from leaking out around the words. "Are you ashamed to be seen with me?"

"I don't only kiss you in the dark . . . do I?"

"Yes . . . you do." Silence again. Fern could hear Ambrose breathing, hear him thinking. "So does it? Embarrass you . . . I mean."

"No, Fern. I'm not ashamed to be seen with you. I'm ashamed to be seen," Ambrose choked, and his hands found her in the dark once more.

"Why?" She knew why . . . but she didn't. Not really. His hand found her jaw and his fingers traced her cheekbone lightly, moving along her face, finding her features, stopping at her mouth. She pulled away so she wouldn't pull him in.

"Not even me?" she repeated. "You don't even want me to see you?"

"I don't want you to think about how I look when I kiss you."

"Do you think about how I look when you kiss me?"

"Yes." His voice was raspy. "I think about your long red hair and your sweet mouth, and the way your little body feels when it's pressed up against me, and I just want to put my hands on you. Everywhere. And I forget that I am ugly and alone and confused as hell."

Flames licked the sides of Fern's belly and she swallowed hard, trying to contain the steam that rose up and burned her throat and drenched her face in shocked heat. She'd read books about men that said things like that to the women they desired, but she didn't know people really said such things in real life. She never thought someone would say those things to her.

"You make me feel safe, Fern. You make me forget. And when I kiss you I just want to keep kissing you. Everything else falls away. It's the only peace I've found since . . . since . . ."

"Since your face was scarred?" she finished softly, still distracted by the things he'd said about her mouth and her hair and her body. Still flushed yet afraid, eager yet reluctant.

"Since my friends died, Fern!" He swore violently, a vicious verbal slap, and Fern flinched. "Since my four best friends died right in front of me! They died, I lived. They're gone, I'm here! I deserve this face!" Ambrose wasn't shouting, but his anguish was deafening, like riding a train through a tunnel, the reverberations making Fern's head hurt and her heart stutter in her chest. His profanity was shocking, his utter, black despair more shocking still. Fern wanted to run to the door and find the light switch, ending this bizarre confrontation playing out in the pitch black. But she was disoriented and didn't want to sprint into a brick wall.

"In the dark, with you, I forget that Beans isn't going to come walking in here and interrupt us. He was always sneaking girls in here. I forget that Grant won't fly up that rope like he's weightless and that Jesse won't try his hardest to kick my ass every damn day because he secretly thinks he's better than I am.

"When I came in today, I almost expected to find Paulie asleep in here, curled up in the corner, having a nap on the wrestling mats. Paulie never went anywhere else when he sluffed. If he wasn't in class, he was here, sound asleep." A sob, deep and hard, rattled and broke from Ambrose's chest, like it had grown rusty over time, waiting to be released. Fern wondered if Ambrose had ever cried. The sound was heart wrenching, desperate, desolate. And Fern wept with him.

She reached toward the sound of his pain and her fingers brushed his lips. And then she was in his arms again, her chest to his, their wet cheeks pressed together, their tears merging and dripping down their necks. And there they sat, comforting and being comforted, letting the thick darkness absorb their sorrow and hide their grief, if not from each other, then from sight.

"This was where I was the happiest. Here in this smelly room with my friends. It was never about the matches. It was never about the trophies. It was this room. It was the way I felt when I was here." Ambrose buried his face in her neck and fought for speech. "I don't want Coach to bring in a bunch of guys to replace them. I don't want anybody else in this room . . . not yet . . . not when I'm here. I can feel them when I'm here, and it hurts like hell, but it hurts so good . . . because they aren't really gone when I can still hear their voices. When I can feel what is left of us in this room."

Fern stroked his back and his shoulders, wanting to heal, like a mother's kiss to a skinned knee, a bandage to a bruise. But that wasn't what he wanted, and he lifted his head, his breath tickling her lips, his nose brushing hers. And Fern felt desire drown the grief.

"Give me your mouth, Fern. Please. Make it all go away."

25
Float across Hannah Lake

"You'll have to help me undress, you know, and I don't think Ambrose can handle it. The sight of my glorious naked body takes some getting used to."

Ambrose, Bailey, and Fern were at Hannah Lake. It had been a spontaneous trip, prompted by the heat and the fact that Fern and Ambrose both had the day (and night) off. They'd hit a drive-thru for food and drinks, but they hadn't gone back home to get their suits.

"You won't be naked, Bailey. Stop. You're scaring Ambrose." Fern winked at Ambrose and said, "You *will* have to help me get him in the water, Ambrose. At that point I can hold him under all by myself."

"Hey!" Bailey interjected with mock outrage. Fern's laughter peeled out and she patted Bailey's cheeks.

Ambrose got behind Bailey and hooked him under the arms, lifting him so Fern could slide his pants around his hips and down to his feet.

"Okay. Set him down for a minute."

Bailey looked like a frail old man with a bit of thickness around his midsection. He patted his belly with good humor. "This little baby helps me float. It also keeps me from falling over in my wheelchair."

"It's true," Fern said, pulling Bailey's shoes and socks from his feet. "He's lucky that he's chubby. It gives his trunk some support. And he really does float. Just watch."

Fern set Bailey's shoes neatly to the side and removed her own sneakers. She wore shorts and a turquoise tank top and made no move to remove those, unfortunately. Ambrose unlaced his boots and unzipped his jeans. Fern looked away, a rosy tinge climbing up her neck and onto her smooth cheeks.

When he was standing in his boxers, he picked Bailey up in his arms without a word and started walking toward the water.

Fern pranced along behind him, shooting instructions about how to hold Bailey, how to release him so that he wouldn't tip forward and not be able to turn onto his back.

"Fern. I got this, woman!" Bailey said as Ambrose released him. Bailey bobbed, almost in a sitting position, butt down feet floating up, head and shoulders well above the surface.

"I'm free!" he yelled.

"He yells that every time he's in the water," Fern giggled. "It probably feels amazing. Floating without anyone holding onto him."

"*Kites or balloons?*" Ambrose said softly, watching Bailey. Floating without anyone holding onto him. Those were the very same words he'd used when Fern had asked him the question long ago. How foolish he'd been. What good was flying if there was no one on the other end of the string? Or floating when there was no one to help you back to dry land? Ambrose tried to float, but he couldn't seem to keep his legs from falling like anchors. He resorted to treading water instead, and the symbolism didn't escape him.

Bailey crowed, "Too much muscle? Poor Brosey. Bailey Sheen wins this round, I'm afraid."

Fern had found the sweet spot and was concentrating on keeping herself afloat, her pink toenails peeking above the surface of the water, her eyes fixed on the clouds.

"Do you see the Corvette?" Fern lifted her arm out of the water and pointed at a fluffy conglomeration. She immediately started to sink and Ambrose slid a hand under her back before her face slipped beneath the water.

Bailey wrinkled his nose, trying to find a car in the clouds. Ambrose found it, but by that time it had shifted and looked a little more like a VW bug.

"I see a cloud that looks like Mr. Hildy!" Bailey laughed. He couldn't point so Fern and Ambrose studied frantically, trying to catch the face before it dissolved into something else.

"Hmmm. I see Homer Simpson," Fern murmured.

"More like Bart . . . or maybe Marge," Ambrose said.

"It's funny how we all see something different," Fern said.

They all stared as the image because softer, less defined, and floated away. Ambrose was reminded of another time he'd floated on his back, staring at the sky.

"Why do you think Saddam had his face plastered all over the city? Everywhere you look you see his ugly mug. Statues, posters, banners every-freakin'-where!" Paulie said.

"'Cause he's 'Suh damn' good-looking," Ambrose said dryly.

"It's intimidation and mind control." Grant, ever the scholar, filled in the answer. "He wanted to make himself seem godlike so that he could more easily control the population. You think these people fear God or Saddam more?"

"You mean Allah," Paulie corrected mildly.

"Right. Allah. Saddam wanted the people to think he and Allah were one in the same," Grant said.

"What do you think Saddam would think if he saw us swimming in his pool right now? And I must say, it's 'Suh damn' fine pool," Jesse stood in the chest-deep water, arms spread on the surface of the water, staring at the ornate fountain that rimmed the far side of the pool.

"He wouldn't mind. He's 'Suh damn' generous, he would invite us to come back whenever we want," Ambrose said. The "Suh damn" jokes had been going on for days.

Their whole unit was splashing around in the huge outdoor pool located at the Republican Palace, now in US hands. It was a rare treat to be this wet and this comfortable, and the boys from Pennsylvania couldn't have been happier if they were actually back home in their very own Hannah Lake, lined with trees and rocks instead of ornate fountains, palm trees, and domed buildings.

"I think Saddam would demand we kiss his rings and then he would cut off our tongues," Beans joined in.

"I don't know, Beans, with you that might be an improvement," Jesse said. Beans launched himself at his friend and a round of water wrestling ensued. Ambrose, Paulie, and Grant laughed and egged them on, but they were all too grateful for the wet reprieve to waste it by joining in on the horseplay. Instead, they floated, staring up at the sky that didn't look all that different than the sky over Hannah Lake.

"I've seen Saddam's face so much I can see it when I close my eyes, like it's burned on my retinas," Paulie complained.

"Just be glad Coach Sheen didn't use the same methods of intimidation during wrestling season. Can you imagine? Coach Sheen's face everywhere we looked, eyes blazing at us." Grant laughed.

"It's weird, when I try to really picture his face, or anyone's face, I can't. I try to pull in the details, you know, and . . . I can't. It hasn't been that long. We've only been gone since March," Ambrose said, shaking his head at the unreality of it all.

"The longest months of my life." Paulie sighed.

"You can't picture Rita's face . . . but I bet you can picture her naked, right?" Beans had stopped wrestling over Jesse's comment about his tongue, and he was wielding it offensively once more.

"I never saw Rita naked," Ambrose said, not caring if his friends believed him or not.

"Whatever!" Jesse said in disbelief.

"I didn't. We only went out for about a month."

"That's plenty of time!" Beans said.

"Does anyone else smell bacon?" Paulie sniffed the air, reminding Beans that he was being a pig again. Beans splashed water in his face, but didn't attack. The mention of bacon had everyone's stomachs growling.

With one last look at the sky, the five climbed out of the stately pool and dripped their way to their piled fatigues. There were no clouds in the sky, no faces to reconstruct in white film, nothing to fill the holes in Ambrose's memory. Unbidden, a face rose in his mind. Fern Taylor, her chin tipped up, her eyes closed, wet eyelashes thick on her freckled cheeks. Her soft pink mouth, bruised and trembling. The way she'd looked after he'd kissed her.

"Have you ever stared at a painting so long that the colors blur and you can't tell what you're looking at anymore? There's no form, face, or shape—just color, just swirls of paint?" Fern spoke again, and Ambrose let his eyes rest on the face that had once filled his memory in a faraway place, a place that most days he would rather forget.

Bailey and Ambrose were silent, finding new faces in the clouds.

"I think people are like that. When you really look at them, you stop seeing a perfect nose or straight teeth. You stop seeing the acne scar or the dimple in the chin. Those things start to blur, and suddenly you see them, the colors, the life inside the shell, and beauty takes on a whole new meaning." Fern didn't look away from the sky as she talked, and Ambrose let his eyes linger on her profile. She wasn't talking about him. She was just being thoughtful, pondering life's ironies. She was just being Fern.

"It works both ways, though," Bailey contributed his two cents. "Ugly is as ugly does. Becker's not ugly because of the way he looks. Just like I'm not devastatingly handsome because of the way I look."

"So true, my floating friend. So true," Fern said seriously. Ambrose bit his tongue so he wouldn't laugh. They were such dorks. Such an odd little twosome. And he had the sudden urge to cry. Again. He was turning into one of those fifty-year-old women who liked pictures of kittens with inspirational sayings printed on them. The kind of woman who would cry during beer commercials. Fern had turned him into a blubbering mess. And he was crazy about her. And her floating friend too.

"What happened to your face, Brosey?" Bailey inquired cheerfully, switching subjects the way he always did, without warning. Okay, maybe Ambrose wasn't crazy about the floating friend.

"It got blown off," Ambrose answered curtly.

"Literally? I mean, I want specifics. You had a bunch of surgeries, right? What did they do?"

"The right side of my head was sheared off, including my right ear."

"Well that's okay, right? I mean that ear had some major cauliflower if I remember right."

Ambrose chuckled, shaking his head at Bailey's audacity. Cauliflower ear is what happened to wrestlers' ears when they didn't wear their headgear. Ambrose never had cauliflower ear, but he appreciated Bailey's humor.

"This ear is a prosthetic."

"No way! Let me see!" Bailey bobbed wildly and Ambrose steadied him before he tipped face first into the drink.

Ambrose pulled the prosthetic ear from the magnets that held it in place, and Fern and Bailey gasped in unison, "Cool!"

Yep. Dorks. But Ambrose couldn't deny that he was relieved by Fern's response. He had given her every reason to run away from him, screaming. The fact that she didn't even flinch eased something in his chest. He inhaled, enjoying the sensation of breathing deeper.

"Is that why your hair won't grow?" It was Fern's turn to be curious.

"Yeah. Too much scar tissue on that side. Too many grafts. There's a steel plate on the side of my head that attaches to my cheekbone and my jaw. The skin on my face was peeled back here and here," Ambrose indicated the long scars that crisscrossed his cheek. "They were actually able to put it back, but I took a bunch of shrapnel to the face before the bigger piece took the side of my head. The skin they put back was like Swiss cheese and I had shrapnel buried in the soft tissue of my face. That's why the skin is so bumpy and pockmarked. Some of the shrapnel is still working its way out."

"And your eye?"

"I took a big piece of shrapnel to my eye, too. They saved the eyeball but not my sight."

"A metal plate in your head? That's pretty intense." Bailey's eyes were wide.

"Yeah. Just call me the Tin Man," Ambrose said softly, the memory of nicknames and old pain making it hard to breathe again.

"The Tin Man, huh?" Bailey said. "You *are* pretty rusty. That double leg yesterday was PA-THETIC."

Fern's hand slipped into Ambrose's and her feet found purchase on the rocky bottom beside his own. And just like that the memory lost its bite. He slid his arm around her waist and pulled her to him, not caring if Bailey gave him grief. Maybe the Tin Man was coming back to life. Maybe he had a heart after all.

They swam around for about an hour, Bailey floating happily, Fern and Ambrose paddling around him, laughing and splashing each other until Bailey claimed he was turning into a raisin. Then Ambrose carried Bailey to his chair and Fern and Ambrose lay out on the rocks, letting the sun dry their clothes. Fern was wearing the most and was definitely the wettest, and her shoulders and nose started to show signs of sunburn, the backs of her pale thighs turning a soft pink. Her hair dried into deep red ringlets, falling down her back and into her eyes as she smiled at him drowsily, half asleep on the big warm rock. He felt a strange falling sensation in his chest and lifted his hand to rub the spot just above his heart, as if he could soothe the feeling and send it away. It was happening more and more often when he was around her.

"Brose?" Bailey's voice cut through his reverie.

"Yeah?"

"I have to go to the bathroom," Bailey informed him.

Ambrose froze, the implications clear.

"So you can either take me home pronto, or you can accompany me to yon forest." Bailey nodded toward the trees surrounding Hannah Lake. "I hope you brought toilet paper. But either way, you're going to have to quit looking at Fern like you want to gobble her up, because it's making me hungry, and I can't be responsible for my behavior when I'm hungry and I need to use the can."

And just like that the mood was broken.

26

Invent a Time Machine

November 22, 2003

Dear Marley,

I've never written you a love note, have I? Did you know Ambrose wrote love letters back and forth senior year with Rita Marsden only to find out Rita wasn't writing them? It was Fern Taylor, the little redhead who hangs out with Coach's son, Bailey. In the beginning, Paulie gave Ambrose the idea to use poetry, but I actually think Ambrose was really enjoying himself until Rita dumped him and told him it had been Fern all along. Ambrose doesn't show a lot of emotion, but he was pretty pissed. We teased him about Fern Taylor for the rest of the year. The thought of Ambrose with Fern is pretty funny. He didn't think so. He still gets real quiet if we even mention her name. It got me thinking that I've never been very good at communicating, and it reminded how far some people will go to get a message across.

We've been on a rotation guarding some prisoners before they are transferred out of Baghdad. Sometimes it takes a few weeks before we have a place to send them. It's amazing the lengths the Iraqi prisoners go to to communicate with each other. They make clay by mixing their chai (tea) with dirt and sand. Then they write little messages on pieces of napkin or cloth and put them inside the clay ball (we call them chai rocks) and let it dry out. Then they toss the chai rocks they've made into different cells when the guards aren't looking. I couldn't think of anything to write today, and that got me wondering if I only had a little slip of paper to tell you how I feel, what would I say? I love you seems kind of unoriginal. But I do. I love you, and I love little Jesse even though I haven't met him. I can't wait to come home and be a better man, because I think I can be, and I promise I'm gonna try. So here's your first official love note. Hope you like it. Grant made sure I used good grammar and spelled everything right. It pays to have smart friends.

Love,
Jesse

● ● ●

Ambrose stood outside Fern's house and wondered how he was going to get inside. He could throw rocks at her window—hers was the one on the ground floor on the back left side. He could serenade her and wake up the neighborhood . . . and her parents, which wouldn't help him get inside either. And he really wanted to get inside. It was 1:00 a.m., and unfortunately, his baker's hours had screwed up his sleep schedule, making rest impossible on the nights he didn't work. He didn't sleep well anyway—ever. Hadn't since Iraq. His shrink told him bad dreams were normal. She told him he had post-traumatic stress disorder. No shit, Sherlock.

But it was the need to see Fern that was messing with his ability to sleep tonight. It had been hours since she'd dropped him off and taken Bailey home. Only hours. But he missed her.

He pulled out his phone, a much more logical option than communicating by throwing rocks or playing musical Romeo.

Are you awake? he texted, hoping, praying her phone was by her bed.

He waited only twenty seconds before his phone vibrated in response.

Yes.

Can I see you?

Yes. Where are you?

Outside.

Outside my house?

Yep. Are you freaked out? I've been told I'm scary looking. I even thought about climbing through your window, but monsters supposedly live under the bed or in closets.

Joking about his face was so much easier now. Fern had made it easier. She didn't respond to his last text, but her light suddenly went on. A couple of minutes passed and Ambrose wondered if she was making herself presentable. Maybe she slept with nothing on. Damn. He should have sneaked through the window.

Seconds later, her head shot out the window and she beckoned him to her, giggling as she held the blind out of the way so he could climb through the narrow opening, standing to the side as he found his feet and straightened, filling her room with his shoulders and his height. The covers on her bed were flung back and a dent in the outline of her head still flattened the center of her pillow. Fern bounced on her toes like she was overjoyed to see him and her hair bounced with her, crimson corkscrews that fell down her back and around her shoulders, dancing against the bright-orange tank top she'd paired with boxer shorts in mismatched colors that made her look like a carnival clown in a state of undress.

Carnival clowns had never made him breathless before, so why was he short on air, desperate to hold her? He filled his lungs and extended his hand in greeting, looping his fingers in hers and pulling her toward him.

"I always dreamed a hot guy would come through my window," Fern whispered theatrically, snuggling into his side and wrapping her arms around his waist like she couldn't believe he was real.

"Bailey told me," Ambrose whispered back.

"What? That sneak! He broke the best friend's code not to reveal secret fantasies! Now I'm embarrassed." Fern sighed gustily, not really sounding embarrassed at all.

"You could have used the front door," Fern murmured after a long silence. She stood on her tiptoes and kissed his neck and then his chin, which was as far as she could reach.

"I've been wanting to climb through your window. I just never had a good enough reason. Plus, I thought it was a little too late to knock on your door. And I wanted to see you."

"You already saw me today, at the lake. I have a sunburn to show for it."

"I wanted to see you again," Ambrose whispered. "I can't seem to stay away."

Fern blushed, the pleasure of his words washing over her like warm rain. She wanted to be with him every minute, and to think he might feel the same was mind-blowing.

"You should be exhausted," she said, always the nurturer, and she pulled him toward her bed and urged him to sit.

"Working nights at the bakery makes it so I can't sleep, even on my nights off," Ambrose admitted. He didn't elucidate on the bad dreams that made it even harder. After a brief silence he added, "Care to share any more fantasies while you've got me here? Maybe tie me to your bed?"

Fern giggled, "Ambrose Young. In my bed. I don't think my fantasies can top that."

Ambrose's eyes were warm on her face as he studied her in the shadows cast by her small bedside lamp. "Why do you always say my full name? You always call me Ambrose Young."

Fern thought for a moment, letting her eyes drift closed as he drew circles on her back with gentle fingers. "Because you were always Ambrose Young to me . . . not Ambrose, not Brose, not Brosey. Ambrose Young. Superstar, studmuffin. Like an actor. I don't call

Tom Cruise by his first name either. I call him Tom Cruise. Will Smith, Bruce Willis. For me, you have always been in that league."

It was the Hercules thing again. Fern looked at him like he could slay dragons and wrestle lions, and somehow, even with his pride tattered and his old image torn down like the toppled statues of Saddam Hussein, she hadn't changed her tune.

"Why did your parents name you Ambrose?" she asked softly, lulled by his stroking fingers.

"Ambrose is the name of my biological father. It was my mom's way of trying to make him acknowledge me."

"The underwear model?" Fern asked breathlessly.

Ambrose groaned. "I'm never going to live that down. Yeah. He modeled. And my mother never got over him, even though she had a man like Elliott who thought she walked on water and would have done anything to make her happy, even marry her when she was pregnant with me. Even let her name me after Underwear Man."

Fern giggled. "It doesn't seem to bother you."

"No. It doesn't. My mother gave me Elliott. He's been the best father a kid could have."

"Is that why you stayed when she left?"

"I love my mom, but she's lost. I didn't want to be lost with her. People like Elliott aren't ever lost. Even when the world tumbles around his ears, he knows exactly who he is. He's always made me feel safe." Fern was like Elliott in that way, Ambrose realized suddenly. She was grounded, solid, a refuge.

"I was named after the little girl in the book *Charlotte's Web*," Fern said. "You know the story, right? The little girl, Fern, saves the little pig from being killed because he's a runt. Bailey thought my parents should have called me Wilbur because I was a bit of a runt myself. He even called me Wilbur when he really wanted to bug me. I told my mom they should have named me Charlotte after the spider. I thought Charlotte was a beautiful name. And Charlotte was so wise and kind. Plus, Charlotte was the name of a Southern belle in one of my all-time favorite romances."

"Grant had a cow named Charlotte. I like the name Fern."

Fern smiled. "Bailey was named after George Bailey, from *It's A Wonderful Life*. Angie loves that movie. You should hear Bailey's Jimmy Stewart impression. It's hilarious."

"Speaking of names and all-time favorite romances, Bailey told me you write under a pen name. I've been really curious about that."

Fern groaned loudly. She shook her fist toward Bailey's house. "Curse your big mouth, Bailey Sheen." She looked at Ambrose with trepidation. "You are going to think I'm some stalker chick. That I'm totally obsessed. But you have to remember that I came up with this alter ego when I was sixteen and I *was* a bit obsessed. Okay, I'm still a bit obsessed."

"With what?" Ambrose was confused.

"With you," Fern's response was muffled as she buried her forehead in his chest, but Ambrose still heard her. He laughed and forced her chin up so he could see her face. "I still don't understand what that has to do with your pen name."

Fern sighed. "It's Amber Rose."

"Ambrose?"

"Amber Rose," Fern corrected.

"Amber Rose?" Ambrose sputtered.

"Yes," Fern said in a very, very small voice. And Ambrose laughed for a very, very long time. And when his laughter rumbled to a stop, he pressed Fern back against her pillows and kissed her mouth gently, waiting for her to respond, not wanting to take what she didn't want to give, not wanting to move faster than she was ready. But Fern pressed back ardently, opening her mouth to his, small hands sliding beneath his shirt to trace the contours of his abdomen, making him groan and wish for a bigger bed. His groan fired her own response, and she tugged his shirt over his head without missing a beat, eager as she always was to be as close to him as possible. Her ardor had Ambrose losing himself in her scent, her soft lips and softer sighs, until he smacked his head against her headboard, knocking a bit of sense back into his love-drunk brain. He scrambled to his feet, grabbing his shirt from the floor.

"I have to go, Fern. I don't want your dad to catch me in his daughter's room, in his daughter's bed, with my shirt on the floor. He will kill me. And your uncle and my former coach would help him. I am still afraid of Coach Sheen, even though I'm twice his size."

Fern mewled in protest and reached for him, snagging him by the belt loops to pull him back. He laughed and stumbled, reaching out to steady himself on her bedroom wall, and his hand brushed a thumbtack, the kind that has a peg, knocking it loose. The push-pin fell somewhere behind Fern's bed, and Ambrose grabbed at the paper so it wouldn't fall too. He glanced at the sheet and his mind gobbled up the words before he had a chance to wonder if it was something he shouldn't see.

If God makes all our faces, did he laugh when he made me?
Does he make the legs that cannot walk and eyes that cannot see?
Does he curl the hair upon my head 'til it rebels in wild defiance?
Does he close the ears of the deaf man to make him more reliant?

Is the way I look coincidence or just a twist of fate?
If he made me this way, is it okay to blame him for the things I
    hate?
For the flaws that seem to worsen every time I see a mirror,
For the ugliness I see in me, for the loathing and the fear?

Does he sculpt us for his pleasure, for a reason I can't see?
If God makes all our faces, did he laugh when he made me?

Ambrose read the words again silently, and he felt a wave rise in him. It was a wave of understanding and of being understood. These words were his feelings. He'd never known they were hers too. And his heart ached for her.

"Ambrose?"

"What is this, Fern?" he whispered, holding the poem out to her.

She eyed it nervously, uncomfortably, her expression troubled.

"I wrote it. A long time ago."

"When?"

"After the prom. Do you remember that night? I was there with Bailey. He asked all of you to dance with me. One of the more embarrassing moments of my life, but his heart was in the right place." A wan smile lifted the corners of Fern's mouth.

Ambrose remembered. Fern had looked pretty—on the verge of beautiful—and it had confused him. He hadn't asked her to dance. He'd refused to ask her to dance. He'd even walked away from Bailey when Bailey had made the request.

"I hurt you, didn't I, Fern?"

Fern shrugged her slim shoulders and smiled, but the smile was wobbly and her eyes had grown bright. Still, after more than three years, it was easy to see the memory pained her.

"I hurt you," he repeated, remorse and realization coloring his voice with regret.

Fern reached out and touched his scarred cheek. "You just didn't see me, that's all,"

"I was so blind then." He fingered a curl that coiled against her brow.

"Actually . . . you're kind of blind now," Fern teased quietly, seeking to ease his guilt with jest. "Maybe that's why you like me."

She was right. He was partially blind, but in spite of that, maybe because of that, he was seeing things more clearly than he ever had before.

27
Get a Tattoo

Iraq

"Let me see your tat, Jess," Beans wheedled, looping his arm around his buddy's neck and squeezing a little harder than could be deemed affectionate. Jesse had spent some of his downtime that morning with a medic who dabbled in tattoos, but he'd been quiet about the results and more morose than usual.

"Shut up, Beans. Why you gotta know every damn thing? You're always in my business," Jesse said, pushing at his pesky friend who was intent on seeing what was inked on Jesse's chest.

"It's because I love you. That's why. I just gotta make sure you didn't get something stupid that you'll regret. Is it a unicorn? Or a butterfly? You didn't get Marley's name wrapped around a rose, did you? She might not be interested when you get home, man. She might be hanging on some other stud. Better not put her name on your skin."

Jesse swore and shoved Beans hard, knocking the smaller soldier to the ground. Beans was up in a flash, his temper hot, his string of obscenities hotter, and Grant, Ambrose, and Paulie rushed to get between the two. The heat was making them all crazy. Add that to the tension that never eased, and it was amazing they hadn't turned on each other before.

"I have a kid! I have a little boy! A new baby boy, who I've never seen, and Marley is his mother! So don't you talk shit about my baby's mother, asshole, or I will beat the livin' hell outta you and spit on your sorry ass when I'm done."

Beans immediately stopped trying to take a swipe at Jesse, and the anger drained from his face as quickly as it had come. Ambrose immediately let him go, recognizing the danger had passed.

"Jess, man. I'm sorry. I was just messin'." Beans rested his locked hands on his head and turned away, cursing himself this time. He turned back, his expression heavy with remorse. "It sucks, man. Being here when you got that goin' on at home. I'm sorry. I just talk too damn much."

Jesse shrugged, but his throat worked rapidly like he was trying to swallow an especially bitter pill, and if he hadn't been wearing eye protection, just like they all were, he might not have been able to hide the moisture in his eyes that threatened to spill out and make the situation even tougher for all of them. Without a word, he began removing his body armor, his fingers sure and swift. It was something they did several times a day, something they wore every time they left base, and it was as familiar to his fingers as tying his shoes.

He lifted his body armor from his chest and tossed it to the ground. Then he loosened the Velcro flap on his shirt and unzipped it, leaving it hanging open as he pulled his undershirt out of his waistband and pushed it up, exposing his chiseled black abdomen and well-developed chest. Jesse was every bit as beautiful as Ambrose, which he pointed out continually. There, on his left pec, written across his heart in careful black stencil, were the words:

My Son
Jesse Davis Jordan
May 8, 2003

He held his khaki undershirt bunched in his fist just below his chin for several seconds, letting his friends stare at the new tattoo he'd been *reluctant to share. Then, without commenting, he pulled his undershirt down, closed his shirt, tucked it in, and pulled his body armor back on.*

"That's cool, Jess," Beans whispered, his voice hollow and gutted like he'd taken a bullet in his chest. Everyone else was nodding, but nobody could speak. They were all fighting off the emotion of the moment, knowing nothing they could say would make Jesse feel any better. Or Beans, for that matter. They resumed their walk back to base in silence.

Paulie fell into step with Jesse and slung his arm around his shoulders. Jesse didn't shrug him off like he'd done a moment ago with Beans. Then, with the words swirling around them in the shimmering desert heat, Paulie began to sing.

I wrote your name across my heart
So I would not forget.
The way I felt when you were born
Before we'd even met.

I wrote your name across my heart
So your heart beats with mine
And when I miss you most I trace
Each loop and every line.

I wrote your name across my heart,
So we could be together,
So I could hold you close to me
And keep you there forever.

The words hung in the air when Paulie was finished. If anyone else had tried to sing, it wouldn't have worked. But Paulie had a gentle heart and a way of communicating that they had all grown accustomed to. The fact that he'd broken into song to comfort his friend didn't faze any of them.

"You write that, Paulie?" Grant whispered, and there was a tremor in *his voice that everyone noted and studiously ignored.*

"Nah. Just an old folk song my mom used to sing. I don't even remember the group that sang it. They had hippie hair and they wore socks with their sandals. But I've always liked the song. I changed the first verse a little, for Jesse."

They walked in silence a little longer until Ambrose started to hum the tune and Jesse demanded, "Sing it again, Paulie."

• • •

"What kind of tattoo should I get? I mean, really? The word *Mom* inside a heart? That's just pathetic. I can't think of a damn thing that's cool without being ridiculous for a guy in a wheelchair," Bailey complained.

The three of them—Ambrose, Bailey, and Fern—were on their way to Seely, to a tattoo parlor called The Ink Tank. Bailey had been begging Fern to take him to get a tattoo since he was eighteen years old, and he'd brought up the subject again a few days ago at the lake. When Ambrose said he would go, Fern was officially outnumbered. Now she was at the wheel, the accommodating chauffeur, as usual.

"Hey, you could get a club, Brosey, like Hercules. That would be cool," Bailey suggested.

Ambrose sighed. Hercules was dead, and Bailey just kept trying to bring him back to life.

"Bailey, you could get an *S*, a Superman *S* inside a shield. Remember how much you loved Superman?" Fern perked up at the memory.

"I would have thought it was Spider-Man," Ambrose said, remembering the fuss Bailey had made over the dead spider when they were ten.

"I gave up on spider venom pretty quickly," Bailey said. "I figured I'd probably been bit by a million mosquitoes, so bugs probably weren't the answer. When spider venom lost its appeal, I abandoned Spider-Man and latched onto Superman."

"He became convinced his muscular dystrophy was a direct result of being exposed to Kryptonite. He had his mom make him a long red cape with a big *S* on the back." Fern laughed and Bailey huffed.

"I'm going to be buried in that cape. I still have it. That thing is awesome."

"So what about you, Fern? Wonder Woman?" Ambrose teased.

"Fern decided superheroes weren't for her," Bailey said from the back. "She decided she would just be a fairy because she liked the option of flying without the responsibility of saving the world. She made a pair of wings from cardboard, covered them in glitter, and rigged up some duct tape straps so she could wear the wings around on her back like a back pack."

Fern shrugged. "Sadly, I don't still have the wings. I wore those things to death."

Ambrose was quiet, Bailey's words resonating in his head. *She liked the option of flying without the responsibility of saving the world.* Maybe he and Fern *were* soul mates. He understood that sentiment perfectly.

"Is Aunt Angie going to ground us from each other, Bailey?" Fern worried her lower lip. "I can't imagine they want you getting a big tattoo."

"Nah. I'll just play the give-the-dying-kid-his-last-wish card," Bailey said philosophically. "Works every time. Fern, you should get a little fern on your shoulder. Not the word—an actual fern. You know, with fronds and everything."

"Hmm. I don't think I'm brave enough for a tattoo. And if I was, it wouldn't be a fern."

They pulled in front of the tattoo parlor. It was quiet—noon wasn't a popular hour for tattoos apparently. Bailey was suddenly quiet, and Ambrose wondered if he was having second thoughts. But as Fern removed the restraints from his chair and he maneuvered himself down the ramp, he didn't hesitate.

Fern and Bailey were all eyes inside the little business, and Ambrose braced himself, just like he always did, for the curious second glances and the blatant staring. But the man who approached them had a face that was so inked in intricate designs that Ambrose, with his marks and scars, looked tame beside him. He looked at Ambrose's scars with a professional eye and offered to add a few embellishments. Ambrose refused, but instantly felt more at ease.

Bailey had chosen to get a tattoo high on his right shoulder where it wouldn't rub against the back of his chair. He chose the words "Victory is in the Battle," the words from the bench at the memorial, the words his dad had repeated hundreds of time, the words that were a testament to Bailey's own life and a tribute to the sport he loved.

And then Ambrose made his own request, surprising Fern and Bailey, peeling off his shirt and telling the tattooed man what he wanted done. It didn't take long. It wasn't a complicated design that required a great deal of skill or a mix of colors. He wrote out what he wanted, neatly, checking that the spelling was right, and handed it to the artist. He chose a font, the letters were stenciled on his skin, and then, without fanfare, the artist began the process.

Fern watched in fascination as, one after another, the names of Ambrose's fallen friends were inked across the left side his chest. Paulie, Grant, Jesse, Beans, one beside the other, neat block letters in a solemn row. When it was finished, Fern traced the names with the tip of her finger, careful not to touch the tender skin. Ambrose shuddered. Her hands felt like balm on a wound, welcome and painful at the same time.

They paid, thanked the tattoo artist and were heading for home when Bailey asked quietly, "Does it make you feel closer to them?"

Ambrose looked out the window at the landscape streaming by—trees and sky and homes as familiar to him as his own face . . . or the face he used to see when he looked in the mirror.

"My face is messed up." His eyes met Bailey's in the rearview mirror, and he reached up and traced the longest scar, the one that ran from his hairline to his mouth. "I didn't get to choose these scars. My face is a reminder every day of their deaths. I guess I just wanted something that reminded me of their lives. It was something Jesse did first. I've been wanting to do it for a while."

"That's nice, Brosey. That's really nice." Bailey smiled wistfully. "I think that's the worst part. The thought that no one will remember me when I'm gone. Sure, my parents will. Fern will. But how does someone like me live on? When it's all said and done, did I matter?"

The silence in the old blue van was thick with empty platitudes and meaningless reassurances that begged to be uttered, but Fern loved Bailey too much to pat him on the head when he needed something more.

"I'll add you to my list," Ambrose promised suddenly, his eyes holding Bailey's in the mirror. "When the time comes, I'll write your name across my heart with the others."

Bailey's eyes swam and he blinked rapidly, and for several minutes he didn't speak. Fern looked at Ambrose with such love and devotion in her face that he would have offered to write an entire epitaph across his back.

"Thank you, Brosey," Bailey whispered. And Ambrose started to hum.

● ● ●

"Sing it again, please?" Fern begged, tracing the longest scar on his right cheek, and he let her, not even minding the reminder that it was there. When she touched his face he felt her affection and her fingertips soothed him.

"You like it when I sing?" he said sleepily, knowing he didn't have much longer before he would have to drag himself into work. Fern had the day off, but he didn't. The trip to the tattoo parlor had taken all afternoon, and when evening fell, he and Fern had said good-bye to Bailey but had struggled to say good-bye to each other. They'd ended up watching the summertime sun set from the trampoline in Fern's backyard. Now it was dark and quiet, and the heat had tiptoed away with the sun, making him drowsy as he sang the lullaby Paulie had taught them in the first months of their tour in Iraq. Jesse's son had just been born, and the tour had stretched out in front of them, endless dust and endless days before they could return home.

"I love it when you sing," Fern said, shaking him from his reverie. She started to sing the song, pausing when she forgot a word, letting him fill in the blanks until her voice faded away and he finished the song on his own. "*I wrote your name across my heart so we could be together, so I could hold you close to me and keep you there forever.*" He'd sung it three times already.

When he sang the last note, Fern snuggled into him, as if she too needed a nap, and the trampoline rocked slightly beneath them, rolling her into the valley his big body made, depositing her across his chest. He stroked her hair as her breaths became deeper.

Ambrose wondered wistfully how it would feel to sleep beside her all the time. Maybe then the nights wouldn't be so hard. Maybe then the darkness that tried to consume him when he was alone would slink away for good, overpowered by her light. He'd spent an hour in a session with his psychologist yesterday. She'd been floored by the "improvements in his mental health." And it was all due to a little pill called Fern.

He had no doubt that she would agree if he asked her to run away with him. Although they would have to take Bailey. Still. She would marry him in a heartbeat . . . and his heart beat enthusiastically at the idea. Fern had to feel the increase in volume and tempo beneath her cheek.

"Have you heard the joke about the man who had to choose a wife?" Ambrose asked quietly.

Fern shook her head where it lay against him. "No," she yawned delicately.

"This guy has a chance to marry a girl who is gorgeous or a girl who has a wonderful voice, but isn't much to look at. He thinks about it and decides that he will marry the girl who can sing. After all, her beautiful voice should last a lot longer than a beautiful face, right?"

"Right." Fern's voice sounded more awake, as if she found the subject matter highly interesting.

"So the guy marries the ugly girl. They have a wedding, a feast, and all the wedding night fun stuff."

"This is a joke?"

Ambrose continued as if she hadn't interrupted him. "The next morning the guy rolls over and sees his new bride and he screams. His wife wakes up and asks him what's wrong. He covers his eyes and yells, 'Sing! For the love of God, sing!'"

Fern groaned, indicating that the joke was lame. But then she started to laugh, and Ambrose laughed with her, bouncing beside her on the trampoline in Pastor Taylor's backyard like a couple of little kids. But in the back of his mind he wondered uneasily if there wouldn't come a point when Fern would look at him and beg him to sing.

28

Be a Hero

Bailey had very little independence. But in his chair, with his hand resting on the controls, he could motor down to Bob's gas station on the corner, to Jolley's to see Fern after work, or to the church in case he wanted to torment his Uncle Joshua with theological hypotheticals. Pastor Joshua was usually very patient and willing to talk, but Bailey was sure he groaned when he saw Bailey coming.

He knew he shouldn't be out as late as he was. But that was part of the thrill too. Twenty-one-year-old men should not have curfews. The only thing he felt guilty about was that when he got home he would have to wake his mom or dad to help him to bed, which took some of the fun out of his late-night excursions. Plus, he wanted to head to the store and see Fern and Ambrose. Those two needed a chaperone. It had started to steam whenever they were together, and Bailey was pretty sure it wouldn't be long before he was the third wheel on wheels. He laughed to himself. He loved puns. And he loved that Fern and Ambrose had found each other. He wouldn't be around forever. Now that Fern had Ambrose, he wouldn't worry about her so much.

He wasn't living dangerously tonight. He'd tried to sneak out without the head lamp, but his mom came running out behind him.

Maybe he would just conveniently leave it at the store when he left. He hated the damn thing. He smirked, feeling like a rebel. He stayed on the sidewalk and streetlights guided his way; he really didn't think he needed a spotlight shining from his forehead. Bob's Speedy Mart was on his way and Bailey decided to stop in, just because he could. He waited patiently until Bob himself came out from behind the register and opened the door for him.

"Hey, Bailey." Bob blinked and tried not to look directly at the light blazing from Bailey's head lamp.

"You can turn that off, Bob. Just click the button on the top," Bailey instructed. Bob tried, but when he clicked the button the light still blazed, as if there was something that had come loose on the inside. He pulled the elastic band around so the light shone from the back of Bailey's head and he could look at him without going blind.

"That'll have to do, Bailey. What can I help you with?" Bob made himself available as he always did, knowing Bailey's limitations.

"I need a twelve pack and some chew," Bailey said seriously. Bob's mouth dropped open slightly, and he shifted his weight uncertainly.

"Um. Okay. Do you have your ID on ya?"

"Yep."

"Okay. Well . . . what kind would you like?"

"Starbursts come in packs of twelve don't they? And I prefer to chew Wrigley's. Mint, please."

Bob chortled, his big belly shaking above his giant belt buckle. He shook his head. "You had me going for a minute, Sheen. I had this picture of you heading down the road with your lip full of tobacco and a case of Bud on your lap."

Bob followed Bailey down the aisles, picking up his purchases. Bailey stopped in front of the condoms.

"I'll need some of those too, Bob. The biggest box you have."

Bob raised one eyebrow, but this time he wasn't falling for it. Bailey snickered and rolled on.

Ten minutes later, Bailey was back on the road, his purchases tucked by his side, Bob laughing as he waved him off, having been thoroughly entertained. He realized belatedly that he hadn't righted Bailey's head lamp.

Bailey chose to head down Center and hit Main instead of cutting down Second East. It was a longer route to the store, but the night was balmy and the air felt good on his face. And he had time. He would give the lovebirds an extra ten or fifteen minutes together before the fun arrived. The silence was welcome, the solitude more welcome. He wished he'd thought to have his dad stick his ear buds in his ears so he could blast some Simon and Garfunkel. But he had been unsuccessfully trying to escape without the head lamp.

The businesses along Main were empty and dark, the black windows reflecting his image back at him as he motored past the hardware store, the karate dojo, and the real estate office. Mi Cocina, Luisa O'Toole's Mexican restaurant, was closed too, the twinkle lights and strung habanera peppers swaying in the light wind, clacking against the mustard-yellow siding. But the building next to Luisa's wasn't closed. Like Bob's Speedy Mart, Jerry's Joint—the local bar—was never closed. A neon-orange light advertised that status, and a few old trucks were pulled right up to the door.

Bailey could hear faint music leaking out from the establishment. He listened, trying to place the song and heard something else. Crying. A baby? Bailey looked around, puzzled. There wasn't a single soul in sight.

He moved forward, crossing the paved entrance to the bar, passing the first few vehicles parked in the long row. Crying again. Parked slightly behind the bar in the gravel that wrapped around the establishment was Becker Garth's black 4x4, complete with jacked-up wheels and a skull and crossbones in his back window. How original. Bailey rolled his eyes. What a douche.

Crying again. Definitely a baby. Bailey veered off the sidewalk and bumped over the gravel toward the 4x4. He could hear his heart beating in his temples, and he felt nauseated. The crying was coming from Becker's truck.

The passenger door was slightly ajar, and as Bailey got closer he could see blonde hair streaming over the edge of the seat.

"Oh no. Oh no. Rita!" Bailey moaned as he maneuvered his chair alongside the opened door. He was afraid he would bump it closed. If he did that, he wouldn't be able to open it again. He lined his chair up so his hand, lying against his armrest was only inches from the edge of the door. He raised his hand as high as he could and wedged it into the opening. He pushed as hard as he could and the door wobbled and then swung slowly open. Bailey's hand fell back to his armrest and his heart fell to his feet. Rita lay unconscious on the seat of the truck, her blonde head hanging off the seat, her hand resting against the door. She'd clearly opened the door but hadn't made it any further. Two-year-old Tyler Garth stood in the foot well, one hand in his mouth, one hand on his mother's face.

"Rita!" Bailey cried. "Rita!" She didn't stir.

Ty whimpered and Bailey felt like whimpering too. Instead, he lowered his voice and tried again, talking to Rita, urging her to respond. There was no blood that he could see, but Bailey had no doubt that Becker Garth had done something to his wife. He couldn't help Rita, but he could take care of Ty. That's what Rita would want him to do.

"Ty Guy. Hey, buddy," Bailey coaxed, trying not to let his terror show. "It's me, Bailey. You want a ride in my chair? You like riding in Bailey's chair, huh?"

"Mama," the child whimpered around his fingers.

"We'll go fast. Let's show Mommy how we go fast." Bailey couldn't lift Ty onto his lap. So he beckoned to him with curled fingers. "Hold my hand and climb into Bailey's chair. You remember how, right?"

Ty had stopped crying, and he looked at Bailey's chair with big blue eyes. Bailey wheeled into the opening, pushing the door wider with his chair. He was so close Ty could literally crawl into his lap. If he would.

"Come on, Ty. I have a treat for you. You can have some candy, and Bailey will take you for a ride in his chair. Let Mommy have a nap." Bailey's voice broke on the words, but the mention of candy was all it took. Ty knelt down in the foot well and climbed over Bailey's armrest and into Bailey's lap. He dug his tiny hand into the little white grocery sack and pulled out the Starbursts triumphantly. Bailey backed away from the door, away from Rita. He had to get help. And he was very afraid that at any minute Becker Garth would come running out of the bar and see him. Or worse, drive away with Rita dying in the front seat of his truck.

"Hold on to Bailey, Ty."

"Go fast?"

"Yeah. We're going to go fast."

• • •

Ty had no concept of holding on. Bailey needed his right hand to drive the wheelchair and his left to punch in 911 on the cell phone that was strapped to his other armrest. He dialed and hit speaker and then put his left arm around Ty, trying to secure him as he crossed the gravel and eased up onto the sidewalk. The 911 operator answered and Bailey started spilling out the details, shouting at his armrest and trying to steer. Ty started to cry.

"I'm sorry sir. I can't hear you."

"There is a woman, her name is Rita Marsden . . . Rita Garth. She's unconscious in her husband's vehicle. He's hit her before, and I think he's done something to her. The truck is parked in front of Jerry's Joint on Main. The husband's name is Becker Garth. Her two-year-old son was there with her. I heard him crying. I have the kid but I don't dare stay with Rita, because her husband could come out any second. And I don't want him to run and take the baby."

"Does the woman have a pulse?"

"I don't know!" Bailey cried helplessly. "I couldn't reach her." He could tell the 911 operator was confused. "Look, I'm in a wheelchair. I can't raise my arms. I'm lucky I was able to get her child out of the truck. Please send the police and an ambulance!"

"What is the license plate on the vehicle?"

"I don't know! I'm not there anymore!" Bailey slowed and turned the chair slightly, wondering if he should go back for the answers the operator was seeking. What he saw behind him made his heart seize in his chest. He was maybe two blocks away from the bar but there were lights pulling out of the lot. It looked like Becker's truck.

"He's coming!" Bailey shrieked, increasing his speed, roaring down the street as fast as he could. He needed to cross over, but that would put him in Becker's headlights. And the headlights were bearing down on him. Tyler was screaming, sensing Bailey's panic. The 911 operator was trying to get him to answer questions and "remain calm."

"He's coming! My name is Bailey Sheen, and I am holding Tyler Garth on my lap. I'm in a wheelchair driving down Main toward Center in Hannah Lake. Becker Garth hurt his wife and he's coming toward us. I need help!"

Somehow, miraculously, Becker Garth drove right past. He obviously didn't expect the guy in the wheelchair to be any sort of threat. Of course, he'd always underestimated Bailey. Bailey's heart leaped in relief. And then Becker hit his brakes and spun his truck around.

He sped back toward Bailey, and Bailey knew there was no way Becker wasn't going to notice the child on his lap. Bailey shot across the two-lane street, veering right in front of the oncoming truck, knowing his only chance was to get to Bob's and relative safety.

Wheels squealed behind him as Becker's truck flew past him again and tried to brake, not expecting Bailey's wild maneuvering.

"I'm turning down Center toward Bob's Speedy Mart!" Bailey screamed, hoping the 911 operator was hearing what he said. Ty had lungs, and he was terrified. At least he was clinging to Bailey like a baby chimp, making it easier for Bailey to hold onto him.

There was certainly no way Bailey could hide. Ty's screams would give them away. There was no time anyway. Becker Garth had flipped around and was coming down Center, pinning them in his lights once more. The black 4x4 rolled up along Bailey's left side. Bailey could see that the passenger side window was down, but he didn't look at Becker. His attention stayed riveted on the road in front of him.

"Sheen! Where the hell do you think you're going with my kid?"

Bailey kept pushing his controls, flying along the darkened street, praying he wouldn't hit any potholes. Hannah Lake had more potholes than streetlights, and the combination was dangerous, especially in a wheelchair.

"Pull over, you little shit!"

Bailey kept moving.

The 4x4 veered over, and Bailey screamed and pulled right on his controls. His chair lurched wildly and Bailey thought for sure it would tip, but it righted itself once again.

"He's trying to run me off the road!" he screamed at the 911 operator. "I am holding his kid and he's trying to freakin' run me off the road!"

The 911 operator was yelling something but Bailey couldn't hear through the roaring in his ears. Becker Garth was drunk or crazy or both, and Bailey knew he and little Ty were in serious trouble. He was not going to live through this.

And then, in the midst of the fear, a sense of calm overtook him. Deliberately, carefully, he slowed the wheelchair to a crawl. His job was to keep Ty safe for as long as possible. He couldn't outrun Becker anyway, so he might as well travel at a safer speed. Becker seemed confused by his sudden decision to slow down and shot past him once more before he punched on his brakes, making his truck spin out on the gravely shoulder of the road. Bailey didn't want to think about what Becker's driving was doing to Rita, unconscious and unrestrained on the passenger side.

And then Becker was coming toward him again, this time in reverse, his slanted taillights like demon eyes hurtling straight for him. Bailey veered right again, but he had run out of road and his chair bumped and slid down the muddy incline into the irrigation ditch that ran parallel to the road. He wasn't going very fast, but that was irrelevant as the chair pitched and wobbled and then fell forward into the murky water that had collected in the bottom of the canal. Tyler was thrown from his arms, landing somewhere in the thick grass on the opposite side of the narrow embankment.

Bailey found himself face down in the water, his hands folded beneath his chest. His right pinky was pinned back and the pain surprised him, making him hyperaware of the beating of his heart, a beat that was echoed by the throbbing in his finger. But Bailey knew a broken finger was the least of his problems. There was only a foot of water in the ditch. Only a foot, at the most. But it covered Bailey's head. He struggled, trying to push up with his hands. But he couldn't push himself up, and he couldn't roll over. He couldn't sit up or climb out.

He thought he heard Ty crying. The sound was distorted by the water, but Bailey's reaction was one of relief. If Ty was crying, he was still alive. And then a door slammed and Ty's cries became distant and disappeared. The rumble of Becker's truck, the loud, souped-up roar that sounded a bit like the ocean in Bailey's ears, receded as well. Bailey's lungs screamed and his nose and mouth filled with mud as he tried to breathe. And the throbbing in his finger faded with the beating of his heart.

29
Ride in a Police Car

Two police cars and an ambulance raced by, sirens blaring, as Fern pedaled home around twelve that night. Her mind was on Ambrose, as usual, when the cacophony of emergency vehicles whooshed past.

"Dan Gable must be stuck in a tree again," she said to herself. She giggled at the thought, although the ambulance for a cat might be a first, even in Hannah Lake. Last time it had been the fire truck. Bailey had seriously enjoyed every minute of it and had praised Dan Gable for days afterward. Maybe that was why Bailey never showed up at the store. Fern flew down Second East and turned onto Center, wondering where the excitement was. To her surprise, there were more police cars than Fern had ever seen at one time lining the road. Cops on foot were spread up and down the street with flashlights in hand. The lights swung back and forth in a purposeful swath, like the officers were canvassing the area in search of something. Or someone, she supposed, curiously.

As Fern headed down the road, a cry went up and officers began running toward the beckoning call.

"I've got him! I've got him!"

Fern slowed and got off her bike, not wanting to be anywhere near whoever "he" was if the police had just captured someone dangerous.

The ambulance was frantically waved down and before it had even come to a complete stop, the back doors flung open and two EMTs scampered out and ran down the embankment beyond Fern's line of sight.

Fern waited, her eyes pinned to the spot where the ambulance workers had disappeared. Nobody came back up for several minutes. Then, when Fern had almost convinced herself to get back on her bike and permanently remove herself from the scene, an officer pushed something up out of the ditch. It was a wheelchair.

"That's weird," Fern mused aloud, wrinkling her nose skeptically. "I thought they would use a gurney."

But the wheelchair was empty, and it was coming up the embankment, not being brought down.

And then she knew. She knew that it was Bailey's chair. And she dropped her bike and ran, screaming his name, oblivious of the shocked reactions around her, to the officers who scrambled to assess the threat, to the arms that reached out to keep her from the scene.

"Bailey!" she screamed, fighting through a sea of uniformed arms to get to him.

"Miss! Stop! You need to stay back!"

"It's my cousin! It's Bailey, isn't it?" Fern looked frantically from face to face and stopped on Landon Knudsen. Landon was a squeaky new recruit to Hannah Lake's sheriff's department. His pink cheeks and blond curls gave him a cherubic appearance, completely at odds with his stiff uniform and the holster around his hips.

"Landon! Is he okay? What happened? Can I please see him?" Fern didn't wait for him to respond to one question before she asked another, needing the answers but knowing that once he spoke, she would wish she'd never asked.

And then the EMTs were pushing the gurney back up the hill, rushing to the open doors of the waiting ambulance. There were too many people around the gurney and Fern was still too far away to make out who occupied the stretcher. Her eyes met Landon's again. "Tell me!"

"We're not sure exactly what has happened. But, yeah, Fern. It's Bailey," Landon said, his face lined with apology.

• • •

Landon Knudsen and another officer that Fern didn't know, an older man who was obviously Landon's senior partner, took Fern to Bailey's house and there informed Mike and Angie that Bailey had been taken by ambulance to Clairemont County Hospital. It was after midnight. Angie was in her pajamas and Mike was rumpled from falling asleep in his recliner, but both were in the old blue van in two minutes flat. Fern climbed in with them and called her parents on the way. They wouldn't be far behind. And then she called Ambrose. In very few words, sanitized and shortened because Angie and Mike were listening, she told him something had happened to Bailey and that they were going to the hospital in Seely.

The police gave them no details but escorted them to the hospital about half an hour north of Hannah Lake with sirens blaring, hastening the journey. It was still the longest half hour of Fern's life. The three of them didn't speak. Speculation was too terrifying, so they sat in silence, Mike Sheen behind the wheel, Angie clutching his right hand, Fern trembling in the single back seat that was positioned behind the empty space designed for Bailey's chair. Fern didn't tell them she'd seen the wheelchair. She didn't tell them that it had been in the ditch. She didn't tell them that she thought it was too late. She just told herself, over and over, that she was wrong.

When they rushed into the ER and identified themselves, the two police officers on their heels, they were led to an empty partition. A thirty-something man in green scrubs with "Dr. Norwood" written on his nametag, dark circles under his eyes, and a subdued expression on his face, informed them that Bailey was gone.

Bailey was dead. He'd been declared dead on arrival.

Fern was the first to break down. She'd had longer to process the possibility, and she'd known. Deep down she had known the instant she saw the chair. Angie was in a state of shock and Mike angrily demanded to be taken to him. The doctor acquiesced and pulled the curtain aside.

Bailey's face and hair were wet and matted with mud, the area around his nose and mouth wiped partially clean during attempts to resuscitate. He looked different away from his chair, like someone Fern had never met. One of Bailey's fingers was bent at an odd angle and someone had placed his thin arms by his sides, making him look even more foreign. Bailey called his arms T-rex arms—completely useless and disproportionate to this rest of his body. His legs were equally thin and the shoe on his right foot was missing. The sock was soaked with mud like the rest of him and his head lamp lay beside him on the gurney. The light was still on. Fern couldn't take her eyes from it, as if the lamp was to blame. She reached for it and tried to turn it off, but the button was flat, permanently pressed down, and it wouldn't release.

"It was the light that helped us find him so quickly," Landon Knudsen offered. But it hadn't been quickly enough.

"He was wearing his light! He was wearing his head lamp, Mike!" Angie collapsed into the chair by Bailey's side and clutched his lifeless hand. "How could this happen?"

Mike Sheen turned on the officers, on Landon Knudsen, whom he'd coached and taught, on the senior officer who had a son who had attended his youth camp last summer. With tears in his eyes and with a voice that had made his wrestlers sit up and listen for three decades, he demanded, "I want to know what happened to my son."

And with very little resistance, knowing full well that it was against protocol, they told him what little they knew.

The 911 dispatch had gotten a call from Bailey. They had an idea of his general location and the fact that he was in duress. Dispatch sent all available units to that location, and within a few minutes, someone saw the light from his head lamp.

Interestingly enough, the band was twisted so the actual light was on the back of Bailey's head, the way a kid sometimes wears his hat with the brim in back. If the light had been on the front of his head, it would have been submerged in water and mud. Bailey had been found in the ditch with his head lamp shining up into the heavens, marking the spot where he lay. The officers would not confirm that Bailey had drowned. Nor would the doctor. Both simply said that an autopsy would be performed to determine cause of death, and with an expression of sorrow for their loss, Bailey's parents and Fern were left alone behind the thin partition, faced with death as life moved on around them.

● ● ●

Sarah Marsden didn't sleep well. She hadn't slept well in years. After her husband, Danny, had passed away she was sure she would sleep like she too had died, delivered from the strain and hard labor of caring for someone who couldn't do much for himself and who was angry and abusive toward anyone who tried to help him.

Danny Marsden had been paralyzed from the chest down in a car accident when their daughter, Rita, was six years old. For five long years, Sarah had done her best to take care of him and her young daughter, and for five long years she'd wondered each day how she could go on. Danny's neediness and his misery took a toll on them all, and when he passed away the day before Rita's eleventh birthday, it was hard to feel anything but relief. Relief for him and relief for herself, relief for her daughter who had only seen her father at his very worst, though if Sarah was being honest, Danny Marsden wasn't a nice man before his accident.

Yet Sarah still didn't sleep well. Not then, and not now, more than ten years later. Maybe it was worry over her daughter and young grandson, because Rita had chosen a man just like her father. The difference was, Becker was able to inflict physical pain as well as emotional pain. It was the bodily harm Sarah worried about most. So when the phone rang at midnight she was immediately alert and reaching for the phone.

"Hello," she answered, hoping Rita just needed to talk.

"She won't wake up!" Becker's voice blared out, making her wince even as she pressed the phone more firmly to her ear.

"Becker?"

"She won't wake up! I went in to get a couple of beers at Jerry's, and when I came back out to the truck, she was just laying there like she had passed out. But she wasn't drunk!"

Fear slapped Sarah across the face and left her reeling from the blow. Staggering, she braced herself against her nightstand and kept her voice steady, "Becker? Where are you?"

"I'm at home! Ty's screaming, and I don't know what to do. She won't wake up!" Becker sounded like he'd had more than a beer at Jerry's, and Sarah's fear swung on her again, catching her in the stomach and doubling her over.

"Becker, I'm on my way!" Sarah was shoving her feet into flip flops and grabbing her purse as she ran for the door. "Call 911, okay? Hang up the phone and call 911!"

"She's tried to off herself! I know it! She wants to leave me!" Becker was howling into the phone. "I won't let her leave me! Rita—"

The phone went dead and Sarah trembled and prayed as she threw herself into her car and squealed out of her driveway. She punched at the keypad on her phone and tried to keep herself together as she gave the 911 operator Rita's address and repeated Becker's words: "Her husband says she won't wake up."

30
Make It to Twenty-One

Ambrose arrived a few minutes behind Fern's parents, and all three were ushered into the ER at the same time the gurney with Rita Garth was pushed through the emergency room doors, an EMT calling out her vitals and giving an update on what measures had been taken en route. A doctor shouted for an MRI, and medical personnel descended on their new patient as Pastor Taylor and his wife stood dumbfounded by the arrival of a second loved one, still unaware of the condition of the first. And then Sarah Marsden was rushing through the doors, little Tyler, wearing a pair of mud-streaked pajamas, in her arms. Becker lurked behind her, seeming distraught and ill-at-ease. When he saw Ambrose he fell back, fear and loathing curling his lip. He shoved his hands into his pockets and looked away disdainfully as Ambrose focused in on the conversation that was taking place.

"Sarah! What's happened?" Joshua and Rachel swarmed her, Rachel taking the filthy toddler from her arms, Joshua putting his arm around Sarah's shaking shoulders.

Sarah had very little to tell them, but Rachel sat with her and Becker in the waiting area, while Joshua and Ambrose went to check on Bailey's status. Pastor Joshua missed the fear that stole across Becker's face and the way his eyes slid to the exit upon the mention of Bailey's name.

He also missed the two policemen that were positioned just inside the emergency room door and the cruiser that had just pulled up at the curb beyond the glass doors of the waiting room. But Ambrose didn't.

When Joshua and Ambrose were led to the little room where Bailey lay, they saw Bailey's parents gathered at his bedside, Fern huddled in the corner, and Bailey lying with his eyes closed on the hospital gurney. Someone had brought Angie Sheen a small plastic tub filled with soapy water, and with loving care, Bailey's mother was washing the mud and grime from his face and hair, gently administering to her son for the last time. It was obvious from the grieving of those gathered that Bailey was not simply resting.

Ambrose had never seen a dead body before. The man was just lying in a heap outside the south entrance to the compound. Ambrose's unit had patrol duty that morning, and Paulie and Ambrose came upon him first. His face was a swollen mass of black and blue, blood was dried at the corners of his mouth and beneath his nostrils. He wouldn't have been recognizable if not for his hair. When they realized who it was, Paulie had walked away from the dead man they all knew and thrown up the breakfast he'd consumed only an hour before.

They called him Cosmo—the a mass of frizzy, curly hair that stuck up and out from his head identical to Cosmo Kramer on the popular American sitcom Seinfeld. *He'd been working with the Americans, feeding them tips here and there, giving them information on the comings and goings of certain people of interest. He was quick to smile and hard to scare, and his daughter, Nagar, was the same age as Paulie's sister, Kylie. Kylie had even written Nagar a couple of letters and Nagar had responded with pictures and a few basic words in English that her father had taught her.*

They had found his bike first. It had been tossed outside the base too, its wheels spinning, handle bars buried in the sand. They checked for a flat and looked around for Cosmo, surprised that he had just abandoned it in the middle of the road that circled the perimeter beyond the concertina wire. *And then they found Cosmo. His dead fingers had been wrapped around an American flag. It was one of those little cheap ones on a wooden stick, the kind you wave at parades on the Fourth of July. The message was clear. Someone had discovered Cosmo's willingness to assist the Americans. And they'd killed him.*

Paulie was the most shaken of all of them. He didn't understand the hate. The Sunnis hated the Shiites. The Shiites hated the Sunnis. They both hated the Kurds. And they all hated Americans, though the Kurds were slightly more tolerant and recognized that America might be their only hope.

"Remember when that church burned down in Hannah Lake? Remember how Pastor Taylor helped organize a fundraiser and everybody kind of pitched in and the church got rebuilt? It wasn't even Pastor Taylor's church. It was a Methodist church. Half of the people who gave money or helped rebuild weren't Methodist. Heck, more than half had never set foot in any church," Paulie had said, incredulous. "But everybody helped anyway."

"There are scumbags in America, too," Beans reminded gently. "We may not have seen it in Hannah Lake. But don't for one second believe there isn't evil everywhere."

"Not like this," Paulie whispered, his innocence making him resistant to the truth.

Ambrose never saw his friends after the blast that killed them. He never saw them laid out peacefully in death like Bailey was. They wouldn't have been laid out. No open caskets for soldiers returning from war, for soldiers who had died from an improvised explosive device that blew a two-ton Humvee into the air and sent another one careening. They wouldn't have looked like Bailey either, as if they were sleeping. Judging from the damage to his own face, they would have been ravaged, unrecognizable.

At Walter Reed, Ambrose saw soldiers who were missing limbs. He saw burn patients and soldiers with facial injuries much worse than his own. And his dreams were filled with limbs and gore and soldiers who had no faces and no arms, stumbling around in a storm of black smoke and carnage on the streets of Baghdad. He'd been haunted by the faces of his friends, wondering what had happened to them after the blast. Had they died immediately? Or had they known what was happening? Had Paulie, with his sensitivity to things of the spirit, felt death take him? Had Bailey?

Such needless death, so unnecessary, so tragic. Grief clogged Ambrose's throat as he stared at Bailey Sheen, at the dirt that matted his hair and the dried mud that Angie Sheen gently wiped from his round face. The toddler Rachel Taylor had taken from Rita's mother was smeared in the same black mud. Bailey was dead, Rita was unconscious, and the bottoms of Becker Garth's pant legs were still damp and caked in dirt. He had done something to his wife. And he had done something to Bailey, Ambrose realized in dawning horror. There was evil everywhere, Ambrose thought to himself. And he was seeing it right here in Hannah Lake.

He strode from the room, fury pounding in his temples, surging through his veins. He crossed the emergency lobby, pushing the swinging doors wide that separated the waiting room from the trauma center, causing the few people who huddled miserably on the metal chairs, waiting for admittance or word on the condition of loved ones, to look up in alarm at the angry, scarred giant who flew through the doors.

But Becker wasn't there. Rachel Taylor still waited by Sarah Marsden's side, but Ty had surrendered to exhaustion across her chest. Rachel still hadn't seen Bailey, still didn't know her nephew had been killed. She looked at him in question, her eyes wide in a face that reminded him of her daughter, reminded him that Fern sat devastated in the room where Bailey lay and he needed to go to her. Ambrose turned around and went back through the trauma doors. Landon Knudsen and another police officer Ambrose didn't know stood just outside the emergency room entrance.

"Knudsen!" Ambrose called out as he pushed through the entrance doors.

Landon Knudsen took a step back and his partner stepped forward and put a hand on his holster.

"Where's Becker Garth?" Ambrose demanded.

Knudsen's shoulders slumped as his partner's back stiffened, their opposing reactions almost comical. Landon Knudsen couldn't take his eyes off of Ambrose's face. It was the first time in three years he had laid eyes on the wrestler he had idolized in high school.

"We don't know," Landon admitted, shaking his head and trying to hide his reaction to the change in Ambrose's appearance. "We're just trying to get a handle on what the hell is going on. We had another cruiser here, but we didn't have every entrance and exit covered. He's slipped out."

Ambrose didn't miss the slide of Landon's eyes, the discomfort and pity that colored his gaze, but he was too upset to care. The fact that they had been watching Becker Garth confirmed his suspicions. In very few words, he laid out the mud he'd seen on the toddler and on Bailey's clothing, as well as the "coincidence" that Bailey and Rita had been brought to the emergency room within a half hour of each other. The officers didn't seem surprised by his synopsis, though they were both vibrating with adrenaline. This type of thing didn't happen in Hannah Lake.

But it had happened, and Bailey Sheen was dead.

● ● ●

Rita regained consciousness within hours of her surgery. She was confused and teary with a headache for the record books, but with the pressure on her brain relieved and the swelling under control, she was able to communicate and wanted to know what had happened to her. Her mother told her what she knew, reliving Becker's 911 call and the trip to the ER with little Ty almost inconsolable in his father's arms. She told Rita that Becker had not been able to rouse her.

"I was sick," Rita said weakly. "My head hurt and I was so dizzy. I didn't want to go to Jerry's. I had bathed Ty and put him in his pajamas, and I just wanted to go to bed. But Becker wouldn't let me out of his sight. He found my stash, Mom. He knows I was planning to leave. He's convinced I have something going on with Ambrose Young." Rita's voice became more measured as the pain killers began to pull her under. "But Fern loves Ambrose . . . and I think he loves her too."

"Did you hit your head?" Sarah pulled Rita back on track. "The doctors said you sustained an injury on the back of your head that caused a slow bleed on the inside . . . a subdural hematoma, the doctor called it. They drilled a little hole in your skull to relieve the pressure."

"I told Becker I wanted a divorce. I told him, Mom. He just looked at me like he wanted to kill me. It scared me, so I ran. He came after me swinging, and I hit the floor pretty hard where the tile meets the carpet. It hurt so bad. I think I passed out because Becker got off me real quick. I had a big bump there . . . but it didn't bleed."

"When was that?"

"Tuesday, I think." It was Friday night when Rita was brought into the ER, late Saturday morning now. Rita was lucky to be alive.

"I dreamed about Bailey," Rita's voice was slurred and Sarah didn't interrupt, knowing she was fading fast. "I dreamed Ty was crying and Bailey came and got him and took him for a ride in his wheelchair. He said 'Let Mommy sleep.' I was so glad because I was so tired. I couldn't even lift my head. Funny dream, huh?"

Sarah just patted Rita's hand and tried not to cry. She would have to tell Rita about Bailey. But not yet. Now she had something more important to do. When she was sure her daughter was fast asleep and wouldn't miss her, she called the police.

31

Always Be Grateful

The window was open. Just like it always was. The wind made the curtains flutter slightly and the blinds banged against the sill every now and again when an impudent gust would make an attempt to come inside. It wasn't that late, just after dark. But Fern had been up for thirty-six hours and she fell into her bed, needing the sleep that would come in fits and starts, interspersed with crying that hurt her head and made breathing impossible.

After they left the hospital, left Bailey in the hands of those who would carry out an autopsy and then transfer him to the mortuary, Fern and her parents spent the day with Angie and Mike at their home, acting as a buffer between the well-wishers and the grieving parents, accepting food and condolences with gratitude and making sure they offered comfort in return. Ambrose went back to the store to help his father and she and Rachel kept Ty with them so Sarah could stay with Rita. Becker had run off and no one knew where he was.

Angie and Mike seemed shell-shocked but were composed and ended up giving more comfort than they received. Bailey's sisters had been there as well, along with their husbands and children. The mood was one of both sorrow and celebration. Celebration for a life well lived and a son well loved, and sorrow for the end that had come without warning. There were tears shed, but there was laughter too. More laughter than was probably appropriate, which Bailey would have enjoyed. Fern had laughed, too, surrounded by the people who had loved Bailey most, comforted by the bond they shared.

When Sarah came to get Ty that evening, reporting that Rita was going to be okay, Fern had stumbled gratefully to her room, seeking comfort in solitude. But when she was finally alone, the truth of Bailey's absence started to push through her defenses, riddling her heart with the pricking pain of precious memories—words he would never say again, expressions that would never again cross his face, places they wouldn't go, time they wouldn't spend together. He was gone. And she hurt. More than she'd thought was possible. She prepared for bed at nine o'clock, brushing her teeth, pulling on a tank top and some pajama bottoms, washing her swollen eyes with cold water only to feel the heat of emotion swell in them once more as she burrowed her face in the towel, as if she could snuff out the knowledge that throbbed at her temples.

But sleep would not come and her grief was amplified by her loneliness. She wished for reprieve, but found none in the darkness of her small room. When the blinds clanked loudly and a flicker of light from the streetlamp outside danced across her wall, she didn't turn toward the window, but sighed, keeping her heavy eyes closed.

When she felt a hand smooth the hair that lay against her shoulders, she flinched, but the flash of fear was almost immediately replaced with a flood of welcome.

"Fern?"

Fern knew the hand that touched her. She lay still, letting Ambrose stroke her hair. His hand was warm and large, and the weight of it anchored her. She rolled toward him on her narrow bed, and found his eyes in the darkness. Always in the darkness. He was crouched by her bed, his upper body outlined against the pale rectangle of her window, and his shoulders seemed impossibly wide against the soft backdrop.

His hand faltered as he saw her swollen eyes and her tear-stained face. Then he resumed his ministrations, smoothing the fiery strands from her cheeks, catching her tears in the palm of his hand.

"He's gone, Ambrose."

"I know."

"I can't stand it. It hurts so bad that I want to die too."

"I know," he repeated softly, his voice steady.

And Fern knew that he did. He understood, maybe better than anyone else could.

"How did you know I needed you?" Fern whispered in broken tones.

"Because I needed you," Ambrose confessed without artifice, his voice thick with heartache.

Fern sat up and his arms enveloped her, pulling her into him as he sank to his knees. She was small and he was wonderfully large and he enfolded her against his chest. She nestled into him, wrapping her arms around his neck and sinking into his lap like a child who had been lost and then found, reunited with the one she loved most.

It was a testament to Ambrose's love for her, the length of time in which he knelt on the hard floor with Fern in his arms, letting her sorrow wash over and through him. His knees ached in steady concert with the heavy ache in his chest, but it was a different pain than he'd felt when he'd lost Beans, Jesse, Paulie, and Grant in Iraq. That pain had been infused with guilt and shock and there had been no understanding to temper the agony. This pain, this loss, he could shoulder, and he would shoulder it for Fern as best he could.

"It wouldn't hurt so badly if I didn't love him so much. That's the irony of it," Fern said after a while, her voice scratchy and thick with tears. "The happiness of knowing Bailey, of loving him, is part of the pain now. You can't have one without the other."

"What do you mean?" Ambrose whispered, his lips against her hair.

"Think about it. There isn't heartache if there hasn't been joy. I wouldn't feel loss if there hadn't been love. You couldn't take my pain away without removing Bailey from my heart. I would rather have this pain now then never have known him. I just have to keep reminding myself of that."

Ambrose rose with her in his arms and settled them both on her bed, his back against the wall, stroking her hair and letting her talk. They ended up curled around each other, Fern flirting with the edge of the mattress, but supported by Ambrose's arms that were wrapped securely around her.

"Can you make it go away, Ambrose? Just for a while?" she whispered, her lips against his neck.

Ambrose froze, her meaning as plain as the devastation in her voice.

"You told me that when you kiss me, all the pain goes away. I want it to go away, too," she continued plaintively, the tickle of her breath against his skin making his eyes roll back in his head.

He kissed her eyelids, the high planes of her cheekbones, the small dollop of an earlobe that made her shiver and bunch his shirt in her hands. He smoothed her hair from her face, gathering it in his hands so he could feel the slide of it through his fingers as he found her mouth and did his best to chase memories from her head and sorrow from her heart, if only for a while, the way she did for him.

He felt her breasts against his chest, her slim thighs entwined with his own, the press of her body, the slide of her hands, urging him on. But though his body howled and begged and his heart bellowed in his chest, he kissed and touched, and nothing more, saving the final act for a time when sorrow had released its grip and Fern wasn't running from feeling but reveling in it.

He didn't want to be a temporary balm. He wanted to be a cure. He wanted to be with her under an entirely different set of circumstances, in a different place, in a different time. At the moment, Bailey loomed large, filling every nook and corner, every part of Fern, and Ambrose didn't want to share her, not when they made love. So he would wait.

When she fell asleep, Ambrose eased himself from the bed and pulled her blankets around her shoulders, pausing to look at the deep red of her hair against her pillow, the way her hand curled beneath her chin. *It wouldn't hurt so badly if I didn't love him so much.* He wished he would have understood that when he'd found himself in a hospital full of injured soldiers, filled with pain and suffering, unable to come to terms with the loss of his friends and the damage to his face.

As he stared down at Fern he was struck with the truth she seemed to intuitively understand. Like Fern said, he could take his friends from his heart, but in purging the memory, he would rob himself of the joy of having loved them, having known them, having learned from them. If he didn't understand pain, he wouldn't appreciate the hope that he'd started to feel again, the happiness he was hanging onto with both hands so it wouldn't slip away.

● ● ●

The day of the funeral, Fern found herself on Ambrose's doorstep at 9:00 a.m. She had no reason to be there. Ambrose had said he would pick her up at 9:30. But she was ready too early, restless and anxious. So she'd told her parents she would see them at the church and slipped out of the house.

Elliott Young answered the door after a brief knock.

"Fern!" Elliott smiled as if she were his new best friend. Ambrose had obviously told his dad about her. That was a good sign, wasn't it? "Hi, sweetie. Ambrose is dressed and decent, I think. Go on back."

"Ambrose!" he called down the hallway adjacent to the front door. "Fern's here, son. I'm going to head out. I need to stop by the bakery on the way. I'll see you at the church." He smiled at Fern and grabbed his keys, heading out the front door. Ambrose's head shot out of an open door, a white dress shirt tucked into a pair of navy slacks making him look simultaneously inviting and untouchable.

His face was lathered on one side, the side untouched by violence.

"Fern? Is everything okay? Did I mess up the time?"

"No. I just . . . I was ready. And I couldn't sit still."

He nodded as if he understood and reached for her hand as she approached.

"How you holding up, baby?"

The endearment was new, protective, and it comforted Fern like nothing else could have. It also made her eyes fill with tears. She clung to his hand and forced the tears away. She'd cried endlessly in the last few days. Just when she felt she couldn't cry anymore, she would surprise herself and the tears would come again, rain that wouldn't stop. She had applied her makeup that morning heavier than usual, lining her brown eyes and laying the waterproof mascara on thick, simply because she felt stronger with it; a sort of armor against the grief. Now she wondered if she should have left it off.

"Let me do that." Fern held out her hand for the razor he wielded, needing to do something to distract herself. He handed it over and sat on the counter, pulling her between his legs.

"It only grows on the left side. I won't ever be able grow a mustache or a beard."

"Good. I like a clean-shaven man," Fern murmured, expertly slicing away the thick white lather.

Ambrose studied her as she worked. Fern's face was too white and her eyes were shadowed, but the slim black dress complimented her lithe figure and made her red hair look even redder still. Ambrose loved her hair. It was so Fern, so authentic, just like the rest of her. He slid his hands around her waist and her eyes shot to his. A current zinged between them and Fern paused for a deep breath, not wanting the liquid heat in her limbs to make her slip and nick his chin.

"Where did you learn to do that?" Ambrose asked as she finished.

"I helped Bailey shave. Many times."

"I see." His blind eye belied his words, but his left eye stayed trained on her face as Fern picked up a hand towel and blotted off the residue, running her hand across his cheek to make sure she'd gotten the shave close and smooth.

"Fern . . . I don't need you to do that."

"I want to."

And he wanted her to, simply because he liked the way her hands felt on his skin, how her form felt between his thighs, how her scent made him weak. But he wasn't Bailey, and Fern needed to remember that.

"It's going to be hard for you . . . not to try to take care of me," Ambrose said gently. "That's what you do. You took care of Bailey."

Fern stopped blotting and her hands fell to her sides.

"But I don't want you to take care of me, Fern. Okay? Caring about someone doesn't mean taking care of them. Do you understand?"

"Sometimes it does," she whispered, protesting.

"Yeah. Sometimes it does. But not this time. Not with me."

Fern looked lost and avoided his gaze as if she were being reprimanded. Ambrose tipped her chin toward him and leaned in, kissing her softly, reassuring her. Her hands crept back to his face and he forgot for a minute what he needed to say with her pink mouth moving against his. And he let the subject rest for the time being, knowing she needed time, knowing her pain was too sharp.

32

Wrestle

There was a hush in the church as Ambrose rose and walked to the pulpit. Fern couldn't breathe. Ambrose hated being stared at, and here he was the center of attention. So many of the people sitting in the packed church were seeing him for the first time. Light filtered down through the stained-glass windows and created patterns around the pulpit, making Ambrose look as if his appearance was marked by a special grace.

Ambrose looked out over the audience, and the silence was so deafening he must have questioned whether his hearing had left him in both ears. He was so handsome, Fern thought. And to her he was. Not in the traditional sense . . . not anymore, but because he stood straight, and his chin was held high. He looked fit and strong in his navy suit, his body a testament to his tenacity and the time he spent with Coach Sheen in the wrestling room. His gaze was steady and his voice was strong as he began to speak.

"When I was eleven years old, Bailey Sheen challenged me to a wrestle-off." Chuckles erupted around the room, but Ambrose didn't smile. "I knew Bailey because we went to school together, obviously, but Bailey was Coach Sheen's kid. The wrestling coach. The coach I hoped to impress. I'd been to every one of Coach Sheen's wrestling camps since I was seven years old. And so had Bailey. But Bailey never wrestled at the camps. He rolled around on the mats and was always in the thick of things, but he never wrestled. I just thought it was because he didn't want to or something. I had no idea he had a disease.

"So when Bailey challenged me to a match, I really didn't know what to think. I had noticed some things, though. I had noticed that he had started walking on his toes and his legs weren't straight and strong. He wobbled and his balance was way off. He would fall down randomly. I thought he was just a spaz."

More chuckles, this time more tentative.

"Sometimes my friends and I would make jokes about Bailey. We didn't know." Ambrose's voice was almost a whisper, and he stopped to compose himself.

"So here we were, Bailey Sheen and me. Bailey had cornered me at the end of camp one day and asked me if I'd wrestle him. I knew I could easily beat him. But I wondered if I should . . . maybe it would make Coach Sheen mad, and I was a lot bigger than Bailey. I was a lot bigger than all the kids." Ambrose smiled a little at that, and the room relaxed with his self-deprecation. "I don't know why I agreed to it. Maybe it was the way he looked at me. He was so hopeful, and he kept glancing over to where his dad was standing, talking with some of the high school kids that were helping with the camp.

"I decided I would just kind of roll around with him, you know, let him shoot a few moves on me the way the biggest high school kids let me do with them. But before I knew it, Bailey had shot in on me, a very sweet single leg, and he attached himself to my leg. It caught me by surprise, but I knew what to do. I sprawled immediately, but he followed me down, spinning around behind me, just like you're supposed to do, riding me. If there had been a ref, he would have scored a takedown—two points, Sheen. It embarrassed me a little, and I scrambled out, trying a little harder than I had before.

"We were facing each other again, and I could tell from Bailey's face he was excited. He shot in again, but I was ready for him this time. I hit an inside trip and Bailey hit the mat hard. I followed him down and proceeded to try and pin him. He was squirming and bridging, and I was laughing because the kid was actually pretty damn good, and I remember thinking, right before his dad pulled me off him, 'Why doesn't Bailey wrestle?'" Ambrose swallowed and his eyes shot to the end of the bench where Mike Sheen sat with tears running down his face. Angie Sheen had her arm wrapped around his and her head was on his shoulder. She was crying too.

"I've never seen Coach Sheen look so pissed and afraid. Not before and not since. Coach started yelling at me, a high school kid pushed me, and I was scared to death. But Bailey was just sitting there on the mat breathing hard and smiling." The audience burst into laughter then, and the tears that had started to flow ebbed with the much-needed humor.

"Coach Sheen picked Bailey up off the mat and was running his hands up and down Bailey's body, I guess making sure I hadn't done any damage. Bailey just ignored him and looked at me and said, 'Were you really trying, Ambrose? You didn't just let me get that takedown, did you?'" More smiles, more laughter. But Ambrose seemed to be struggling with emotion, and the crowd quieted immediately.

"Bailey just wanted to wrestle. He wanted a chance to prove himself. And that day in the gym, when he took me down, was a big moment for him. Bailey loved wrestling. Bailey would have been an amazing wrestler if life had just handed him a different set of cards. But that's not the way it worked out. But Bailey wasn't bitter. And he wasn't mean. And he didn't feel sorry for himself.

"When I got home from Iraq, Coach Sheen and Bailey came and saw me. I didn't want to see anyone, because I was bitter, and I was mean, and I felt sorry for myself." Ambrose wiped at the tears that were slipping down his cheeks. "Bailey wasn't born with the things I have taken for granted every day of my life. I was born with a strong body, free of disease, and more than my fair share of athletic talent. I was always the strongest and the biggest. And lots of opportunities have come my way because of it. But I didn't appreciate it. I felt a lot of pressure and resented the expectations and high hopes people had for me. I didn't want to disappoint anyone, but I wanted to prove myself. Three years ago I left town. I wanted to go my own way . . . even if it was just for a while. I figured I'd come back, eventually, and I'd probably wrestle and do what everyone wanted me to do. But that's not the way it worked out," Ambrose said again, "is it?"

"Bailey told me I should come to the wrestling room, that we should start working out. I laughed, because Bailey couldn't work out, and I couldn't see out of one of my eyes or hear out of one of my ears, and wrestling was the last thing I wanted to do. I really just wanted to die, and I thought because Paulie and Grant and Jesse and Connor were dead, that that was what I deserved."

There was a sense of mourning in the audience that surpassed the grief over Bailey's death. As Ambrose spoke the names of his four friends there was an anguish that rippled through the air, an anguish that had not been exorcised, a grief that had not eased. The town had not been able to grieve for their loss, not entirely. Nor had they been able to celebrate the return of one of their own. Ambrose's inability to face what had happened to him and to his friends made it impossible for anyone else to come to terms with it, either.

Fern turned her head and found Paul Kimball's mother in the crowd. She clutched the hand of her daughter, and her head was bent, bowed with the emotion that permeated the air. Coach Sheen buried his face in his hands, his love for the four dead soldiers almost as deep as the love he felt for his son. Fern longed to turn and find the faces of each loved one, to meet their eyes and acknowledge their suffering. But maybe that was what Ambrose was doing. Maybe he recognized that it was time . . . and that it was up to him.

"Two days after Bailey died, I went to see Coach Sheen. I thought he would be heartbroken. I thought he would feel the way I've felt for the past year, missing my friends, asking God why, angry as hell, basically out of my mind. But he wasn't.

"Coach Sheen told me that when Bailey was diagnosed, it was like the whole world stopped turning. Like it was frozen in place. He said he and Angie didn't know if they would ever be happy again. I've wondered that same thing over the last year. But Coach said, looking back, that what felt like the worst thing that could ever happen to them turned out to be an incredible gift. He said Bailey taught him to love and to put things in perspective, to live for the present, to say I love you often and to mean it. And to be grateful for every day. It taught him patience and perseverance. It taught him there are things that are more important than wrestling."

Coach Sheen smiled through his tears, and he and Ambrose shared a moment with the whole town looking on.

"He also told me Bailey wanted me to speak at his funeral." Ambrose grimaced and the audience laughed at his expression. He waited for them to grow quiet before he continued. "You know I love wrestling. Wrestling taught me how to work hard, to take counsel, to take my lumps like a man and win like one too. Wrestling made me a better soldier. But like Coach Sheen, I've learned there are things more important than wrestling. Being a hero on the mat isn't nearly as important as being a hero off the mat, and Bailey Sheen was a hero to many. He was a hero to me, and he was a hero to everybody on the wrestling team.

"Shakespeare said, 'The robbed that smiles steals something from the thief.'" Ambrose's eyes shot to Fern's and he smiled softly at the girl that had him quoting Shakespeare once again. "Bailey is proof of this. He was always smiling, and in so many ways he had life beat, not the other way around. We can't always control what happens to us. Whether it's a crippled body or a scarred face. Whether it's the loss of people we love and don't want to live without," Ambrose choked out.

"We were robbed. We were robbed of Bailey's light, Paulie's sweetness, Grant's integrity, Jesse's passion, and Bean's love of life. We were robbed. But I've decided to smile, like Bailey did, and steal something from the thief." Ambrose looked out across the mourners, most whom he had known his whole life, and cried openly. But his voice was clear as he closed his remarks.

"I'm proud of my service in Iraq, but I'm not proud of the way I left or the way I came home. In a lot of ways, I let my friends down ... and I don't know if I'll ever forgive myself completely for their loss. I owe them something, and I owe you something. So I'll do my best to represent you and them well by wrestling for Penn State."

Gasps ricocheted around the room, but Ambrose continued over the excited response. "Bailey believed I could do it, and I'm going to damn well do my best to prove him right."

● ● ●

1995

"How many stitches did you get?" Fern wished Bailey would pull off the gauze taped to his chin so she could see for herself. She'd run straight over when she'd heard the news.

"Twenty. It was pretty deep. I saw my jaw bone." Bailey seemed excited about the seriousness of his wound, but his face fell almost immediately. He had a book on his lap, as usual, but he wasn't reading. He was propped up in his bed, his wheelchair pushed to the side, temporarily abandoned. Bailey's parents had purchased the bed from a medical supply store a few months before. It had bars along the side and buttons that would raise your upper body so you could read or your feet so you could pretend you were in a rocket ship shooting into space. Fern and Bailey had ridden on it a few times until Angie had firmly told them it wasn't a toy and she never wanted to catch them playing spaceship on it, ever again.

"Does it hurt?" Fern asked. Maybe that was why Bailey was so glum.

"Nah. It's still numb from the shot." Bailey poked at it to show her.

"So what's wrong, buddy?" Fern hopped up onto the bed, wiggling her little body next to his and pushing the book aside to make more space.

"I'm not going to walk again, Fern," Bailey said, his chin wobbling, making the gauze pad shimmy up and down.

"You can still walk a little though, right?"

"No. I can't. I tried today and I fell down. Smacked my chin really hard on the ground." The bandage on Bailey's chin wobbled again, evidence to his claim.

For a while, Bailey had only used his wheelchair when he got home from school, saving his strength so he could leave it at home during the day. Then the school day got to be too much, so Angie and Mike changed tactics, sending him to school in his chair and letting him up in the evenings when his strength would allow. But slowly, incrementally, his evening freedom became more and more limited and his time in the chair increased. Apparently now, he wasn't walking at all.

"Do you remember your last step?" Fern asked softly, not savvy enough at eleven to avoid direct questions that might be painful to answer.

"No. I don't. I would write it in my journal if I did. But I don't know."

"I bet your mom wishes she could put it in your baby book. She wrote down your first step, didn't she? She probably wishes she could write down your last."

"She probably thought there would be more." Bailey gulped and Fern could tell he was trying not to cry. "I thought there would be more. But I guess I used them all up."

"I would give you some of my steps if I could," Fern offered, her chin starting to wobble too. They cried together for a minute, two forlorn little figures on a hospital bed, surrounded by blue walls and Bailey's things.

"Maybe I can't take steps, but I can still roll," Bailey wiped at his nose, and he shrugged, abandoning his self-pity, his optimism rising to the surface the way it always did.

Fern nodded, glancing at his wheelchair with a flood of gratitude. He could still roll. And then she grinned.

"You can't walk and roll, but you can rock and roll," Fern squealed and jumped off the bed to turn on some music.

"I can definitely rock and roll." Bailey laughed. And he did, singing at the top of his lungs while Fern walked and rolled and boogied and leaped enough for both of them.

33

Don't Be Afraid of Dying

Bailey's final resting place was nestled to the left of his Grandpa Sheen, Fern's grandpa too. Jessica Sheen laid just beyond, a woman who died of cancer when her son, Mike, was only nine years old. Rachel, Fern's mother, had been nineteen when her mother died, and she lived at home and helped her father raise her little brother, Mike, until he graduated from high school and left for college. As a result, the bond between Rachel and Mike was more like parent and child than brother and sister.

Grandpa James Sheen was in his seventies when Fern and Bailey were born, and he passed when they were five years old. Fern remembered him vaguely, the shock of white hair and the bright-blue eyes that he'd passed down to his children, Mike and Rachel. Bailey had inherited those eyes as well—lively, intense. Eyes that saw everything and soaked it all up. Fern had her father's eyes, a deep, warm brown that comforted and consoled, a deep brown the color of the earth that was piled high next to the deep hole in the ground.

Fern found her father's eyes as he began to speak, his slightly gravelly voice reverent in the soft air, conviction making his voice shake. As they listened to the heartfelt dedication, Fern felt Ambrose shudder as if the words had found a resting place inside of him.

"I don't think we get answers to every question. We don't get to know all the whys. But I think we will look back at the end of our lives, if we do the best we can, and we will see that the things that we begged God to take from us, the things we cursed him for, the things that made us turn our backs on him or any belief in him, are the things that were the biggest blessings, the biggest opportunities for growth." Pastor Taylor paused as if gathering his final thoughts. Then he searched out his daughter's face among the mourners. "Bailey was a blessing . . . and I believe that we will see him again. He isn't gone forever."

But he was gone for now, and now stretched on into endless days without him. His absence was like the hole in the ground—gaping and impossible to ignore. And the hole Bailey left would take a lot longer to fill. Fern clung to Ambrose's hand, and when her father said "amen" and people began to disperse, Fern stayed glued to the spot, unable to move, to leave, to turn her back on the hole. One by one, people approached her, patting her hand, embracing her, until finally only Angie and Mike remained with Ambrose and Fern.

Sunlight dappled the ground, bending around the foliage and finding the floor, creating lace made of light and delicate shrouds over the heads of the four who remained. And then Angie moved to Fern and they clung to each other, overcome with the pain of parting and the agony of farewell.

"I love you, Fern," Angie held her niece's face in her hands as she kissed her cheeks. "Thank you for loving my boy. Thank you for serving him, for never leaving his side. What a blessing you've been in our lives." Angie looked at Ambrose Young, at his strong body and straight back, at the hand that enveloped Fern's. She let her eyes rest on the sober face marked by his own tragedy, and she spoke to him.

"It always amazes me how people are placed in our lives at exactly the right times. That's how God works, that's how he takes care of his children. He gave Bailey Fern. And now Fern needs her own angel."

266 • Amy Harmon

Angie placed her hands on Ambrose's broad shoulders and looked him squarely in the eye, unashamed of her own emotion, demanding that he listen. "You're it, pal."

Fern gasped and blushed to the roots of her bright red hair, and Ambrose smiled, a slow curve of his crooked mouth. But Angie wasn't done, and she removed one of her hands from Ambrose's shoulder so she could pull Fern into the circle. Ambrose looked over Angie's blonde head and locked eyes with his old coach. Mike Sheen's blue eyes were bloodshot and rimmed in red, his cheeks wet with grief, but he tipped his head when Ambrose met his gaze as if he seconded his wife's sentiments.

"Bailey was probably more prepared to die than anyone I've ever known. He wasn't eager for it, but he wasn't afraid of it either," Angie said with conviction, and Ambrose looked away from his coach and listened to a wise mother's words. "He was ready to go. So we have to let him go." She kissed Fern again and the tears fell once more. "It's okay to let him go, Fern."

Angie took a deep breath and stepped back, dropping her hands, and releasing them from her gaze. Then, with an acceptance born of years of trial, she reached for her husband's hand, and together they left the quiet spot where the birds sang and a casket waited to be blanketed in the earth, secure in the faith that it wasn't the end.

Fern walked to the hole and, crouching down, she pulled a handful of rocks from the pockets of her black dress. Carefully, she formed the letters *B S* at the foot of the grave.

"Beautiful Spider?" Ambrose said softly, just beyond her left shoulder, and Fern smiled, amazed that he remembered.

"Beautiful Sheen. Beautiful Bailey Sheen. That's how I'll always remember him."

● ● ●

"He wanted you to have this." Mike Sheen placed a big book in Ambrose's hands. "Bailey was always designating his belongings. Everything in his room has a specified owner. See? He's written your name on the inside."

Sure enough, "For Ambrose" was written inside the cover. It was the book on mythology, the book Bailey had been reading that long ago day at summer wrestling camp when Bailey had introduced Ambrose to Hercules.

"I'll leave you two for a minute. I think I'm okay . . . but then I come in here and realize that he's really gone. And I'm not okay anymore." Bailey's father tried to smile, but the attempt made his lips tremble and he turned and fled from the room redolent with Bailey's memory. Fern pulled her legs up and rested her chin on her knees, closing her eyes against the tears that Ambrose could see leaking out the sides. Bailey's parents had asked them to come by, that Bailey had belongings that he had wanted them to have. But it could wait.

"Fern? We can go. We don't have to do this now," Ambrose offered.

"It hurts to be here. But it hurts not to be here too." She shrugged and blinked rapidly. "I'm okay." She wiped at her cheeks and pointed to the book in his hands. "Why did he want you to have that book?"

Ambrose flipped through the pages of the book, not pausing for the mighty Zeus or the big-breasted nymphs. With the book heavy in his hands and the memory heavy in his heart, he kept turning until he found the section and the picture he'd thought of many times since that day.

Face of a Hero. Ambrose understood it so much better now. The sorrow on the bronze face, the hand on a breaking heart. Guilt was a heavy burden, even for a mythological champion.

"Hercules," Ambrose said, knowing that Fern would understand.

He raised the book so Fern could see the pages he perused. When he held it upright, turning it so she could see, the thick pages fell forward, fanning out before he could smooth them back, and a folded sheet of paper fluttered to the ground.

Fern leaned down to retrieve it, sliding it open to ascertain its importance. Her eyes moved back and forth and her lips moved as she read the words printed on the page.

"It's his list," she whispered, her voice colored with surprise.

"What list?"

"The date says July 22, 1994."

"Eleven years ago," Ambrose said.

"We were ten. Bailey's last summer," Fern remembered.

"His last summer?"

"Before he was in a wheelchair. Everything happened that summer. Bailey's disease became very real."

"So what does it say?" Ambrose crossed to Fern and sat beside her, looking at the sheet of lined paper with the fringe still attached, where Bailey had ripped it from a notebook. The handwriting was juvenile, the items listed in a long column with details listed out to the side.

"*Kiss Rita? Get married?*" Ambrose chortled. "Even at ten, Bailey was in love."

"Always. From day one." Fern giggled. "*Eat pancakes every day, Invent a time machine, Tame a lion, Make friends with a monster.* You can tell he's ten, huh?"

Ambrose chuckled too, his eyes skimming the dreams and desires of a ten-year-old Bailey. "*Beat up a bully, Be a superhero or a super star, Ride in a police car, Get a tattoo.* Typical boy."

"*Live. Have courage. Be a good friend. Always be grateful. Take care of Fern,*" Fern whispered.

"Maybe not so typical," Ambrose said, his own throat closing with emotion. They were quiet for several long moments, their hands entwined, the page growing blurry as they fought the moisture in their eyes.

"He did so many of these things, Ambrose," Fern choked out. "Maybe not in the typical way, but he did them . . . or helped someone else do them." Fern handed Ambrose the page. "Here. It belongs in your book. Number four says *Meet Hercules*." Fern pointed at the list. "To him, you were Hercules."

Ambrose pressed the precious document back between the pages of the Hercules chapter, and one word leaped from the page. *Wrestle.* Bailey hadn't clarified the word, hadn't added anything to it. He'd just written it on the line and moved to the next thing on his bucket list. Ambrose closed the book on the pages of long ago dreams and ancient champions.

Hercules had tried to make amends, to balance the scales, to atone for the murder of his wife and three children, the four lives he had taken. And though some would say he was not to blame, that it was temporary madness sent by a jealous goddess, he was still responsible. For a time, Hercules had even held the weight of the heavens on his shoulders, convincing Atlas to surrender the weight of the world to his willing back.

But Ambrose wasn't a god with superhuman strength and this wasn't ancient mythology. And some days, Ambrose feared he more closely resembled a monster than a hero. The four lives he felt responsible for were lost, and no amount of labor or penance would bring them back. But he could live. And he could wrestle, and if there was a place beyond this life where young men lived on and heroes like Bailey walked again, when the whistle blew and the mat was slapped, they would smile and know he wrestled for them.

34
Catch a Bad Guy

Fern returned to work a few days after Bailey's funeral. Mr. Morgan had covered for her for almost a week and he needed her to come back. It was easier than staying home and moping, and Ambrose would be there at the end of her shift. By ten o'clock Fern was exhausted. Ambrose took one look at her and told her to go home. Which prompted tears and insecurity from Fern, which prompted kisses and reassurances from Ambrose, which led to passion and frustration, which led to Ambrose telling her to go home. And the cycle repeated.

"Fern. I am not going to make love to you on the bakery floor, baby. And that's what's going to happen if you don't get your cute butt out of here. Go!"

Ambrose dropped a kiss on her freckled nose and pushed her away from him. "Go."

Fern was still thinking about sweaty sex on the bakery floor when she walked out of the employee entrance at the back of the store. She almost couldn't stand to leave him. Being apart had become torture. Soon Ambrose would be leaving for school. And with Bailey gone and Ambrose far away, Fern didn't know what she was going to do with herself.

The thought caused a flood of emotion that had her turning back toward the employee entrance, eager to return to his side. She wondered what Ambrose would do if she followed him. She could register for school and get a student loan. She could live in the dorms and take a couple of classes and write in the evenings and follow him around like a puppy, the way she'd done her whole life.

Fern shook her head adamantly, took a fortifying breath, and walked toward her bike. No. She wasn't going to do that. In recent days she had thought about what came next for them. She had made her feelings known. She loved Ambrose. She had always loved him. And if Ambrose wanted her in his life permanently, not just as a temporary distraction or a safety net, he was going to have to be the one to say the words. He was going to have to ask.

Fern knelt by her bike where it was chained to a downspout and clicked the combination absentmindedly. Her mind was far away, wrapped in Ambrose and the thought of losing him once more, and she reacted slowly to the sudden rush of footsteps coming up behind her. Steely arms wrapped around her and shoved her to the ground, causing her to lose her grip on her bike so it teetered and toppled beside her.

Her first thought was that it was Ambrose. He had surprised her in the dark before, just outside the employee entrance. But it wasn't Ambrose. He would never hurt her. The arms that gripped her were thinner, the body less corded with muscle, but whoever it was, he was still much bigger than Fern. And he intended to hurt her. Fern shoved frantically at the weight that pressed her face into the sidewalk.

"Where is she, Fern?" It was Becker. His breath reeked of beer and vomit and days without a toothbrush. The immaculate Becker Garth was coming undone, and that scared Fern more than anything.

"I went to her mother's house but it's dark. I've been watching it for two days. And she's not at home! I can't even get in my own house, Fern!"

"They left, Becker," Fern wheezed, trying to keep the terror at bay. Becker sounded hysterical, like he had lost his sanity when he'd forced Bailey off the road. The police didn't think Becker knew that they had Bailey's 911 call. Maybe he had thought he could just come back home now that the dust had settled and nobody would be the wiser.

"WHERE ARE THEY?!" Becker grabbed Fern's hair and ground her cheek into the sidewalk. Fern winced and tried not to cry as she felt the burn and scrape of the concrete against her face.

"I don't know, Becker," Fern lied. There was no way she was telling Becker Garth where his wife was. "They just said they were leaving for a couple days to get some rest. They'll be back." Another lie.

As soon as Rita had been discharged from the hospital, she'd given her landlord notice and Sarah had put her house up for sale with a local realtor and asked that it be kept private. Rita was devastated by Bailey's death and they were afraid. With Becker unaccounted for, they didn't feel safe in their homes, in their town, and they liquidated everything they could and had decided to take off until Becker was no longer a threat, if that day ever came.

Fern's father had arranged to have their belongings sold and what couldn't be sold was kept in a storage unit owned by the church. He'd given them $2,000 in cash, and Fern had dipped into her own savings account. In less than a week, they were gone. Fern had been so afraid for Rita. She hadn't thought she needed to be afraid for herself.

Fern heard a snick and felt a slide of something cold and sharp against her throat. Her heart sounded like a racehorse at full speed, echoing in the ear that was pressed against the sidewalk.

"You and Bailey turned her against me! You were always giving her money. And Sheen tried to take my kid! Did you know that?"

Fern just squeezed her eyes shut and prayed for deliverance.

"Is she with Ambrose?"

"What?"

"Is she with Ambrose?" he screamed.

"No! Ambrose is with me!" Just inside the door of the bakery. And so, so far away.

"With you? You think he wants you, Fern? He doesn't want you! He wants Rita. He's always wanted Rita. But now his face is all messed up!" Becker spit the words into her ear.

Fern felt the nick of the blade against her skin, and Becker moved the knife from her throat to her face. "And I'm going to cut you up so you match. If you tell me where Rita is, I'll only mark up one side, so you look just like Ambrose."

Fern squeezed her eyes shut, panting in panic, praying for deliverance.

"Tell me where she is!" Becker raged at her silence and backhanded her. Fern's head rang and her ears popped and for a moment she lost herself, floating out and beyond, a momentary reprieve from the terror that gripped her. Then Becker was up and dragging Fern by her long red hair before she could get her feet under her, pulling her over the curb, crossing the street, and moving across the field that extended into the dark trees behind the store. Fern scrambled, crying against the pain at her scalp, trying to stand. And she screamed for Ambrose.

● ● ●

"Do you feel that?"

The words came into Ambrose's mind as if Paulie stood at his shoulder and spoke them in his ear. His deaf ear. Ambrose rubbed at his prosthetic and stepped back from the mixer. He flipped it off, and turned, expecting someone to be standing there with him. But the bakery was silent and empty. He listened, the silence expectant. And he felt it. A sense of something wrong, a sense of foreboding. Something he didn't have a name for and couldn't explain.

"Do you feel that?" Paulie had said before death had separated the friends forever.

Ambrose walked out of the bakery toward the back door, the door Fern had exited less than ten minutes before. And then he heard her scream. Ambrose flew through the exit door, adrenaline pulsing in his ears and denial pounding in his head.

The first thing he saw was Fern's bike, laying on its side, the front wheel pointing into the air, the pedals holding the front half up in a slight tilt, freeing the big wheel to spin slightly in the wind. Like Cosmo's bike. Smiling Cosmo, who wanted his family to be safe and his country to be delivered from terror. Cosmo, who died at the hands of evil men.

"Fern!" Ambrose roared in terror. And then he saw them, maybe one hundred yards away, Fern struggling with someone who held his arm around her throat and was dragging her across the field behind the store. Ambrose ran, sprinting across the uneven ground, his feet barely touching the earth, rage pouring through his veins. He closed the gap in seconds, and as Becker saw him coming he yanked Fern up against him, shielding himself. In a hand that shook like someone who was strung out and beyond reason, he held a knife out toward Ambrose as Ambrose hurtled toward him, closing in fast.

"She's coming with me, Ambrose!" he shrieked. "She's taking me to Rita!"

Ambrose didn't slow, didn't let his eyes rest on Fern. Becker Garth was done. He'd killed Bailey Sheen, left him lying in a ditch, knowing full well he couldn't save himself. He'd abused his wife, terrorized her and his child, and now he held the girl Ambrose loved like a rag doll, shielding himself from the wrath wrapped in vengeance that was coming for him.

Becker cursed viciously, realizing that his knife wasn't going to prevent a collision with Ambrose. He dropped Fern, releasing her so he could escape, and screamed as he turned to run. Fern screamed as well, her fear for Ambrose evident in the way she staggered back to her feet and spread her arms as if to stop him from hurling himself into Becker's knife.

Becker had staggered only a few steps before Ambrose was on him, knocking him to the ground the way Becker had knocked his wife to the ground. Becker's head collided with the dirt the way Rita's head had collided with her kitchen floor. Then Ambrose let loose, fists flying, pummeling Becker like he'd done in ninth grade when Becker Garth had terrorized Bailey Sheen in the men's locker room at school.

"Ambrose!" Fern cried from somewhere behind him, anchoring him to her and to the present, slowing his fists and calming his rage-fueled barrage. Standing, he grabbed Becker's long hair, the hair that looked like Ambrose's old locks. And he dragged him, the way Becker had dragged Fern, back to where Fern was swaying on her feet, trying not to collapse. He released Becker and pulled Fern into his arms. Becker fell in a heap.

"Don't let him get away. We can't let him find Rita," Fern cried, shaking her head and clinging to him. But Becker wasn't going anywhere. Ambrose swept Fern up in his arms and carried her back to the store where her bike still lay, its front wheel still spinning gently, impervious to the drama that had played out nearby.

Fern's face was bloody along her throat and blood oozed from an abrasion along her cheekbone. Her right eye was already swollen shut. Ambrose sat her gently against the building, promising her he would be right back. He grabbed the wiry bike lock that dangled from the downspout, and digging out his phone, he called 911. While he calmly told the 911 dispatcher what had transpired, he hog-tied Becker Garth with Fern's bike lock in case he regained consciousness before the cops arrived. Ambrose hoped he did. He hoped Becker woke up soon. He wanted him to know how it felt to be trapped on his back in the dark, unable to move, knowing he couldn't save himself. The way Bailey must have felt in ninth grade in a black locker room, lying in his toppled chair, waiting for rescue. The way Bailey must have felt, face down in a ditch knowing his attempts to help his friend would cost him his life.

Then Ambrose walked back to Fern, fell to his knees beside her, and pulled her into his lap, wrapping his arms around her gently, humbly. And he whispered his thanks into her hair as his body began to shake.

"Thank you, Paulie."

35

Take Care of Fern

Prom 2002

Fern fiddled with her neckline for the hundredth time since arriving and smoothed her skirt as if it had suddenly become wrinkled since she'd smoothed it four seconds ago.

"Do I have lipstick on my teeth, Bailey?" she hissed at her cousin, grimacing in a parody of a smile so he could see the two white rows of perfect, straight teeth she had suffered three long years in braces for.

Bailey sighed and shook his head no. "You're fine, Fern. You look great. Just relax."

Fern took a deep breath and immediately started nervously biting the lip she had just covered in a new coat of coral red lipstick.

"Crap! Now I know I have lipstick on my teeth!" she wailed in a voice pitched for his ears alone.

"I'll be right back, okay? I'm just going to go to the girl's room a second. Will you be okay without me?"

Bailey raised his eyebrows as if to say, "Are you kidding me, woman?"

Fern hadn't been gone for five seconds before Bailey was shooting across the dance floor toward the circle of wrestlers he had been wanting to talk to since arriving at the prom with Fern.

Ambrose, Paulie, and Grant had come without dates. Bailey didn't know why. If he had a chance to ask a girl to prom, hold her in his arms, smell her hair, and stand on his own two legs and dance, he wouldn't let the opportunity pass him by.

Beans and Jesse were there with girls, but their dates were huddled a little way off in a serious discussion about shoes, hair, and dresses—their own and everyone else's.

The five friends all saw Bailey coming at breakneck speed in his wheelchair, weaving in and out of dancers on the floor like a man on a mission, and they smiled in greeting. They were good guys and always made him feel like they didn't mind having him around.

"Lookin' good, Sheen." Grant whistled.

Paulie straightened Bailey's bow tie just a smidge, and Ambrose walked around his chair, giving him the once-over.

"You come stag like the rest of us?" Ambrose asked, stopping in front of Bailey and sinking to his haunches so Bailey didn't have to strain his neck to make eye contact.

"Speak for yourself, man. I am with the lovely Lydia," Beans crooned, his eyes on his date.

Lydia was pretty cute, but she kind of let it all hang out, and Bailey thought she'd be prettier if she had a little of Rita's secrecy. Rita showed just enough to suggest it only got better beneath her clothes. Lydia showed so much you wondered why she even bothered with clothes. But Beans seemed to appreciate that about her.

"Marley looks good." Bailey complimented Jesse's girl, and Jesse waggled his eyebrows. "Yes, she does, Sheen. Yes, she does."

Marley's dress was pretty revealing too, but she wasn't as voluptuous as Rita or Lydia, which made it seem less so. She was slight like Fern, but she had long black hair and an exotic slant to her eyes and cheekbones. She and Jesse had been a couple since sophomore year, and they looked good together.

"I'm here with Fern." Bailey got right to the point, not wanting Fern to come back and see him working the crowd on her behalf. Ambrose immediately rose back to his feet and Bailey sighed inwardly. Ambrose acted like Fern was a Russian spy who had tricked him into spilling the country's secrets instead of a girl who had written him a few love letters and signed someone else's name. His reaction made Bailey wonder if maybe he had feelings for Fern after all. You didn't get that angry over something that didn't matter.

Bailey looked at Paulie and Grant and forged ahead, hoping Ambrose would hear him out. "You guys that don't have dates, would you ask her to dance? Fern's always taking care of me, but it would be nice if she could dance with someone besides her cousin at her senior prom."

Ambrose took a few steps back and then turned and walked away without saying a word. Grant and Paulie watched him go, matching stunned expressions on their faces.

Beans burst into laughter and Jesse whistled low and slow, shaking his head.

"Why does he always act like that whenever anyone says a word about Fern?" Grant wondered, his eyes still on his friend's retreating back.

Bailey felt his face grow hot and his collar felt too tight all of a sudden. It took a lot to embarrass Bailey. Pride was a luxury a kid like him couldn't afford and have any kind of life, but Ambrose's rebuff had embarrassed him.

"What is his problem?" Bailey asked, baffled.

"I think he has a thing for Fern," Beans said, as if that was the most outrageous thing ever.

Bailey shot Beans a look that made Beans stop short and clear his throat, swallowing his laughter.

"I would really appreciate it if you guys would dance with her. If you think you're too damn good for her then never mind. It's your loss, definitely not hers," Bailey said, the heat of embarrassment morphing into anger.

"Hey Bailey, no problem, man. I'll ask her to dance." Grant patted his shoulder, reassuringly.

"Yeah, I'm in. I like Fern. I'd love to dance with her," Paulie agreed, nodding.

"Me too. I love Fern," Beans chimed in, his eyes gleaming with mirth. Bailey decided to let it go. It was just Beans. He couldn't seem to help himself.

"You know I got your back, Sheen. But if I dance with her, she's going to know something's up," Jesse said regretfully. "Marley's my girl, and everyone knows it."

"That's okay, Jess. You're right. I don't want to make it too obvious." Bailey heaved a sigh of relief.

"So what you gonna do while we're keeping Fern busy?" Beans teased.

"I'm going to dance with Rita," Bailey said without pause.

The four wrestlers immediately burst into whoops and laughter as Bailey smirked and pivoted his chair around. Fern had just walked back into the gymnasium and was turning this way and that, looking for him.

"You guys take care of Fern. I'll take care of Rita," he called over his shoulder.

"We'll take care of her. Don't worry," Grant reassured, waving him off.

"We'll take care of her," Paulie repeated. "And I'll take care of Ambrose. He needs someone to look after him too."

● ● ●

"Can I stay?" Ambrose cleared his throat. It was so hard to ask. But he couldn't leave. Not now. They had all been up most of the night, and dawn was only an hour away. Elliott Young had taken over at the bakery, and Joshua and Rachel Taylor had rushed to their daughter's side when they got the call. It had only been two weeks since they were awakened and told to come to the hospital not knowing what had happened to Bailey. It was clear by their panic-stricken faces followed by their grateful tears that they had expected the worst.

Fern and Ambrose were questioned at length by the responding officers, and Becker Garth was taken to the hospital in an ambulance and then remanded into police custody. Fern had refused to go the hospital but had allowed the police to take pictures of her injuries. She was bruised and scraped, and she would be sore in the morning, but now she slept in her own bed, and Ambrose was standing by the front door, his hand on the knob, asking Joshua Taylor if he could stay the night.

"I don't want to leave. Every time I close my eyes, I see that bastard dragging her away . . . sorry, sir." Ambrose apologized, although he really wasn't sure what other word he could have used to describe Becker Garth.

"That's okay, Ambrose. My sentiments exactly," Joshua Taylor smiled wanly. His eyes roved over Ambrose's face, and Ambrose knew it wasn't because of his scars. They were the eyes of a father, trying to ascertain the intentions of a man who was clearly in love with his daughter.

"I'll make you a bed down here." He nodded once and turned, walking away from the door, motioning for Ambrose to follow. He moved as if he'd aged ten years in the last week, and Ambrose realized suddenly how old Joshua Taylor really was. He had to be twenty-five years older than Elliott, which would put him at seventy. Ambrose had never really thought about Fern's parents, never really looked at them, the way he'd never really looked at Fern until that night at the lake.

They must have been fairly old when Fern was born. How would it feel to discover you were having a child when you never thought you would? How the pendulum could swing! Such immeasurable joy at welcoming a miracle into the world, such unfathomable pain when that child is taken from the world. Tonight Joshua Taylor had almost lost his miracle, and Ambrose had witnessed a miracle.

The Pastor took a flat sheet, a pillow, and an old pink quilt out of a linen closet, walked into the family room, and began making up the couch as if he'd done it a hundred times.

"I've got it, sir. Please. I can do that." Ambrose rushed to relieve him of the duty, but Fern's father waved him off and continued tucking the sheet securely into the cushions and folding it in half so Ambrose could tuck himself inside like a taco.

"There. You'll be comfortable here. Sometimes when I've got a lot on my mind and don't want to keep Rachel awake, I come down here. I've spent a lot of nights on this couch. You're longer than I am, but I think you'll be fine."

"Thank you, sir." Joshua Taylor nodded and patted Ambrose on the shoulder. He turned as if to leave, but then paused, looking at the old rug that snuggled up to the couch where Ambrose would sleep.

"Thank you, Ambrose," he answered, and his voice broke with sudden emotion. "I have often worried that when Bailey died, something would happen to Fern. It's an illogical fear, I know, but their lives have been so entwined, so connected. Angie and Rachel even discovered that they were pregnant on the same day. I worried that God had sent Fern for a specific purpose, a specific mission, and when that mission was fulfilled, he would take her away."

"The Lord giveth and the Lord taketh away?"

"Yes . . . something like that."

"I've always hated that quote."

Joshua Taylor looked surprised, but continued on. "Tonight, when you called . . . before you even spoke, I knew something had happened. And I prepared myself to hear the news. I've never told Rachel about this. I didn't want her to be afraid with me." Joshua looked up at Ambrose, and his large brown eyes, eyes so like Fern's, were filled with emotion.

"You've given me hope, Ambrose. Maybe restored my faith a little."

"Restored mine too," Ambrose admitted.

Joshua Taylor looked surprised once more and this time he sought clarification. "How so?"

"I wouldn't have heard her scream. I shouldn't have. I had the radio on. And the mixer. Plus, I don't hear all that well to begin with," Ambrose smiled, just a wry twist of his lips. But this wasn't a moment for levity, and he immediately became grave once more. "I heard Paulie, my friend Paulie. You remember Paul Kimball?"

Joshua Taylor nodded once, a brief affirmation.

"It was like he was standing right next to me, speaking into my ear. He warned me—told me to listen. Paulie was always telling us to listen."

Joshua Taylor's lips started to tremble, and he pressed a hand to his mouth, clearly moved by Ambrose's account.

"Since Iraq, it's been . . . hard . . . for me to believe that there is anything after this life. Or, for that matter, any purpose to this one. We're born, we suffer, we see people we love suffer, we die. It just all seemed so . . . so pointless. So cruel. And so final." Ambrose paused, letting the memory of Paulie's voice warm him and urge him forward.

"But after tonight, I can't say that anymore. There's a lot I don't understand . . . but not understanding is better than not believing." Ambrose stopped and pinched the bridge of his nose. He looked at Joshua Taylor for affirmation. "Does that make any sense at all?"

Joshua Taylor reached for the arm of the nearest chair and sat abruptly, like his legs could no longer bear his weight.

"Yes. Yes. It makes perfect sense," he said quietly, nodding his head. "Perfect sense."

Ambrose sat too, the old couch welcoming his weary frame into her folds.

"You're a good man, Ambrose. My daughter loves you. I can tell."

"I love her," Ambrose said, but stopped himself from saying more.

"But?" Pastor Taylor asked, the many years of listening to people's problems making him highly aware when someone was holding back.

"But Fern likes to take care of people. I'm worried that my . . . my . . . my . . ." Ambrose couldn't find the words.

"Need?" Joshua Taylor supplied delicately.

"My ugly face," Ambrose corrected abruptly. "I'm worried my disfigurement makes Fern want to take care of me. I'm not exactly beautiful, Pastor. What if one day Fern sees me as I really am and decides my need for her isn't enough?"

"Your father came and saw me once, a long time ago. He was concerned about the same thing. He thought if he looked different your mother wouldn't have left."

Ambrose felt an immediate surge of pain for his father and a corresponding flash of anger for the woman who had discarded him for an airbrushed underwear ad.

"Can I suggest to you what I suggested to him?" Joshua Taylor asked gently. "Sometimes beauty, or lack thereof, gets in the way of really knowing someone. Do you love Fern because she's beautiful?"

Ambrose loved the way Fern looked. But he wondered suddenly if he loved the way she looked because he loved the way she laughed, the way she danced, the way she floated on her back and made philosophical statements about the clouds. He knew he loved her selflessness and her humor and her sincerity. And those things made her beautiful to him.

"There are a lot of girls who are physically more lovely than Fern, I suppose. But you love Fern."

"I love Fern," Ambrose readily agreed, once again.

"There are a lot of guys who are needier . . . and uglier . . . than you in this town, yet you're the first guy Fern has ever shown any interest in." Pastor Taylor laughed. "If it's all about altruism, why isn't Fern out looking to start a home for wayward ugly men?"

Ambrose chuckled too, and for a moment, Joshua Taylor looked at him fondly, the lateness of the hour and the brush with death giving the conversation a surreal cast that invited candor.

"Ambrose, Fern already sees who you really are. That's why she loves you."

36
Go to Penn State

Fern was subdued as she helped Ambrose pack. She'd been subdued all week. The trauma of Bailey's death and Becker's attack had taken its toll, and now with Ambrose leaving, she didn't know how it was going to feel to wake up tomorrow, completely alone for the first time in her life. Ambrose had helped to temper Bailey's loss. But who would temper Ambrose's?

She caught herself refolding his shirts, rewinding his socks, fiddling with things he'd put in one place, unintentionally putting them in another so when he turned to retrieve them they were gone.

"I'm sorry," Fern said for the tenth time in the last half hour. She moved away from the open suitcases before she could do more damage and began making Ambrose's bed, simply because she had nothing better to do.

"Fern?"

Fern continued patting, smoothing, and fluffing and didn't look at Ambrose when he said her name.

"Fern. Stop. Leave it. I've just got to climb back in it in a few hours," Ambrose said.

Fern couldn't stop. She needed to keep doing, keep busy. She bustled into the hallway, looking for the vacuum so she could tidy up Ambrose's room. Elliott was working a swing shift at the bakery, covering for Ambrose on his last night at home, and the house was quiet. It didn't take her long to find the vacuum and a dust cloth and Windex too.

She buzzed around Ambrose's half-empty room, hunting dust bunnies and wiping down every available surface until Ambrose sighed heavily and, zipping his last suitcase, turned on her with his hands on his hips.

"Fern."

"Yeah?" Fern answered staring at a section of the wall where the paint looked suspiciously light. She had scrubbed too hard.

"Put the Windex down and step away slowly," Ambrose commanded. Fern rolled her eyes but stopped, fearing she was doing more harm than good. She set the Windex down on Ambrose's desk. "The rag too," Ambrose said. Fern folded the rag and set it beside the Windex. Then she put her hands on her hips, mimicking his stance.

"Hands in the air, where I can see 'em."

Fern put her hands up and then stuck her thumbs in her ears, waggling her fingers. Then she crossed her eyes, puffed out her cheeks, and poked out her tongue. Ambrose burst out laughing and swooped her up like she was five years old and tossed her on his bed. He followed her down, rolling over so he pinned her partially beneath him.

"Always making faces." He smiled, running his finger along the bridge of her nose, across her lips, and down her chin. Fern's smile faded as his finger crossed her mouth, and the despair she'd been busily avoiding crashed down on her.

"Wait . . . what's that face?" Ambrose asked softly, watching the laughter fade from her countenance.

"I'm trying really hard to be brave," Fern said quietly, closing her eyes against his perusal. "So this is my brave, sad face."

"It is a very sad face." Ambrose sighed, and his lips found hers and briefly caressed her mouth before pulling away again. And he watched the sad face fall and break into tears that leaked out beneath her closed lids. Then Fern was pushing him off, fighting out of his arms, scrambling for the door so she wouldn't make him feel bad and make it harder for him to go. She knew he needed to go. Just as much as she needed him to stay.

"Fern! Stop." It was the night at the lake all over again, Fern rushing away so he wouldn't see her cry. But he was quicker than she was, and his hand shot out, pinning the door closed so she couldn't leave. Then his arms were around her, pulling her up against him, her back to his chest, as she hung her head and cried into her palms.

"Shush, baby. Shush," Ambrose said. "It's not forever."

"I know," she cried and Ambrose felt her take a deep breath and bear down, gaining control over herself, willing her tears to ebb.

"I wanted to show you something," Fern said abruptly, wiping her cheeks briskly, trying to remove the residue of her grief. Then she turned toward him and her hands rose to the opening of her shirt and she began to undo the row of white buttons.

Ambrose's mouth immediately went dry. He had thought about this moment countless times, and yet with all the turmoil and loss, he and Fern had only flirted with the edge, as if they feared falling over. And privacy was hard to come by while they both lived at home, the kind of privacy he wanted with Fern, the kind he needed with her. So passion had been bridled and kisses stolen, though Ambrose was finding it more difficult every day.

But she only made it about five buttons down before she stopped, sliding her shirt open over her left breast, just above the lace of her bra. Ambrose stared at the name printed in very small letters in a simple font across Fern's heart. *Bailey*.

Ambrose reached out and touched the word and watched goose bumps rise on her skin as his fingers brushed against her. The tattoo was new and lightly rimmed in pink, not yet scabbed over. It was maybe an inch long, just a little tribute to a very special friend.

Fern must have been confused by his expression. "I felt like such a badass getting a tattoo. But I didn't do it to be hardcore. I just did it because I wanted . . . I wanted to keep him close to me. And I thought I should be the one . . . to write him across my heart."

"You have a tattoo, a black eye, and I just saw your bra. You are getting to be very hardcore, Fern," Ambrose teased gently, although the fading black eye made his blood boil every time he looked at her.

"You should have told me. I would have gone with you," Ambrose said as he pulled his soft gray T-shirt over his head, and Fern's gaze sharpened just like his had moments before.

"Seems we both wanted to surprise each other," he added softly as she looked at him. The names were spaced evenly in a row, just like the white graves at the top of the little memorial hill. Bailey didn't get to be buried with the soldiers, but he stood with them now, his name taking a position at the end of the line.

"What's this?" Fern asked, her fingers hovering above a long green frond with delicate leaves that now wrapped around the five names.

"It's a fern."

"You got a tattoo . . . of a fern?" Fern's lower lip started to tremble again, and if Ambrose wasn't so touched by her emotion, he would have laughed at her pouty little girl face.

"But . . . it's permanent," she whispered, aghast.

"Yeah. It is. So are you," Ambrose said slowly, letting the words settle on her. Her eyes met his, and grief, disbelief, and euphoria battled for dominion. It was clear she wanted to believe him, but wasn't sure she did.

"I'm not Bailey, Fern. And I'm not going to ever replace him. You two were inseparable. That worries me a little because you're going to have a Bailey-sized hole in your life for a long time . . . maybe forever. I understand holes. This last year I've felt like one of those snowflakes we used to make in school. The ones where you fold the paper a certain way and then keep cutting and cutting until the paper is shredded. That's what I look like, a paper snowflake. And each hole has a name. And nobody, not you, not me, can fill the holes that someone else has left. All we can do is keep each other from falling in the holes and never coming out again.

"I need you, Fern. I'm not going to lie. I need you. But I don't need you the same way Bailey did. I need you because it hurts when we're apart. I need you because you make me hopeful. You make me happy. But I don't need you to shave me or brush my hair or wipe syrup off my nose." Fern's face collapsed at the memory, at the reminder of Bailey and the way she had lovingly cared for him.

Fern covered her eyes, covering her anguish, and her shoulders shook as she cried, unable to muscle the emotion back anymore.

"Bailey needed that, Fern. And you gave him what he needed because you loved him. You think I need you. But you aren't convinced I love you. So you're trying to take care of me."

"What *do* you want from me, Ambrose?" Fern cried from behind her hands. He pulled at her wrists, wanting to see her face as he laid it all on the line.

"I want your body. I want your mouth. I want your red hair in my hands. I want your laugh and your funny faces. I want your friendship and your inspirational thoughts. I want Shakespeare and Amber Rose novels and your memories of Bailey. And I want you to come with me when I go."

Fern's hands had dropped from her face and though her cheeks were still wet with tears, she was smiling, her teeth sunk into her lower lip. The teary eyes and the smiling mouth were a particularly endearing combination, and Ambrose leaned forward and tugged her bottom lip free with his teeth, gently nipping, softly kissing. But then he pulled away again, intent on the subject at hand.

"But the last time I begged someone I loved to come with me when they really didn't want to go, I lost them." Ambrose wrapped a strand of Fern's red hair around his finger, his brow furrowed, his mouth turned down in a wistful frown.

"You want me to come to school with you?" Fern asked.

"Kind of."

"Kind of?"

"I love you Fern. And I want you to marry me."

"You do?" Fern squealed.

"I do. It doesn't get better than Fern Taylor."

"It doesn't?" Fern squeaked.

"It doesn't." Ambrose couldn't help laughing at her incredulous little face. "And if you'll have me, I will spend the rest of my life trying to make you happy, and when you get tired of looking at me, I promise I'll sing."

Fern laughed, a watery, hiccupping sound.

"Yes or no?" Ambrose said seriously, reaching for her hand, the ultimate either/or question hanging in the air between them.

"Yes."

37

Get Married

The stands were packed with blue and white and Fern felt a little lost without a wheelchair to make arrangements for and sit beside, but they had good seats. Ambrose had made sure of that. Her uncle Mike was on her left, Elliott Young on her right, and beside him, Jamie Kimball, Paulie's mom. Jamie had worked the front counter at the bakery for years, and Elliott had finally gotten the nerve to ask her out. So far, so good. Another silver lining. They needed each other, but more importantly, they deserved each other.

It was the last duel of the season for the Penn State Nittany Lions, and Fern was so nervous she had to sit on her hands so she wouldn't resume her bad habit of shredding her fingernails. She felt this way every time she watched Ambrose wrestle, even though he won a whole lot more than he lost. She wondered how Mike Sheen endured this torture year after year. If you loved your wrestler, and Fern did, then wrestling was absolutely agonizing to watch.

Ambrose hadn't won every match. He'd had an impressive year, especially considering his long absence from the sport and the disadvantages that he started the season with. Fern had made Ambrose promise to enjoy himself, and he had genuinely tried. No more trying to be Mr. Universe or Hercules or Iron Man or anything but Ambrose

Young, son of Elliott Young, fiancé of Fern Taylor. She took a deep breath and tried to take her own advice. She was the daughter of Joshua and Rachel, cousin of Bailey, lover of Ambrose. And she wouldn't trade places with anyone.

She hadn't gone with him when he left for school. They'd both known it wasn't possible right away. Fern had finally scored a three-book deal with a respected romance publisher and had deadlines to meet. Her first novel would be out in the spring. Ambrose had been convinced he had to slay his dragons on his own two feet—no metaphoric shield or minions to keep him company.

Ambrose had been afraid and admitted as much. The discomfort of curious gazes, the whispers behind hands, the explanations that people felt they were owed all grated on him. But it was okay too. He claimed the questions gave him an opportunity to get it all out in the open, and before long, the guys on the wrestling team didn't really see the scars. The way Fern never saw Bailey's wheelchair. The way Ambrose finally looked beyond the face of a plain little eighteen-year-old and saw Fern for the first time.

The Penn State head coach had made Ambrose no promises. There was no scholarship waiting when he arrived. He told Ambrose he could come work out with the team and they would see how it all shook out. Ambrose had arrived in October, coming in on the block, a month behind everyone else. But within a few weeks, the coaches at Penn State were impressed. And so were his new teammates.

Fern and Ambrose started writing letters again, long e-mails filled with either/or questions both tender and bizarre, designed to make the distance seem trivial. Fern always made sure to close her letters with her name in bold and all in caps, just to make sure Ambrose knew exactly who they were from. The love notes kept them laughing and crying and longing for the weekends when one or the other would make the trip between Hannah Lake and Penn State. And sometimes they met somewhere in between and lost themselves in each other for a couple of days, making the most of every second, because seconds became minutes and minutes became precious when life could be taken in less than a breath.

When Ambrose ran out on the mat with his team, Fern's heart leaped, and she waved madly so he would see them all there. He found them quickly, knowing what section they were sitting in, and he smiled that lopsided grin that she loved. Then he stuck out his tongue, crossed his eyes, and made a face. Fern repeated the action and saw him laugh.

Then Ambrose rubbed his chest where the names were written, and Fern felt the emotion rise in her throat and touched the name over her own heart. Bailey would have loved to see this. If there was a God and a life beyond this one, Bailey was here, no question in Fern's mind. He would be down on the floor scouting out the competition, taking notes and taking names. Paulie, Jesse, Beans, and Grant would be there too, lining the mats, watching their best friend do his best to live without them and cheering him on, just like they always had. Even Jesse.

● ● ●

Fern and Ambrose were married in the summer of 2006. The little church that Joshua and Rachel Taylor had dedicated their lives to was filled to capacity, and Rita was Fern's maid of honor. She was doing well, living back in Hannah Lake now that Becker was in jail awaiting trial, charged with several counts in three separate cases.

Rita had been granted a divorce, and she threw herself into planning a wedding that would be remembered for years to come. And she outdid herself. It was perfect, magical, more than even Fern could have imagined.

But the flowers, the food, the cake, even the beauty of the bride and the dignity of her groom weren't what people would be talking about when it was all over. There was a feeling in the air at that wedding. Something sweet and special that made more than one guest stop and marvel, "Do you feel that?"

Grant's family was there, and Marley and Jesse Jr. too. With Fern at his side, Ambrose had eventually made the rounds to all the families of his fallen friends. It hadn't been easy for any of them, but the healing process had begun, though Luisa O'Toole still blamed Ambrose, refused to answer the door when he came by, and didn't make an appearance at the wedding. Everyone deals with grief differently, and Luisa would have to come to terms with her grief on her own time. Jamie Kimball sat at Elliott's side, and from their clasped hands and warm glances, it was easy to predict there might be another wedding before long.

Little Ty was growing up fast and sometimes he still liked to crawl up in Bailey's chair and demand a ride. But at the wedding, no one sat in Bailey's chair. They placed it at the end of the front pew in a place of honor. And as Fern walked down the aisle on her mother's arm, her eyes strayed to the empty wheelchair. Then Ambrose stepped forward to take her hand, and Fern couldn't see anything but him. Pastor Taylor greeted his daughter with a kiss and placed his hand on the scarred cheek of the man who had promised to love her and cleave to only her, as long as they lived.

When promises were made, vows spoken, and a kiss delivered that made the audience wonder if the couple would hang around for the festivities afterward, Joshua Taylor, with tears in his eyes and a lump in his throat, addressed the gathering, marveling at the beauty of the couple who had come so far and suffered so much.

"True beauty, the kind that doesn't fade or wash off, takes time. It takes pressure. It takes incredible endurance. It is the slow drip that makes the stalactite, the shaking of the Earth that creates mountains, the constant pounding of the waves that breaks up the rocks and smooths the rough edges. And from the violence, the furor, the raging of the winds, the roaring of the waters, something better emerges, something that would otherwise never exist.

"And so we endure. We have faith that there is purpose. We hope for things we can't see. We believe that there are lessons in loss, power in love, and that we have within us the potential for a beauty so magnificent that our bodies can't contain it."

Epilogue

". . . and Hercules, in great pain and suffering, begged his friends to light a huge fire that reached into the heavens. Then he threw himself on the fire, desperate to extinguish the agony of the poison that had been rubbed on his skin.

"From high on Mount Olympus, mighty Zeus looked down on his son, and seeing the torment of his heroic offspring, turned to his vindictive wife and said, 'He has suffered enough. He has proven himself.'

"Hera, looking down on Hercules, took pity on him and agreed, sending her blazing chariot from the sky to lift Hercules up and take him to his place among the gods, where the much-beloved hero still lives on to this day," Ambrose said softly, and shut the book firmly, hoping there wouldn't be pleas for more.

But silence greeted the triumphant finish, and Ambrose looked down at his son, wondering if somewhere between the twelfth labor and the end the six-year-old had fallen asleep. Vivid red curls danced around his son's animated face, but the big dark eyes were wide open and sober with thought.

"Dad, are you as strong as Hercules?"

Ambrose bit back a smile and swooped his little dreamer up in his arms and tucked him into bed. Story time had gone long, it was way past bedtime, and Fern was somewhere in the house dreaming up her own story. Ambrose had every intention of interrupting her.

"Dad, do you think I could be a hero like Hercules someday?"

"You don't have to be like Hercules, buddy." Ambrose flipped off the light and paused at the door. "There are all kinds of heroes."

"Yeah. I guess. Good night, Dad!"

"Good night, Bailey."

The End

Bonus Content

Interviews with Ambrose Young 2002 and 2007

2002—Interview with Ambrose Young on ESPN's *Off the Mat*

SPORTSCASTER: Welcome to a special edition of *Off the Mat*. We're here at the Giant Center in Hershey, Pennsylvania, on the night before day one of the Pennsylvania State Wrestling Tournament. It's not often we on *Off the Mat* cover high school wrestling, but it's not every day that the sport of wrestling has such a dominant talent at such an early age. High school senior Ambrose Young from Hannah Lake, Pennsylvania, is a three-time state champion who will be competing this weekend for his fourth state title. No Pennsylvania wrestler has ever claimed four state titles, all in the upper weights. If Ambrose is successful over the next few days, he will make history. Ambrose Young is being scouted by every Division I wrestling program in the country, and we have him here to talk about this tournament and what comes next in his already storied career. Hello Ambrose, thanks for being here.

AMBROSE: Thank you for having me. (*Shifts nervously in his chair.*)

SPORTSCASTER: Ambrose, you could do something very few wrestlers in the history of our sport have ever done. How does that feel?

AMBROSE: Right now . . . it feels . . . exhausting. (*Laughter erupts from the set and the small crowd gathered around the press pit.*)

SPORTSCASTER: (*Laughing heartily.*) Lots of pressure, I'm sure.

AMBROSE: (*Nodding quietly, almost grimly.*) Yes sir. The expectations . . . my own and everyone else's . . . can be pretty heavy.

SPORTSCASTER: How do you combat it? What are some of your techniques for staying focused on the prize?

AMBROSE: I work as hard as I can in the wrestling room, year round, so that I won't disappoint myself, my team, or my community on the mat. And I try not to take anything for granted.

SPORTSCASTER: Have you taken a look at your competition? Do you know the strengths and weaknesses of your opponents?

AMBROSE: I try not to focus on my opponents. Sheen, uh Bailey Sheen, Coach Sheen's son, and the team's stat man—loves that shi—uh, stuff. He tells me what I need to know, what to look for, but I try to ignore the competition, for the most part. It's too easy to doubt myself and question my abilities. For me, it's better to just work hard and be coachable.

SPORTSCASTER: Any thoughts about where you're going to go, what school you're going to wrestle for, when this is all over?

AMBROSE: (*Hesitates and looks at his hands. A voice from the crowd yells out, "Penn State, baby!" Ambrose smiles and shakes his head. "Quiet down, Sheen," he calls back, and the crowd laughs.*)

SPORTSCASTER: Was that the stat man?

AMBROSE: Yep. The one and only, Bailey Sheen.

SPORTSCASTER: So does Bailey Sheen have inside information? Is it Penn State?

AMBROSE: Maybe. I . . . uh. I haven't decided. I like Iowa. (*Cheers erupt.*) I like Oklahoma State. (*Catcalls and clapping.*) And maybe . . . maybe I won't wrestle at all. (*Crowd falls silent and the sportscaster's mouth falls open slightly.*)

SPORTSCASTER: Is this breaking news? Are you making an announcement? You do realize the heart of every wrestling coach in the country just stopped, don't you?

AMBROSE: Nah. No announcement. I just . . . need to focus on what I have to do here. What I have to do in the next couple of days. And then I'll think about what comes next.

SPORTSCASTER: On a personal note, this has been a hard time for a lot of people. With the attacks on September 11th, sports has taken a backseat in a lot of people's minds. What have the last few months meant to you?

AMBROSE: (*Shrugs and is silent for several seconds.*) The things that were so important before, just aren't as important anymore. But at the same time, we have to go on, you know? I guess I . . . feel different . . . I think a lot of people do. Life changed that day . . . and it doesn't seem like it will ever be the same again.

SPORTSCASTER: We definitely have to go on. You're right. And so many kids who are coming up in the sport look up to you and what you've accomplished. What do you have to say to them?

AMBROSE: I . . . I'm not sure. I guess . . . work hard. You gotta love the sport. If you don't . . . (*He shrugs and raises his hands helplessly.*) If you don't . . . then figure out what you do love.

SPORTSCASTER: Do you love the sport, Ambrose?

AMBROSE: Not lately . . . but the sport loves me (*He chuckles nervously, the crowd laughs, and the sportscaster smiles indulgently. The sportscaster clears his throat and switches topics, steering the interview away from Ambrose's obvious discomfort.*)

SPORTSCASTER: Have you ever watched *Off the Mat* before, Ambrose?

AMBROSE: Yes, sir. I'm a fan.

SPORTSCASTER: Good answer. (*Laughter.*) So, you know how this next part works. It's the lightening round. Some of the questions are the same questions we ask every wrestler who comes on *Off the Mat*, and there are a few sent in by our viewers. Ready, Ambrose? (*Ambrose nods and shifts in his chair.*)

SPORTSCASTER: Tournaments or duals?

AMBROSE: Tournaments. There's more going on, so less crowd attention is paid to any one match.

SPORTSCASTER: Takedowns or escapes?

AMBROSE: Takedowns—does anyone ever say escapes? (*Sportscaster laughs.*)

SPORTSCASTER: Weigh-ins or wrestle-offs?

AMBROSE: Weigh-ins. Wrestle-offs can be stressful, but weigh-ins are painful.

SPORTSCASTER: Penn State or Oklahoma State?

AMBROSE: No comment.

SPORTSCASTER: (*Grins and shrugs.*) You can't blame me for trying. Ankle pick or arm drag?

AMBROSE: Ankle pick. It takes more energy, but it's so satisfying when you do it right.

SPORTSCASTER: Food or sleep?

AMBROSE: Food. You know my dad owns a bakery, right?

SPORTSCASTER: First thing you're going to eat after the tournament is over?

AMBROSE: One of everything. (*Laughter.*)

SPORTSCASTER: And this question is from one of your female fans. (*Hoots and hollers from the onlookers.*) Blondes or brunettes?

AMBROSE: (*Pauses momentarily and then answers in a rush.*) Red-heads. (*His cheeks grow ruddy, and he clears his throat.*) Nah. Just kid-ding. All of the above.

SPORTSCASTER: Ambrose, thank you for being here. (*Leans forward to shake his hand.*) May there be more pins—and redheads—in your future.

2007—Interview with Ambrose Young on ESPN's *Off the Mat*

SPORTSCASTER: We're here with four-time Pennsylvania high school state champion and 2007 NCAA Division I National Champion, Ambrose Young. Ambrose has become one of the most inspiring figures in college sports. An Iraqi War Veteran, he's started his own foundation called Making Faces, a charity that works with returning vets who need facial reconstruction after sustaining injuries, much like Ambrose himself experienced in Iraq. Welcome, Ambrose. Thank you for joining us today on ESPN's *Off the Mat*.

AMBROSE: Thank you for having me.

SPORTSCASTER: It hasn't been an easy road, has it?

AMBROSE: No sir. It hasn't. But I'm convinced there's no such thing.

SPORTSCASTER: You were a standout high school wrestler, highly recruited. You had an undefeated record for your sophomore, junior, and senior years, and you were a four-time state champion. But you decided to go to Iraq. Tell us about that.

AMBROSE: 9/11 hit me pretty hard. I was a senior in high school that year. My mom worked in the North Tower and the events hit very close to home. It was something I just felt like I had to do. I was pretty naïve, I admit. There's a lot I regret about that decision, but I don't regret serving my country or the things I've learned in the process.

SPORTSCASTER: For our viewers, Ambrose and several men from his unit were out on patrol and hit a roadside bomb. Several men were killed and Ambrose was seriously wounded. Some of those men were your friends, is that right?

AMBROSE: Jesse Jordan, Grant Nielson, Paul Kimball, and Connor O'Toole were their names. They were all killed. They were my best friends. We wrestled together at Hannah Lake, grew up together, and we served together.

SPORTSCASTER: You came back to Hannah Lake a changed man.

AMBROSE: Yeah. Changed. Messed up. I really wished I had died with them. I was pretty angry for a while.

SPORTSCASTER: Did you ever think you'd wrestle again?

AMBROSE: (*Laughs and shakes his head.*) I *knew* I wouldn't. I can't see out of my right eye. I can't hear out of my right ear. I was majorly messed up, out of shape, and definitely didn't want to be in the public eye in any way.

SPORTSCASTER: So what happened?

AMBROSE: Fern Taylor happened.

SPORTSCASTER: Your wife?

AMBROSE: Yeah. My wife. Along with some other pretty important people. Coach Sheen—my high school wrestling coach—and his son, Bailey. I owe them everything. They were convinced I could do it. They convinced me.

SPORTSCASTER: Coach Sheen is very well respected but he's had his share of tragedy, hasn't he? He lost his son, Bailey, in 2005, correct?

AMBROSE: Yeah. We lost Bailey and wrestling lost its biggest fan.

SPORTSCASTER: You're still affected by that, aren't you?

AMBROSE: We miss him every day. He and my wife were incredibly tight—she is Coach Sheen's niece—so they were family as well as friends. Bailey died a hero. Life goes on, but yeah. We miss him. (*Ambrose clears his throat and looks at his hands. Sportscaster takes a minute to let him compose himself.*)

SPORTSCASTER: Speaking of life going on—you and your wife are expecting a child any day. Congratulations!

AMBROSE: Thank you. We're pretty excited. We just have to cross our fingers that he or she doesn't decide to make an appearance during the NCAA tournament.

SPORTSCASTER: We're all crossing our fingers that doesn't happen. Before we let you go, we have the lightning round—twenty seconds until the whistle blows and the match (or the interview) is over. These are questions from wrestlers on Montpelier Junior High's wrestling team, about a half hour from Hannah Lake. These are wrestlers from twelve to fourteen who really look up to you. You ready?

AMBROSE: Ready.

SPORTSCASTER: Favorite color?

AMBROSE: Red.

SPORTSCASTER: (*Looks up in surprise.*) Red? Penn State and Hannah Lake's colors are both blue.

AMBROSE: Yeah...but my wife's hair is red. (*Laughter from camera crew.*)

SPORTSCASTER: I seem to remember a question in our first interview with you about redheads . . . is this just a coincidence?

AMBROSE: (*Scratches his head.*) I forgot about that. Uh. No. No coincidence. (*More laughter.*)

SPORTSCASTER: Favorite wrester?

AMBROSE: Dan Gable.

SPORTSCASTER: Favorite Olympic moment?

AMBROSE: John Smith's gold medal match, 1992, in Barcelona. I watched it with my dad.

SPORTSCASTER: Nickname?

AMBROSE: Brosey, Brose.

SPORTSCASTER: Hercules?

AMBROSE: (*Rolls his eyes.*) Yeah. That too. Next question. (*Laugher again.*)

SPORTSCASTER: Favorite food?

AMBROSE: I'm a wrestler so I'm always hungry. I just like food. And lots of it. Did you just hear my stomach growl?

SPORTSCASTER: Favorite cartoon? Remember these questions are from kids.

AMBROSE: Scooby Doo. That dog knew how to make a sandwich. Did I mention I'm hungry?

SPORTSCASTER: This last question is from Billy Jackson, captain of the Montpelier Hawks. He wants to know who your hero is and why?

AMBROSE: Bailey Sheen. He never gave up. Never let life beat him. Died a hero.

SPORTSCASTER: (*Smiles and leans forward to shake Ambrose's hand.*) Ambrose Young. You're an inspiration. Thank you for being with us today.

Acknowledgments

With every book, the list of people that deserve thanks and accolades grows exponentially. First, I need to thank my husband, Travis. Travis is a wrestler, and I'm convinced the sport of wrestling builds good men. Thank you for your support, T. Thank you for making it possible for me to be a mother and a writer.

Thanks to my children, Paul, Hannah, Claire, and little Sam. I know it's not easy when I'm off in my head playing with my characters. Thank you for loving me anyway. To my extended family—Sutorius and Harmon both—thank you. Mom and Dad, thank you for letting me hide in your basement and write, weekend after weekend. I love you both so much.

A special acknowledgement goes to Aaron Roos, my husband's cousin, who suffers from Duchenne muscular dystrophy. Aaron just turned twenty-four and is going strong! Thank you, Aaron, for your candor, your optimism, and for spending the afternoon with me. Bailey really came alive because of you. To David and Angie (Harmon) Roos, Aaron's parents—I am so moved by both of you and respect you so much. Thank you for your strength and your example.

To Eric Shepherd, thank you for your military service and for looking out for my little brother in Iraq. And thank you for giving me a glimpse of what it's really like for the soldiers when they're gone and when they come home.

To Andy Espinoza, retired police sergeant, thank you for your help with police procedure. You have been wonderful on the last two books. Thank you!

Thanks to *Cristina's Book Reviews* and *Vilma's Book Blog*! Vilma and Cristina, you are my Thelma and Louise. Thank you for taking the cliff with me and promoting *Making Faces* with such enthusiasm and class. And for *Totally Booked Blog*—Jenny and Gitte—you ladies put *A Different Blue* over the top, and I will be forever grateful for your belief in me and for always giving it to me straight.

There are too many loyal readers and bloggers to thank, but know how much I appreciate all of you for some truly humbling support. Thank you.

To Janet Sutorius, Alice Landwehr, Shannon McPherson, and Emma Corcoran for being my first readers. To Karey White, author and editor extraordinaire (check out *My Own Mr. Darcy*) for editing *Making Faces*. To Julie Titus, formatter and friend, for always making time for me. To my agent, Jane Dystel, for believing in me and taking me on.

And finally, to my Heavenly Father for making even ugly things beautiful.

About the Author

Amy Harmon is a *New York Times, Wall Street Journal,* and *USA Today* bestselling author of ten novels. Her books are now being published in thirteen languages around the globe.

She knew at an early age that writing was something she wanted to do and divided her time between writing songs and stories as she grew. Having grown up in the middle of wheat fields without a television, with only her books and her siblings to entertain her, she developed a strong sense of what made a good story.

For more information about Amy and her books, visit:
Website: http://www.authoramyharmon.com/
Facebook: https://www.facebook.com/authoramyharmon?fref=ts
Twitter: https://twitter.com/aharmon_author

Books by Amy Harmon:

Young Adult and Paranormal Romance
Slow Dance in Purgatory
Prom Night in Purgatory

Inspirational Romance
A Different Blue
Running Barefoot
Making Faces
Infinity + One
The Law of Moses
The Song of David

Romantic Fantasy
The Bird and the Sword

Historical Fiction
From Sand and Ash